"A distinctive and often agreeable spin to the story of Camelot. Focusing on Merlin rather than the usual Arthur, King weaves his tale by combining bits of folklore and mythology with both sheer invention and historical fact. . . . Action fans wil thrill to his frequent and well-told accounts of battles, both material and magical . . . Creative plot twists abound." —*Publisher's Weekly*

"Drawing on an ancient Norse, Celtic, and Roman myths, King crafts an unusual blend of history and legend that should appeal to fans of the Arthurian cycle." —*Library Journal*

"This is a unique retelling of the story of Merlin has fully developed characters and plenty of action. Recommend this fantasy to readers ready to move beyond T. A. Barron's *The Lost Years of Merlin* series." —*VOYA*

"If you want a sumptuous fantasy feast by a fearless author, try *Mad Merlin*." —John Dalmas

Mad Merlin

J. ROBERT KING

A TOM DOHERTY ASSOCIATES BOOK
NEW YORK

This is a work of fiction. All the characters and events portrayed in this book are either products of the author's imagination or are used fictitiously.

MAD MERLIN

Copyright © 2000 by J. Robert King

Edited by Brian Thomsen

A Tor Book
Published by Tom Doherty Associates, LLC
175 Fifth Avenue
New York, NY 10010

www.tor.com

Tor® is a registered trademark of Tom Doherty Associates, LLC.

ISBN: 0-812-58427-9
Library of Congress Catalog Card Number: 00-025946

First edition: July 2000
First mass market edition: August 2001

Printed in the United States of America

0 9 8 7 6 5 4 3 2 1

Acknowledgments

First and foremost, I want to thank my editor, Brian Thomsen. He's the one who first encouraged me to "write your Merlin book." He also edited it and found a home for it. Brian is the reason this book exists. From the bottom of my heart, thanks!

A hearty thanks goes also to Tom Doherty and all his splendid Associates, for their commitment to excellence and their fostering of excellence on this project.

And of course I must thank all the great storytellers who have kept the memory of Arthur and Merlin alive—from Geoffrey and Malory to Tennyson and Steinbeck and White and many more—I'm deeply indebted to you all.

BOOK ONE

Madness

*For Elias
the infant King who saved me*

Prologue

Everyone seems to know me. After fifteen hundred years, they remember me. Everyone knows Merlin. I am, of course, delighted.

You're smiling in recognition, aren't you?

There was a time when I didn't even know myself. I was mad. I was lost. The secret of my past was hidden even from me. To discover that secret, I walked an arduous and perilous road. I would not have survived that journey, except that I had a friend at my side, a young man everyone also knows.

This is the story of how we found out who we were. This is the story of King Arthur and mad Merlin. . . .

1

The Heath Road

*G*o fetch mad Merlin!" griped Ulfius to himself. "Go fetch mad Merlin!"

The warrior was incensed. He yanked gauntlets from his hands as he strode up the heath road. Next, his helmet came off, spilling sweaty black curls to his shoulders. Droplets spattered his ring mail and glinted angrily in the afternoon sun. The Pendragon emblazoned on his tabard seemed to be spewing steam. Even the roadside gorse bushes looked frustrated. "Why do I get all the rotten jobs?"

In truth, there were no good jobs in Uther Pendragon's army. Trench digging was one of the king's favorite pastimes. Trenches for soldiers and for soldiers' waste. Trenches to drain swamps and fill moats. Whenever Uther felt the slightest bit discontented, another ten trenches got dug. Just now, the king of Britannia was very discontented. He wanted Igraine, Duchess of Dumnonia. Two leagues' worth of siege tunnels and a hundred tuns' worth of latrines had not won her for him. Igraine's husband, Duke Gorlois, remained with his noble retainers in Castle Terrabil, uncowed by all the impressive digging. And so—

"Go fetch mad Merlin!"

Ulfius glowered. Dark brows lowered stormily over steel-gray eyes. He was too old for this duty. At thirty-two, he was a seasoned fighter. He had fought for Ambrosius. He had fought against Vortigern. And now, he was Uther's man. They were the greatest rulers Britannia had seen since the time of the Romans—if any ruler could be called great since the Romans. There had been Constantines and Caesars, true, but in name only. Even King Uther ruled only the lower third of the isle, and that tenuously. And whenever he or any other self-proclaimed king of Britannia grew vexed or perplexed, he sent for Merlin.

The mad mage was purported to reside above. The hill had a terrifying aspect. It seemed a giant's head—a Pictish giant with savagely shaved temples and a violent shock of hair at its crown. Although sheep cropped the grass on the sides of the hill, they avoided the top. There, green blades reached a man's hips and heath brushed his shoulders. It was a mad place, and even the sheep knew it. It was like many other such places in Britannia. Whenever a Roman road crossed desolate ground outside a city or fort, the route attracted beggars and tinkers and vagabonds. They huddled in what might loosely be considered a society—lunatics, brigands, demoniacs, and the occasional Caledonian. They lay there in wait of travelers too weak or stupid to defend themselves, or too soft-minded to resist tossing them a few coin.

That's where Merlin would be, among the outcasts. That's where Ulfius headed.

It was a weary climb. Ulfius fastened the gauntlets to his skirt of tasses. With each step he took, the metal gloves clanged against his left cuisse. He'd been advised not to ride his horse. Horses incited the lunatics. They thought a man on a horse was rich. Madmen fought with nails and teeth, sharp rocks and sticks—a dirty battle. And what honor was there in killing madmen?

"More honor than in becoming one," Ulfius growled. Sweat nettled his neck. His mail-quilt seeped slowly. His hipslung gauntlets kept coming unhinged and falling to the ground. He himself was coming unhinged. "Ah, there are the grubbers now."

Beyond a corner of scrubby gorse, a squalid panorama opened. Hovels crowded both sides of the road. The best and tallest were round shelters of stick and sod, in the style of Celtic barbarians. Others were built of barrel sections, ruined wagons, remnants of crate, and whatever other debris could be tricked from passersby. A few shelters were no more than holes dug in the ground, with husks of oak bark perched above them to keep rain out. The folk who dwelt in them would have found Uther's latrines spacious and bright.

The fairer structures dribbled gray soot from their roofs, evidence of a fire within and of a mind able to control fire. These would be brigands poised for highway robbery, or perhaps tinkers—wandering tricksters with the blood of Old Pharaoh in their veins. Even now, some of the inhabitants poked ruddy faces from their hovels. Eyes gleamed avariciously with the reflection of Ulfius's armor.

The lesser denizens of the heath emerged too. Those who had anything to sell brought it with them as they trundled toward the road. Chipped amphorae, stained scarves, worn-out bits, torn saddle blankets, skins said to contain ardent spirits, confiscated writs—anything that might bring Roman coin. The worst of the lot had nothing to sell—madmen, demoniacs, lepers, and the accursed. Beggars. They clawed their way as best they could from their foul holes.

Ulfius simultaneously felt his stomach sink and his bile rise. The next moments would be tricky. Merlin would be one of these tattered lunatics, yes, but to find him Ulfius would have to ask a brigand or a tinker. They ruled the heath—the more able and ruthless preying upon the less so. For all its disease and starvation and squalor, the heath bore a remarkable resemblance to Britannia as a whole.

Tyranny and want. They were the only means left to unite the people.

Ulfius carried no Roman coin. That's what they really wanted. Other mints were mixed with iron. Pendragon shillings were as debased as the rest, but they were all Ulfius bore. Twenty shillings filled a pouch beneath his mail shirt. He had the uneasy premonition that shillings and shirt both would be gone soon enough.

He approached an old tinker woman who sat beside bundled faggots of oak. She was a toothless hag. Her skin was baked into cracked lines, and her eyes were little more than slits of white.

"Firewood," she croaked as Ulfius stopped before her. "Firewood."

Ulfius waved an off-putting hand. "Thank you, no. I don't need firewood—"

"Everybody needs firewood." The woman's ragged clothing smelled of smoke and age.

"I'm looking for someone—"

"I'm someone—"

"A lunatic. The man I'm looking for is a lunatic, and you certainly aren't a lunatic," Ulfius flattered.

"Neither am I a man, but you didn't mention that," she replied.

A crowd of beggars was gathering, their hands held out imploringly to Ulfius. Each poured a lament past putrid teeth. One tried to snatch away his gauntlets.

Ulfius slapped the fingers. "Get back!"

The beggars cringed. They were well acquainted with the applications of fear. The effect lasted only a moment before they pressed again toward the soldier, their din resuming.

Ulfius shouted over them to the woman, "Do you know where I might find Merlin?"

The crone replied, "I sell firewood."

Ulfius fished the coin bag from about his neck and jingled it once. "Were I to buy some firewood, might you tell me where to find Merlin?"

"I might," the crone replied. "A Roman silver piece per bundle."

"A Roman silver—!" Ulfius began in indignation. Gathering himself, he smiled. "I haven't any Roman coins, but—" he gingerly plucked a shilling from the drawstring pouch "—I *do* have Pendragon coinage."

She spat. "I'd not surrender good oak for your Pendragon coin. And I'd certainly not surrender Merlin for it. Go back to your stockades."

Ulfius waved his hand, only then noting that his right gauntlet had disappeared among the pawing throng. "No. You misunderstand. I don't want to imprison Merlin. I want to hire him.

"*I'm* Merlin!" interrupted a man wearing Ulfius's left gauntlet.

The soldier grabbed back his gauntlet and considered the thief. He was white-haired, wild-eyed, rag-cloaked, gaunt, and craven. Ulfius had last seen Merlin a decade before, from a distance, but the sorcerer had looked no better than this.

"You are Merlin?"

Another lunatic, slightly more tattered and scrofulous than the first, answered, "No, *I* am Merlin."

The cry was picked up through the dingy crowd. "No, I am Merlin!" "I am Merlin!" "I am Merlin!" Every idiot on the heath suddenly was the mad mage. Even the tinker with the firewood put in her bid. She was one of the few Ulfius could immediately eliminate. Most of the others could have been he. They pressed up around him, shouting, pawing, begging—each addled mind trying to use the name to his or her advantage.

"Enough!" Ulfius shouted, drawing his sword and waving it above their heads.

Lunatics fell back, trembling. The shouts ceased on their lips.

"That's better. You all may look like Merlin, may sound like him and even smell like him, but only one of you could be he. Therefore, I propose a contest. The winner, the true Merlin, will receive this bag of coin and accompany me to aid Uther Pendragon—there to receive great riches."

A happy sound moved among the tattered throng.

"Any losers, though—any who falsely claim to be Merlin and waste my time in proving the lie—will be slain immediately upon discovery. Now, who among you is he?"

The heath was silent save for two idiots—the two who had first laid their claims. Perhaps one was the mage. Perhaps neither was. Perhaps both were too mad to understand the consequences of a lie.

Ulfius was chagrined. What honor was there in killing lunatics?

He sheathed his sword and waved the men toward a clear spot, where the grass had been trampled flat. "Let's spread out a little bit, provide some room. There we are, and may the best Merlin win." That proposal sent a shiver through

Ulfius. "Right, then. Merlin One—that is your official contest title—you must prove your magical might by lifting . . ." Ulfius cast his glance around the trammeled spot. His eyes settled on a likely stone, half buried among tall grasses. "Yonder stone overhead, using only enchantment."

The madman clumped over to the spot and squatted, staring at the smooth curve of the stone. He rumpled his brow. "It'll be quite a feat—"

"Not greater than the great Merlin," Ulfius pointed out.

"No," Merlin One allowed with a kind of growl. "No, indeed." He cracked his knuckles, spit on his hands, and launched into a dance.

Ulfius crossed arms over his chest—and noted both his gauntlets were missing. He snarled and studied the crowd. The gloves were nowhere to be seen. Only wide, imploring eyes greeted him. *Someone* in this press of unwashed bodies had a knack for sleight-of-hand.

Merlin One did not. He culminated his summonation spell with a series of ineffectual hand gestures. Giving up, he said, "The stone is too large. It is too well lodged."

Ulfius felt his stomach clench. What could he do with this wretch? "You can't possibly be the true Merlin."

Merlin One snorted. With renewed vigor, he resumed his artless clog dance.

Merlin Two watched with impatient amusement. "What do you expect from the son of an incubus?"

And then, what no one expected occurred. The rock shifted. It more than shifted. It jiggled and struggled up from the embrace of earth and grass.

Ulfius gaped in astonishment. The stone was rising from the ground.

Though momentarily stunned immobile, Merlin One resumed his dance. He accentuated the shoving motions that had given the stone its first magical jolt. It more than jolted now. The ground rumbled. The grassy verge around it split. The rock that emerged shrugged off crumbling earth to reveal an edge four feet—eight feet—twelve feet in length. Its lower reaches were wet and black.

"Merlin?" Ulfius gasped, disbelieving.

The block, twice the height of a man and perhaps equal to one of the Avebury megaliths, broke free of the soil. A gaping hole lay beneath it. Mud sloughed from the edges of the stone, falling into the hole.

Merlin One stood to one side of the mammoth rock and gestured excitedly at it. "Do you see? I *am* Merlin. I *am* Merlin!" He seemed as surprised by this conclusion as anyone. "Where would you like me to put the stone?"

Breathless, Ulfius shrugged and muttered, "Anywhere."

A pernicious impulse jagged across the madman's eyebrow. He crooked a pair of index fingers toward Merlin Two. Without hesitation, the massive stone slammed down atop the astonished impostor. A dark pool seeped out from beneath the stone.

"You said the false Merlin would die immediately," Merlin One reminded.

"I . . . I . . . You killed him!" Ulfius gabbled.

The stone shifted again. It vaulted up suddenly from the bashed ground where it had landed. In the well beneath it, blood and mashed bone reassembled themselves. Merlin Two formed under the hovering stone. Humors fled into once-ruptured membranes, which sealed themselves into a pair of glowering eyes.

Merlin Two was displeased with the result of the contest. He clapped his hands together. A sound like lightning came from him. The megalith split into two halves, a pair of hands poised to smash a fly between them.

Merlin One was that fly.

There came a second gory moment. The first Merlin sprayed out evenly across the others gathered there.

"You—you killed . . . *You* are Merlin?"

The drops lingered for a mere instant on the uplifted faces. Red liquid converged in the gap and hurled the halves of stone apart. Merlin One re-formed. He too was angry. He flung his hands up. The two hunks of stone leaped outward.

Ulfius had to duck to avoid being walloped by a slab of

rock. When he rose, he found himself in the midst of an impromptu spell battle.

Merlins One and Two were at the heart of it, but every last lunatic competed. Lightning bolts lashed from one woman's hands. A putrid cyclone made its unwanted way through the crowd. A few of the idiots grew great fangs and claws. Others transformed into half animals.

"They cannot *all* be Merlin!"

2

Of Stumps and Dreams

He's a soldier. Most certainly. And he searches for me. He has the Look. Sharp-eyed and dark-browed, sweaty and put-out before he had even put in—this man has the Look.

Now his look changes. He suddenly seems a child. He suddenly seems the child.

The boy haunts my dreams. His face is the color of the moon. Antlers top his golden hair. Twin rivers issue from his eyes. His tongue is a sword that juts for leagues and leagues. In one hand he holds a cup of gold. It makes him seem the boy Christ, but he is not the Christ. In the other hand, he holds the keys to hell. He is not the boy Christ. He haunts my dreams, and now he stands there on the heath, asking my name.

All white hair and tatters, Merlin sat on a shattered oak stump and watched the heath. He could hear none of what transpired. The oak grove lay in the lee of the hill, so Merlin had dispatched a family of field mice to spy. They gathered friends, and soon a long line of tiny creatures stretched through the grass. The rodents' voices were shrill in the extreme, and their messages were maddeningly garbled. Even so, Merlin could piece one thing together. "The soldier is definitely looking for me."

"Never trust field mice," came a pulpy voice.

Merlin did not startle. He was used to Loki's antics. The god of chaos often visited him. Never appearing, Loki would only speak out of birdsong or the crackle of sticks underfoot. Just now, he'd chosen to speak through the very stump on which Merlin sat. Perhaps it was poor etiquette to sit on a conversation partner, but Merlin knew Loki wouldn't mind. The god and the madman understood each other.

"Never trust field mice," the stump repeated. "I let a family of mice live in me once. They had promised not to gnaw, though they did, day and night. Do you know what it's like to have something gnawing your insides day and night?"

"Yes, Loki. Now hush," Merlin said, delivering a gentle thump. This did the trunk more damage than he had intended, for it was rotten. Merlin dragged white mats of hair back from his ear and cupped an age-worn hand there. "The mice say the Moon brothers are claiming to be me. They say all the mad folk are claiming to be me. The shiny warrior has challenged them to levitate a stone from the ground." Merlin blinked. His eyes were bright blue beneath flocculent brows. "That is why David capers now. He is trying to raise the stone. Do you see?"

"Of course not," said Loki. "This stump has no eyes."

Out on the heath, an ancient stone was dislodging itself from the ground and slipping upward. Its rumble reached even the oak grove.

"Are you lifting that stone, Loki," Merlin asked, "or am I?"

"I am," Loki replied. "Let the warrior think someone else is you. Warriors are always trouble."

"But he looks so like the boy—" Merlin objected "—the one in my dreams."

"Ah, the Christ."

"The boy is not the Christ," Merlin growled.

"Oh, yes, the not-Christ. The boy with the sword tongue

and the antlers. Even a sightless stump can see that this soldier looks nothing like the boy."

"But he might know the boy. He might know about the keys—"

"The keys to your madness?" Loki interrupted. "Oh, give that up, Merlin. Without madness, who are you? Without madness, who is Merlin?"

"Who is Merlin?" the old man echoed, defeated. It was a fair enough question. He could not remember what he had done an hour ago, let alone who he really was. He could not remember where he had been, whom he had spoken to. He remembered history as though it had been his own life, and forgot his own life as though it were history. Gods and mortals, myths and truths were indistinguishable in his mind. Dreams infused his days. Dreams and nightmares. It was a miserable state, but the only state he had. "Who is Merlin?"

He waved an off-putting hand. The gesture was ill-timed. On the distant heath, the monolith fell and crushed Brynn Moon.

Merlin startled, clutching the stump. The stump startled, too, but had nothing to clutch. A tiny wail of dread came rippling down the mouse line. As the piping sound of despair reached Merlin's ears, he waved his hand again.

The stone bounded up like a man embarrassed he had fallen. Brynn bounded up too. Smashed ribs re-formed and shattered halves of vertebrae embraced their counterparts. Blood drops and puddles arched up through air to make channels through knitting muscles. In a moment, the smashed madman was rebuilt. A coo of approval came among the jabberings of the mice.

"That was well done," said Loki.

"How did you know what I did?" Merlin protested. "You don't have eyes."

"The mice told me."

"You don't trust mice."

"Yes, but you do, and you are dreaming me."

"Damn," said Merlin.

This happened all too often. Merlin would be in the midst

of something wonderful and find it all a fancy. Even his most cogent moments were tinged with delusion. On the other hand, his most delirious dreams touched on deep realities. Somewhere in that mass of mad confusion lay the secret of Merlin's identity, the truth of his past. Try as he might, he could never puzzle it out. Cipher lay upon cipher in a great wall of mystery that enclosed him. It grew higher each day.

"You're certain you're a dream, Loki?" Merlin asked in disappointment. "You and the mice and the Moon brothers and the shiny soldier?"

"Oh, the soldier is real. But as to me and the mice—we're likely just fleas and chiggers."

"You seemed chiggerish."

"Well, Merlin. Will you just sit here and talk to me, knowing I'm a dream, or will you go out there to that shiny man and find out what he seeks?"

In answer, the mage sent a blazing thought out across the heath. The distant stone split in half and clapped around the remaining brother.

"If this is a dream, I want to enjoy it."

Merlin re-formed the rag-garbed lunatic and began sketching lines of lightning from his fingertips. Smoke and screams filled the heath. Wails of despair came. Blasts of energy flung bodies up into the air. It was a typical dream—all that leaping blue-white energy. Soon Merlin was bored.

He flung some animals into the mix. Field mice were nice creatures, even if they were only dreamed. Rabbits and stoats were nice too —especially when they were three stories tall. They bounded in ludicrous display among the arcing rills of magic. Tinkers and lunatics fled before the giant beasts, only to be trampled.

Merlin's dream was running out of characters. But not for long.

He enlarged one girl into a giantess, complete with titanic clothes and a colossal switch. He made her lash the crowd with it. Where the switch struck, idiots changed. Two sprouted the hindquarters of horses and pranced—angry centaurs. Two others became snake-bodied monsters. One man who was struck in the face grew an elephant's trunk. He used it to grab away the giantess's switch. Others joined the attack. A hoary spider web flowed out from another, cocooning the titan.

"You know how it is," Merlin said with a distracted yawn. "When a fancy is pleasant, you don't want it to end."

"I know how it is," Loki replied excitedly in the face of the mayhem. "This is why we are such good friends. We understand each other, and you put on a splendid show."

"Yes," Merlin said, standing and stretching. "Well, as you say, there is a real soldier up there, and he looks like the boy. I must meet him. Farewell, Loki."

"Farewell, Merlin," the stump replied. "I hope you find the boy with the keys. I hope you find your future king."

Merlin waved good-bye and walked up from the grove onto the mad, thick heath.

At times, it was pleasant to be sopping with magic. Merlin could do most anything he could imagine. He *had done* most everything he imagined. He cared nothing for riches or fame. Merlin preferred to make stumps talk, to imbue crickets with songs in Lydian mode, to teach cats to smile. . . . Each small enchantment helped a hostile outer world conform to his inner mind.

At other times, the burden of magic was unbearable. It shot through flesh and bone, blood and brain, until he heard stumps speak but not people. It enervated his body for days and weeks on end while it led mind and soul on terrifying inner quests. He knew these to be dreams only when he died, for unlike others, madmen can die in their dreams.

And so, Merlin marched up from the Loki-stump to the shiny warrior. He amused himself as he went.

"That woman there—she seems almost a Diana." Merlin waggled his fingers, and a bow grew in her hand. The line of mouse informants around her transformed into leaping hinds. "And where there is a Diana, let there also be a Venus." Merlin chose the oldest, lankest, back-bentest crone in the group to garb in the habiliments of the love goddess. He also equipped her with the advantages, both physical and metaphysical, of the queen of love. "And look, there, that red-haired Caledonian with the brawling arms?" A casual thought from Merlin gave him a mighty sword that flashed fire and slew birds dead in flight anywhere above the heath. "Last of all among the children of the gods, let that golden-haired lad mount up on a fiery chariot." Horses formed from wicker and whimsy. Reins shaped themselves from beams of light. The chariot itself became the embodied sun, the lad none other than fiery Phaeton.

Merlin neared the scene. If it had seemed chaos before his spellwork, now it seemed pure hell. The giantess, tangled in her web, was blindly crushing her comrades. Diana was shooting men through the heart with arrows less kind than Cupid's. Venus was backed against a rock by a sword-proud Mars. Above it all, Phaeton bore the inconstant and destroying orb of the sun. They were dying in dozens, but what matter was it? They were dreams.

Oh, thought Merlin's bitterly, and what battlefield would be complete without ravaging Valkyrie? Since the sack of Rome, even Romans could claim the soul-gathering maidens of Saxony for their own.

Merlin nodded toward a group of beggar girls. The five children rose. Their gray rags changed into golden finery. They began to scream in terror. Shouts turned into the song of goddesses. Horned helms topped their braided heads. Spears sprouted in their hands. Spectral chariots and horses formed before and beneath them. They swooped over the field of the fallen, drawing corpses up into the air. The girls let out bellows of such despair that Merlin's heart would have bled for them had they been more than dream.

Ah, it was a lovely thing to be mad. At least there was little boredom in it.

Merlin walked into the midst of the wild mayhem. Untouched by the conflagration all around, he approached the scowling warrior and spoke:

"I am Merlin. I am the man you seek."

•   •   •

"I am Merlin," said the wizened old man to Ulfius. "I am the man you seek."

Ulfius stared, dumbfounded, at the new arrival. His eyes shifted involuntarily to the chaos that filled sky and land before him. Two score of the heath's inhabitants lay dead already, heads smashed open or throats severed or hearts seized in despair or guts run through by arrows or spears. A veteran of five campaigns, Ulfius had never seen such carnage. Ulfius fixed his eyes on the wild white hair of the man before him. "You are author of all of this?"

The man nodded. "It is my dream."

Without thought, Ulfius's hand flew and struck the man's face. The slap was loud, and the force of it whirled the beggar to one side. "Then, for the love of God, cease it!"

The moment skin struck skin, the crazy circus of atrocity paused. The man, clutching one reddened cheek, straightened and stared into Ulfius's eyes with a look that was both penetrating and dissipated. "It is not a dream?"

Ulfius flung his hand out. "The blood is real enough!"

White despair ghosted over the old man's face. "The stump had said it was a dream." He made a sweeping gesture.

Aerial creatures came crashing down. Giant figures shrank. Monsters regained human form. The dead drank in whatever blood or brain they had lost. All stood up and stared. Arrows dissolved from their stomachs and chests. Blood seeped from ragged clothes back into veins.

"I am a little confused," Merlin said sadly—yes, Merlin, for this must surely be the mad mage that Uther sought. "Who summons me?"

Ulfius found himself dropping to one knee. "I am Ulfius, noble retainer of King Uther Pendragon. You are wanted down in the king's tents, for council of war."

The old man seemed to consider. "Real war, or dream war?"

"Whichever," Ulfius replied wearily. He stood. "Uther summons."

"Well, then," said Merlin, seeming both relieved and resigned, "I go."

3

A King's Larder

No sooner had Merlin spoken than he scratched his beard and vanished.

Ulfius was left to stand there, blinking.

The beggars gaped at him. They were even more tattered than before—jangled, exhausted, and confused. Many of them had been killed and resurrected, including the two idiots who had claimed to be Merlin and died thrice over. They all had crept from their squalid hovels with hopes of improving their lot, and now would creep back into them, terrified to emerge again.

"Is anyone injured?" asked Ulfius.

The crowd shook their heads, mouths and eyes hanging open in astonishment.

"Right," Ulfius said. He slid his sword back into its scabbard. Only then did it occur to him where the departed mage had gone. Ulfius bolted upright and glared down the road. "Don't take your horse," he hissed under his breath. Feeling the need of a hasty departure, Ulfius bowed to the throng. "Thank you for your aid." Without further ado, he headed quickly down the high road, toward the siege of Castle Terrabil. His clothes dripped sweat as he went. "Go fetch mad Merlin. . . . Don't take your horse. . . . The stump told me it was a dream. . . ."

The return trip had the virtue of being downhill. Still, during every jolting step of the journey, Ulfius imagined the horrors Merlin initiated below: Uther garbed as a Rhine maiden, trenches overflowing with current jam, Castle Terrabil brought to hideous life, Duke Gorlois turned into a mad pig. . . . The possibilities were endless, as were the steps on that league-long hike from the heath to the siege army.

As debased as Britannia had become under Uther's rule, at least it remained orderly. If Merlin started flinging spells for Uther, madness would reign. Perhaps Ulfius could stop it all, if he were quick enough. Perhaps he could divert Merlin. . . .

Ulfius rounded a long, slow curve onto a plateau above the sea. The ground ahead had been churned by shovels and mud-mired carts. Tents spread in flapping crescents on either side of the road. Beyond lay the assembly grounds. Cook fires smoldered, and men paused on their way between the tents and the trenches. Ulfius shuddered at the thought of the trenches—worm halves, mud, surly warriors, and not a woman for leagues. Beyond, Castle Terrabil crouched on a massif above the sea.

"Merlin could be anywhere here—"

A violent rustle of canvas caught Ulfius's eye. In the royal pavilion beside the cook tent, something thrashed. A large crowd gathered. Grimy soldiers stared in stunned silence, broken by occasional whoops, laughs, and catcalls. Tent poles shuddered under unseen assaults. Linen flapped agitatedly. A warning shout went up. Something large and metallic crashed down. Mud-encrusted men danced outward to avoid a sloshing tide of red.

"Uther's wine kegs!" Ulfius realized. He ran full tilt down the road. His iron-shod boots clacked on paving stones. He reached the edge of the crowd and clawed his way inward.

There, at the back of the king's dining pavilion, a ragcloaked badger was busily scrabbling among barrels in the royal larder. Merlin. His lungs heaved excitedly. His hands pounded on a barrel head. Wood splintered. A white puff of flour billowed into the air. As though unfamiliar with the uses of the stuff, Merlin scooped a batch of it into his mouth, chewed experimentally, and coughed, spreading a plume across the chairs and tables.

"No, no, no, no!" Ulfius shouted. He clambered over tumbled furnishings much to the amusement of the watching crowd. "No, Merlin. You mustn't!"

The mage looked up. His beard was white with flour except where dribbles of grease darkened it. A side of bacon, newly discovered, was clutched in one hand. Two bites were already missing from the meat. The madman stood there, chomping and making circular gestures that indicated he would speak once his mouth was clear. "There you are. Uther's not here. I smelled food."

In his wine-soaked rags, the man's wretched starvation was obvious. The furious reprimand on Ulfius's lips died away. He approached gently and pried the side of bacon from Merlin's grasp. "There, there. Don't ruin your appetite. I'm sure the king will want to feast you."

"Oh, I can eat forever," Merlin said, patting the warrior's arm. A change came over his face. Even through the mask of grease, flour, and jam, a beatific light shone. "You think Uther will be glad to see me?"

Ulfius looked the lunatic up and down. He had not previously noticed the cake smashed between his toes. "He'll be delighted."

"God damn it! Who in hell's fury is ransacking my pavilion!" came an unmistakable shout from the far end of the tent.

The king had arrived.

"Back to digging, you whoresons!" the king advised the idle crowd before storming into the pavilion. "I'll have a pound of flesh for every ounce missing from my private stores—"

Though Ulfius knew that an entire pound would come from his own flesh, he rallied himself. Brushing the worst of the flour from his companion, he turned Merlin to face the king. "Allow me to introduce you."

Uther arrived. He never entered a place. He always arrived. Often he arrived mantled in blood. Other times, the blood only swelled at his face and neck, wishing to burst forth. Meaty hands, massive arms, and aggressively black hair and beard—Uther was a great clenched muscle in a hauberk of shiny mail. He bellowed, "What is the meaning of this outrage!"

Ulfius managed a courtly bow. "King Uther of Britannia,

may I present to you the mighty mage Merlin."

The king bit back a blast of rage. Profanities swirled in the blood vessels of his eyes. He glared at the intruder—noting breakfasts, dinners, and desserts exhibited across his form—and then turned toward Ulfius. "You're quite certain?"

"The very gods of Rome and Saxony have descended to tell me so," replied Ulfius. He watched happily as the king struggled to master his affronted pride. "May I add that I have seen this man crush men under huge stones, burn them alive, and make them slay each other with fiery chariots—only to put them back together like a set of wooden soldiers when he was all done?"

Uther listened. Rage gave way to respect, and then to fear. Fear turned to frustration when the king contemplated the Roman wine spilled across the floor. "Well, then, master Merlin . . . thank you for answering my summons."

Merlin bowed. His back was smeared with custard. "Thank you for feasting me."

"Yes," replied the king. "Perhaps we should get you cleaned up and retire to my private tent?"

Merlin looked enraged. "I'm not done eating!"

Ulfius interceded. "Given the . . . ardor of the wizard's hunger, I would suggest staying here—far away from your private tent and the valuables within."

"Quite right," said the king. His face had gone from bright red to a shade of feverish pink. "Yes. Ulfius, make a place for us at one of these tables."

The warrior hopped to, setting up toppled chairs and wiping away spatters of apple butter. He fetched a folded cloth of red samite and laid it across a table. He draped matching seat covers on the arms and back of the chairs.

All the while that Ulfius worked, mage and king regarded each other. Uncomfortable smiles lifted the corners of their mouths but never quite reached their eyes.

Ulfius concluded his preparations and gestured for the king to sit. "Here we are. Here we are."

Uther sank grandly into the wooden chair, his mere presence transforming it into a throne. "You may sit in my company, Merlin."

The wizard nodded and smiled with his eyes. "And you may sit in mine." Uther scowled, and Merlin quickly added, "Your Highness." Before he settled into place across from the king, he darted off to nip a wheel of cheese. As he slumped into the seat, weathered hands clutched inexpertly at the cheese, breaking off great hunks. Teeth bit through wax and cheese, both.

Ulfius meanwhile withdrew to an anonymous distance. His previous dealings with each man convinced him this would be a confrontation best observed from afar.

"I do not know how much Ulfius has told you," the king began quietly.

Merlin chewed heartily and made a face as he swallowed a ball of wax. "He was kind enough to tell me I was not dreaming the battle on the heath. I appreciate perspective on such matters. I can never be quite clear what is real. Even a dream can say it is real."

"Yes," Uther said, confused. "Well, the battle down here, on the plain—it is no dream. It's a border war. Duke Gorlois refused a royal summons. It's treason." He leaned forward, conspiratorially. "Truth be told, it's a border war, but not over land. Over a woman! Igraine! She's one to boil the blood!"

"Boil the blood . . ." Merlin said through a strange smile. He closed his eyes, and a look of ecstasy stole across his features. "Yes." Merlin nodded avidly. "Boil the blood." He motioned to Ulfius. "How about a flagon or two of wine?"

Ulfius shrugged a question at his king, asking for permission. Uther reluctantly nodded.

While the warrior fetched a pair of flagons, Uther struggled to reclaim the thread of his narrative. "Where was I? Oh, yes, Igraine . . . Her husband is a traitor—Fortune smiles—and we are besieging his castle to bring him out. Once Duke Gorlois is defeated, Igraine can be mine."

"I once knew a woman who could boil blood," interrupted Merlin. He paused to delicately draw a wrangled bit of wax from his mouth. "Well, not a woman exactly. She was a cow. Then there was another woman who could freeze blood— ugly physiognomy, you see?"

"I want your help, Merlin," the king pressed. "Britannia requires your help. Gorlois is a traitor, but canny, and well armed, well provisioned. I need you to break through his walls. Bring him out to me. Alive, of course, so he can be properly gibbeted."

"Very nice. I like giblets." He leaned back in his seat as Ulfius placed before him a goblet and a flagon of foamy red from Gaul. Reaching out with cheese-crumbly fingers, Merlin grabbed Ulfius's sleeve. "Giblets, please."

"Raw, or boiled?" Ulfius asked as he set a goblet of wine in front of the king.

"Surprise me." Merlin drew the king's flagon and goblet over too. "Did you want any, Uther?"

"Enough delay," said the king, pounding on the table. "Will you do it? Will you deliver Gorlois to me?"

"Oh, yes," said Merlin, "if you wish. . . . Of course, you will be destroyed."

The king gabbled, staring at the filthy vagabond before him. At last, he gathered the wit to roar, "What?"

Merlin downed the first tankard of ale in one prolonged swallow. He hoisted the next one and slurped more gently. "Oh, I can bring him to you. I could walk through the air to where Gorlois is and snatch him up and bring him here for trial and execution, but he has a smell about him—a skunk smell. That's what will happen if I drag Gorlois out to you. You'll end up stinking, and he'll lope away, free. You'll lose allies. He will gain them. He will besiege you in your own castle, and in the end, Ulfius here will eviscerate you." Merlin's eyes again rolled into his head. "Ah, viscera. Have you any blood sausage or haggis in this store of yours?"

Uther was too enraged to hear the question. He stood from his spot, tipping the heavy wooden chair back with his knees. "What! What are you saying?"

"I have visions. The future and the past are much clearer to me than the present. If you send me to fetch Gorlois, the future is not pretty." Merlin pivoted in his chair, seeing his latest entree arrive.

Ulfius brought a platter with raw chicken giblets and strands of link sausage. As he placed the plate on the table, Merlin laughingly pantomimed evisceration.

King Uther glared at Ulfius, looking at once hurt and furious. "You traitor! Merlin here says you will kill me!"

Ulfius backed away. "Sire, these rantings—they are whimsy, mere fancy."

"You consider eviscerating me to be whimsy? Fancy?"

Ulfius stumbled backward over a set of chairs. "No, sire, I—"

"And you!" the king roared, drawing his sword. "You come in here and ransack my personal pantry and gulp down my personal wine and have the audacity to refuse my personal demand that you fetch Gorlois?"

"I didn't refuse," Merlin said blandly, his mouth full of a wine-and-cheese mush, "only that if I did, Ulfius would kill you."

The king released a shriek of rage and hauled hard on his sword. It leaped over his head in a gleaming arc that would slice the chomping wizard in half. The blade flashed and descended and struck.

Steel clanged on steel. Ulfius's sword had jabbed into the space between the king and Merlin. The edges of the blades skirled angrily. Uther leaned inward, intent on killing Merlin. Ulfius gritted his teeth and struggled to hold aloft the wrath of the king. Between them, metal shuddered and groaned.

"How dare you!" the king demanded.

"Don't kill him, sire," Ulfius pleaded. The words sounded ridiculous in his own ears. Only an hour ago, he would have sold Merlin to a renderer to turn into soap. Now, he was committing treason to save the man's life. To make matters worse, Merlin sat there, oblivious. He had floated out a pot of leeks from the pantry and was fumbling about, trying to get hold of one. An errant stroke of one hand flung up a leek, and the thing tumbled through the air, striking Uther in the pate.

"Regicide! You're conspiring to kill me!"

"No, Your Highness. He is . . . he is only a starving madman."

"He's mad, and I'm furious," Uther hollered. He hauled his sword back and took a lateral swing at the old man's neck.

Again, Ulfius interposed his blade. "Give him a chance, sire. I have seen wonders from him. And his heart is good."

"His heart, aye?" asked the king.

He pivoted his blade and rammed it toward Merlin's chest. Steel sank deep into flesh—pig's flesh. Merlin had levitated the gnawed side of bacon over to himself and was worrying a white edge of fat.

"Perhaps a few jiggers of spirits," the wizard suggested to himself. He stood and tottered back toward the gaping pantry.

The side of bacon remained, skewered, on the blade of Uther Pendragon. Growling, the king won free, and the fatty meat dropped to the floor. Mead gushed from the panty.

Uther stalked toward it. Murderous light shone in his eyes.

Ulfius leapt in the way, sword wavering before him. "Please, sire."

"Out of my way!"

"He has Otherworld powers. They say he's the son of an incubus." It was not enough, and Ulfius began to improvise. "God has cursed him with the mark of Cain—you cannot kill him. And don't anger him. He can fling out his bones like porcupine quills. His blood is acid, and his urine is fire."

The king was apoplectic. "I want to kill him!"

"Sire, no," Ulfius said. "I'll take him out of here, far away, and you'll never see him again."

Uther lowered his sword, blinking thoughtfully. A wrathful breath fled him. "If you put it that way—"

Lowering his guard, Ulfius replied, "I'm so glad you see—"

The king bulled past, intent on cleaving the bent shoulders of the man who predicted his doom.

4

Visions of the Pendragon

Merlin dug doglike in an overturned barrel of pickles. He wanted a big one. The big ones would be on the bottom. A bit of vinegar and garlic was just the thing to cut a too-sweet wine and a too-bland cheese. The rye spirits had just not done the trick, and the king had had only three bottles of the stuff. Pickle juice sogged the elbows and knees of his ragged robe. That meant a few more hours of savoring once he was tossed out.

They would toss him out, of course. They always did. They would try to kill him, first, but Merlin was a hard creature to kill. He had been hanged, drawn, quartered, gibbeted, immolated, crucified, buried, drowned, strangled, backstabbed, bludgeoned, and once even flung from a siege engine. And those were only mortal abuses. He'd also been struck by lightning, carried away in a waterspout, eaten by sharks, and buried in an avalanche. Man or beast or god, none had been able to grant him quietus. Certainly Uther Pendragon couldn't kill him—

Unless, of course, all those memories of deathless death were only fancies. And fancies or no, getting killed was painful.

"Ah, here it is," declared Merlin with satisfaction, lifting a prodigious pickle from the dark brine.

"Ah, here you are," declared Uther with rage. He hurled his sword tip at the wizard's stooped back.

Merlin whirled. Steel rang on pickle. The knobby cucumber had become as hard as iron. The wizard did not exactly hold the vegetable, but suspended it before him on tracers of magic. Trembling fingers leaked streams of green motes. The pickle whirled and flung back the king's blade. It advanced. The two fought viciously.

It was an oracular moment. Merlin saw past green skin and pickle juice, past the king of Britannia and his ludicrous struggle. He saw to Duke Gorlois in Castle Terrabil, and beyond him, to Duchess Igraine at Tintagel. The mad mage's mind drove even beyond her—through her—to the wheeling white skies and the destiny in those skies.

A figure moves. It is mountain-massive but white and quick like lightning. It soars among clouds and dives through lakes of black water. It darts, swift and smooth, a yarn shuttle among the raveling strands of Albion. It is a boy, yes—the boy, but in the form of the Pendragon. Uther? Pure and crystalline? No. This boy rises beyond and through Igraine, beyond and through two castles besieged, past Gorlois and through Uther. The boy is the son of Uther.

The boy must be made. At whatever cost, this quicksilver boy with his bunch of keys and his tongue like a sword and antlered head and sanguine goblet—he must become reality. He will be my reality. The child of the Pendragon will save me. He has the keys to my madness. He will save me and all of Britannia. The quicksilver boy must become reality.

Then the dream was gone. Merlin was left gaping. His fleecy eyes hung wide. His mouth mimicked them below. How to realize this dream? If he brought Gorlois to Uther, the king would be killed by Ulfius himself. If he enspelled a corridor into Castle Terrabil, Uther would later die by poisoning in the castle gardens. Whether from thorn or tampered food or blowgun, Merlin saw the man crumple, hands balled to his clenched belly, and die. A similar fate awaited should Merlin spirit Igraine into the king's hands, fingers even now full of strangled pickle. But if—

"Your Highness." Merlin interrupted with a discreet cough into his fist.

The king glanced up from the cucumber he held. An expression halfway between fury and desperation clutched his face. "What?"

"I cannot bring Gorlois to you, but—"

"Guards! Armsmen! Cavalry! Infantry! Slay this man!"

Into every flap of the pavilion, warriors flooded. They charged. Their expressions transformed from voyeuristic glee to angry duty. Swords hissed out of scabbards. Boots kicked up dirt. Shouts converged on the vinegar-soaked madman.

Ulfius did his best to wave them off but was pushed brusquely aside.

Imploring, Merlin flung his hands outward. "Perhaps another plan—"

The front rank of soldiers charged across the pavilion's floor and sank into a trough of blood pudding that appeared beneath them. They thrashed in dread of drowning.

The next warriors leaped the broad trough and continued the charge. From all directions, they swarmed Merlin. Swords and battle-axes descended. They flashed into the space where the mage stood. Steel met steel in a deadly storm.

The wizard, though, was gone.

Blades withdrew. Warriors backed up, astonished.

Where the mad mage had been, a mouse in ratty clothes now stood. Its tiny hands were spread beseechingly, and its little voice harped in minuscule fury. A few armsmen stepped forward to cleave the creature.

Even before they could lift their weapons, Merlin swelled up and outward. Each miniature jag of hair widened into a bristle. The creature's nose lengthened into a long gray trunk. Whiskers melded into a pair of tusks. A mammoth? In moments, its vast shoulders flung back the armsmen. Its tusks tore through the pavilion roof overhead.

All the while that the beast grew, its voice expanded as well. "The implication of bringing duke or duchess to you would be death, but there is still a way that you can have the duchess—"

An armsman in rusty hauberk lunged at the pachyderm.

His sword lanced deep into the beast's neck. Blood gushed forth. Ignoring tusks, the man clung hard to the hilt of his sword and wrenched at it to tear the wound wider.

The mammoth's voice failed. Its eyes rolled in white anguish. It thrashed at the impaling blade.

More warriors, emboldened by the first, drove their swords into the poor beast's sides. They shouted encouragement to each other. Their weapons jabbed inward like thirsty tongues. Blood answered steel.

Merlin was sliced through. Swords pierced his hide and entered his ribcage and crossed in his organs. His flesh was in tatters. Death seeped from every tissue. Pain sank its claws into his heart.

He wouldn't die, of course. He couldn't die except in his own dreams, but he could feel pain, vicious in every tissue. And pain had a way of unhinging him. The fragments of mind and body came into chaotic conjunction, seeking a new form. There, amid flapping tabards—purple dragons on fields of gold—he saw his salvation.

A surge of primordial energy raged through him. Bristles flattened to scales. Hair jagged out in a mangy mane. Snout shrank and widened. Eyes grew from black to red. Ears peaked. Wings unfolded. Tail became a great, lashing scourge. The arching neck of the Pendragon rose up to fling back the torn roof of the pavilion. Releasing a fiery roar, the great wyrm unfurled its wings and hurled the armsmen away. Its beaked maw darted down to pluck swords from its side. Its tail meanwhile cleared a space behind it. With each blade yanked from its wounds, the massive beast slapped its tail on the earth, sending up dirt clouds and shaking the whole encampment.

The armsmen who had wounded Merlin ebbed back in a cringing tide. Retreating and advancing groups collided. They fell in rings all around the towering monster. Beyond them, others dropped to their knees and gazed in hope and dread at the beast.

"The Pendragon!"

"The deliverer!"

"He will fight for us!"

Merlin heard these speculations. They rose, multifarious, in his wheeling mind. The Pendragon would fight for them, would deliver them. . . .

"Behold, the Pendragon!" Merlin shouted.

A furious growl answered this last comment, a growl from Uther himself. "I am the Pendragon, not this . . . this overgrown toad!"

"Overgrown toad!" A look of furious indignation cross the dragon's face. It yanked the last of the swords from its hide, which healed behind the emerging steel. Merlin flung the weapon away, and it clanged in the wreck of the king's pantry. "Overgrown toad! I've a mind to slay the lot of you, beginning with the king and working on down to the last squire and stable hand! But I came here not to slay—but to save. And apart from the Pendragon, Albion will not be saved!"

Uther lowered his guard for a moment. "So, you will bring Gorlois to me?"

"No. I will not bring Gorlois to you," Merlin said. "But you are not after Gorlois. You are after Igraine."

"You will bring her to me?"

"I will take you to her," said the dragon. Even as he spoke, Merlin began to revert to his native form. Already, the scaly face of the wyrm had transformed into the querulous eyes and shaggy beard of the mad mage. "For a price, of course."

5

Three on a Tear

That night beneath a starry sky, three horsemen rode full-tilt across the plains of Dumnonia. Ghosts of steam rose from warm fens into the chill air. Claws of mist dragged across black stifles. Perhaps the Dumnonian dead were rising in outrage. Perhaps the land herself protested their mission. Whatever warnings they whispered, though, were lost to the ravenous clamor of hard-shod hooves.

Ulfius trailed the other two riders. In place of his Pendragon armor, he wore the livery of Duke Gorlois. He also bore the face of Gorlois's chamberlain, Jordanus. The man had a mop of red hair, a broad beard, and bushy mustaches. He was more a descendant of barbarous Dyfed than civilized Rome. Even Ulfius's horse seemed half-savage, barded in green and red.

Just ahead rode Merlin, disguised as Brastias, the hulking castellan of Tintagel. He had devised these magical semblances and every other particular of this lunatic spree. The sorcerer cast an avid grin toward Uther.

The king was plainly worried. Though he had submitted to this whole scheme, the battle in the pantry was fresh in his mind. Merlin was powerful, yes, but also insubordinate. There was no more dangerous combination—power and insubordination. Uther had not become king by being a fool, and now his throne was in the hands of a fool. But for Igraine, he would do anything. Done up like blond-haired Gorlois, Uther crouched low aback his galloping steed. He rode like a man braced in the joust. Had he a lance, it would have been leveled before him, with a shield riding low upon his shoulder. Clearly, he intended conquest.

Ulfius's accusing eye turned back at last upon himself. His comrades might be forgiven their indiscretions. They both had their lunacies. Ulfius, on the other hand, was of sound mind and unblemished honor. His complicity in all this was criminal. He shook his head. In the rumbling hooves and coiling mists, Ulfius suddenly realized he would be trapped here, between the beggar and the king, until one or the other died.

"Or until I die," Ulfius muttered bitterly, "which seems most likely."

The three horses galloped up the twisting road that led to the gatehouse of Tintagel. A small garrison manned the fortification. Beyond its portcullised arches lay a drawbridge, the only navigable route onto the peninsula. The drawbridge crossed a fifty-foot chasm, with only a rocky ridge below. At the far end of the bridge stood another gatehouse in the curtain wall of the castle.

"There will be ten men at the first gatehouse," Ulfius shouted. "Armed men. We mustn't slip up. We must talk as little as possible. We must remember we are Duke Gorlois, Chamberlain Jordanus, and Castellan Brastias—"

"Yes, yes," the king growled impatiently. "Now shut up."

In a clamor of hooves, the party reached the looming bridge gate of Castle Tintagel. A portcullis of black oak and iron barred the way. Jags of upended slate topped the field-stone walls all around. Even the ivy bristled with thorns. This was a barbarian castle, beyond the reach of Rome and civilization. Until now, it had been beyond the reach of Uther too.

A dark party of armsmen—avatars of this place of mossy black stone—emerged from the gatehouse. They spread themselves before the portcullis. Visors were lowered. Teeth clenched behind clamped lips. Eyes glinted in forbidding warning. Hands clutched Pagan great swords.

The captain of the armsmen stepped forward. His red-and-green livery seemed black beneath the stars. He unhooded a lantern and stared angrily at the arrivals. "Identify your-selves!" He lingered on the vowels and clipped glottal stops.

Ulfius suddenly realized his midlands accent would be conspicuous.

The king commanded, "Clear the way. It is Duke Gorlois. We have defeated Uther. His forces lie decimated. We broke through. Chamberlain Brastias, Castellan Jordanus, and I have ridden here to bring the news."

"Chamberlain *Jordanus*," Ulfius corrected, struggling to sound Dumnonian, "and Castellan *Brastias*. We are weary with fighting and giddy with victory."

"And eager to see our lady."

With each new utterance, the captain blinked in confusion. He lifted the lantern, shining it across the faces. "Your looks are right, but not your voices. Your voices slosh with the Thames."

"Ach," replied Ulfius, "so much time spent among those midland bastards! They tried to steal our lands, and now have stolen our tongues!"

"Bastards," agreed Uther.

A grim smile lit the captain's face. "What is the fate of their king?"

"Evisceration!" Merlin piped up. Uther flung a murderous glance his way, but the madman continued, "It was quite a sight!"

The captain shrugged, chuckling. "Well, good news, at the least. Welcome home! Shall I signal for a bath to be drawn? The kettles should be put on straight away—"

"No," Uther replied, nudging his mount toward the yet-closed gate. "No, I want to see Igraine!"

The captain broke in. "It's only that you are rather ... *potent* in your unwashed—that is, in your ... battle armor, and—"

"I want to be potent!"

"Raise the portcullis!" shouted Ulfius. He feared one more turn of conversation would bring them all to the gibbet. "Raise the portcullis!"

The captain relayed the order, seeming just as glad to end this uncomfortable interview.

Uther heeled his steed up to the grid of wood and iron even as it began to rise in its track. The black walls let out a toothy rattle as chain and cog engaged. Ulfius and Merlin likewise urged their mounts forward. Uther's beast crowded the gate, its nose nearly getting caught as the thing rose. The moment its head could slip beneath the sharpened spikes, Uther kicked it forward and, ducking, followed. Merlin and Ulfius made their way within.

The stony vestibule beyond was riddled with murder holes. In them Ulfius glimpsed eyes and what seemed eyes but turned out to be arrowheads. At the far end of the passage, a drawbridge was lowering, revealing blue wedges of night. Shouts sounded above, hailing the approach of the king. On the curtain wall across the chasm, giant rectangles of light played, illumination flung from lanterns unhooded. With a boom, the drawbridge settled into place. The way was clear out onto it, and the door in the curtain wall was opening.

"It's not too late," replied Ulfius. "We could turn about right now, race into the hills—"

Uther dug heels into the side of his horse and sent it bolting over the drawbridge. Merlin followed close behind.

Ulfius felt himself deflate. He pursued at a sedate pace. By the time he caught up to his comrades, they were already dismounting in the courtyard. A passel of drowsy and hastily arrayed servants were relieving the men of their mounts and burdens.

One of these, a young man with hair cropped just above his shoulders, was struggling to explain things to the king. "At this hour, she would be in your apartments."

"Which way?" asked Uther avariciously.

"Which way?" the youth wondered.

Ulfius broke in. "Lead the way. The duke needs help shucking his armor. He needs someone to carry it."

"I can clean it, as well," the youth offered.

"No, just leave it in the duke's chambers with him."

The boy cast an admiring glance at the false Gorlois. "Eager for your lady's company—"

"Hop to, boy," Uther said, slapping the young man's back.

As they set off into the deeps of the place, Ulfius's attention turned to another such conversation.

"Have you seen them? About knee-high. Lovely legs. Pale skin. Delicious."

"Seen whom?" the groggy armsmen asked.

"The lamb shanks? And the sausages. And the pasties. Who has been keeping the larder since I went to war?"

"Why, Claudias. He is acting castellan—"

"Surprise inspection," Merlin said. "Take me straight away to the larder. Don't alert Claudias. I must see that all is in order. Otherwise, there will be more than sides of beef hanging there!"

"Of course," said the armsman. He fiddled at his belt for

a jumble of keys. "This way. Yes, I have the key right here. This way."

Delighted, Merlin slapped the rump of his horse. It whinnied and reared. Its fore hooves spun, and it screamed in a voice like a woman's. The dark company of retainers snatched for the horse's reins and yanked it to ground. Their growls sounded murderous next to the horrible wailing of the horse.

The sound rooted Ulfius to the flagstones. He glanced involuntarily toward the high tower where Igraine would surely have her chambers. Candlelight was awakening there, and with it a woman—a fair and virtuous woman, the object of a lustful king and a deceiving son of an incubus. The poor creature. To preserve her honor, she had withdrawn from the world, and her husband had gone to war against the king of Britannia. Now, all her virtue would be stolen from her without even her knowledge. She would be quickly bathing, of course, and trading glad, amazed jokes with her chambermaids. Then would come the horrible moment of truth. The ravenous wolf disguised as her husband would attack. He would fling back the door and burst through. He would hurl her tender flesh to the floor. In whatever state of gritty halfnakedness he had achieved, he would vault atop her. There would not be screams, but only because he would forbid it— he who was her husband and her captor and her husband's hated foe, all in one.

"I cannot allow it," Ulfius swore to himself. He released the traces of his own mount and strode toward the archway where he had seen Uther and his guide disappear. "By all that is holy, I cannot allow it."

He started up the stairs, lost his footing, and spilled across their base. Scale mail rattled like a crashing wave.

"Chamberlain!" shouted a young girl. She pelted across the dark courtyard to help the fallen man. Her small, warm hand clutched his fiercely. "Are you all right?"

"No," replied Ulfius frankly. He huffed a breath and stared up the forbidding spiral before him.

"Is it true, Jordanus? Is my father home?" the girl asked excitedly.

Ulfius stared at her. In the moonlight, she was as pale as porcelain. She had long black hair and wide eyes. Slim shoulders shivered in her nightshirt. He thought at first she must be cold, but realized then it was excitement.

"Is the war over? Is Father home?"

"Oh, sweet dear Morgause," Ulfius said, stroking the child's cheek.

"I'm Morgan," she said, drawing back from him and staring strangely. "Morgause is in Lothian. What's wrong with you, Jordanus?"

Ulfius shook his head and laughed exhaustedly. "Forgive me, Morgan. I am not myself. . . ."

Hope drove the shadows from her face. "He's here, isn't he?"

"Dear child, it's too late for you to be awake. Go back to bed and dream sweet dreams—"

"He *is* home," she declared eagerly. Flashing past him, she ascended the tower stairs.

"Wait!" Ulfius shouted after her. His objection brought only happy giggles from the fleeing girl. "Wait, Morgan. Come back!"

Ulfius followed. His iron-shod footsteps echoed on the stairs with savage monotony, like the rasp of sheers. It was bad enough what would happen to Igraine, but for Morgan to witness it all—

"Morgan, stop!" Ulfius gasped. In his armor, he couldn't keep up. "Please, Morgan, stop!"

The girl disappeared around the corner of the spiral.

Ulfius clutched his chest, laboring up the stairway. How high could this tower be? He had almost convinced himself to give up—that if the duchess's chambers were so lofted as this, God himself was responsible for what took place next.

"Father! Father!" Morgan shouted. She flung back an ornate door of oak and silver gilt and strode into the room.

"Wait!" Ulfius stumbled through, just behind her. He

clutched Morgan's shoulders and tried to pull her back, hissing, "You shouldn't see this violence."

A coifed head appeared from the bed's veils and looked gently at Ulfius and Morgan. Igraine was a lovely vision. Her eyes were azure in the light of a hundred candles. Her mouth was a ribbon of red samite. Her skin was pale silk. Her bare shoulders were as luscious as cream. And she smiled. That was the great miracle of it. She smiled.

"What violence, dear Jordanus?"

Confused, Ulfius blinked stupidly at her. "Your husband. He was on his way. He—"

"He has arrived," she said. A slender hand reached back to draw a smiling Gorlois—a *faux* Gorlois—to the edge of the bed. "And the violence of which you spoke?"

"W-well," stuttered Ulfius, "I s-suppose I assumed . . . given the king's—that is, the duke's state . . . that, well, a certain . . . brusqueness might be evidenced—"

"Father! You are back!" Morgan said happily. She pulled free of Ulfius's nerveless fingers and ran toward the image of her father.

"Out!" Uther shouted, pointing at the girl. "To bed with you!"

Morgan stopped midstep. Her breath caught short in a near sob. "But I want to see you. I want to kiss you."

"You heard me, child! Out!"

Eyes slivering in anger, Morgan seemed to see through the guise. She hissed, "You aren't my father!" She backed slowly away. "You're a devil."

"Out!"

Morgan turned and fled. Her bare feet pattered sadly down the stairs.

"And you, loyal servant," Uther said with a growl. "You will begone too." The naked man stepped from the bed and strode toward Ulfius. He lifted Ulfius by his shoulder plates, carried him to the open door, and tossed him down the spiral stair.

And Ulfius had thought the way up had been long.

6

Barrels and Broken Sieges

Tintagel was well stocked. Venison, pork, mutton, duck, goose, wild boar, eel, and even a bit of dolphin; wheat rolls, rye bread, oat cakes; sea salt, exotic cinnamon, honey, rosemary, sweet basil, clover, garlic chives, thistle blossom, mustard seed; cabbages, carrots, leeks, red onions, dried peas and beans; mead, ale, bitters, beer, wine, and spirits from the highlands; even medicinal worts and saps and powdered essences. Taxonomy did not matter to Merlin. It was all delicious. He had found a big bowl and a grinder and sat astride them both, feeding item after item into the macerating mouth of the thing. A multifarious ooze came out the other end, seasoned with spices and poisons. Occasional splashes of liquor made the stuff a regular mush. Merlin tasted his concoction by sinking a ladle in it, hoisting the thing to his lips, and letting the thick mess gush down his throat. A good portion of it painted the beard and neck of his Brastias semblance.

"Castellan, I would gladly prepare something for you," an agitated cook said. In one hand he held aloft a lantern, the only illumination in the large, wet cellar. The other hand raked through his standing black hair.

Merlin looked up. A gray slug of mush slithered down his black-bearded cheek. "Do you know this recipe?"

The cook gabbled, "Know the recipe? Know the recipe? Of course not! I studied in London. I am a Roman-trained vintner, a Frank-trained baker, and a Celtic-trained butcher." He paused, his whole form jiggling in agitation. "What you do with food—this I have never seen!"

"Watch and learn," the madman replied.

"I could have fed twenty men with what you have in that bowl."

"You can have whatever I don't finish."

Releasing a shriek of exasperation, the cook turned away. His hands quivered as he stomped up the cellar stairs. Light retreated with him.

Merlin blinked pleasantly at the vanishing illumination. The mush would be just as tasty in the dark.

Except that darkness never came. With a perfunctory motion, another figure snatched the cook's lantern. An ominous voice said simply, "He's down there?"

"Yes."

The second figure descended. As frayed as the cook had seemed, this new arrival looked downright battered. Jambeaus and sollerets hung loose from his shaky ankles. Cuisses and brassards were bashed as by countless bludgeons. Under a shirt of chain mail, the man's chest was caved in and panting. Bruises crossed his face, and his red hair, beard, and mustaches drooped in sweaty lines. He reached the bottom of the stairs, raised the lantern, and let out a solemn groan.

"Is that you, Ulfius?" Merlin asked lightly.

"Yes," the lantern man replied with profound regret. "Yes, it is."

"You wouldn't know it. You look a right barbarian." Merlin took another gulp of his concoction and held a ladleful out to his comrade, who demurred. Merlin shrugged. "Who did you find to fight with at this hour?"

"The stairs," Ulfius replied sullenly. He marched across the cellar to a low pile of barrels and sat down. The lantern seemed infinitely heavy. When he set it down, he heaved a terrific sigh and plunged his head into his hands. "What are we doing here, Merlin?"

"Eating," the mage responded without pause. Despite his black-bearded disguise, he looked very Merlinesque in his mask of ground food. He hiked a thumb up toward the tower. "Eating and trysting."

"That tells why you and Uther are here, but why am I here?"

"To keep us from getting killed." Merlin smiled blissfully and sampled more of the venison-cake-ale concoction. Pleasure spread like springtime sunlight over his features. "You really must try some of this."

Green-gilled, Ulfius watched the madman. "Why don't you just conjure food? Why do you spend your magical might turning yourself into a mouse or a Pendragon when you could just make yourself a perfect meal?"

Merlin's lips pursed, and he shook his head. "Food is different."

Ulfius considered the gruel draping the madman's front. "Yours certainly is."

"All food is," Merlin said. "It's difficult to conjure—not a being, but a becoming. Say you are hunting a hart. It is a creature, a living being. You down it with an arrow. Now it is food. Then you eat it, and it becomes a part of you—a living being." He snorted, pleased with his explanation. "Food is like fire—the process of something becoming something else." He smiled. "Food is different."

Unimpressed, Ulfius said, "What about fire? I've seen you wield it expertly."

"Fire?" Merlin's eyes wandered in their sockets, as though he were searching for a thought he'd tucked away, expecting never to need it. "Fire is different."

A hiss of irritation escaped Ulfius.

Merlin hoisted a dripping ladle. "Do you see this stuff? It is primordial, full of life, vibrant as fire, glorious as chaos!" A particularly fibrous glob slipped from the spoon and pasted itself on Merlin's side. Undaunted, he declared, "I could no more conjure this than I could conjure the child that Uther is even now getting on Igraine."

Despair as thick and gray as Merlin's stew oozed over Ulfius. "A child. I'd nearly forgotten. Cruel fortune to bring a child out of all this trickery and nonsense."

"Not cruel," said Merlin's setting the ladle down for the first time. His eyes glowed with a faraway gleam, as though he were seeing the distant lakes of Rheged. "He will be such a child. He will arise like life itself. He will unite the land, Ulfius. He will unite all of us, even me. He will save us. Yes, it is a foul meat grinder he comes from, a great chaos of violence and trickery, lust, deviltry, collusion, deceptions—but none of that matters. All of that is food, a process changing one life into another. And what a life!"

Ladle forgotten, Merlin reached in and scooped goo with both hands. He scraped the paste into his lips. Trailing sludge striped his cheeks. He looked like a mud-painted Pict. The madman's eyes closed in delight as he swallowed, and he held his dripping hands high in adulation.

The scene transforms. It is not gray stew that drapes me, but blood. It is not a dark and dingy cellar where I kneel, but a fire-flickering battlefield. My armor is still Dumnonian, and I still wear the form of Castellan Brastias, but I am elsewhere.

A black band of men in Pendragon livery rushes up an embankment.

I slump to the ground. I bury my face in a twist of dry grass beside a dead man.

The soldiers arrive. One kicks the dead man in the ribs. The body groans. A pair of swords jab through its chest, ending with a gurgle of air. A third blade strikes the man's head from his shoulders.

Another soldier turns toward me. He kicks.

I hold back the agonized roar. The man could likely not kill me—except of course that this is a dream—but he could hurt me plenty. I lie still and silent. A second kick follows, and a third.

"He's dead," the soldier says. He shifts his feet, voice clambering out over tumbled grass and fallen warriors. "There's more over there. Make sure all of Gorlois's soldiers are dead before you spend time looking for the duke. We're not after a live prisoner. We're after a dead rebel."

Dark laughter answers from the warriors around.

"Thrash those grasses down there. You'll likely scare up a few more of these conies. Stab anything that moves."

Footfalls announce the departure of half the group. Three men remain. A warm stream spatters my back. Ignominy soaks into ring mail and quilted camise.

"If I'd known Gorlois would sally out tonight, I'd not have drunk so much ale." The man laughs.

"Nobody could've guessed," another responds. *"What kind of warrior would leave his entrenchment to attack us in ours?"*

"Gorlois. That's what kind," the third says.

"He must've heard about Uther and Merlin going to Tintagel. That must've been what lured him out."

"Just as well. He'll be dead before dawn, if he's not dead already, and we can all get back home before the rains come."

"Uther'll fancy another's wife by Samhain, and we'll be out here again before Imbolc."

Their leader motions toward the east. *"We're not done here, tonight. We've got lots of Dumnonians to flush and snare. When Uther's back from his night of sport, we'll have sport of our own to show him."*

Amid murmurs and the sound of swords slashing through brush, the three depart.

Sodden and quivering, I rise slowly from the clutch of grass where I had lain. Hands grip me, and I whirl, ready to fight.

There is no one there, only the spangled night. Out of the cold heart of it comes a familiar voice, worried. *"Merlin! Merlin, are you all right?"*

I see only a Dumnonian hillside—leagues of trenches and armies of dead. Uther's war machines are wreathed in orange fire. A wide swath of dead warriors leads from the nearby battle to the open gates of Castle Terrabil. The fortress bleeds soot into the sky. A sickle moon drags its point through the shuffling sea.

•   •   •

"Gorlois led a charge," Merlin blurted bleakly.

The hands on his shoulders tightened. Ulfius shook him. "Wake up, Merlin. It's only a dream."

"Gorlois led a charge. His forces are decimated."

A pause came. "How do you know this?"

"Brastias," Merlin said, panting. "I can see through his eyes."

The band of Pendragon warriors hunches at the base of the hill. The leaders jab swords into a bank of holly. A yelp comes. A bloodied warrior scrambles up from the leaves. Uther's men set to with swinging blades. The warrior bears the first two wounds before crumpling to one knee. The next hail of steel unmakes him. He falls amid holly. He rolls once in anguish and lies still.

"Our forces have taken the field?" asked Ulfius in hope.

"They are cleansing it," replied Merlin. "They are killing every last Dumnonian."

More silence came. "Why don't they just surrender?"

"Perhaps they have. Uther told them to take no prisoners," Merlin noted hollowly. "He wants Gorlois dead. He wants Igraine to himself."

The stillness that came after that was bleak. "It gets worse and worse. One man's lust means a thousand men murdered." He hissed again, though this time with rage instead of irritation. "And what of Gorlois? Does he live?"

Merlin pulled away from the man's grasp and stooped back down into the murk of dream. His hands moved as though among dewy grass. He laid hold of something. He turned it over.

"Gorlois is dead." The words fell heavily out of him as though they were tied to a stone.

The vast black battlefield dropped away from his eyes. The dead, the atrocities, the dream. Grass turned to stone. Blood became meat gruel. The true figure of Castellan Brastias gave way to his image.

Merlin swooned. Gentle hands laid hold of him and steadied him.

"You're sure what you saw? Gorlois is dead?" Ulfius asked.

Merlin only nodded. He raised haunted eyes toward the warrior. "Atrocity."

A fragile, hopeful light dawned there.

"He will have quite a life, Ulfius. The child that comes from this meat grinder—he will have quite a life!"

7

Birth of a King

*G*o watch the birthing!" Ulfius growled to himself. He sat in a cordwained corner of the royal bedroom. "Go watch the birthing! Why do I get all the rotten jobs?" He knew why. One glance toward the canopied bed, and he knew why: Uther was a coward.

Throughout this longest of days, Queen Igraine had languished there. Midwives circled and prodded with the eager intensity of strappado artists around a well-tempered rack. It was agony. Every groan sent a twisting dagger into Ulfius's gut. Every scream raked his brains to rags. Never before had he put much stock in Eve's temptation by the snake. Now, witness to the curse of God laid upon women—he believed.

"Uther! Uther, you slick snake. You putrid scrapegrace!" she shouted in one of her more lucid moments. Perhaps this morning had been the wrong time for Uther to tell Igraine about the deception that had conceived their child. "And you, Ulfius—you spreading canker!" she shouted his way. "You vile vulture. What kind of devil's deal did you make to have a claim on this child?" It had also been the wrong time to tell her she couldn't keep the boy.

Ulfius buried his face in his hands. He had worn his shiniest suit of ceremonial armor, wanting to instill a state of decorum to the proceedings—and to deflect any physical assault. Even so, the suit was hot in that agonied room. Every insult the queen hurled his way made him bake all the more.

She'd been wronged, absolutely. Even though King Uther's lust for her had deepened to love, it did not excuse that mad night nine months ago. Even though the wedding of king to duchess had made this child legitimate, it did not excuse the intentional siring of the bastard to begin with. And even though the child of Igraine would, if Merlin was right, one day unite all the land, that did not give the mad mage the right to steal the boy away.

As wrong as Uther and Merlin were, it was always Ulfius who facilitated their depravity. After all, who was sitting like a vulture in the birthing room even now?

"All the rotten jobs . . ."

Then it happened. At long last, after hours' worth of advice about medicinal plasters and prayers to the Virgin Mother and invocations of household spirits, the real screaming began. The midwives seemed to take this as a good sign. They chanted instructions about pushing and ceasing. They pumped the poor woman's arms and legs and played her bare belly as though it were a Caledonian drum wheel. When these ministrations were done, one lady offered the queen a broom handle to cling to. Igraine summarily took it up and used it on her assistants. She threw the handle away and instead clutched the bowed heads of a pair of helpers.

With one more almighty roar, she heaved. Water and something that looked like blue samite emerged. On that glorious tide rode the unifier of Britannia. Old-woman hands caught the purple child and peeled back the placental robes.

"A boy!" she shouted excitedly. "A boy!" She laid the child's chest across her arm and gently patted forth the mucous plug in his throat. Using a tanned pig bladder, she sucked the child's nose clean. A hearty bellow came from the lad.

Ulfius sat up. For the first time that day, he felt excitement, even joy. There was something primordial and powerful in that cry. This child would be a force. This child would unite the clans and kings and usher in an age of peace. He emptied his tiny lungs with each shout, paused only a moment to suck in more air, and roared again.

Ulfius stood and wandered from the leathery confines of his corner abode. It was a foolish time to do so. Midwives swarmed in waspish frenzy. The baby cried out at full voice. Sheets and floor yet bore the potent woman-magic of after-birth. Even so, Ulfius was drawn to the squalling babe. He was drawn as men of old were drawn, told by magi this child would be a king. Where all the previous moments of this day had been awash in female mystery, that boy child was male mystery incarnate, and Ulfius was drawn. In five quick, quiet strides, he was at the midwife's side.

Igraine pled to hold the child Ulfius had come to carry away.

"Give me the child," Ulfius said. His voice rang with command, though he had not intended it.

The midwife looked angrily at him, but in Ulfius's face she saw a beaming hope that could not be denied. Lifting the boy child, she gave him over.

Ulfius received the babe. He was large already, the purple of his skin banished by air and light. His bellows continued, only amplified by the terrified fury of the mother. Ulfius heard none of it. He could only stare into those gray-blue eyes.

"Welcome to the world, child."

It was not paternal love that moved through Ulfius, but pious fealty—the impulse of a true soul in the presence of its sovereign.

"Maggot! Cradle-robber! Fomorian!"

Instead of steering out of the storm of maternal anger, Ulfius headed toward Igraine. Her rants quieted as he approached. With reverent motion, he lowered the babe into her arms. Fury still reddened her skin, but tears of relief cooled angry cheeks. A smile lit her face. She drew swaddling blankets around the infant and held him there beside her. Coos replaced shouts. Hands that had wielded a broom handle now caressed the baby's limbs.

Tearful, Igraine looked into Ulfius's dark eyes and

pleaded, "You will not take him. You will not."

Only then did the glow depart the warrior's figure. He bowed his head. "It is your husband's will, dear queen."

"Let him be damned!" she growled.

"He is your king," Ulfius replied.

"This baby was mine before Uther was my king, before he married me and made the boy legitimate." Her expression softened again to pleading. "Ulfius, if ever you chose bravery over cowardice, choose it now. Do not take my baby."

Ulfius bowed his head. He was tired of being caught between a mad king and a mad mage. Treason, though, was a greater wrong than cowardice. "I must, dear queen. Uther will not be denied. Merlin will not be denied."

"That Satan-spawn. He was stolen from his parents and now wants to steal my child from me," she hissed bitterly. "Changeling thief!"

"My queen, I swear, I will do all in my power to assure this child is reared well, is brought up in nobility and love, is trained to be king," pledged Ulfius. He'd had no notion of this vow a moment before it was spoken, but did not regret it.

Her eyes testing his, she relinquished the babe. "As long as you live, you will labor to guard my child, my Arthur?"

"As long as I live," Ulfius replied solemnly. He took the swaddled child. Arthur had ceased crying and stared into the eyes of his protector. "Welcome, young Arthur." He wrapped the babe more firmly in his arms, bowed just slightly to the queen, pivoted, and made his way out the door. The queen's racking sobs followed him out.

There were spiral stairs beyond—the queen's quarters in Castle Albion were duplicates of those she had kept at Tintagel. Ulfius descended. With each footfall, he wondered how he could remain true to his vow and yet carry out the task before him.

He rounded a corner, and a small hand grasped him, stopping him dead. Ulfius looked downward. A pair of great brown eyes returned his stare. Morgan.

The girl child set her lips in a precocious pouting rose. "Is this my brother?"

Ulfius took a shuddering breath, but managed a smile. "Why, yes, Morgan. This is Arthur."

Her ivory brow furrowed. "Arthur? Named after Uther? Why is he not named after my father?"

Crouching on the stair, Ulfius allowed the girl to gaze into the swaddling clothes. "Uther is your father now, my dear."

"He is not. He never will be," Morgan said levelly. She peered past the folds of cloth. Her nose curled, and she fairly growled, "But Uther *is* the father of this . . . this creature."

Ulfius protectively drew the cloth up beside Arthur's face, and he stood. "Well, then . . . I had better be on my way. . . ."

Morgan still had not released Ulfius's tabard. "I saw him that night, you know. I saw that Uther was disguised as my father. I saw, and nobody believed me. I can see things others cannot. I saw—"

"Please, Morgan," said Ulfius, tugging away from her, "I must go."

Her eyes narrowed. At last she released the hem, raising her hand to point accusingly. *"You* were there too. You were Jordanus, weren't you?"

Ulfius retreated down the stairs, his heart thrumming in his chest.

"I see! I see what no one else sees! Uther is not my father. Arthur is not my brother. They never will be!"

The child's imperious voice rang in Ulfius's ears as he staggered to the base of the tower stair. The doorway opened to the lady's garden. Striding quickly, Ulfius followed a path among roses and irises, reached another slanting stair, and descended it to an ivy-encrusted postern gate.

He looked behind him. There was no sign of the poor young girl. Morgan was rightfully angry, of course. She saw what others did not. Clear vision in a world of atrocity was not a blessing but a curse.

Ulfius turned back around. The ironwork barrier before him was ancient. Its broad bars were thickened by carbuncles, rusted shut. Black paint further encrusted the device

until its iron seemed as rampant as the wild bellflowers growing beyond it.

Of course, Merlin was nowhere to be seen.

The warrior stood there, peering out at the dark curve of
forest that lay beyond. A breeze brought the sweet scent of
peat. A bird flitted among alder boles. It skipped into and
out of slanting rays of sunlight. A toad in some distant bier
gave sullen complaint. Leaves shifted. Of Merlin, though,
there was not a sign.

Ulfius lifted the quieted child toward the monstrous gate.
"Merlin, come claim the child now, or I take him back to
his mother's breast."

The mage appeared. He did not so much arrive as appear,
assembling himself from wood sorrels and gentians. The rags
and narrow shoulders, the starved figure, the ratty beard and
hair . . . his eyes were last to slip into being from whatever
place he had been. They glimmered in covetous anticipation
and swam with strange visions.

In seeing those eyes again, Ulfius drew back. He pulled
the babe out of Merlin's reach. "Merlin. I thought you
wouldn't come."

The tattered old mage took a step forward. "You mean,
you hoped I wouldn't."

Ulfius retreated again. "What do you know of caring for
a newborn?"

An avid gleam filled Merlin's gaze, and his hands reached
out like a pair of claws. "I am just a newborn. I take care of
myself."

Ulfius critically studied the old man's figure. "What are
you going to feed him?"

"Food," Merlin replied. He tugged at the swaddling
clothes. "Like I feed myself."

"He needs milk—mother's milk," Ulfius said.

"I'll conjure some."

"You can't. You said food was different. You said it re-
sisted magic."

"Interesting idea." Merlin struggled to wrap his arm

around the bundle, but Ulfius did not let go. "Release the child. He is mine!"

There was enough desperate anger in that command that Ulfius gave Arthur into Merlin's inexpert grasp. "Why, Merlin? Why do you even want the boy? You said yourself he will unite the land, will save it. Why jeopardize this miracle child?"

Merlin's gaze flared. "Because he will unite me, too! He will unite me!" The mage turned to the postern gate. A covert gesture flung golden fire into the jammed lock. Motes of rust popped from the old metal. They glowed into sparks and hailed away from the mechanism. In moments, the lock shone as new. Some of the sparks formed themselves into a spectral key, which inserted itself and turned. The latch opened, and the door swung slowly wide. "Do not try to follow us, Ulfius. I warn you." The dead sincerity of his words shone through the mad storms in his eyes. "Do not try."

Ulfius opened his mouth to reply, and was surprised by what he said, "His name is Arthur."

"What?" asked Merlin as he fled like a miser with a pot of gold.

"The babe. His name is Arthur."

Arthur. Your name is Arthur. Your eyes, Arthur, they are twin gushing streams of blue. Never have such eyes been in all the world. Not even the eyes of the boy Christ were this way. And your hair, spun gold. Here are the nubs where your antlers will grow. They will be wide-spreading and rake the heavens. And the flashing sword that issues from your mouth—the piercing sound that slices league on league to bring all the world beneath your sway—it cleaves soul from spirit and joints from marrow. . . .

What is this? Where is the cup you are to bear in your right hand? Cups do not grow from fingers as antlers from heads. Cups are things apprehended. Now I apprehend. You do not have the cup, but you shall have it. You do not yet know where it is, but you shall know. And where are the keys for your left hand? They are to be apprehended, too? You will know where to seek the keys. You will find them for me.

Oh, dear sweet Arthur, how strange you are. A child of mad dreaming. How strange you and I are.

Merlin had not gotten a stone's throw from the gate before the child began to cry. Its little wails filled the dense wood. The other creatures quieted to listen. Marsh hares ran for their warrens. Foxes pricked their ears. Wolves loped from dens to see what poor, miserable creature was caught in the evening forest.

Merlin trundled onward. Children like motion. Besides, Ulfius would follow. He was incapable of not following. He would follow, and Merlin would have to escape.

A pair of silvery eyes, kin to the child's own, watched from a leafy glen. Merlin released a long howl that sent the forest creature bolting. The sound occasioned only a louder, more sustained complaint from the child. Merlin lifted Arthur from his side, where he had been carried in one arm like a bundle of wood, and held the child before him.

Arthur was stunning—that much was sure—with his lupine eyes. He was also becoming a torment. His blood-mottled forehead was clenched in rage. His mouth poured out laments. Tiny hands quivered impotently.

"There, there," Merlin said.

A thin tendril of green magic slid from between his teeth, upward into an ancient elm. The probing enchantment searched along the convolutions of oozy bark, discovered its quarry, and returned bearing the iridescent creature. The magic tendril deposited a large locust on the child's cheek. Merlin smiled in satisfaction and nodded his head, commanding the bug to sing. It complied. As loud and startling as steel on a whirring whetstone, the song hushed the child.

Satisfied, Merlin clambered down the path. Ahead, the trail gave out onto a pasture. Merlin hurried into the clearing. Night deepened across the sky. Clouds crouched on the nighttime horizon. The heavens above seemed a giant serpent's belly, scaly and sinuous. From the woods around came shuffling noises. Wolves, certainly, thinking the child's cries the sound of a wounded hare—but also bigger footfalls, more conscious and less deft. It could have been no one but Ulfius.

The mage's mind spread in enchantment on the darkling wind. It sought among stalks of grass and decorous mounds of sheep shit. There were allies here. The shepherd's cairn at the peak of the low rise teemed with little beasts. They responded as ever they did to Merlin's summons, with querulous voices, too shrill to make any but emotive sense.

He stooped by the roadside and spoke quietly to the creatures gathered below him. "I know you fear owls, but none will bother you if you clamber on my pursuer. I want you only lightly to nip him. Don't hurt him. He is a good man. Only send him running back to the castle."

The reply was a cooing agreement. Only one nestling offered a wail of complaint.

The gist came clear to Merlin. "Ah. You are more a singer than a warrior," Merlin said. "I understand. A filid among fighters." He lifted the dissenting mouse from among the weeds at the base of cairn and set the creature on Arthur's chest.

It was a fastidious white mouse with little pink eyes. Its paws drew daintily through its whiskers. Preparatory to its own concert, the mouse seized the singing locust, bit its head off, and swallowed the rest in three quick gulps. Its fur riffled in satisfaction.

Arthur, deprived of his nursery song, wailed.

The mouse began to sing. Its music was all the sweeter for a full belly. Arthur quieted again. Merlin started on his way. The mouse sang on, evoking dark holes and flitting moths, crowded nests and the fearful sound of paws digging. Its compatriots meanwhile marched out through the grasses toward Ulfius, who even then emerged darkly from the wood.

"And he was worried I could not care for the child," Merlin muttered as he strode into the gathering night.

8

Flight by Sea

Dawn approached.

Arthur had been crying nonstop since midnight.

After the white mouse, Merlin had required concerts of a garter snake, three barn cats, a gray wolf, and even a bandit with the misfortune of leaping on the man. None had silenced the baby. Shrieks and wails, growls and sobs, screeches and yowls. Merlin's magical attempt to endow himself with a nursemaid's accouterments only resulted in a neck-slung pair of wineskins—useful for him but pointless for the child. His midnight inquiry at a peasant hovel asking after a maid with full breasts got his head nearly cleaved by an ax. He fled, and the wails continued.

"And I thought I could care for this child," Merlin lamented. "He is madder than I! Volatile, fearless, indomitable, vociferous—utterly beyond persuasion!" Arthur was more than a handful. For sheer idiocy, he was a whole heath road of lunatics rolled into one. "He's not even old enough to be mad!" griped Merlin to himself. "And I hoped *he* would save *me.*"

At the darkest corner of night, Merlin wondered if he had been mistaken about the nature of this child. What if the prophecies of the boy's destiny were only more delusions, only fancies of a jumbled and hopeless mind? What if Merlin was slaying himself and the child, and for nothing at all?

He kicked viciously at the dirt path. Morning gathered like a golden cat just over the hills. It would soon pounce, bringing with it daytime and villagers with threshers and soldiers with spathas. There would be mobs and prisons and the gibbet—again. Merlin might have given up just then, but on the road behind, there came a brief thrashing sound and a muffled curse. He glanced back to see, in a little well beside an oak, a tattered and tormented figure, struggling hopelessly to hide.

As long as Ulfius pursued, it was easy enough to keep going, for sheer amusement.

With a childish giggle Merlin turned and scuttled away down the road. Little puffs of dirt arose from each footfall. He had the presence of mind to infuse the dust with magic. Puffs curled into the air and swarmed slowly toward Ulfius.

A small sound of dread came from the well beside the oak. Dust coalesced around it in a dingy cloud. Coughing began.

In a particular pique, Merlin paused to do a little jig, sending even more magical puffs up to add to the cloud.

Sneezing, coughing, and spitting, Ulfius no longer struggled to conceal his curses. "Damn you, incubus spawn! You'll die of exposure! You'll kill the child! He needs his mother. *You* need his mother. Damned warlock!" His fury was interrupted by a fit of sneezes.

Merlin sniggered. He hurried down the path, around a berm of clover, and into a ravine.

At the base of it lay a beautiful sight—a narrow, deep, and slow-moving river. The verges were overhung with willows. Mosses clung to the elm boughs. Holes filled the muddy banks, and tiny sets of eyes gleamed within. Best of all, though, was the small fishing dinghy overturned beside the rocky ford.

> "A river to bear us,
> A wind to sing us,
> A boat to rock us,
> A welcome tomorrow!"

Merlin ambled downward, hugging the child tightly to his wineskins. "Water will save us, child. It saved me before and will save us now."

Arthur ceased crying a moment to stare into the mad face above him.

Merlin took this as a sign. He kicked the overturned boat upright, simultaneously dumping from it the oars, nets, and prawn traps stowed beneath. The hull rolled in the mud. Hoisting the babe high, Merlin clambered over the gunwales and sat in the boat's prow. He settled Arthur in place before realizing the boat was still beached. Climbing out, he heaved the craft into the water.

It went with sudden alacrity. The stern pulled away from Merlin's hand and into deep water. He made a desperate grab for it and splashed down into a hole in the riverbed. Cold black water closed over his head.

Though placid-seeming without, the water moved with a quiet and restless might. It shoved Merlin down in sucking darkness. He lifted his head and could make out, small and triangular on the silvery surface, the dinghy drifting steadily away down the flood.

Enough was enough. Merlin raked his hands through the coursing tide. Fingers trailed long bubbles that solidified into schools of darting fish. Another sweep of his arms lengthened the things into water snakes and eels. A third, and the riling mass of cold muscle and silver scale enwrapped the tattered mage and bore him upward.

His head broke the surface. Hair and beard streamed water. The creatures he had evoked clung all about him like sodden locks. Coiling, they hoisted him from the river and bore him along in the boat's placid wake. He reached the stern and climbed in with no more difficulty than if the dinghy had been on land. He sat. The creatures wriggled away from him. Some slipped over the sides. Others hid themselves beneath the planks or around the sleeping babe. An unlucky few found themselves clutched in the wizard's hands and shoved between his strong, bright teeth.

For the first time in hours, the trip looked more promising.

The euphoria did not last. The dawning day turned dastardly. Sunlight glared mercilessly into the little tub. At first, it gave welcome warmth to the drenched wizard. Steam rose in

ghosts from his rags. But once warp and weft were baked
dry, the skin beneath them began to bead with drops of
sweat. New moisture entered the cloth. Merlin dragged strag-
gles of hair across his face to cool the burning sensation, but
found his own breath too strong to endure.

"Where are we going?" he wondered aloud for the first
time, blinking sleepily at the trees that craned over the waterway. In truth, he knew what he fled—Uther and his violent
kingdom, hilltops of madmen, years of beggary and starvation and idiocy. Arthur was the pot of gold that would purchase his way out of deprivation, and yet Merlin hoarded
that gold, had no idea how to convert this fortune into happiness and ease. He laughed at his own lunacy. The king of
Thebes and Herod of Palestine sought to change their fate
by slaying the prophesied boy. Merlin sought to assure it by
adopting him. "Where are we going, you ask? We are going
to our destiny."

That was as much mind as he had left. More glaring than
the sun and more nettling than his sweat, sleep couched him
in prickly delirium. Merlin wanted to stay awake, wanted to
be certain Ulfius could not follow, but sleep would not be
denied. Arthur himself was at last snoring hard. Sweet leth-
argy drifted out from him in waves.

"What harm, to sleep awhile, in the bosom of the river?"
Merlin slid down from the stern seat. Tarred planks cradled
him. The river rocked him. Reeds and willows sang him to
sleep.

Or, if not to sleep, to delirious dream.

He had fled this way countless times. It was as instinctual
as breathing. There was always a clear threat to escape,
whether or not there was a clear salvation to escape to. Hay
wains and horses, herds of swine and fishing boats—whatever vessel was on its way out of destruction could carry
Merlin along.

The last time he had escaped by boat, the vessel had been
much larger. The gunwales of the little dinghy swelled outward and upward to accommodate the vision. Beneath Merlin's curled back, planks extended into a large expanse of

floor. Rows of benches sprouted out of chine braces. Chains rankled at the base of them. Holes along the rail grew long oar handles, even now dragging forward in unison. No hands clutched those oars save the hands of magic, but they drove tirelessly forward. The prow of the ship curled into a glaring dragon head. Salt billows broke against the prow and sent spray arcing back to the stern, where Merlin stood.

He pounded the drum. Each time the mallets struck skin, waves of dweomer leaped out to propel the oars. He had clutched those drumsticks tightly in his hands from the moment he had boarded the ship and burned away its mooring lines. Invisible oarsmen had plied their posts ceaselessly since then. The square-rigged sail had helped at first. Just beyond Saxony it had captured Eurus, the East Wind. In time, though, the restless god had torn his way right through the canvas.

Still, Saxons pursued. Someone always pursued.

Merlin turned his gaze out past the dragon-tailed stern. The stormy North Sea was dark with coming night. All across its icy expanse, Saxon ships prickled. Their oars moved like centipede legs. Their sails bore the emblems of strange gods. Though they were leagues back, the scent of their hatred was strong on the east wind.

They wanted Merlin. They wanted him dead. They had tried to kill him back in Asgard. Perhaps they would have succeeded were it not for the great sword at Merlin's belt. It was the sword that the Saxons had really wanted. A god-killing sword, they called it. Without equal.

Merlin turned fore. The sun was abandoning him. The moon would aid the Saxons. This sort of thing never used to happen. Now even wind and wave fought him. He could have expected as much from the water, but the air?

"Enough, Eurus! Enough!" Merlin raged into the eastern storm. "You ripped my sail to rags, and now you bear the Saxons along? Do you want my blood as much as they?"

Out of the petulant east came a voice, huge and roaring like a waterfall. "Who could not want your blood?" Behind the ship, a face formed of gray cloud and black night. The visage rolled inward.

To himself Merlin grumbled, "I'd forgotten how ugly you were."

"What?" the east wind growled.

Merlin smiled tightly and shouted, "What of old alliances? What of allegiances?"

"Alliances? Allegiances?" The aerial god hurled a gale down from the hateful night.

Wind lashed brutally across Merlin's ship. The sea sucked its belly away. A deep trough of water opened fore. The ship bobbed corklike down into it. Rags of sail rattled angrily. Loose lines lashed the deck. Merlin faltered at the drum, struggling only to hold on. Oars went slack and dragged dead through foamy water. The ship lulled in the trough, and Merlin wondered for one horrible moment whether it would drive right on down to sunless depths. Then it mounted up the opposite wave. Merlin clutched the stern rail to avoid being flung overboard. With terrific motion, the ship crawled up the watery slope.

Eurus glared balefully at the refugee ship. "Alliances? Allegiances? You betrayed us! Every last one of us! You left us to die!" Another easterly blast raked the vessel.

Merlin stooped to shelter by the rail. His free hand clutched the hilt of the god-killing great sword. He shouted into the teeth of the storm, "What do you mean? We were friends. Allies."

"Friends?" the wind answered. Its fury redoubled. "Allies? We were much more than that, or don't you remember?"

He did not. Merlin could hardly remember a week at a stretch. How could he remember years, centuries? Everything was in fragments, a shattered urn. "I will make it up to you. I will make it right!" He did not know what he had done wrong, let alone how to fix it, but it was the prerogative of mortals to make bad-faith deals with gods.

"You cannot make it right," the wind hissed. "You know that as well as I do. You can never make anything right again."

That much, at least, sounded familiar.

As the ship topped the next wave, something sinister appeared in the east. It seemed a cobra, slithering over the surface of the wave and towering into the clouds.

A waterspout. The black column of liquid tore across the middle of the lead Saxon vessel. Even at this great distance, the impact of water and wind against the hull was deafening. The spout shattered wood, twisted metal, snapped the mast, and flung the sail full in the water. The ship would have capsized had it remained afloat long enough. Instead, bow and stern parted company in a ragged wound of wood. The two sank into separate watery graves.

With malevolent intent, the waterspout turned toward Merlin's ship. Eurus impelled the spout on his killing breath.

This was the end, then—to die in desperate flight, in confusion and madness, slain not by Saxons but by sea.

By sea . . .

"If you would kill me, Eurus, do it yourself!" shouted Merlin over the pitching stern. "Don't cower behind the mighty sea!"

The taunt worked. The eastern sky gathered itself in pulchritudinous rage. Clouds boiled and flung themselves across the pitching water. Eurus's face formed and dissolved and formed again. His mouth opened in a roaring chasm. He would swallow the ship whole—the ship and the mad mage and his god-killing sword.

As the irresistible sky closed in blackness over Merlin and his ship, he drove the blade upward into the heart of the heavens. A roar of agony cascaded down from the storm. Hail and lightning and rain as thick as rock poured down around him. Impaled on the god-killing sword, Eurus flailed in his death throes. Winds bled into the sea. Waves lashed the sky. The world turned to churning mist.

Merlin clung on all the while. He was sure he would die in the midst of it. It was ironic that killing a god was just as deadly as being killed by one.

•   •   •

Merlin awoke in just such a nighttime tempest. The great Saxon galley was replaced by a little dinghy. The North Sea became this wide river, vast and deep. Its edges were lost to darkness. Rain, hail, wave, and wind ravaged the tiny craft, swamping it.

Worst of all, though, Arthur lay silent and still in the bow.

Merlin let out a yip of fear. He jolted up from the stern and crawled to the motionless bundle there. The baby's face was awash in pelting sleet. His fists were cold and rigid against his little chin. Merlin lifted the bundle. The feverish warmth that had suffused it was utterly gone. The child was as cold as a drowned cat.

A dead weight hung in the old man's chest. It felt as though his heart had turned to stone. The child in his arms was equally stony.

"It matters little, this dead thing," Merlin muttered to himself. He could reassemble a man from mush and bone meal. He could breathe life back into this child as easily as—breathing.

Merlin leaned over Arthur and let a hot exhalation wisp from him. The air was charged with a red gleam. Motes chased through the vapors. Tiny particles of power eddied about the child's nostrils and flowed slowly downward. They sank into his pellucid skin. In moments, the child's eyes would open and crimson motes would cascade into the dark pupils and light them too. In moments . . . Merlin's magic had never failed. . . . At least not that he remembered. He could always raise the dead—

Except when there was a curse. . . .

The life-giving breath dissipated. The child lay utterly still.

Merlin wailed again. In clumsy hands, he clutched Arthur to his chest. "Live, child! Live. If you die, I die—Albion dies." Again, his mind was racked with thoughts of Herod and the king of Thebes, who sought to avert fate by slaying a child. In seeking to ensure fate, Merlin had slain the only vessel that could bring it about.

"I am mad," he said in despair. "I am and always shall be mad!"

"Yes, you are and ever more shall be mad," came a pattering voice. It chuffed and hissed in the pounding rain.

Head drooping above the babe, Merlin groaned. "Loki, you have done this to me. You have cursed the child."

"Not I," the god assured in a crackling voice. "The curse is from other powers of this land. I told them about your sword-mouthed boy Christ."

"He was not—*is* not the boy Christ."

"The land disagrees. A savior with a sword for a tongue and a blood cup and the keys to hell?" Loki circled the dinghy in a swarm of hail. "He is another Christ, another conqueror come to drive the old gods farther below. The land will not welcome him. It has cursed him."

"What of the antlers? What of the rivers that issue from his eyes? They are of the land!" Merlin said, pleading. "Half of this child is from ruthless Uther, yes, but the other half is from gentle Igraine—"

Loki's toothy smile shone in the chattering rain. "It is not my judgment. The powers of the land reject your Arthur. They curse him."

Merlin sank atop the still babe, hot tears mingling with cold rain on Arthur's face. The old man groaned. He had dreamed of this child for years, but he had held him for only moments. And now, Arthur was gone forever. Merlin sought the boy in his dreams. Surely, if he could see Arthur there, he could break this curse. Surely . . .

In the darkness of that huddled hull, a bright vision came to him.

She is strong and wise, this child. Her feet fold among roots of oak. Ivy garbs her as Eve of old. Her face is bright and beaming as the moonlight, and a wreath of holly adorns her head. So beautiful and powerful and pure a child there has never been in Albion. Her heart, in its red compass, holds all the land from Eire to Essex, Dumnonia to Caledonia. . . .

Tuatha, she is. Not a ruler, but the power of a ruler. She

*is the land. She will hold the keys to Arthur's heart. And her
name will be Guinevere. . . .*

It was a bright-beaming moment, ingenuous. This vision was
not Arthur, but another. She was the one who could lift the
curse of the land, who could bring Arthur back to life. She
was nothing yet—a bright strand in an otherwise black tapestry. To bring her into being would save Arthur, but to bring
her into being would take trickery. . . . Trickery like that at
Tintagel.

"Oh, Loki," Merlin groaned piteously, "they have bested
us both!"

A hush came momently to the storm, and then, "Us—
both?"

"Yes. They have spurned my Arthur and have spurned
your offer."

"My offer? What offer?"

Merlin lifted an incredulous face to the rain. "You are the
god of bargains, are you not? Did they give this judgment
without allowing you to bargain?"

The pelting drops grew angry. "They did."

Merlin shook his head. "Then they have bested us both."
Hissing hail answered. Each stone struck water and cracked
angrily. "Unless—"

"Unless—?"

"No, it is only more madness—"

"Speak!" the storm commanded.

Merlin shrugged. "Arthur is fated to rule, but he cannot
rule a land that rejects and curses him. Without a strong
hand, all ends in blood. Britons and Britannia both die.
But . . ."

"Say on—"

"But the throne of Britannia is wide enough for two—for
the one fated to rule and she whom the land chooses to empower him. As Arthur is carried from a king's cradle into

the wild, the gods of the wild might carry one of their own into the cradle of a king."

"A faerie changeling?"

"Yes. There are king's cradles enough here about. Find one with a newborn girl and switch her. It is easily done."

"A fey queen to Arthur's king?"

"Yes. Should the land save Arthur this night, he will be betrothed this very hour to the Tuatha child. She and he will rule together. That is our bargain."

A riffle of suspicion moved through the storm. Loki hissed, "How does this bargain benefit me?"

Merlin's brow knotted. "He who cannot be king would do well to be king-maker."

"Yes," Loki answered out of the roaring rain. "Yes . . ." There was only a moment's absence, but a moment can be a lifetime for a god. "I have conveyed your message. Of course, I have added terms of my own to sweeten the union. I am god not of bargains, but of bad bargains, and to this bad bargain, the powers of the land have agreed. . . ."

On one wind-lashed leg, Merlin suddenly felt a warm stream. Any other man would have held the child away from him at that moment, but Merlin clenched him all the tighter. For him, the sensation was more welcome than warm mead.

"You live, Arthur! I live! Albion lives!" A cold shudder moved through the child. "Thank you, O land! Thank you, Loki!"

"Remember who mediated this bargain," Loki hissed on the failing rain. "I have made Arthur, and can as easily un-make him."

"Yes," Merlin said. "Yes, I will remember."

Then Loki was gone. The storm eased, but still the river flexed its cold sinews all about. Loki always came to Merlin garbed in mad confusion, and he left just the same. Perhaps he did not come or leave at all, but dwelled ever in the chaos-corners of Merlin's mind. The old man did not know; he did not care. Only one thing mattered now—

"Arthur, you live." He stared into the blue, clenched face of the boy. "But for how long?"

The ragged lunatic clutched the comatose child to his breast. Beneath them, the boat was swamping. Waters raged. Merlin did all he could think of doing. He leaped into the turgid river and struggled to swim to shore.

9

Of Wolves and Druids

*F*or a young man seeking adventure, the Roman ruins at Chertsey-on-Thames rarely disappointed. Tumbled columns, burned-out foundations, roads lined with milkweed and beggarticks, vaporous ghosts along the river, haunted archways, shattered statues . . . the place held a palpable sense of danger.

Just last week, Kay had fought a wolf pack among the abandoned columns. The beasts might even have been the spawn of the She-wolf that suckled Romulus and Remus. Well, in truth, they were not feral wolves, but wild dogs—even more vicious since they do not fear man. Kay had been hard pressed by fifteen or so. He'd killed ten with his spatha before the others fled. That did not sound so noble, though, killing dogs. He hadn't really killed them, only wounded them sore, and not with a sword, but with a stout branch like the one he now clutched. And not ten but two. But they *were* wild dogs, all three of them. The collars meant nothing. Often pets went wild and banded together to run sheep. All that tail wagging had been only a ruse. It was their way of getting close enough to strike.

"Who am I fooling?" Kay asked himself, kicking a chunk of shattered cornice across the weed-filled plaza. Young shoulders slumped in resignation beneath a haystack of blond hair. Kay wrinkled his handsome features into an unhandsome scowl. Father always spoke of Saxon invaders in the east, all-out war, Pagan uprisings, petty kings killing petty kings. The only Saxons Kay ever met, though, were peaceful Christian farmers. You can't battle a peaceful Christian farmer. That was no more noble than killing friendly dogs. "What's the point of even having a sword in this day and age?" Kay wondered bitterly. Perhaps that was why he didn't yet have one.

Next moment, he ardently wished he did. A hissing wail like that of a gorgon came from the waterfront. Kay froze. That was the power of a gorgon—any who looked into her eyes would turn to stone. Perseus had fought Medusa using a mirror, and here was Kay with neither mirror nor sword.

But he had courage. He'd not slain twenty wolves bare-handed in this very spot only to turn away from a single gorgon. Courage would turn this stout stick into a spatha—no, better yet, into one of those huge bastard swords the Caledonians so specialized in. And faith would be a buckler before him—or one of those shoulder-high shields with the big blood-red crosses on the front and the arrows sticking in it. Then, of course, his linen tunic would become a breast-plate of righteousness, and his trousers the girdle of virility, and his family rings the gauntlets of . . . the gauntlets of big knuckles.

Keeping his back toward the hissing sound lest he be turned to stone, Kay cautiously retreated into battle. He glanced down at his sandals, shushing over the Roman-laid road. Half crouching, he stole from the plaza to the water-front. Wherever possible, he hid himself behind curtains of foxglove or along piles of cut stone. To cross an open zone, he clutched fistfuls of goldenrod behind his backside and moved very slowly.

The noise grew louder as he went. It was a vicious wheeze. Calculating and cruel. The gorgon would hiss a long breath out, and then draw another in through phlegmy lungs. There would be poison sacs in that horrid throat. Poison sacs and the fingers and toes of her last victims.

Kay clutched the goldenrod all the tighter. He could still

retreat—or actually, advance—out of here. Already Father tired of his wolf story, and Kay needed another. The decision was made for him next moment. He stepped back onto an unseen stair and obligingly tumbled. Head over goldenrod, Kay sprawled with an aching groan at the base of the stair—

Just beside the gorgon! The sawing hiss was nearly deafening now. The thing's cold, sodden robes pressed up against Kay's face. The serpent lay in coiling malice just beneath him. Encased in its sinuous flesh was the skeleton of a man. Kay pushed away from the repellent creature and shrieked. He forgot himself, his eyes flashing over the hateable glare of that grotesque face.

The woman's withered flesh was haloed in a mass of roiling snakes, as white as maggots. Her skin had a sepulchral cast. Her eyes glared like blood-red suns. A forked tongue darted from her hoary lips as she hissed—

Kay flung his arms up to shield his eyes, but too late. Already petrified, he posed there, statue-still. The agony of death was on him—the knowledge he would never again see Father or Mother or home. Cold rain would crack against his stony skin. Snows and ice would shatter him. And what of the ignominious pigeons? A heartfelt groan escaped him.

A groan?

He could breathe. More than that, he could move. His first impulse was to run, but into his mind returned that petrifying vision. The gorgon had looked a bit manlike, in fact. Those snakes might have been only a white beard and hair pasted down by water. Hmm. Mustering an extreme measure of courage, Kay glanced down at the monster—

No monster, but an old, snoring man. And what was that bundle in his arms? Kay pulled back a blanket to find a dead child.

"They were surrounded by Saxons when I found them. I killed sixteen of them and drove the others off!" Kay explained that evening to his father.

Ector was a great striding shadow in the stairway ahead

of him. The snoring man hung limp in his grasp. Arms and legs scraped along the walls. Ector took the steps three at a time. Ever since Kay had led his father to the ruins, Ector had gone grimly silent. His actions were determined and purposeful. He seemed a great black bear, wheezing as he trundled to the infirmary of the castle.

Blond-headed and slight, Kay was nowhere near to being his father's shadow, but he trailed the man as closely as one. Kay stopped his jabber occasionally to look down at the child in his arms. The babe had not been dead, after all. It was still breathing, but Kay feared it might die any moment.

"Where do you think they came from? Do you think they were left from when the place wasn't a ruin? Maybe they were trapped in it for hundreds of years."

Ector reached the top of the stairs and flung back the door. The room beyond glowed with lanterns. The castle chirurgeon, the village midwife, a priest from the Woking bishopric, a nursemaid, and Ector's wife, Diana, were waiting there. They had laid sheets across a pair of raised pallets in the center of the room, spread new green rushes on the floor to soak up any humors spilled in the following administrations, readied cranial drills and bone saws and leeches, laid in jugs of rye spirits for pain relief, gathered sulfur and pitch and charcoal, and even brought Diana's needlepoint set in case any wounds needed stitching. Beyond the row of high windows, a just-risen moon disappeared behind twilight clouds.

Blond and bright-eyed, Diana hurried toward the door. She still possessed the grace of her youth, though now had seen nearly thirty-five years. As her husband deposited the old man on one raised pallet, Diana took the baby from her son and headed toward the other.

"It's still alive," Kay said hurriedly. "I'm wondering if it is a faerie child."

"All right, all right, Kay," Diana told him, meaning both that she had heard him and that he should now be quiet.

Kay caught half the message. "What if they are Saxons? What if they are invaders?"

"All right, Kay," his mother repeated. She drew the swaddling cloths from the babe, wrung a clean white rag in a steaming basin of water, and began wiping the creature's mud-crusted limbs. "He's hardly breathing." She set a hand across the baby's chest. "And has hardly a pulse." She stooped down to kiss the baby's forehead. "Fever."

Kay hovered beside the pallet. "Do you think he's been poisoned?"

Diana shook her head in amazement. "No, just starved and sunburned and parched—look how dry his tongue is."

"I've heard that tinkers do this," Kay said. "Steal babies and then lie down with them and wait for someone to save them so that they can get into the house just to rob it."

"Who told you that?" Diana asked.

Kay shrugged. "Nobody. Just seems likely."

His mother flung a glance toward the old man lying naked now on the opposite table. "He doesn't look like a tinker. He looks like a—like a lunatic."

Ector, the priest, and the chirurgeon stared at the still figure. Gray-garbed and serious, the healer used tongs to draw leeches from a jar and stick them in place. Despite his relative youth, the chirurgeon had thinning hair, a hawkish nose, and a grave aspect. The priest was his physical opposite—an older man with a great gut and a mass of black hair. He used oil to make the sign of the cross on the man's pate. Meaty hands clutched the patient's bared shoulders, and the priest denounced whatever demon possessed him. Ector, for his part, held the patient's feet and pumped his legs vigorously.

Skin twitched with long black leeches. Ribs trembled under exorcisms. Legs flapped in emulation of an overturned frog. The patient looked more miserable than when Kay had found him.

"I've heard lunatics do that, too," Kay said, "steal babies, I mean."

The midwife and nursemaid arrived beside Diana and Kay. The two women cooed. Hands old and young converged to stroke the child's cheek.

Diana smiled gently as she finished cleaning and swaddling him. "He needs to be held and fed. He needs a woman's arms."

The nursemaid bent downward, her black hair falling in a gentle curtain around the boy. She cradled him, purred something in his ear, and lifted him. Already the child's troubled face seemed to ease. "There, there, sweet baby. There, there."

"Druids do that too," Kay said, elaborating on his theory, "steal babies, I mean, and send them downstream. Or maybe that was pharaohs. Do you think he is Moses? Or, if he came from the river, maybe he is a water sprite."

The nursemaid had discreetly moved aside the folds of her robe and positioned the child's head within. Small sounds of suckling came. "All he needed was a woman's arms."

"He's not bleeding fast enough," the chirurgeon said testily at the other table. He retrieved a long knife from his leather satchel of implements. Often these same tools assisted him in extracting confessions in the dungeons of London. "There is too much bad blood. Just too much."

Still clutching the man's head, the priest said, "Evil blood. Not just bad blood, but evil blood. Do you see the folds of skin in his forehead? Just here between the eyes VI-VI-VI? That is the mark of the beast." This observation was followed by loud prayers and the production of a small leather scourge from the priest's belt. "He is lucky I was once an ascetic. I can banish demons of flesh and soul."

"You're both mad," Ector claimed from the man's feet. The rigors of his gymnastic program had redoubled. The old man's legs now bounded up in opposition to each other, his knees alternately thumping against his chest. "He needs to wake up. He's stopped moving and can't start up again. He just needs to wake up."

The old man floundered beneath their none-too-gentle ministrations.

Beyond the windows, clouds deepened across the sky and boiled down to scrape along the ground. A cold and irritable wind swept up off the fields and into the infirmary. It brought the threat of rain. Distant thunder accompanied the unconscious flopping of the old man.

A violent seizure clutched him. His eyes rolled in their sockets. His hands lashed out and caught the head of the chirurgeon. Those arms proved stronger than they looked, hauling the healer down against the mess of cuts and leeches there.

Ector tried to pry the chirurgeon loose, only to get a mule kick in his jaw. He went down like a flour sack.

The priest raised his flail to flog the demon into submission. Just as the iron-tipped thongs of leather reached their height behind his head, lightning jagged in from the window. Blue-white power leaped into the scourge and shot down leather straps, burning them away to nothing. Energy coursed through the priest. He was limned in divine fire. Charges crackled back and forth across his still frame. Then the bolt vanished.

The priest stood there, smoldering. A black line marked his arm. Tepid little fires traced the path of lightning through his clothes. Eyes wide and jaw hanging loose, the priest made small gasping sounds.

Outside, more lightning cracked the sky. Flashes showed turbid clouds looming low over the fields. Thunder set a continuous rumble in the air. Wind pitched treetops. The ground shook. The whole world seemed to be undergoing the same torments as the old man.

"I told you he was a druid," Kay said happily. He watched in wonder as gray tendrils of smoke rose from the shoulders of the priest. "He's tied to the land, somehow. Whatever you do to him happens to all of us!" He smiled proudly at his realization and stared around the room, looking for approval.

Ector could not praise his son, for he lay facedown on the flagstones. Nor was the priest in any shape to offer comment. Small puffs of smoke came from his nostrils with each breath. Neither had the chirurgeon heard Kay. He had only just struggled free of the lunatic and was busy plucking leeches from his face. The nursemaid and midwife were too distracted caring for the child.

That left only Kay's mother, who looked up with long-suffering eyes.

The lunatic bucked for a moment on the table. Simultaneously, wind ravaged the treetops and hurled hail down on the castle.

Incredulous, the young man set hands on his hips. "See what I mean?"

"All right, Kay!"

The lad was incensed. At last, a real adventure was staring him in the face, and no one would believe it. Here was a dying druid and a faerie child. Their very moods shaped the actions of those around. Their pain or pleasure reshaped the land. And all the adults could tell him was "All right"?

"He's *my* druid," Kay said in sudden pique. "And he's *my* baby too. I found them. I get to say what happens with them—"

"Kay," his mother interrupted sternly, "don't wake the baby."

Don't wake the—Kay stomped from the room, slammed the door, and vaulted down the stairs. He reached the door at the bottom and flung it wide.

Outside, a crazy storm raged. Sleet and hail poured down in brief fury, then gave way to warm gusts of wind, which in turn surrendered to cold stillness, and then more rain. Clouds mounded over each other like bloodthirsty Saxons. Lances of lightning split the night three and four times a second. Thunder bellowed.

Kay charged out in it. He lifted his fists toward the raging sky and shouted, "I'm right! I'm right!"

And then, he saw something that terrified him more than rain or hail or lightning. There atop the rolling clouds, figures moved. He glimpsed them outlined in sudden flashes of light—titanic figures and battling gods. They strove in primordial conflict above the world. This was no Christian tableau, no vision of Siloam or Golgotha. This was a Pagan scene, rife with forbidden grandeur, flawed heroes, and antediluvian gods: Jove, Mars, Apollo, Diana, Athena, Saturn. . . .

"I'm right," he said more quietly. He withdrew to the doorway, shut it, and locked it tight. "I'm right."

10

The Monster Awakes

The storm lasted seven days, as did the old man's coma. All the while that clouds crashed across the dark skies, the man thrashed in delirium on his bed. Whenever he clutched at his wounds, hands of lightning probed the aching belly of the clouds.

On that first night, the adults had at last listened to Kay. They accepted the connection between man and storm. Midwife, nursemaid, and Diana took the place of their fallen male counterparts and tended the agonized man. They replaced scourges and leeches with tender fingers and bandages. Ector eventually awakened from his sore-jawed sleep. He rose to see his wife cradling the old man as she had the baby. The storm outside eased for a time. Priest and chirurgeon both advised that this man be turned out of the castle, perhaps even exiled or executed. He was at best a Pagan monster, and at worst a demon. Ector pointed out that further privations would only worsen his sufferings and deepen the storm. Kay sensibly asked where they could find anyone stupid enough to carry the man into exile. Diana had forbidden any further discussion, saying the old one was probably the baby's grandfather.

From that time forward, they called the man Grandfather. The baby they called Pryderi, after the divine lad stolen at three days old from Rhiannon in Pagan lore. Pryderi ate and woke and slept in the hour-long cycles of newborns.

Grandfather did not fare as well. His privations ran deeper. His torments at the hands of healer and priest had been worse. In flickering eyeballs, mad delusions showed clear. Occasionally, he would shout imprecations in the barbaric tongue of Saxons. His fists flailed rhythmically in air as though pounding a drum. He ground his teeth and tore his bedclothes to rags and foamed at the mouth. While the family fell in love with tiny Pryderi, they grew more fearful of Grandfather. What endless storms would be unleashed should he die? What further destruction would be caused if he lay forever in coma?

What horrors would result should he awaken?

After seven days of lashing rain, with every spare board nailed over a window and every spare pot gathering drips, the storm halted in midthunderclap.

Kay watched an unstoppable surge of lightning stop. It seemed like an old man on a creaky stair—it rambled halfway down the sky, halted to remember why it descended, and then slowly climbed back up. The clouds themselves dispersed in the next moments. Their woolly mats rolled back. Sky blue pierced through. The sun seemed almost cruelly bright in that sudden dawn.

Kay marveled. The courtyard beyond his hastily boarded-up window looked disheveled from sleep. Grassy patches were sunk beneath chill water. Paths had become mud-sloughs. Querulous faces peeped out each window.

New thunder sent them ducking back. The clamor began with the cracking of wood, followed by clattering iron pots and an avalanche of pottery. In the aftermath of the noise came the disconcerting gush of wine flooding from a staved barrel. Avid gibbering accompanied the clangor.

The faces that had retreated from the windows returned and stared toward the castle cellar. It could be none other than Grandfather, awake.

Kay's eyes widened in excitement. "Who is he? Who is the babe? What adventure awaits?" Rubbing his hands together, Kay turned to the treasure chest beside his pallet and searched for a weapon. He might, after all, have to kill

Grandfather, if he turned out to be a devil. Kay's hand settled on his practice sword, a sharpened stick. "If that demon kills me, Father will rue the day he denied me a true blade."

Carried on the fleet feet of youth, Kay reached the cellar before anyone else. He splashed through mud and yanked hard on sodden hatches to heave them upward. Light poured down over a miserable creature.

Grandfather sat down there, an inch of dark wine covering the floor around him. He had pulled a string of smoked fish from the rafters and bit through scale, meat, and bone. Strong teeth made a pulp of it. He interrupted his fierce chewing to scoop wine from the floor. The sanguine stuff dribbled from his cupped hand into his beard, washed white by Kay's mother in the last days.

Diana arrived next moment. She stood, shocked, behind Kay.

Ector, his squire, the castellan, and a half-dozen armsmen came close on her heels. They all stood amazed in the mud.

Grandfather looked up at them and seemed to surface from a deep place of delight. "Hello," he said, squinting toward the light. "Good food."

An incredulous look passed among the owners of all that food.

Kay declared, "He's a Fomorian! Who else could eat as much?"

Ector moved to the head of the group. He crouched and crooked a finger, as though trying to coax a strange dog. "Come on up out of there, Grandfather."

"Not likely," came the immediate response, along with a wine-flinging shake of the old man's head. "There's three more fish, and a batch of fresh mushrooms—"

"We haven't been properly introduced," Ector continued.

Grandfather chomped into a large radish. The bitter root brought tears to his eyes, but he spoke through them. "Ah, yes. The name is Merlin."

Ector thoughtfully nodded his head. "And I am Ector, Duke of Chertsey. This is my wife, Duchess Diana, and my son, Kay." He scratched a shock of black hair. "How did you end up in Chertsey?"

Merlin seemed to consider. His hands dropped away from his mouth, and a gnawed fish tail jutted in his grasp. "Yes. How?"

Ector laid a hand on Kay's shoulder. "My son found you in the Roman ruins. It looked like you'd washed up out of the river."

"That's how," Merlin replied. He pointed an emphatic finger. "That's how. I came by boat. I was fleeing the Saxons."

"The Saxons!" Kay enthused.

"The Saxons?" Ector asked.

"The Saxons," Merlin affirmed. "They were chasing me across the North Sea. I'd stolen one of their dragon ships. There were about fifty more that came out after me."

"Fifty dragon ships!" Kay said, rubbing his hands.

Merlin nodded deeply, hunks of bread pushing his cheeks out as he chewed and swallowed. "Last thing I remember was a storm at sea. I'd not have survived it except that I killed a god."

"Killed a god!" Kay clutched the sides of his head in delight.

For the first time, Grandfather Merlin's gaze settled on the lad. His swarming eyes cleared, replaced by intense focus. He took the boy's measure. There was approval in his gaze. When he continued his story, he spoke with sober deliberation. "I had a sword. A great sword, bigger than these Roman spathas—a giant, two-handed blade, like the Saxons themselves wield. It was that sword that killed the god Eurus, lord of the East Wind. It was that sword that brought the Saxons behind me. Wotan wanted it."

"Wotan!" Kay exclaimed.

"I'd been his guest," Merlin said. He leaned against a wine-soaked bag of grain and settled into the tale. "He rules over the kingdom of Asgard—a beautiful place, like nothing you have here in Albion—"

"Britannia," Ector corrected.

"Yes, here in Britannia. Asgard is full of palaces of gold

and silver. It sits on a mountain in the clouds. From his throne in Valhalla, Wotan can see all of heaven and earth. Lovely. Even to get to that city, you have to cross a bridge of light in the middle of the air. Did I tell you it was built by giants—?"

Kay's interruption was itself interrupted by his mother's hand, clamped over his mouth.

"Wotan made a deal with them to build it and then cheated them out of their asking price. He's been gathering warriors ever since, fearing the giants will come back to take revenge. He sends virgin women out on horseback to lure warriors back to Asgard. Once they get there, they aren't disappointed. They spend all day cutting each other to ribbons, and then at the end of it, they get put back together. Every night they feast on roast boar and drink mead given by a magic goat. Then they sit around all night telling Wotan about all the people they've killed." Merlin sighed gustily, ripped a hunk of bread from a loaf, and said, "Ah, it was a wonderful place."

Ector blinked quizzically. "This King Wotan of the Saxons sounds . . . familiar. . . ."

Kay ducked away from his mother's hand and asked, "Why were they chasing you? They sound wonderful!"

"That sword," said Merlin. He'd gone back to eating and spoke around mouthfuls of bread. "That god-killing sword. Wotan wanted it and was scared of it. It would help against the giants when they returned. I wouldn't give it up. It was mine. I didn't have much, but I had that sword. Wotan demanded it. I told him to try to take it." Merlin waved a dripping hand in the air and let out a laugh. "All those warriors, though—useless against me when I had that sword. I killed fifty of them in that first fight—"

"Fifty!" Kay said.

"And fifty more as I fled down the rainbow bridge. I slew the crew of a dragon ship and sailed from the fjord and out on the North Sea. Fifty ships followed me—"

"Fifty and fifty and fifty!" Kay proclaimed.

"And I sailed all the way here, to Albion—"

"Britannia."

"Yes, and the Saxon ships landed behind me. And that is how the Saxons came to this isle," Merlin finished. He bit off two more hunks of bread and scooped handfuls of wine into his overfull mouth.

Kay's look of delight dimmed. While Grandfather Merlin spoke, his thoughts swam with god-killing swords and North Sea battles, virgins on horseback and magical she-goats, days of deadly combat and evenings of feasting on boar. The old man talked with such certainty, Kay could not help believing. Even the fifty slain in the great hall and the fifty slain on the rainbow bridge and the fifty ships in the fjord did not seem unreasonable. But this business of the Saxon invasion! That could have been nothing but a downright lie. That one lie unraveled the whole unlikely story. Kay felt duped.

"Wait. The Saxon invasion? The Saxon invasion!" Kay declaimed. "That was over a hundred years ago!"

Merlin blinked in thought. "I've done a few other things since then."

"Father asked how you got to Chertsey. You can't have come by way of dragon boat! You couldn't even have sailed a dragon boat up this far!"

"Well," Grandfather Merlin replied passively, "I came by way of boat, somehow. I remember a storm. I remember the thing swamping." He shrugged.

"Unless you're over a hundred years old, you couldn't have been around for the Saxon uprising, and if you had been, you would have known it was the Romans who brought them here to begin with, as legionnaires, and that they rebelled, not invaded. And if it was this sword they were after, where is it? Why didn't you have a sword when I found you? Everything you've said is a lie!"

"No—" Merlin said, breaking in for the first time. "No. A delusion, perhaps, but not a lie."

"Oh, you're mad!" Kay said spitefully. He regretted the words as soon as they were spoken, and turned away from Merlin.

Wine sloshed sullenly around the man's knees. The gleam was gone from his gaze. The focus was gone too. His eyes were twin kaleidoscopes in his skull. He seemed suddenly small and sad. "Yes, mad."

Duchess Diana drew her young son back from the head of the group. "Forgive us, Grandfather. We are only wanting to find out the truth. We want to know what happened to you and the baby."

"The baby?" Merlin asked, querulous.

Diana smiled sweetly. "Yes, the baby. The swaddled baby you had with you."

Merlin startled. He stood, dripping wine. His hands quivered in distress. "Where is he? Is he safe? Where is he? Where is Arthur?"

"Safe," Diana replied soothingly. "He is safe."

Merlin clambered up the stairs. He was an unwholesome sight, streaming a dirty liquid that seemed blood. His garments were further speckled by food that hadn't had the presence of mind to reach the madman's mouth. Bread crumbs sifted down from lashes and brows to settle on cheeks. "I want to see him. Take me to Arthur. I must see him!"

Despite the wine and food, Diana graciously received the man's arm and led him away from the cellar. The crowd around, replete with stable hands and cooks and dogs, fell back as she escorted him along.

Merlin's demeanor turned almost apologetic as they went. "It's just that he is everything in the world to me."

Diana gently patted his hand. "Yes, Grandfather. I understand."

11

The Impossible World

In the next weeks and months, Merlin became Grandfather to all who dwelled in Castle Chertsey.

Ector, always the pragmatist, considered Merlin and Arthur to be merely sojourners in need of hostel. The ancient codes of hospitality required that Ector welcome them, lodge them, feed them, clothe them, and treat them as favored guests. The armsman-duke did precisely that.

Kay was the opposite. He provided the guests nothing and required of them everything. Of Arthur, Kay required patient attention. He spent long hours telling the baby of his magnificent exploits and putting on shows of stick-fencing. Of Merlin, Kay required recitations of more stories. He'd forgiven the old man the excesses of his first round of tales. Merlin could not distinguish truth from falsity, and implausibility made his stories only more engaging.

"My father was a cannibal," Merlin said one winter morning six months later.

He sat at the breakfast table with Duke Ector, Duchess Diana, Kay, and Ector's five highest-ranking warriors. All eyes rose to stare at Merlin. He was using his fingers to lift hunks of whipped egg into his mouth, and missing half the time. He was a regular nuisance at table, eating portions fit for ten armsmen in their prime and sending another ten portions to the castle dogs in a sporadic spray of steaming particles.

"An infanticidal cannibal," Merlin elaborated with a blinking smile.

Ector's black brows looked especially dark in the chill air of winter as he leaned across his own pile of steaming eggs. Fork in one hand and knife in the other clanked down beside his wooden plate. "I'm not sure this conversation is suitable for breakfast—"

"Oh, he didn't eat them for breakfast. He ate them for dinner. One night, around a table just like this, he snatched them up and bit their heads off and swallowed them."

Diana dropped a linen napkin over her breakfast and set a hand over her mouth.

Kay gazed adoringly at the old man. "Did he eat you too?"

"No," Merlin said simply. "I was too young. I was the youngest. Not a mouthful, yet. But I saw what happened to the others and didn't want it to happen to me, so I was careful not to eat too much. Father used to push food on me, wanting me to grow plump, but I always slipped it to the dogs."

Ector looked at his own well-fed canines. "That's where you learned the trick."

"Once I got old enough, I met a woman named Metis who was a terrible cook. Whatever she made, no matter how good it tasted at first, always made you throw up. She's the one they named emetine after. I got her to cook a dinner for Father, and he threw up my brothers and sisters, and he was still wiping his lips when we killed him and took over the household." Merlin shrugged, chewing on a hunk of jerky that hung out of his mouth and flopped like a living thing. "Nice way to inherit an estate."

Kay was nearly drooling in delight. Diana withdrew. Unflappable Ector made the mistake of scooting his wife's plate to him and digging into her meal. He was halfway done when he realized Merlin and Kay both had stopped to gaze at the hungry man.

"They're just eggs!" Ector declared through a mouthful.

All of Merlin's stories were of that variety—lurid, amusing, and impossible, but told with complete conviction. He believed his stories. What was even more disconcerting was that these ravings had a sense of continuity among them. As ridiculous as they were, the accounts joined together to create a consistent—if impossible—world. Merlin spoke of dividing his father's estate among him and two brothers. It was a mad division—Merlin got the sky above it all, one brother got the sea around it all, and the third got the caves beneath it all. As to the land itself, they shared that. When Kay asked where Merlin's kingdom lay, he said that they stood in it. He was king of everything from the Blessed Isles to the land of the Aethiopians.

"You were emperor of Rome?" Kay asked.

Merlin's face drew into a solemn scowl. "I suppose I was."

Kay only laughed, slapping his knees. "Ah, yes, Emperor Merlin! I remember you!"

It was like having two babbling infants in the family. Except that Arthur grew up, and he did so rapidly.

By the time Kay got a wooden practice sword, Arthur was old enough to totter around him, jabbing with a stick. It was excellent practice for Kay. Learning not to skewer his little brother taught Kay balance and finesse. Skipping away from Arthur's unsteady advance taught him agility and footwork. When summer rolled around and the castle gardens were redolent with bees, Kay had become skilled enough he could slice the tiny insects in half.

They were quite a trio in the coming days of fall. Among brown grasses and yellow elm leaves, the old man, the young man, and the babe went on constant excursions. Kay swaggered along with his wooden sword, constantly cautioning his two companions to stealth and silence. Occasionally he would rush forward to ambush deer sleeping in the grass, or to hack away at particularly sinister stumps. Merlin would never heed these calls to silence. He admonished Kay not to frighten deer since they might be transformed and tormented huntsmen, and not to batter stumps, who have had a bad enough life as it was. Merlin's objections eventually taught Kay discretion in his selection of targets. Arthur offered observations of his own, nonsense sounds that were a disturbing imitation of Merlin's own vocal style.

Arthur prattled on through that winter and the next. Gradually, he added more words and more sense to his sayings. At three, even he could tell the difference between reality and Grandpa's stories. That didn't stop him from listening. Arthur sat for hours at a time on Merlin's lap. Grandfather had found a tower attic with a rocker of black lacquer. On its back was carved a mysterious head that Merlin called Boreas, the North Wind ("not the one I killed") for the curls emerging from mouth and brows. Kay called the figure the Pagan Pan. Arthur called it only "goat man." In that strange seat, Merlin would sit with Arthur. They huddled beneath blankets. Their breath sent mist whirling up beneath the encroaching roof line. Cold winds rattled the small window. Swathed together in quilts and stories, the two were warm.

"You were born to save me, Arthur," Merlin told the boy

gravely. A chill breeze seeped around the ill-fitting window. "You were born to save me and all Albion."

"Britannia," the child corrected, as he had heard others do countless times. Arthur's golden baby hair had given place to brown locks. His early days of squalling were replaced by a quiet precociousness. Arthur lifted a small hand to caress Grandfather's white beard. "You're safe, Grandpa. I'll make you safe." He pantomimed a sword swipe. "I and Kay and Father and Mother will make you safe."

"Oh, it is not with swords that you save me, Arthur," Merlin said gently. The slates moaned with cold. "You let me tell my stories. You and Kay listen. All others think them mad ravings, lunatic delusions. But not you."

"They are your stories," Arthur said firmly.

"They are my stories," Merlin echoed. "And they are real. Somehow. I am not making them up, Arthur. I *remember* them. If I could only remember enough of them, I would know who I am."

Arthur turned suddenly to look at the old man. A warm wave rose from the blanket that enfolded them both. "I know who you are. You are Grandpa."

"Yes," Merlin said softly. "I am Grandpa."

Arthur knew no more than that—Merlin was his grandfather, Ector his father, Diana his mother, and Kay his brother. There was no sense in telling him the rest. For that matter, no one, not even Merlin, knew the rest. Merlin had vague memories of a battle on a hilltop, something about a pickle that defended him from a lustful tyrant, men digging latrines around a Terrible Castle, a friend who had a stranger's face, and a woman raped by a man who looked like her husband but was not and was. All of this, the last part especially, seemed not just nonsense but *dangerous* nonsense. Merlin did not confess these memories to Arthur, but he believed them to be true.

It was the only secret he kept from Arthur. Merlin worked hard to hide his sorcerous talents from his hosts, but not from the child. Arthur was his complete confidante. From the earliest days, Merlin had flown him around the room on invisible hands, painted pictures in air to illustrate his stories, put on miniature fireworks shows in their attic hideaway, made mice speak and spiders sing, conjured unseen minstrels and spectral hounds. One of Arthur's favorite friends was a sarcastic stool in the stables.

When they played hide and seek, Merlin often turned invisible and walked around behind the boy.

At last, Arthur simply stopped searching, waved his hands in the air, and latched hold of Merlin's airy cloak. "Come out, Grandfather, I know you're there!"

With a gentle laugh, Merlin reappeared and embraced his grandson. "You found me. Good boy."

Merlin hid these enchantments from his host family. The storms that accompanied his all-too-common nightmares unnerved them enough. If they knew about Merlin's true power, they would likely bring back the exorcist. . . . If they knew, perhaps they would be more likely to believe his stories.

"That's what your stories are, Grandpa Merlin," Kay noted one summer day as he sparred with a wooden dummy in the castle practice yard. "They are pearls—inside, there's a kernel of truth, an irritating little hunk of sand that you've worried over for decades until they are smooth and soft."

Merlin looked up from a book he was reading—or appearing to read, though the thing was held upside down and he was turning the pages backward. "Pearls? My stories. Origins in irritation. Pearls . . . ?"

"Yes," said Arthur, "pearls! That's what they are! Maybe there's only a little truth in them, but they're better than the truth. Prettier." Arthur danced on the opposite side of the practice dummy and sent a slim stick in to jab at his brother. Arthur was five now, and he idolized Kay.

There was much reason to. At sixteen, Kay had trained in arms use for four years and was a muscular, daring, and powerful swordsman. His blond mop of hair was a golden delight to the maidens about Chertsey. Today, shirtless and sweating, Kay hacked fiercely. His blade sliced Arthur's stick in half and notched the side of the quintain. He yanked the steel free, and a hunk of wood tumbled in air.

"Yes, pearls. That's what they are, Grandpa," Kay said, panting. He leaned on his blade. "You're a poet. You take something small and common and let it roll around in your head for years until it's turned into something big and beautiful."

"You should make a necklace of your stories for Mother," said Arthur. "All pearls, with a big diamond in the middle."

Merlin considered. His eyebrows seemed more ivory than white in the summer sunlight. "Yes. I should. Except, you see, Arthur, I shattered the diamond long ago. That's where all the sand came from for the pearls."

Kay slung his sword on the belt at his waist and swaggered to the well. A bucket and ladle rested on the edge. Instead of drinking from the ladle, he upended the pail over his face and felt the cool water splash over him. "Too bad. Not much work for poets these days. Now, for warriors, on the other hand—" He stretched. "As long as there are petty kings and Saxons in the east, there will be plenty of demand for warriors."

"Grandpa is more than a poet," objected Arthur. "He's a powerful wizard. Show him, Grandpa! Show him!"

Merlin sighed, "I know a little prestidigitation—"

Kay's barking laughter caught him short. Along with battle prowess and a brawny build, Kay had gained a warrior's arrogance. "It takes more than sleight-of-hand to defend a realm, to build it up out of petty dukes. It takes might of arms."

"Grandpa is not just a wizard. He's an oracle. He can tell the future!" Arthur insisted. "He can tell you what you will be doing tonight."

Kay laughed again. He blinked at the white-haired old man. "Well, how about it?"

"Tonight?" Merlin asked innocently. "You'll be awake a while, and then asleep. At the end of sleeping, you'll wake up."

Strutting across the practice grounds, Kay tousled Arthur's hair and slapped Merlin's back. "Well, there, you're wrong. Tonight, Father will be back from fighting. He's bringing with him the king's chamberlain. The man will test me for sword skill and, when I pass, will induct me in the order of arms. It's not likely I will be sleeping tonight at all—not for a whole week."

"Uther's chamberlain . . ." said Merlin in a wondering, far-away voice. "That title sounds familiar."

"I'll have my own sword and lance and the right to ride a horse into battle. My own horse! Of course I'll need a squire. That'll be you, Arthur, once you can lift a saddle onto a horse. And if I ever need a tinker to do sleight-of-hand, or a poet to sing my praises—"

"One who makes little deeds into great pearls—" Arthur enthused.

"What's the name of the chamberlain?" Merlin asked.

"He's a veteran campaigner," Kay said offhandedly. "Fought for Ambrosius and Uther both. Oafius or Dufius or Ulfius or something."

"Ulfius," Merlin wondered aloud. "I feel I should know that name." He shrugged. "I'll be glad to meet him. Perhaps he knows something more about my past."

"Cook is preparing a special feast for the chamberlain. It will be my crowning glory!"

Merlin stood, brushed off his robes, and walked distract-edly toward the kitchens. "I'll make sure they set my place beside the chamberlain."

A look of green horror came over the young warrior's face as he watched Merlin go.

12

Conferring Arms

Ulfius was numb all over. His backside was numb from the saddle, and his head from Duke Ector's ceaseless talk of Kay—

"—and, of course, there was the time he was determined

to leap the falls of a small creek near our home. He wanted to do it at the height of the rainy season. He got his wish. Snow melt was followed by five inches of rain overnight, and in the morning, the falls were two feet deep and twelve feet across. That didn't stop Kay. He is about as reck—as fearless as anyone you could meet. Why, there was the time when he found an old man and a baby starving in a Roman ruin nearby our castle—"

"Did you say you had another son?" Ulfius asked, rubbing his temples.

"Oh, yes, but he's too young to fight. Still, he adores his older brother, Kay—"

Ulfius sat up taller in the saddle in an attempt to reintroduce blood flow to certain areas. Ector took the posture to mean a heightening of interest, and redoubled the volume of his narrative. After three days on the road, Ulfius knew nothing could drown out Ector when he put his belly into the tale—not even fifty-four horse hooves on a wooden bridge.

Just now, the party crossed the drawbridge of Castle Chertsey. The gate loomed up before them. Beyond the portcullis, Ulfius glimpsed a lovely vision—by all likelihood the blond-haired Duchess Diana. She had a matronly grace, refined rather than ravaged by her years.

"—considered for the priesthood, but I said, 'Not my first-born son!' "

"Excuse me, Sir Ector," said Ulfius, standing in the saddle, "but is this the beautiful wife you have told me so much about?"

With an amused look, the duchess replied lightly, "Yes, and you must be Chamberlam Ulfius."

He bowed low even as the portcullis rattled slowly upward in its tracks. Once the massive thing had risen, he dropped from the saddle, fell to one knee, and took her hand. He opened his mouth to greet her—and his jaw dropped as though never to close again.

"Merlin!" Ulfius gasped under his breath. Beside Diana stood the madman Ulfius had sought for five years.

In that time, Ulfius's vow to Igraine had weighed heavily on him—as had the queen's disapproval. Even Morgan berated him daily. With one breath she would disparage Ulfius for losing Arthur, and with the next disparage Arthur himself. And now, to have Merlin standing there—alive, well dressed, at home among a respectable family in a respectable castle (with a downright *superlative* young warrior)—it all gave Ulfius hope he might find the prince within.

Merlin's face was the most beautiful and horrible thing Ulfius had seen in years.

Duchess Diana gazed down quizzically at Ulfius. He still clutched her hand.

"Forgive me, Duchess," Ulfius said, blushing. "After hearing so many speeches I . . . I seem to have nothing to say."

Diana drew Ulfius up from his knee and said, "Your speechlessness honors me, Chamberlain. It has been a long while since my husband has been speechless." She glanced with fond reproof at Ector. Then to Ulfius she said, "Welcome to Castle Chertsey. There'll be feasting tonight, and drinking and, I do fear, a bit of bragging!" She turned and led the way through the gate.

Ulfius took up his steed's reins and followed. In a few paces, he reached the tottering old mage and drew up beside him. He was glad for the clamor of hooves on stone to mask their words from other ears.

"Hello, Merlin," Ulfius said, nudging the wizard.

The mage gave a small start and turned delirious eyes his way. "Hello?"

"It's Ulfius," the warrior said. "Remember? I fetched you to break the siege of Castle Terrabil."

Merlin gave a shrugging nod. "How are things in the castle?"

"How are things in the—?" Ulfius echoed, stunned. "Don't you remember me? Don't you remember who I am?"

"Oh, I remember," said Merlin, a defensive jag lifting one eyebrow. "You are Ulfius. You came here to see Kay."

Ulfius was astonished. He stared into the madman's face. Delirium scrolled over Merlin's features. Fragments of recognition tumbled in his eyes, mixed with shards of fancy and delusion and doubt. He was lost again, this all-powerful mage. How many decades, how many centuries had this man wandered the world, the mysteries of the ages filling his pockets and yet his fumbling fingers unable to grasp them?

Ulfius grabbed the lunatic's arm. "Merlin, listen—I don't care whether or not you remember me, but tell me you remember Arthur. Tell me he is safe."

Affronted, Merlin pulled his arm away. "Of course he's safe. Of course I remember Arthur. How could I forget my own grandson?" With that, the old mage hastened his steps. In moments, he was beyond the reach of Ulfius and his slow-stomping horse.

Ulfius stared after him. Incredulous, he shook his head. It was going to be a strange visit, indeed.

Who is this man Ulfius? He has no face. Where eyes and nose and mouth should be, there are windows . . . bony orbits and sockets. . . . I cannot see him, but only through him.

In his eyes, antlered Arthur dwells. A crown rests immovable around nubs of horn. This man seeks Arthur, to make him king.

In his mouth dwells another creature—a young woman with skin like moonlight and raven hair and eyes like tidal pools, swarming with scaly things. This one seeks Arthur too, but not to crown him, only to bury him.

And in his nose—the organ that tells what is wholesome from what is rotten—there is not a window but a mirror. In it dwell I. I see myself there. But I am gaunt and tattered and filthy. Unwholesome. Rotten. Mad.

Who is this man Ulfius?

Despite his every attempt to see Arthur, Ulfius always ended up with an eyeful of Kay. Yes, the youth was impressive. He was perhaps too chiseled and idealistic for Uther's meat-grinder battalions, but certainly he deserved induction into the rights of weaponry. Ulfius had been convinced of that after a five-minute demonstration of Kay's sword skill. Even so, a display of horsemanship followed, and an exhibition of wall and tree climbing, of suiting and unsuiting armor, of swinging across moats, of hurling stones and logs, of setting and striking tents, of catching a "wild boar" (only a greased piglet), and of every other task Kay imagined a fighting man doing. The young man had even arranged for a scullery maid to pretend to be trapped in a tower so that he could scale the thing. He was halfway up when Ulfius, using the interior stairs, reached and opened the unlocked door and "rescued" the maid.

Through it all, Ulfius saw nothing of Arthur or, for that matter, Merlin.

It was a thoroughly done-in Ulfius who was led to the castle's high hall for Kay's coming-of-age banquet.

The place was impressive, with stone walls rising two stories to a hammer-beam ceiling in black oak, draped with long banners. Two candle chandeliers poured light and occasional tallow onto the long tables below. The board was spread with bleached linen and runners in red samite. On those runners lay a roast boar with an apple in its mouth. Wooden tankards sat beside stoneware plates. Silver forks lay to one side and flannel napkins to the other. Guests and family gathered, each directed to a seat that befit his or her station. Trenchers were brought out and sliced open. Steam rose from the fresh-cut bread. A pork stew with onions, leeks, carrots, and cabbage was ladled into the loaves.

A small ensemble of players—rebecs and gitterns and fifes—began a lilting tune. Their music rose sweetly up from their corner and ventured out to mingle with happy conversation and tendrils of steam.

Ulfius settled into his seat and heaved a sigh. At least in savory foods, there might be some respite from the ubiquitous warrior Kay.

Then, the tenor began to sing:

"Once lived a lad so noble and true,
And Kay was his name, so strong through and through"

It was Kay, himself, who was singing.

"That ladies and lads always gave him his due,
   Singing terry terry terry, too-rah, terry too-rah rah rah!"

This latest affront was more than Ulfius could bear. His patience snapped like a dry twig.

"Terry too-rah! Too-rah!" shouted Ulfius, standing with hands clenched at his sides.

The song staggered to a halt, as did servants and conversation. Echoing silence filled the hall, broken only by the gassy sound of the boar settling atop its platter.

Ulfius looked around, undaunted by all the astonished attention. "Good! Now that I have all ears and eyes, let me announce that I find Kay to be utterly suitable to join the king's regiments. Without further ado, and with no ceremony whatsoever, I confer upon the lad the honor of sword and horse. There! Finished! Kay is grand! He can fight! He can ride! Now, let's celebrate his ascension! Let's eat some pig and dance a jig and hope to die before morning!"

His voice echoed away into silence. The servants still feared to move. The players refused to play. Ector himself moved with grave aspect toward the musicians' dais where his son stood.

Spirit wilting in him, Ulfius let out a sheepish, "Too-rah."

This whimper was drowned out by Kay's ebullient cry. "I did it! I ascended the heights of glory. I am a noble warrior! I am a retainer to the king!"

Joyful cries surrounded him, and the icy stillness that had gripped the room fractured and shifted into warm motion. Ector lifted his son high on his shoulders. Musicians broke into an instrumental rendition of "Kay the Brave." More guests and family members took their seats amid a flurry of platters and linen. Despite all the happy activity, only scowls were directed toward the inscrutable king's man.

Ulfius slumped down into his chair, deflated. He sucked down his ale and pounded the tankard on the table, requesting another draught. He would drink much tonight, and eat much, and sleep late into the morning, and leave orders with the stable that he wanted to roll out of bed and into the saddle and fly across the green hills of Winchester and never return to this madhouse—

Then Arthur walked in. The boy was in nightclothes, angelic in white linen. It was unmistakably Arthur. His small face combined the fey beauty of Igraine with the powerful lines of Uther. He was all the more unmistakable for the bearded old man that appeared behind him, trying to grab his nightshirt and drag him back into the hall.

Ulfius stood from his place so rapidly his chair barked to the floor behind him. He hurried across the hall to catch the child before Merlin could whisk him away for another five years. "Arthur! Wait! I want to meet you."

The sound of his voice was drowned out by the clamor of music coming from the dais. Behind Ulfius, servants righted his chair. All around the room, eyes disdainfully followed the mercurial emissary of King Uther. He didn't care. He strode rapidly to the doorway.

Young Arthur had won his tug-of-war with the old mage and was striding into the room. His simple white shift against the dark and ornate spaces made him glimmer like a young martyr. His eyes were bright, his face solemnly glad.

Ulfius reached the child and dropped to one knee before him. The rush of emotion was just as it had been when he first held the child, five years before. There was majesty in this boy, an undeniable sense of kingdoms to come and glory ripe upon every tree—a lifetime of brilliance sketched against an age of darkness.

Ulfius took the boy's hands in his own and said, "Arthur, I am so glad to see you—" He had almost said "again," but stopped himself short.

The boy's silvery eyes glimmered in the ceremonial darkness. "You are Ulfius, then, from the court of King Uther?"

"Yes, Arthur."

"I would very much like to see the king's castle, someday," said the bright-eyed boy.

"You will, Arthur," Ulfius responded with sudden certainty. "You will."

Merlin interposed himself. His frail arm, garbed in linen and brocade instead of gray rags, wrapped around the boy. "Come along, now, Arthur. It's past your bedtime."

"But I just met Chamberlain Ulfius, from the king's court," Arthur objected quietly as Merlin drew him back toward the door.

Ulfius caught Merlin's sleeve and insistently pulled him about. Making sure the prince could not hear, he whispered into the old man's ear, "Don't you remember who Arthur is? He is the son of the king and queen. He is the prince!"

Merlin whirled and stared with shock and fear into the eyes of Ulfius. "It doesn't matter. This is his family. This is his home. He's not going back with you."

Ulfius eased his grip on the old man. Merlin was right. If Arthur were taken to court, he would never survive to be king. "Yes. This is his family. I will not take him away from here, from you. . . . But I have sworn to Queen Igraine that I will guard and guide Arthur as he grows."

"What are you whispering about?" Arthur asked.

"I will stay," Ulfius heard himself blurt, loud enough for Merlin and Arthur both to hear. "I will stay. I will teach Arthur—Greek and Latin, swordsmanship, horsemanship, history, sums, geometry. . . . I will prepare him for his role."

"What role?" asked Arthur.

Merlin's gaze had retreated to interior spaces. He drew a deep breath that seemed to clear away some of the cobwebs within him. "Yes. I will allow it—if you keep secret who he is—"

"Of course—"

"I will recommend you to Ector—"

"Recommend whom to Ector?" came a booming voice. Ector had approached the kneeling courtier, the five-year-old, and the doddering old fool. The black scowl across Ector's meaty features made his mood obvious. His glare leaped from Merlin to Ulfius and back again. "Recommend whom?"

"This man," Merlin said, "Ulfius—he would like to stay on to teach Arthur—"

"Teach Arthur?" Ector exclaimed. Anger rimmed his eyes. "Teach *Arthur?* You, who cannot spare a moment to hear about my firstborn son, Kay, who has prepared every possible proof of his virtue? Do you pay any attention to the true warrior in the household? Are you at all interested in the sword prowess, the climbing ability, the overall luster of this lad? Do you give him a moment's consideration? And then, after so passively ignoring his every attempt to impress, you induct him without sword to the shoulder or ceremony of any sort, only to run over here and bow to a mere child eleven years Kay's younger and pledge yourself to teach him?" The man trembled in red fury.

"He'll do it for free," Merlin supplied unhelpfully.

Both Ector and Ulfius glared at him.

Ulfius rallied quickly and climbed to his feet. "On the contrary, Duke Ector, I was so stunned by each and every of Kay's displays of prowess, I was struck dumb. The glazed look in my eyes was not one of boredom, but of abstracted amazement. I found myself like the minuscule cricket locked within the basilica at Canterbury, hearing divine music that makes my own song a mere scraping of legs." *Why do I always get the rotten jobs?* "I, in fact, had determined after mere moments that the lad should be inducted, but let his proofs continue out of sheer amazed ecstasy at witnessing them. When I heard Kay sing, no longer could I hold back my adoration. I declared him a warrior on the spot, lest I get too weak-kneed in confronting him to be able to gently and *safely* convey a sword to the lad's neck—that is, to his shoulder."

Mollified slightly at this display, Ector went from scarlet to mauve. "Why then this hullabaloo?"

"I thought, Duke Ector," continued Ulfius, "that if so splendid a figure of manhood should rise from this family, why not a second? And should not this second son have every advantage of letters and numbers, history and law, as well as physical instruction?"

Ector's face was colored now more by blush than anger. He whispered in aside, "Truth be told, Arthur is not of my blood—"

"Not as bloody-minded as Kay," Merlin interrupted, giving Ector a waggle of his brows, "but still should prove an equal warrior."

"Quite," agreed Ector. He drew a deep breath and assumed yet another shade of red—sanguine glee. "But, as you required such displays of sword work from Kay before admitting him, I will require the same display from you!" Ector drew a gleaming great sword of ornate Saxon design. The blade raked free of its scabbard and glimmered in the dim space.

The clamor in the room died.

Ulfius swallowed, wondering if he could talk his way out of this one. The glad wroth of Ector's black brows convinced him he could not.

Ulfius drew his own sword, no great, six-foot-long Pagan thing but a short Roman gladius. The blades were superior for fighting in tight formation alongside equally armed comrades, but in these one-on-one duels, the gladius was ludicrously inadequate.

It evoked a gurgle of fearful laughter from the crowd.

Compressing his lips in grim irritation, Ulfius strode to an empty place in the great hall. He bowed his head once, and said, "I hope, Ector, that I can impress you as much as your son impresses me."

With fiery joy in his eyes, Ector brought his great sword whirling in a huge overhead arc. It crashed down onto the gladius.

Ulfius's hand jangled near to falling off.

The duke of Castle Chertsey said, "I hope so too."

While Ulfius and Ector began their martial conversation, Merlin nipped away to examine the sumptuous banquet. Wild boar and apples! Tankards of ale and mead! Steaming trenchers of vegetable stew! A feast fit for Asgard!

Merlin slurped Ulfius's trencher dry and conveyed dripping hunks of bread into his gullet.

The sharp ring of sword on sword filled the air. Ector was a bear with a rod of lightning in his grasp. Ulfius was a hedgehog armed with a limp dandelion.

Ah, yes—in that aspect, Ulfius seemed very familiar.

Ector brought his great sword around in a slow arc. Ulfius struggled to dance aside. In the end, he had to fling up his overgrown dagger to turn the blow. The great sword landed; Ulfius took flight. He came down on the table, nearly atop the roast boar. He and the beast traded a sympathetic look. A roar from Ector put an end to this communion. Ulfius retreated. The boar did not. Ector's great sword caught the beast just above the hip and sliced one haunch clean away.

He seems earnest, Merlin thought idly.

As the great sword won free, Merlin sent subtle magic out to ease the severed haunch from the rest of the carcass. Timing the spell to the movement of Ector's sword, he made the hunk of meat vault across the table and land sloppily in his plate. In greasy fingers, he lifted the thing and took a great bite. Brown sauce and crackling stuck to his beard. It was a lovely beast.

Perhaps the chamberlain could use some help, Merlin thought, casting a spell.

Ulfius was even then retreating under a storm of skirling steel. His weapon was too puny to turn back the crashing massiveness of Uther's blade. He turned the gladius in a hopeless attempt to parry. The great sword smashed through and staved his left brassard. Ulfius staggered back and made a desperate feint to drive off his attacker. The gladius flashed outward, seeming to grow until its tip struck Ector, impossibly distant.

The duke retreated. He looked in disbelief at the small red cut on his hip. "How did you do that, Ulfius?"

"Sword work," the man gasped out apologetically. He regained his feet and his ground, moving to the center of the floor. "I'll teach the same trick . . . to Arthur."

Arthur, for his part, watched in a mix of admiration and worry.

Ector panted. "Well, now . . . you said you'll be teaching more than swordsmanship. . . . What of sums and geometries? What is the cube root of two and thirty added to two and thirty?" It was a dirty trick, followed up with a bullish charge, sword raised high.

Caught in the moment of calculation, Ulfius was not set to receive the charge. He lifted his blade and deflected the brunt of the attack, but was sent spinning into a keg of ale. Worse, yet, his gladius lopped the tap from the keg's bung, and golden ambrosia poured over his head.

"I'll have some of that," Merlin decided. He dropped the boar haunch and ambled to the spot. Merlin reached down and hauled Ulfius out of the way. "Four," Merlin whispered, flinging him aside and kneeling in the onslaught of the ale.

"Four," Ulfius said, staggering back into combat.

His gladius tangled with the great sword. Sparks leapt through the air.

Ector growled, impressed. "Tell me about the Peloponnesian War."

Another dirty trick, thought Merlin as he swallowed. That old fight was eight hundred years ago and five hundred leagues away. He drew his mouth away from the stream, stuck a finger in the sweet gush, and sent an enchantment out through the air toward Ulfius.

As the man smashed aside another whistling attack, he spoke in an old voice that reeked of barley water: "The Peloponnesian War was fought between Athens and Sparta, and their allies. Pericles led Athens to early victories until he and many of his folk died due to plague. In the end, Sparta starved Athens into submission. It happened about four hundred years before the Nazarene was born."

This answer only enraged Ector. He drove the scholar before him until Ulfius's back was pressed against a rock wall. Two more strikes of the great sword, and Ulfius's gladius flew free. The tip of the Saxon sword came to rest just beneath his chin.

"Submit," Ector said, temples pulsing. "I have proved the better warrior."

"Bosh," Merlin muttered to the ale cask. He made a small sign.

Ulfius leaped straight into the air, clutched the trailing end of a banner, and swung across the great hall. His voice broke out in a shriek of terror that resolved itself into a song:

"To battle Ector through the night
   Is best left to Dian-er.
   His public sword is long and bright.
   His private's just a dagger!"

A gasp of horror followed this ditty, beginning from the man who sang it and spreading through the room.

Ector roared, "You'd best win this match, Ulfius, or you'll never live to see dawn!" He rushed in the wake of the swinging man, who had traded one banner tail for another. Ector impotently swung his sword behind the retreating heels of his tormentor, growling absurdly and stumbling over chair and table, guest and dog.

In one particular sprawl, he landed atop a serving maid and somehow—magically—got tangled in her dress. She shrieked, rushing in underthings out one end of the garment, as Ulfius angrily clambered in the other end. He rose, draped unevenly, and let out a yell of animal fury.

The sound of his rage echoed with small titters of amusement among the gathered crowd. A pair of heels swung tantalizingly past.

Ector took a wild swipe. His great sword spun him about and hurled him into the vacated lower half of the boar. One knee sunk in a tureen of carrots. One hand buried itself in a sloshing pitcher of mead. The duke of Castle Chertsey rose. For a helm, he wore the torso and head of the boar.

Merlin took a moment away from ale foam to admire his handiwork.

Ector let out one final bellow of rage. The sound was

distant and pathetic, emerging around the apple in the boar's teeth.

The crowd could no longer hold their mirth. A great peal of laughter echoed through the hall. The players began their song. Kay took up the lyrics. Servants danced with dignitaries. Dogs lapped eagerly at a frothy pool.

In its midst sat a very drunk, very satisfied old mage.

13

Battles in the North

Set me down here!" King Uther growled, pointing to the grassy hilltop. "Here!"

Uther was accustomed to riding into battle on a horse, not on a camp chair. His attendants had even strapped him in. Yesterday, the ailing king had fallen out as they trekked up the abutment. This morning, the attendants were taking no chances.

"Ulfius would have come up with a better solution," Uther groused as they carried him to level ground. His chamberlain had been gone for two years now and was sorely missed. "Idiots! Set me down!"

The armsmen did. Pages and varlets swarmed in their wake, carrying medicinal spirits, cushions, blankets—countless measures meant to ease Uther's pain. Nothing could soothe a warrior-king who could no longer make war.

"I should be down there," Uther hissed through grinding teeth.

The plains beside the Humber Firth were ranked with his troops. Two thousand pike men fought in a killing line toward the shimmering water. Their Roman-style hasta spears glinted silver and red in the morning. In their tight formation, they mowed down Angles. Though the four thousand invaders fought like berserkers, they had little organization and less strategy. A week ago, Uther's pike men had received a charge of Angle heavy horse and slew their cavalry to a man. Now, Britannia's troops had trapped the Angle infantry against the Humber Firth and were grinding them to mash.

"Why don't they bring in their ships?" Uther asked himself. Over a hundred dragon ships lay offshore, anchored with no sign of receiving their beleaguered forces. "Why don't they retreat to their ships?"

"Angles don't retreat," one of the armsmen offered. The blond-headed warrior was himself of High German extraction, though his family had been Romanized two centuries before. "They fight like madmen. You cut one down the middle, and the half with the heart fights on. Lop off his head, and he doesn't even notice. I once killed an Angle three times in one afternoon."

"Shut up," Uther advised.

The other armsman considered this an opening. "They're probably afraid we'd break through and capture their boats. They'd rather die than give up their boats."

"Shut up!" Uther commanded. "I can't think with all this yammering."

He studied the battle below. A phalanx of elite Britons stabbed into the heart of the Angles. Long scutum shields were arrayed before, beside, and atop the advancing Britons. Those shields were proof against bow fire and sword work, both. In moments, the phalanx would cut the Angle forces in half.

"Why don't they retreat? They'll be slaughtered. They must know something we don't—"

A warning shout came from the Briton encampment behind Uther.

The armsmen turned, their eyes darkening.

Horns sounded the to-arms. Canvas rustled. Boots pounded. A collective groan came, punctuated by shouted orders.

Uther craned to see, but the straps held him prisoner. "What is it? Turn me, damn you!"

The armsmen crouched to lift the ailing king. "More armies. They bear the colors of Sussex and Essex."

At last, Uther saw. The south road swarmed with Saxons. They advanced steadily from the wood, a black tide of them. There must have been five thousand. Perhaps ten.

"Order a retreat," Uther hissed. A courier frantically scribbled the message. "Bring our troops back from the firth. Fall back to Barrow. There are trenches and walls at Barrow. Fall back and fortify the town!"

The young courier was white-faced. "Yes, my king." He bowed and ran fleetly down the hill.

Another messenger took the place of the first, and Uther said to him, "Take a horse, a quick one, before they close off the south. Ride to the garrison at Caistor. Order all able soldiers to join us at Barrow. Send messengers throughout the land with a summons. Draft it yourself. Make it clear—all able soldiers must come or face execution. Seal it with this ring. Bring all of Britannia, lad. Bring them all, or Britannia ceases to be."

As the courier headed toward the stables, Uther coughed raggedly. Doom swept toward him from the south. "A trap. They lured me into a trap." A grim smile edged across his lips. "Well, at least I'll die like a warrior, and not like a wasting worm."

"Can't we practice in the great hall?" Arthur asked as he swung the narrow plank that served him as a sword. He was seven now, and had endured two years of climbing and gymnastics training. This bright morning was the first time he'd handled anything like a sword. "I want to chop up a roast boar and swing from the banners."

Ulfius smiled patiently. "I don't imagine your father would want me to teach you those tricks."

"He won't know," Arthur piped. "He's off fighting for the king."

"Yes, and with your father and brother away, you are the man of the castle. You should avoid tomfoolery."

Arthur whacked a much-battered quintain. The plank jangled and dropped from nerveless fingers. "Ow! That damned thing fights back."

"Damned thing?" Ulfius said, amazed. "Where did you hear such language?"

Teacher and student simultaneously glanced toward Merlin, who sat by the courtyard well. Grandfather was occupied with a harmless bit of magic. He drew buckets of water up the well, idly transformed the liquid into mead, and then shared ladles of it with the castle dogs.

"Have you been teaching the boy to curse?" Ulfius asked in exasperation.

Merlin looked up and blinked behind aggressive eyebrows. "Somebody has to. How can he be a warrior and not curse? I heard you curse the very day I met you."

"And I've been cursing ever since," Ulfius said. At least Merlin now remembered that first day. He now knew who Arthur was and who he must become. "Well, enough of cursing and sword-swinging. We've more Periclean history—"

Arthur visibly slouched. His footsteps became heavy. "Ughh. And what does Pericles have to do with anything? Who needs to know about Pericles in the middle of a sword fight?"

"Ulfius does, for one," Merlin said placidly.

Ignoring him, Ulfius said, "Tell me what you remember about the Roman world view."

"Oooh!" Arthur flung his hands down, slung his head forward, and did a little dance of dissatisfaction. "They thought Britannia was the Elysian Fields, and thought everybody on this island was happy, and that if you jumped in the North Sea you'd float right on around to the land of the Aethiopians. What difference—"

His tirade was interrupted by the arrival of a horseman beyond the portcullis of the main gate. The man had been riding hard, and his horse foamed around bit and saddle as he pulled it to a stop. The beast let out a wild shriek.

"Who could that be—?" Ulfius began. He turned to see. Young Arthur had already lit out for the gate. "Arthur, get back here. He may well be a Saxon!"

Merlin brought up the rear, a pack of loose-legged dogs bounding stupidly in his wake.

Arthur had run so rapidly across the courtyard, he sent up a cloud of dust. Without thought to his own safety, he rushed up to the portcullis.

The horseman beyond was already shouting to the men on the wall above, who threatened him with short bows.

"Acchh! Put those damned things away!" the rider yelled. He wore the purple and gold Pendragon livery of Uther's army, the cloth limp with sweat. He held high a folded parchment with a great red glob of wax on it. "Don't you see? I've got a letter with the king's seal."

"Let me see," Arthur cried. "Let me see!"

The rider impatiently held the paper out toward the boy in the archway, but shouted to those above, "This letter gives me dominion over you and every other able armsman in the castle. The more trouble you are to me now, the more trouble I'll be to you later!"

Arthur said, "It is the seal. Let him in!"

Ulfius arrived and confirmed Arthur's story. "It is the seal, but keep the gate closed until we read the letter." He reached through the bars of the portcullis.

The armsman presented the letter with an irate swipe of his hand. "There. Crack it. Read it. Confirm it. Then lift this gate!"

Ulfius took the letter and opened the seal. He unfolded the parchment. Merlin and his dogs arrived. The mage, the warrior, and the boy peered at the missive:

From King Uther Pendragon, Heir to Ambrosius, Ruler of Britannia, Keeper of Law, Protector of Britons, Scourge of Saxons, et cetera.

To those who dwell in Castle Chertsey and the lands around, particularly armsmen pledged to the family of Ector,

Greetings.

As ever, your King fights hard on your behalf against the

Angle and Saxon plague, and is even now engaged and brutally pressed by foes along the banks of the Humber at Barrow. His victory will mean the land's security, and his defeat would mean a wave of Pagan destruction.

Therefore, the King commands any able armsmen to march in company forthwith to join the defenders of Lriton. Any who do not comply will be brought before the King upon conclusion of the war to make an accounting for his absence. The penalty for disobedience will be absolute.

King Uther

Ulfius lowered the note, stunned. Were he to join the battle, he would have to account for his long absence, and Arthur's whereabouts would become known. Were Ulfius to remain behind, Uther's envoy would imprison him, and Arthur would be discovered. Either way, Ulfius could not protect the prince.

Arthur clutched the note and sounded out each word written across it. His efforts were hampered by the drunken dogs that nuzzled him.

"Open the gates!" the horseman demanded. "If the king falls, we all become slaves to Saxons."

Delirium crawled over Merlin's features. His lips twitched beneath ragged whiskers.

"Open the gates," shouted Ulfius to the guards above. "Let this man in. Open the gates!"

Fear is the worst passion—fear and dread. They are sad creatures with the pinions of pigeons. Hawks watch them, and they know how strong hawk beaks are and how weak pigeon necks are.

A white flock of fear and dread circles my bed. Above them are the hawks, the Valkyrie. They gather the souls of the dead. They stoop on fallen fighters and scoop them in their beaks and bear them away to Wotan. They come for me.

I know how weak my neck is.

Wotan will sweep across the isle until I am dead and the god-killing sword is his. Saxons will rush in a bloody tide across the country. The Saxon gods will course through skies and seas, rivers and woods. They will bring death to all Albion—all Britannia. To me.

Merlin riled on his pallet. He could not sleep. The pigeons were thick between him and the rafters. He could little breathe for all their down in the air. Their sad cooing was like rain on the rooftop. In his fits of terror, they were his only companions.

Or nearly so.

Falling feathers sketched out an unkind face in the dark air. A voice assembled itself from the sobs of birds. "It has been awhile since last we spoke, Merlin. It has been awhile since you have been backed into a corner so dark."

Heaving a sad sigh, Merlin said, "Loki, old friend."

"Old friend? You honor me," Loki replied, his voice tremulous with coos. "But how can we be friends? You forgot about me a long while."

"Arthur is healing me," Merlin explained pensively. "I am remembering more. The antlered child is hunting down the keys of madness. He is opening lock after nested lock."

"Yes. Your visions of Arthur are coming true. And your visions of Guinevere and Morgan too—"

"Guinevere and Morgan?" asked Merlin in genuine puzzlement.

"Your visions of Wotan will come to pass as well," Loki said. Fear shuddered through the dove song. "He will sweep across this land. Death and mayhem will follow in his wake." There was a keen smile in the floating feathers. "I'm looking forward to it."

"Of course you are," Merlin returned sullenly. "Wotan is your god."

"I am my own god!" The pulse of startled wings joined bird calls. Slowly the pigeons settled, and so did Loki's mood. "But I enjoy chaos, and you've done little to provide any lately. Madness suits you much better than this . . . this bleating hope."

A bitter smile crossed the old man's lips. "Madness will return soon enough. Already, Wotan's wings whistle in my ears. . . ."

Loki said quietly, "There are two kinds of madness, Merlin. There is lunacy, and there is rage. It is lunacy to brood here among passive pinions. You are Merlin. Transform yourself—no simple pigeon, no falcon or hawk, but a drake, a dragon, a Pendragon! Choose rage. Take the battle to Wotan before he brings it to you."

Merlin blinked. A rank breath filled him. "Yes." In sudden decision, he rose from his cot. "Yes, Loki. You are right. If madness is returning, I will seize it. I will grab it before it grabs me. Your insight changes me, Loki."

"Only repay me in chaos—"

"I shall," Merlin answered. He released a great roar—a sound worthy of a dragon. The pigeons took sudden flight. Their flailing white wings filled the air and their coos became shrieks. Out the windows, out the door, away from the madman they went. Soon, all were gone. Only a flurry of feathers remained—and a transforming figure.

Merlin's nightcap grew into a great rumpled hat. It extended into a mantel across his shoulders. His thin linen nightshirt lengthened and darkened into purple war robes. Pockets appeared across the cloak. Within them materialized arcane substances—jiggers of blood, jerked hunks of flesh, powdered bone, mouse brainballs, falcon skulls, poison quills. . . . and all of it was lit by Merlin's blazing eyes.

He reached down by his bedside and grasped a twisted walking stick that Arthur had given him. Clutching the bough, Merlin transformed it. Fury like blood seeped from every tissue. It stained the wood dark. It infused dry fibers and revived them. Gnarled oak grew and twisted into a tall staff. Pictish runes etched themselves across scratched bark. Talismans of pigeon feather and hawk feather and dragon leather formed and attached themselves to the staff. Motes of red power circulated about its head.

Merlin took the staff, flung back the door, and descended a winding stair. At its base was another door, leaking light and noise. Merlin hurled it back.

In the garrison beyond, a company of two hundred fighting men gathered. The broad chamber was alight with torches. Shadows milled at soldiers' feet. The warriors were caparisoned to march at dawn.

The door banged on the wall. Merlin emerged. The clamor dropped to silence, and warriors stared. Even young Arthur—who wore a too-large coat of mail, a skirt of tasses and tuille, mail leggings, and war boots—gazed in wonder at the old man.

Most of the soldiers there had considered Merlin to be simply daft. A few had seen his minor conjurations. Only Ulfius could have anticipated this.

"I go ahead of you," Merlin said solemnly. "Make your best time behind. Wotan will not win. Wotan cannot win."

With that, the fire-eyed wizard flashed away.

Merlin arrived in a much different place.

It was a large and darksome tent, lit not by angry torches but by the decorous glow of tallow and wick. The men in this space were grave, soft-robed—priests instead of warriors. The space had a smell of luxury. Incense curled in the air, and lavish rugs covered the ground. Samite partitions separated room from room. Velvety murmurs softened every corner. The down-turned heads and eyes all bent with grave aspect toward the silken doorway of the king's chamber—

Until the mad mage arrived. Red magic dappled his figure. Numinous creatures crawled across his rumpled headdress. As soft as a whisper, he appeared in the midst of that dolorous throng. There came a moment of shock, and then guards surrounded him.

Merlin merely raised a hand. An unseen barrier arced around him and stayed the armsmen. "I am Uther's mage," he explained simply. "I have come to kill Wotan."

The guards were stunned. The priests murmured prayers and touched crosses.

Merlin whirled and strode, staff in hand, into the chamber of Uther.

The king was dying. He lay on a soft couch of pillows and blankets, his hearty figure ravaged, complexion cadaverous, eyes sunken. Despite the heat of the summer evening, he shivered in woolen blankets.

Another priest, this one in black robes and wearing a small cap of ermine, knelt at the king's bedside. In one hand he clutched a broken loaf of bread, and in the other a chalice. The priest glanced up when Merlin entered. A look of angry suspicion crossed his silvery brows. "What is the meaning of this?"

"I am Uther's wizard," Merlin said levelly.

"Uther's wizard?" the priest echoed. "What would a Christian king want with a Pagan mage?"

"Merlin!" Uther interrupted. His voice was as ravaged as his face. "Why have you come?"

"I've come to kill Saxons. I've come to kill Wotan." His eyes blazed. "I've come to return you to your throne."

The priest gaped.

"Kill Saxons if you will, but you are too late for me, Merlin," the king sighed raggedly. "I am dying."

Merlin strode to the bedside. He stared intently, as though gazing through the withered king. "You must get up, Uther Pendragon. You must be king."

The priest tried to ward Merlin away. "He cannot get up. I am performing extreme unction—"

Merlin grabbed the bread and bit deeply into it, washing it down with the whole contents of the chalice. Through an oozing mass of dough and wine, he commanded, "Get up!"

"That is the body and blood of Christ!" the priest protested.

"Get up! If Uther falls, the nation falls, and death sweeps over us all. Get up!" Merlin demanded. He reached down and ripped the blankets back from Uther, only to see the man's withered legs.

The king was little more than a skeleton. His skin clung to him like wet paper. Beneath it ran a web of cold blue veins. Where once there had been lusty health was now concave ruin.

In his withered figure, Merlin saw the land. Dead trees, cracked plains, razed villages, tumbled walls—the very grass too ragged to cover the shattered bones of the earth. A dead king would mean a dead land, a carcass swarming with Saxon maggots and ghosts.

"Do you see?" the priest asked emphatically. "He cannot get up. He cannot lead his men. He cannot fight!"

"You are too late, Merlin," Uther said. "Too late for me, and for Britannia."

"Death," the mage replied. "Death and death and death."

Uther took a long, shuddering breath and asked. "Does my son live?"

Mention of Arthur drove the riling flames from Merlin's eyes. He circled around the bedside and knelt. His face still glowed feverishly. "Arthur is well. He is a handsome child, and smart. He has your intensity and the queen's gentility. If he lives, he will be a great king."

"If he lives?" Uther repeated in startlement. "Is he ill?"

The wizard's eyes became faraway. "No. But his land is. If you die now, Uther, your son will never be king. He will not survive the month."

Into the hush after those words, the distant desperate sounds of battle intruded. Men roared. Steel clashed. Horses shrieked. War engines groaned. Fires chewed up grasslands and men and all.

"Do you hear that, Merlin?" asked the king, waving a hand beside his ear. "What madness, fighting by torchlight." He gave a low, hopeless laugh. "All that stands between the invaders and the nation is that dying army and this dying king and you, Merlin."

Merlin nodded. Wine ran sanguinely down his white beard. "I would let the nation be damned—it is nothing but the tattered remains of Rome, who stole it from the tattered remains of Albion, who stole it from the tattered remains of the Tuatha Dé Danann. I would let the nation be damned. But if we—if warriors and kings and mages—are all that stand between death and Arthur, I say we must stand."

The priest said, "But he cannot—"

Merlin angrily waved him off. "Get out of here. Where are your miracles? It's up to the Pagans to save the king! Out!" His eyes flared again.

Cringing, the priest retreated from the chamber.

Merlin leaned forward and grasped Uther's withered arm in a wine-stained hand. "I will find you a litter. I will array you for battle and put you on a litter and drag you out where the men can see your courage, that you are not afraid to die. We can yet beat death at its own game. For Arthur, we can."

Uther looked up into the beaming eyes of the mage and said, "Yes."

14

Spells by the Humber

These damned Angles did not understand sleep. Nor did they realize they couldn't simultaneously wield a two-handed sword and a torch.

Ector did. His Saxon great sword remained sheathed, a blood-spattered spatha in his right hand and a torch in his left. He liked to see the men he killed. There was something comforting about knowing they were just men and not demons of darkness. Tall, square-jawed, bearded men.

Ector drove his blade up beneath the leather hauberk of one Angle and lifted the man bodily from the ground. The man's face was close enough to his that they might have kissed. Torchlight showed a red rain from gasping lips. Ector hurled the brute. He landed atop a charging comrade.

Taking a step back, Ector spit blood.

The Pagans were rising up the rill, out of the darkness, hurling themselves over the headwall.

Kay was up there. He had volunteered for the most dangerous post, along the earthwork southern defenses of ruined Barrow. There, he and his contingent had met charge after charge of Saxons. They came with ludicrous blades so heavy the Saxons could scarcely breathe to heft them after clambering to the hilltop. In shoulder-to-shoulder formation, the Britons had turned them back until well past midnight.

Now it was nearly fourth watch. The gibbous moon was deserting them. The torches were burnt to nubs and guttering. Still the Angles and Saxons came on. They could fight without light—without strategy or worthwhile armor or usable swords. They fought with bloodlust and will.

After gulping two breaths, Ector stepped back into battle. He impaled yet another comer. The thrashing man screamed something in the Angle tongue and tried to bite Ector's ear. He thrust the man away, into the onslaught of a Pagan sword. The descending blade clove the Angle nearly in two. Great sword and spatha met in the bloody midst of the dead man.

Spatha hopelessly fouled, Ector released it and rammed his torch in the face of his newest attacker. Black beard and bristly hair whooshed in flame. Burning, the man staggered back. Ector pursued, marching atop the cleft Angle. He dropped his torch and drew the great sword from his hip. The night wrapped him. He brought the sword moaning down. It cleaved plate and mail. The burning man fell atop his comrade, their severed halves intermingling.

Ector roared, a sound full of fury and fight. He hefted his bloodied great sword. Gore garbed him. He wondered if this lust for death was the true purpose of Saxon arms. With dark-attuned eyes, Ector gazed out across the hosts of the foe. An endless black army of them rose up the hill. There would be more blood, more halved warriors, more spectral images of dark gods before this battle was ended.

He would slay until morning, if he lasted that long. If

Britannia lasted that long. Without king or God or sorceries, how could they?

Ector whirled the blade in a deadly ring and waded deeper into melee.

Using his staff for support on the rutted ground, Merlin labored beside the pony cart where the king's litter lay.

A cadre of warriors accompanied them, not only to guard the king's person but to hold high the torches that showed him to his troops. They passed first through the beleaguered encampment, en route to the front lines. The sight was meant to rally the men—Uther in full armor, waving a sword, willing to fight even from his sickbed. The torches, though, made the procession funereal. In their light, the king was more shadow than flesh. His hoarse shouts and waggled sword were the ravings of a senile man.

Merlin was not helping. He tried to lead the soldiers in a war chant, but the only ones he remembered were in Latin. Someone else started a bawdy tavern tune. Though it lifted spirits, it did nothing for the dignity of the king. Wherever the aimless parade ventured, hands gripped hilts a little less tightly, rage drained away before waves of incredulity, and Uther was transformed from the suffering king to the foolish jester.

A pair of arrows thrummed down out of the black air and embedded on either side of Uther's head.

"Dowse those torches," Merlin ordered in a pique. His eyes blazed.

Armsmen smothered the torches in a nearby puddle. The caravan came to a halt.

"It's no use," Uther said despondently. His voice rang through the hollows of his armor. "The sight of me can only dishearten my men and hearten my foes."

Merlin turned to gaze at the swale below. There, the battle raged brutally.

Lit by torches beneath a staring moon, Britons, Saxons, and Angles massacred each other. Twelve thousand warriors fought that night. They clustered at the base of the hill like a giant monster—inky and violent and unrelenting. Barbaric battle-axes rose and fell in a brutal rhythm. Sprays of blood momently caught the light. Gladii leapt up in short, eviscerating stabs. Men screamed. The living climbed over the dead. Warriors hid beneath corpses or used them as shields or knelt to harvest souvenirs. In the darkness, they all were monsters. Briton and Saxon and Angle, they all were monsters.

There was no time for reinforcements. This battle would be done before dawn.

Merlin rolled up the purple sleeves of his battle robe and said, "The king has failed, and the army is failing. Let us see if the mage can succeed."

His fingers danced in the ravening air. From them leaped tracers of sorcerous might—blue lightning and red fire. Great billowing waves belched out over British helms. Magic curled down to crackle and whoosh amid the invaders. An iridescent cloud of smoke rose from the conflagration. Backlit in the enchantment, armor melted and bodies settled to bone and ash.

Merlin cast the king a smile, invisible in the darkness. "That's a rather nice one, I think—" His observation was cut short by a descending swarm of arrows that thudded to ground beside him. The old man snorted, seeing that one shaft had pinioned his foot. He reached down, broke off the arrow, and yanked his foot upward. "Perhaps something less traceable."

He produced a shard of tusk from his war stole. Rubbing it between his fingers, he spoke arcane words and grunted like a boar in battle frenzy.

There seemed to be no effect—until a flash of light illumined a line of Britons, transformed into pigs. Snorting, they charged into battle.

Merlin growled. That was not the desired effect. He swept his hand outward. The arms and armor of the opposing Saxons transformed into fragrant truffles. British pigs fell hungrily on their Saxon foes, eating away swords and armor and all. Squeals of delight and angry curses came from that corner of the battle.

The mad mage was not satisfied. There had to be more devastating effects. Merlin reached back into the chaotic depths of his mind, a man rummaging through a bag of junk. Fingers of thought passed over idols—hard-edged, cold, angry, near-forgotten idols. There was among them a young man who shone like the sun, his every movement lyrical, his very gaze the penetrating eye of Future.

Merlin drew the image forward. The spell rolled out like a carpet. It struck a British soldier. The man was haggard and mantled in blood, scarred and unshaven. Magical power lashed over him. Armor and clothes were stripped away in a rending flash. His sword transformed into a long, slim bow with giant arrows. Naked in the midst of retreating warriors, his flesh was infused with a marbled light. Hair across his body burned away, leaving only the matted and close-cropped locks on his head. Beneath his skin, fat melted and muscles flared. Next moment, his whole being swelled outward. He grew. Six feet tall, eight feet, ten, twelve, fifteen . . . His eyes beamed across the battlefield, searing away Saxons in their compass.

Phoebus Apollo, for it was he, nocked arrows and let fly. Wherever his lightning shafts struck ground, sizzling energy danced out to impale the warriors around. Saxon arrows answered, but pinged uselessly off his stony flesh. From his mouth came a Latin war chant. It terrified Saxons.

The Britons also cringed away. This gleaming presence was unknown to them—centuries removed from Rome. The spectral archer was no god of theirs, but a Pagan sorcery that quelled their hearts. With a groan of dread, they fell back.

Kay was fighting two Angles when one of their horrific gods appeared on the battlefield.

Naked and glorious, the shimmering figure loomed up in their midst. He clutched a giant bow, and his eyes blazed luciferously.

"Preserve!" Kay exclaimed.

His sword faltered. One of the Angles surged in to attack. The warrior's battle-ax descended like Thor's thunder. Kay shied back, but not quickly enough. He felt the blade bite viciously into his shield arm. Ring mail shattered and showered away from the blow. Blood followed afterward. Dragging his shield in a flagging grasp, Kay staggered back. The Angle did not pursue. Beneath red brows, his eyes glowed with the unholy vision of the archer.

Kay took advantage of the Angle's fear to make his own ragged escape. Nerveless fingers lost hold of the shield. He couldn't get a breath. He couldn't reach the retreating line of defenders. . . .

The black hordes of Saxony swarmed around their god, ready to sweep the field. How could the Britons last? How could they stand against this Pagan god of war? What good would the bleeding Nazarene be to armies of men with swords? Was that to be their fate, martyrdom? To save the Saxons by spilling their own blood?

Despair swept over him in a dread cloud. Kay fled back toward burned-out Barrow and the languishing armies of Britannia.

Merlin climbed up the cart where the dying king of Britannia lay. He stared with dismay into the rout he had caused.

Though the giant Phoebus Apollo slew Angles and Saxons in their hundreds, barbarians fought onward, as though accustomed to divine company. It was the Britons who fled. In their minds, there was no divine being but Christ or Satan, and this most certainly was not Christ.

"Not working," Merlin roared. "Not working!"

He clambered down among the pillows that couched the dying king. Unknowing, he kicked a cushion over Uther's face. Merlin reached ground and turned to see a rumpled and apparently headless king.

"How have they—? Who has—?" Merlin cried, clutching the sides of his head. "All is lost! The king is dead!"

"Not yet," came a wry but muffled voice from beneath the pillow. "But soon enough."

Merlin rushed to fling the pillow free. Its fringe had wedged in the king's visor. The cushion pulled Uther's helmet sideways. There was a momentary tug-of-war between the mage's hands and the king's neck. At last, the hands relented. Merlin laid the tangled pillow to one side, pried up the king's visor, and stared into sad, sunken eyes.

"Not dead yet," Uther said, "but soon."

Merlin studied the ravaged brows, the withered visage, the hopeless gaze. "They do not need sorceries. They do not need to be turned to pigs and gods. They need their king, Uther."

"Their king is dead," said Uther. "I will never rise from this pallet—"

Already, Merlin knew what he would do.

He backed away from the reclining king, drew up his sleeves, and reached into the moonless heavens. Power cascaded into his fingertips. From each of the stars above, rays of quintessence filtered down. The spiderweb strands of light twined in Merlin's hands. A magical fabric formed, as strong and sleek as samite. The robe of light whirled in air and descended across the reclining king. Illumination sank into every line of his armor, every turn of metal and seam of cloth. His figure glowed and straightened. Magical energy raced across his form until the whole of his being was traced out by it.

A man of light leaped up from the man of flesh.

Before the reclining king, his glowing semblance stood, projected in air. This was no sixteen-foot-tall figure of marble, but a hundred-foot-tall image of light—no naked god, but a mortal king in warrior's panoply. And, emblazoned across that panoply was the unmistakable image of the Pendragon. King Uther. The spectral figure was made all the more imposing by the strange, fringed object that hung menacingly from his raised visor.

Uther looked up at the enormous semblance, as huge as a titan of old. Amazement filled his face. His hand strayed to the tassels jammed in his helmet, and he struggled to work the pillow free. Simultaneously, the glowing titan lifted its hand to yank away the pillow.

"Yes, that's it, King Uther," Merlin hissed. "Move, and the simulacrum will move. March, and he will march."

Uther and his luminous doppelganger pulled the cushion free and tossed it aside. The numinous pillow careened down amid Saxons, pinning them under its smothering weight. The king laughed. The spectral giant laughed. The king made walking motions with his legs. The colossus strode toward the welling sea of barbarians.

They bunched back, uncertain whether this creature of light could harm them or not.

The giant Uther marched into their midst. His foot came down atop shaggy heads, crushing them as though they were grapes in a vintner's basin. Saxons shrieked at the gory sight. They stumbled back against their comrades. The giant's other foot crashed down. More Saxons crumpled.

A moan rose from the invading armies. It swept in waves out among them. It was as though an icy tide rolled through a hot sea. Bloodlust cooled. Morale shattered.

On the next thunder stroke of Uther's stride, the proud armies turned to flee into the darkness, back to their ships, or to the swamps that had spawned them.

Kay had fallen thrice in his retreat. All was lost. There was another giant, now. God had abandoned Britannia.

Someone grabbed Kay's shoulder and hauled him to a halt.

He whirled, jabbing his spatha toward the warrior's stomach.

A Saxon blade knocked it aside, and the warrior growled in a familiar voice. "Son, son! You mistake your friend for your enemy!"

"Father!" Kay gasped. He sheathed his bloody blade, let fall his shield, and clutched his knees, panting. "Titans . . . they have brought . . . titans from Saxony." He gestured outward with his wounded arm. "How are we . . . to fight . . . gods!"

Ector laughed. It was a heartening sound. "No. You mistake your friend for your enemy. Behold the giant—he is our king, Uther! He wears the Pendragon livery!"

Even as he said it, the titan scooped up a handful of Angles and hurled them through the starry sky. Shouting and flailing, the barbarians tumbled through the air to land in the sea, beside their dragon boats.

Ector stooped to lift his son's shield and place it in his hand. "Come. Our king wants us to drive them back to their ships. Let us, you and me, lead the charge."

Grinning happily, Kay straightened. He took two more fortifying breaths and then lifted his spatha. "For Uther!"

Side by side, they charged the retreating line of Saxons.

Behind them welled a tremendous roar. The beleaguered warriors of Britannia rallied and charged.

15

Death of the Pendragon

Just north of Peterborough, Ulfius and his contingent caught sight of a huge army on the grassy horizon.

The army was descending the York-London Road, and they numbered in the thousands. Helms glinted savagely in the sunshine. Banners etched black rectangles against the bright sky. Toothy polearms bobbed in air. Along the infantry's flanks rode two columns of horse. Their muscular line, fused together in a long trail of dust, seemed a giant serpent slithering its way southward.

"The question is whether they are friend or foe," Ulfius said to young Arthur, riding a pony beside him. "Are they our folk returning victorious on the road from Barrow? Or are they Angles sweeping southward to destroy us? The problem is, we cannot know until we are too close for safe retreat."

"What does it matter?" asked Arthur bravely, brandishing a stick as though it were a blade. "We'll meet them either way. If they are our folk, we will celebrate the victory. If they are our foes, we will bring them down to defeat."

"Not two hundred against two thousand, we won't," Ulfius said. His eyes grew intense. "Arthur, I want you to turn your pony around and make for that stand of alder, there—"

"Behold!" shouted a sentry ahead, "the purple and gold blazing of the Pendragon crest!"

Ulfius lifted a hand visorlike over his eyes and said, "Yes! They fly the banners of Uther. Your fath—your king is hence. Go to the alders and wait for my signal." Standing in the saddle, he shouted, "Best speed!" Ulfius pressed heels to his steed. The horse broke into a gallop.

At seven, Arthur was already an able horseman. He kicked his pony, driving it neck-and-neck with Ulfius's charger. The rest of the mounted contingent surged up behind them. They sent a cloud of dust up from the overgrown Roman road into the cluttered sky. The timid alders where Arthur was to hide rattled with the report of eight hundred hooves.

Ulfius glanced at that stand of trees, and then at the young man riding beside him. "What are you doing?" he shouted.

Arthur looked up, his young eyes clear. "Keeping pace!"

"You were supposed to wait for my signal!"

Arthur pointed up the road, "I think they are waiting for your signal too."

There, before them, the infantry had halted and were spreading out along the road, setting pikes to receive a charge. The cavalry meanwhile bolted out ahead of the rest. They lowered their lances and thundered down the road toward Ulfius.

The warrior reined in his steed and held up a hand, calling for a halt. The two hundred horsemen behind him hauled hard on reins. Horses whickered and shrieked, struggling for purchase on the weedy road. They came to a jumbled halt. Many of the mounts reared. The air was charged with dust and spinning hooves. Ulfius, at the head of the confusion, hastily made the hand signs for parley.

Onward rushed the lancers. Their leveled weapons converged like arrows from Gwynedd longbows.

Ulfius stood in the saddle and waved both hands overhead, repeating the signals.

Still the chargers converged.

Ulfius ordered his own forces to retreat, at the same time forming the parley signal. Neither side responded, the riders of Chertsey too shrouded in dust to escape, and the horsemen of Uther bent on attack. The massacre was inevitable.

"Father!" shouted Arthur, standing atop his pony and waving. "Over here, Father!"

The horseman at the head of the lancers—a huge bear of a man—suddenly lifted his lance, flung back the visor of his helm, and stood in the saddle. He waved off the others. Lances rose into the air—lightning diverted before striking. Hooves sparked on Roman stone as the contingent slid to a stop. Out of the resultant dust cloud, the lead lancer emerged. He proceeded toward Ulfius and Arthur. The rider's right-hand warrior came along with him. They unlaced their helms and drew them away from great shocks of hair—black and golden.

"Father! Brother!" Arthur shouted, waving.

"Ector! Kay!" gasped Ulfius in astonishment. Sweat formed a drenching waterfall across his eyes. He slumped against his mount's mane and took a few deep breaths.

Ector rode his horse up before the jumbled assembly. He marched it up and down. "What is the meaning of this?" he barked.

Ulfius turned his slump into a bow. "Forgive us, Ector. We were so glad to see that you were forces of the Pendragon, I forgot to signal—"

"No," interrupted Ector, "I mean, why is Arthur with you? What reason have you for bringing a child into battle?"

Ulfius blinked in thought. The truth of the matter was that Arthur was not destined for battle. He was along so that Ulfius could keep him out of battle. At times such as these, the safest place for Arthur was aback a fast horse. Even so, he could tell Ector none of this. By way of answer, Ulfius smiled stupidly and shrugged. "Merely a miscalculation." He hastened to add, "But it matters little now, given that Uther is victorious—"

"Britannia is victorious," Ector answered solemnly, "but Uther—he languishes even now on a litter. He led us to victory at Barrow, but at the cost of health and life." Ector's eyes were grave beneath bristling brows. In a low voice, he said, "He struggles to reach London." The bleak wag of his head told the rest of the tale.

Swallowing, Ulfius quickly determined how he would accomplish the next feat. "I want to see him. I was once his chamberlain. There are matters he must know of." Ulfius flicked a glance at Arthur.

"He will not halt," Ector said. "He is intent on London."

A new approach occurred to Ulfius. "Clearly you and Kay have proven yourselves at Barrow, now leading the king's own cavalry. Tell Uther you would have him meet your son, Arthur. Tell him that, and he will halt."

The big man glanced between Ulfius and his son. A gentle emotion shone within the warrior. "I will tell him. If he will halt, you may see him. You and Arthur."

The king lay abed in a hastily erected pavilion. Curtains of samite and velvet bore ghosts of dust from the quick setup. Some cords hung loose across the regal space. Others strained, overtight. At the verges of the tent, mallets still thudded sternly atop wooden spikes.

"He's in here," Ulfius said gently to Arthur. He gestured past the royal guards, into the closed flap of the king's chamber. "He is waiting for us."

Arthur nodded solemnly. The young man had been stripped of his overlarge armor and dusty trail clothes. Ulfius had emptied his canteen to wash Arthur, and had hunted up a clean tunic and Pendragon tabard. The tunic was an ankle-length gown on the boy, and the tabard seemed almost a priest's chasuble. The final effect was imperfect. Even so, Arthur seemed to grasp the absolute significance of this moment. He was about to meet a dying king, to encounter destiny. Arthur put aside his childish giggling and even his pretended bravado. He donned a solemn, beatific expression.

"I'm ready," he said, and stepped through the tent flaps.

Ulfius turned his eye on Ector, standing there as dusty and disheveled as the tent.

The big man had not thought to get cleaned up, but he had removed his helm and run dirty fingers through his hair. Though he had unflinchingly charged into battle for Uther, Ector now seemed hesitant to duck into the tent that held the king. "You go first."

Ulfius nodded and went in.

Taking a breath, Ector followed.

The space within was cool and dark, though the peak of the tent caught the bright afternoon sun and seeped heat downward. In the chill murk of one corner, there was a cushion-strewn pallet. A figure in shapeless robes lingered beside it.

"Hello, Grandfather," Arthur said.

"Hello, Arthur," replied Merlin. He smiled fondly, a small shower of bread crumbs coming from his whiskers. He turned toward the figure on the pallet and spoke quietly. "Here he is, sire, the boy we have spoken of. You have never before seen him, not even at the postern gate, but I think you will recognize him."

Arthur approached. His feet were quiet on the rugs laid there. His shoulders and head glowed golden beneath the radiant roof.

Uther struggled to his elbows to look at the child. He caught only the merest glimpse before slumping back into the cool pillows. His breathing came in long, ragged gasps as though he had just climbed a cliff face.

Arthur dropped to his knee at the foot of the king. "My king."

Uther gestured toward the boy. "Rise. Come to the bedside, that I might see you."

Even as Arthur rose and went with Merlin to the king's side, Ulfius and Ector reached the foot of the bed and knelt.

Arthur stood, gazing down at the withered man who was king of Britannia. Bright-eyed and unabashed, the boy studied the care wrinkles in the man's face, the frown lines from nose to mouth, the dagger-shaped cleft between his eyes. Arthur's scrutiny was so intense, he seemed to be reading the history of the nation, etched in runes across Uther's flesh.

The king returned the look. Arthur's young face was untouched by years, not a word written across it. Uther instead traced the lines of the future in those bright, silvery eyes. "Tell me you are a good son."

"Oh, he is, sire," Ector broke in fervidly where he knelt. "He will be another Kay when grown. He is clever and obedient and brave—"

"I am asking him," the king interrupted quietly. He took Arthur's hand in his own. "Tell me, Arthur, tell me you are a good son."

Arthur nodded. "I am, Your Highness."

Gladness welled in the king's eyes. The craggy wilderness of his face seemed for a moment at risk of crumbling away. "Tell me you are a true-hearted Briton. Tell me you will fight for our land, our people, against the Angles and Saxons."

"Oh, I will, sire," Arthur assured. He patted the man's hand. "That is why I ride north with Ulfius, to fight the Saxons."

Ector nervously interjected, "He is eager, my king, but will of course be conferred with the rights of arms and horse before going into battle."

Ignoring the comment, the king said fondly, "Your mother will be so proud."

"Already, she is," Arthur said, his voice holding no hint of boast.

Uther added, "And your father. He is proud as well."

"And my grandfather," Arthur said. "I have a very proud family."

The tears welling in Uther's eyes at last spilled forward. They ruined the imposing lines of his face and traced feverish red paths down his pale features. A shudder of dread moved through him. He gripped Arthur's hand all the more tightly.

The boy did not shy back. His young jaw clenched in concentration. In moments, the fit passed, and the king lay in a sweaty pallor.

Ector cleared his throat uncomfortably. "Arthur, we should leave the king to rest. We have taxed him enough—"

"I have a son too," Uther growled out. "He is just your age."

"I would like to meet him, sire," Arthur said quietly.

"He is a good son, a good and true-hearted Briton. He will fight the Angles and Saxons when I am gone. He will fight for our land. He will fight great battles that will make my victory two days ago seem small. He will reverse the defeat I suffer even today."

"I would very much like to meet him, sire."

Uther shook his head sadly. "Oh, you cannot." He took a shuddering breath. "The very day he was born, this son of mine, I gave him into the hands of my court mage, to be reared away from the corruption of the royal castle. He has, from that time until this, grown in the house of a great noble warrior, believing himself to be the child of that man." The king glanced to the foot of the bed, where Ector knelt. The duke stared into faraway spaces, and his jaw was dropping slowly open. "And the secret now is more important than ever. Until my son is old enough to lay claim to my throne, he must not be known abroad, lest he be killed by petty kings, grasping for the crown."

Arthur's eyes grew sad. "Still, he should be here, with you so sick. He should be here to soothe you, help you grow well again."

The king smiled and gripped Arthur's hand. "It is a beautiful thought, my child, but I will not be growing well. In fact, this audience I hold with you, I fear, will be my last."

As if prompted by these dark words, a fit of coughing lay hold of the king. He spasmed for some moments in the folds of his deathbed. His hold on Arthur's hand grew only weaker with each convulsion.

The boy clung to the king. The violent seizure etched new

words in Uther's face—in a thousand barbarous tongues was written the name of Death.

When it was done, Uther slumped down amid the cushions. His skin was waxy and spotted with cold sweat. Liquid rattled in his lungs.

"Sire!" Ector said, standing with sudden urgency. He wrung his hands, and his complexion looked no better than the king's. "Your son—he will be taken care of. I will make certain of it."

Arthur glanced in confusion between his father and the king. "Father knows where your son dwells, sire?"

In a voice that sounded as though it came through layers of cerements, Uther said, "I believe he does."

A sudden resolve hardened the features of Arthur. "Then he will take me to meet him."

The last words spoken ever by Uther Pendragon were, "I believe he someday will."

16

Arthur's First Battle

Three years after the death of King Uther, Merlin crouched with Arthur in the Roman ruins near Chertsey. They had come here for a history lesson. Pupil and teacher had been in an old cellar picking among shattered amphorae when the army arrived.

They were black-coated followers of Andraeus, self-styled emperor of the Midmarch. Andraeus was one of a hundred petty kings using his private army to raid the land. Being a pretender to the scepter of Rome, the young rebel had understandable designs on these and any other Roman ruins in the heart of the country.

Ten-year-old Arthur took umbrage. He peered out over the foundation wall and sneered at the hundred-some warriors.

"Look at them. Ragged, filthy rats. They think they can invade my father's dukedom? They think they can take my ruins?"

Merlin tugged him down. "Let them see you, and they'll take your head too."

Arthur allowed himself to be pulled back only momentarily before again lifting his tousled head to glare at his foes. "Ah, Grandfather, we're a match for these numbskulls."

In fact, he was right. Since his audience with the dying king, Arthur had applied himself dutifully to his studies. Ector, Kay, Ulfius, and Merlin had pursued his education fervidly. The result was an athletic ten-year-old who was a sword-match for any boy of sixteen. Arthur was also better educated in history, mathematics, Latin, alchemy, and military strategy than most nobles. Add to that Merlin's magical might, and the two of them could have taken on a much larger contingent than this. Still, the old mage wished to keep his powers—and his grandson's identity—secret from the outside world. Even Arthur did not yet know he was a prince.

"Yes," Merlin responded, "our skulls are at least as numb as theirs." He hoped the sarcasm was sufficient to divert the young man's attention. "Let's find a way out of here to warn your father."

"How about this way?" Arthur asked, vaulting up out of the hole. He lifted a large stone and hurled it into the midst of the craven band.

The rock struck Andraeus in the solar plexus and knocked the breath out of him. Even as he fell to the ground, magical fingers lay hold of the stone. Propelled on tendrils of purple fire, the thing bounded from one body to the next. It ricocheted off four others, knocking them flat before rattling to a stop.

"Get out of here, you flea-bitten curs!" Arthur advised, hands on his hips.

Though his single stone had felled five of the warrior band, there were ninety-five others. Beneath tattered hauberks of black leather, their shoulders had a cocksure set.

Andraeus rose in their midst, hands on his sides as he

struggled for breath. He had skin as pale as bone and a shock of black hair. Once he could get a lungful, he roared, "You little stoat!" He drew his spatha and began to advance.

Throughout the band, steel hissed into air. Warriors followed their emperor.

The young prince hefted a hunk of broken cornice. He brandished it above his head.

The brigands snickered. They had crossed twenty paces of paving stone, halfway to Arthur, before Merlin arose. He seemed a tattered phoenix. Gray robes spread outward across his gaunt frame. Eyes smoldered in the dark folds of his hood. A belt of twine trailed golden in his wake.

His sudden surging presence halted the brigands in their tracks. A gasp of dismay came from them.

Merlin vaulted the foundation wall and lighted in a great rush of cloth beside the rock-toting boy. His robes settled magnificently about him. His eyes glowed violently in the afternoon sun.

Andraeus struggled to maintain his arrogant sneer, but his paper complexion showed a tinge of green. "And who are you to defy the emperor of the Midmarch?"

"Arthur," cried the boy defiantly, "son of Duke Ector, ruler of Chertsey—"

"Not you," Andraeus broke in. He jabbed his spatha toward Merlin. "You."

"He is the ancient sorcerer Merlin. He has walked the four corners of the world, fought beside Odysseus and Caesar, battled Wotan with a god-killing great sword, made a king of Ambrosius and Uther, and saved Britannia from Angle invaders," Arthur boasted, rock still uplifted in his grasp. "He has lived for hundreds of years, and will live hundreds more. That is the man who dares oppose you."

"Merlin? Where have I heard of this Merlin?" Doubt verged in Andraeus's gaze, but he pulled bravado up about him like a cloak. "Ah, yes. Uther had you. And Ambrosius. And now this little dolt. Always the king-maker but never the king, Merlin? You are rather like the hunting dog that flushes and chases prey to a corner, but waits for the master to make the kill. So, this child holds your leash these days, Merlin?" Andraeus stepped forward. "Perhaps I might hold it. Perhaps you have the wisdom to know a true emperor when you see one."

Before Merlin could respond, Arthur hurled his rock. It rushed toward Andraeus's head. The young man ducked. The stone would have sailed harmlessly by, but Merlin flung a spell. Magic fingers caught the cornice and halted it just above the brigand's pate. Scintillating particles of power coursed over the jagged stone, suspending it out of reach.

Andraeus struggled to snatch the cornice. He batted at it with his sword. Ever graceful, the rock veered tauntingly aside, only to hover once again above the man.

"You are no emperor, no king," Arthur said. "Merlin knows who the son of Uther is. He is waiting until the prince comes of age. Then Merlin will install—"

"Enough!" interrupted the mage. "Begone, you brigands. You are no army. You are no emperor."

Andraeus stopped swinging at the cornice and stared in sudden realization at Merlin and Arthur. "A king-maker and a noble boy . . . I see. But it takes more than the blood of Uther to make a true king." With that, he lifted high his spatha and cried, "Charge!"

Merlin reached out one arm to snatch up Arthur. The other arm hurled itself downward. A blast of power roared from extended fingers. Merlin and Arthur rose into the air.

Below, Andraeus skidded to a stop. His men barged into him. The emperor and his lieutenants tumbled into the foundations. They crashed achingly to the ground atop amphora shards. Merlin's spell blast created lines of force that tore hair and clothes and armor, battering the warriors to ground.

The mage soared overhead. Arthur chose this moment to let fall two more stones. They dropped into the column of swirling magic, drew the glowing dweomer in veils around them, and plunged to impact a pair of helmeted heads. Each stone skipped across the throng, tumbling many of those who had stayed up after the first blast. The emperor of Midmarch's army shrank to a mound of angry black ants.

"Hurrah, Grandfather," Arthur shouted gladly. "We showed them. They won't be strutting about Chertsey any longer."

Wind roared through Merlin's white eyebrows, splaying them out like fir boughs. "I fear you are mistaken," he replied. "They know who I am, now."

Arthur waved him off, spitting down into the rushing magic. He was gratified to see the glob of spittle break into hundreds of beads of water, which pelted onto the army. "They don't know who you are. We don't even know who you are."

"They know who you are," Merlin said.

"Yes. They know I am Ector's son, and they will keep their distance."

"No. They know more about you than that, and they will come looking for you. We cannot allow them to depart this place, knowing what they do. Our work here is not concluded."

Arthur's face darkened as he glanced at the beleaguered foe below. "It seems hardly sporting to kill them, Grandfather."

"Oh, we'll not kill them," Merlin said. He lifted his hand overhead and made another gesture. The arcane power rolling from his fingertips changed, turned webby, and whirled into a gossamer net. The great dome of power filled with air and eased them gently downward. "But we must convince them they do not know us, not really."

Below, the windblown soldiers clawed up from the foundations. Andraeus rose first. His shouted commands were lost to distance, but the fury in his voice was not. He gesticulated toward the descending pair and dispatched his forces out over the ruins to surround them.

Arthur watch it all with mild curiosity. He trusted his grandfather implicitly. This deadly business seemed to him no more than a game. "It looks that the trick will be to remain alive long enough for them to change their minds."

"You have grasped the heart of it, child," Merlin said gently. "Did you notice any bowmen among them?"

"No."

"No, indeed. Archers would have meant foresight. I'll secure a safe spot from which to organize the rest of this."

They drifted toward a foundation filled with tumbled limestone columns. His hands full, Merlin waggled his nose at the largest blocks of stone. Twin gouts of sorcery emerged from his nostrils and broadened into overlapping cones. Glowing power bathed the segments of the column. They rolled languidly. Their edges ground together like giant teeth. Ponderous and slow, they lolled out of their troughs and bounded into the air.

The first stone, largest of all, landed in the center of the pediment it had occupied in days of yore. The next vaulted into place atop the first, and the third and forth, until a Corinthian column stood in the center of the square. An acanthus-leaf capital topped it.

Last of all, from shards of stone in the midst of the foundation, a long-lost figure reassembled itself. Rocks joined to form the legs of a rearing beast, a noble torso, and an equine head. Beneath its forehooves crouched a cowering beast, being ridden down. There was a rider, too, shattered among those foundation stones, but Merlin's magic ceased before it reconfigured.

"After all, we need someplace to sit," Merlin noted.

The pair landed none-too-gracefully astride the rearing horse and grappled its marble reins as though they were leather. Merlin whirled his free hand overhead, dispersing the floating magic that had held them aloft. He cracked his aching fingers.

"You are getting heavy, Arthur."

The boy flexed his biceps. "Muscle is heavier than fat."

Even then, Emperor Andraeus and his army of a hundred converged on the ruined plaza. They came from three sides, roaring. Iron-shod feet clacked on old paving stones. They reached the base of the pillar and banged their swords against it.

"A waste of steel," Arthur observed.

Andraeus shouted in rage. "Come down, you pigeons, you gray geese! Come down and fight like men."

As the last of the warriors hastened into the plaza, Merlin rose to his full height atop the rearing horse. He lifted one hand. Around it, magical energy coalesced. It crackled and spat like a wheel of lightning bolts. The blue jolts arced from finger to finger, from hand to head, and danced violently. Wisps stretched in slim vortices down to touch the warriors between the eyes and tousle their hair.

"Impressive," Arthur allowed. "Even for you, Grandfather."

"More impressive to them," Merlin said. "If any of these has any true claim to Roman lineage, they will know who I appear to be."

Arthur peered down past the cracked mane of the statue. At the pillar's foot, the black crowd of warriors shied back. Even above the drone and crack of lightnings, Arthur could hear their gasps and hisses.

"It is the sky god, Jove-Belenus!" one of them shouted.

"He rules among the ruins!"

"If the sky god opposes Andraeus, how can he be emperor?"

Andraeus interrupted them. "He is no god. He's a conjurer. A trickster." The emperor slapped his lieutenants' faces. "He's bewitched you. Turn your eyes away from his glamour!"

Even as he said so, Andraeus gazed sickly at the vision. He was losing his army and his bid for kingship—all because of an old charlatan and a smart-mouthed boy.

Turning, Andraeus spotted his salvation, a broad timber—the king beam of the garrison stables. "Here! Here! If Jove-Belenus is here at all, he is in this beam. He has given us this ram to knock down the pillar and the pretender god atop it. Give a hand! Clear it! Hoist it! Bring it down!"

High overhead, Merlin watched crews of men break from the main body of the army and swarm on all sides of the king beam. Like rows of ants, they tore the beam free of the fallen superstructure and hoisted it to their shoulders.

"No one has respect for the old gods anymore," Merlin said ruefully. "Not even false emperors. Ah, well, I shall have to be more convincing, then."

He leveled his hand. The wheel of lightning whirled onto its side. Bolts of energy leaped in a great dome over the gathered army. A thousand jags of lightning cracked through the air and descended. Where energy struck ground, sand fused to glass, dust jetted up, and slim shafts opened into the earth.

In the center of this circle, the black-garbed army quailed. Men looked about to see who had been struck dead by the rain of fire, but none had. Those carrying the ram paused and sniffed the metallic air.

"He can kill any of us at will!"

"If he can, why didn't he?"

"More trickery," Andraeus said. "More illusion. He has no true power, only glamours and deceit! Bring down the column!"

He and his warriors charged the pillar. The ram boomed against it. Chips of stone shattered away. The column swayed.

For the first time, Arthur looked concerned. "Any more spells, Grandfather?"

"The last one isn't finished," Merlin replied simply.

From each smoking shaft in the ground, figures emerged. Wraithlike, they rose from the old Roman garrison. Ghosts filled the tumbled basilica. Specters danced out of the legionnaire graveyard. They emerged from the smoky shafts and lurched in toward the army of Andraeus.

"He commands the dead!"

"He *is* Jove-Belenus, truly."

"How else could he have fought beside Caesar!"

"No!" Andraeus shouted in their midst. His men released the ram. It ripped itself from Andraeus's fingers. "Don't be fooled. These creatures are more phantasms, more lies—"

A unison moan of rage came from the ghosts. It was enough. The army of the Midmarch broke apart, each man fleeing for whatever escape presented itself. In moments, the plaza was empty aside from Andraeus. Then, with a final glance toward the top of the pillar, he too fled.

Arthur smiled in satisfaction as he watched them go. "I did not know you could summon ghosts," he said offhandedly.

"I cannot." Merlin said. "Andraeus was right. It was all simply phantasm and illusion."

17

Into the Sacred Pool

They rode—three horsemen aback hearty Iberian steeds. Fitted out with stirrups, saddles, bags, and light barding, the horses charged across the Midmarch. Arthur leaned avidly against his steed's neck. Merlin flanked him and chattered away through the hoof-churned air. On the other side, Ulfius kept sober pace with them both.

Fourteen years ago, Ulfius and Merlin had made a very different ride with Arthur's father. Now Uther was dead, and Britannia had no king. Prince Arthur still did not know he was destined for the throne, and he would not be ready to rule for years yet. On that long-ago ride, Dumnonian ghosts had dogged their hooves. Today, the ghosts had taken on flesh. Bandits and pretender kings stalked the Thames Valley. The sunny grasslands were rife with highwaymen and danger. Perhaps it had been a mistake to bring the prince so far from the fastness of Chertsey.

Ulfius ground his teeth grimly. The trip had been his own idea.

"I think it is time you saw the west country," Ulfius had said to Arthur one morning over tea and eggs in the great hall. "It was the country of Uther. It is an important part of Britannia. There is much of history and destiny there. I have gotten leave from your father to make it an extended trip. . . ."

Arthur had voraciously gobbled down a few more hunks of bacon, guzzled scalding tea, and stood from his seat. With an overfull mouth—he'd unfortunately learned his eating habits from Merlin—he said, "I can have my horse saddled by midmorning."

"Wait, wait," Ulfius had urged. "This needs planning. I'll prepare cases for collecting plants and such—many of them are useful for poultices. I'll map a route that will take us by historical sights—earthworks and battlefields—"

"Battlefields!" Arthur had enthused, retreating across the hall to the arms mounted over the fireplace. He began pulling at a battered lance carried by Ector in the cavalry charges at Barrow.

"Now, sit back down and finish—"

"I'll wear my new travel cloak," Merlin had pitched in.

"This is to be an opportunity for instruction—"

"Adventure!"

"Mayhem!"

And that had been that.

For three days, they had traveled the summer countryside and camped beneath the stars. Throughout the day, Ulfius had shoved beneath Arthur's nose every bloom he could find, identifying medicines, spices, and poisons. Throughout the night, Ulfius had struggled to impress upon Arthur the importance of knowing the names and positions of stars for navigation. Merlin had been no help in these endeavors. For every flower Ulfius identified, Merlin had some sad and pointless tale of a pair of lovers turned to mulberries. For every constellation Ulfius had pointed out, Merlin had rehearsed an impromptu drama of weeping virgins and watchful hunters.

All the while, Arthur had grown only the more infected with notions of adventure, valor, heroism, and horsemanship. He had developed the perilous habit of riding close to thickets in order to thrash them with his wooden sword, charging over any bridge that presented itself and claiming it in the name of Chertsey, exhorting flocks of sheep to "stand strong and fight for Britannia." In a land full of highwaymen and danger, such frivolous pursuits could prove deadly.

Today, Ulfius sensed, all this magely muggery and youthful dreaming would come to a disastrous head.

"Behold! A raging waterfall! A cataract into a pool more treacherous than Charybdis itself!" Arthur proclaimed. He pointed ahead to a fast-running stream cut deep in the grassy meadow. The channel gave itself over to a none-too-gentle waterfall. The stream was a lance-length across, and the falls a lance-length high. The waters beneath churned and sent up a fine spray before disgorging into the lower grasslands beyond. "Leap your horse over it, Merlin! I challenge you!"

"Here's where the trouble begins," Ulfius muttered.

Merlin reined his steed up beside the flow. The water was swift. Rills on top turned to white foam. Beneath, shadows lurked blackly among mossy stones. "It looks to me to be a fey place."

"Fey? Fah!" Ulfius said.

"How can you tell?" asked Arthur.

"There is a freshness to fey places," Merlin said wistfully. "Energetic. Alive."

"Did you know," Ulfius interposed, "that freshwater mussels filter water? An average mussel can filter a gallon a day. A spring like this, so clear and fresh, must be a place with mussels."

Arthur glanced between the two men. In the eyes of one, bright spirits drifted in hypnotic dance. In the eyes of the other, little mollusks sucked and jetted water through grotesque organelles. Arthur shook his head. "I said, 'Leap your horse over it!' "

"I'm a friend to fey spirits," Merlin thought aloud.

"We'll have to find a shallow ford upstream," Ulfius said. "Perhaps there will be pools with freshwater prawns—"

"I said—" Arthur began, but gave up, wheeling his steed and galloping back the way they had come.

Ulfius watched the lad go, clouds of pollen rising from the trail he carved through the grass. "You would do well to teach him something real once in a while—something he can use when he is out of provisions and needs food, or when he is injured and needs a poultice."

Merlin also watched the young prince. Arthur reached a low crest, turned, and charged his horse down the pasture, back toward the river. "You would do well to teach him something unreal once in a while. A man who is to be king needn't worry about poultices and river prawns. He must learn about kings and gods, heed their mistakes, and learn to avoid them."

"He's planning on leaping the river—" broke in Ulfius.

"He hasn't the horse for it—" Merlin said, clucking as Arthur closed on them.

"He has the will for it!" Ulfius turned his mount to block the path to the river. Standing in his stirrups, he shouted out, "Arthur, stop this nonsense!"

Merlin kicked the flanks of his mount and charged headlong toward the boy. He cut out along the meadow toward Arthur, hoping to divert him from the babbling shores.

Astride his steed, Arthur only laughed. He drove the beast all the harder.

Merlin gritted his teeth. His horse's hooves hammered the grassy ground. The steed darted in and lowered its head as though it were a ram. It was too slow.

Arthur flashed out past him. The bay's glossy sides gleamed in the noontime sun. In a tempest of sinew, pelt, and hoof, the boy and his mount stormed around the mage and toward Ulfius.

The armsman's mount pranced nervously. Ulfius hauled hard on the reins, keeping the champing beast in place. A wall of muscle on the stream's bank, man and mount were unmovable.

Arthur had no choice. He veered downstream. His mount leaped. It soared out above the rushing torrent. Only then did Arthur realized he and his horse surged straight out over the waterfall.

The young prince hung for a moment above the frothing waters. His bay steed depended magnificently from him.

Then beast and rider plunged down the foamy cascade. They splashed into the turbid pool at its base. The horse's belly struck the waves like a hand slap. A great well of liquid formed, Arthur sitting dry in the midst. The walls of the watery canyon closed. With a clap, horse and boy disappeared. A plume of water shot up above them.

"Arthur!" called Ulfius frantically from atop the falls.

Merlin rode up beside him, so swift he seemed ready to leap the falls himself, though his steed planted its hooves and fought to a standstill. "Arthur!"

The two men stared down into the tumbling pool. Amid white bubbles and blue-black depths, there was no sign of him—not gold hair or metal gleam or tabard flash. Still, *something* moved beneath the waves. Something dark and sleek.

"A serpent, belike," Merlin said, dismounting.

"No serpent, but Arthur's bay," replied Ulfius, pointing.

The drenched horse swam beneath the surface, gaining the muddy verge of the pool. It broke the surface. Saddle and packs streamed. The rider was nowhere to be seen.

"Might as well be a serpent," Merlin said. He waded out to the head of the waterfall.

Ulfius loosened a rope from his pack. "Here. Throw this down to him."

Not waiting for the rope, Merlin pinched his nostrils between two fingers and leaped, over the falls. As huge as the horse and rider had seemed, suspended over that small cataract, Merlin seemed larger still. His riding cloak bunched out on the wind to the size of three or four horses. In the midst of those voluminous folds, Merlin's old face and white beard seemed small. Then, robes, face, and all were swallowed in the spray of water.

Standing in the saddle, Ulfius glimpsed the mage's robe, like a gray octopus beneath the waves. Then, it too was gone. The horse stamped impatiently beneath the noble warrior. He patted the creature's neck, soothing it. "Arthur knows how to swim. He's likely only playing a trick. Or he has found a trove at the bottom. It would be his luck to plunge into a waterfall and find a place where the old Celts used to make offering of gems and weapons and such."

The horse whickered in dubiety and stared at the flood.

"And even if he cannot float, he could walk from a pool like that. He'll walk out with mussels in his pocket for an afternoon snack," he muttered unconvincingly.

Merlin had called this a fey place. This pool might be a vertical passage down from the true world to the Otherworld of spirits. As impossible—as un-Christian—as such a belief was, it soon seemed the only explanation for their long absence beneath the waves.

Cursing in fear for Arthur and Merlin and in hatred of his own God-damned luck, Ulfius flung himself from the saddle, splashed out atop the waterfall, and dove headfirst after his friends.

The scene was particularly beautiful in the moment that he hung suspended above the water. He had the rebel thought that he would very much like to stay here awhile. Then, Ulfius plunged into the black, bubbling, frigid depths.

It *was* a fey place. He felt it in the thousand pressing rivulets that snaked through cloak and armor. It was energetic, as Merlin had said, using the old Greek word. It was alive. Bubbles swarmed him. They sang in small, savage tones against his skin. The stream reached up and hauled him deeper down. Bright bubbles fled aloft, water pixies shunning the cold below. Other beings surrounded him now, black and silky, graceful and brusque. They battered him as he descended. Surges of current like impatient hands wrapped arms or legs and bore him downward. Then, as his lungs despaired of ever again tasting fresh air, he ran up against another pair of bodies.

"Ah, there you are," said Merlin impossibly through the black tide. "Now we can be under way."

Ulfius tried to respond, but hot air flooded out and cold water flooded in. It didn't matter. Dark creatures clustered around Ulfius. He clung to them as they ascended. In moments, the cloud of bubbles scintillated. On the shouldering might of the water spirits, Ulfius, Merlin, and Arthur vaulted up from the surface of the waves. They were tossed free, landing on the grassy verge beside the pool.

There, Arthur and Ulfius clung to the ground, vomiting water and panting.

Merlin crawled to his feet and sent jets of water from his nose. He extended arms to his sides and gazed dejectedly at his riding cloak. "It'll never fit right again."

Ulfius ignored him. As soon as he had the strength, he rolled to gaze into the chaotic pool. There was no sign of their rescuers, only floating crescents of foam over a rolling deep. "What were those things?"

"They were pocket sleeves!" Merlin groused, flinging his arms down. "They were pocket sleeves!"

"No," Ulfius answered with a sneeze. "What were those things that rescued us?"

Merlin looked up, distracted. "Oh, those. You would call them merrow. Scots call them selkies. They are water spirits. Merefolk. Seal-spirits. Not so common in fresh water, but we were lucky they were here. Lucky they weren't kelpies. Kelpies like to drown men."

Ulfius shook his head, stunned.

Once Arthur had stopped coughing, he was smiling. He let out a great whoop and rolled to his back, kicking up his heels. "Ah, what adventure! Grandfather Merlin, you have such friends!"

At that, Merlin looked a little peeved. "Well, friends of a friend, at any rate. They saved us, yes, on condition that we make a small detour."

"Detour?" sputtered Ulfius. "Detour? This horseplay has cost us the better part of a day. What do they want us to do? Where do they want us to go?"

"Not far. An old friend of mine, Brigid, mistress of the lake, asks that we pay her a visit."

"Mistress of what lake?" Ulfius asked.

"Avalon."

Luckily for the three bedraggled travelers, the town of Frome lay only half a day away. It would have been a dreary half-day ride, in wet things and on spooked mounts, except for the excitement of the selkie rescue and the pool to the Otherworld. Merlin had insisted the pool led straight down into an underground realm of earth, where ruled the Tuatha Dé Danann, former kings of Eire and western Britannia. Arthur, always eager to hear his grandfather's tales, had coaxed the telling from him. Ulfius had felt required to interject at intervals how impossible all of this nonsense was, and continued his objections until Arthur had pointed out that they had survived the pool through the impossibility of fey assistance. That had shut up Ulfius while the three trooped to Frome.

The small farming community lay within a shallow swale on the wide Sherborne Plains. The situation was lovely. Thatched cottages dotted fields of green. Archways showed a mild acquaintance with Roman architecture, while slate-stacked walls told of the ancient building practices of Celts. Most pleasant of all, at the center of the village was a two-story hostel.

Poised on the London-Cadbury road, the inn was the most prosperous enterprise in town. It was built of local red brick and timber hauled in from the forests westward. It had a slate roof—a marvel for private construction—four gables, and six chimneys, where it got its name. The Six Chimneys happened to have an empty room and took silver of any mint. And for each of its chimneys, the hostler kept a mastiff—guardians in an unsure land. The security offered by those dogs heightened every other amenity. With horses stabled, brushed, watered, and fed, and packs and clothes hung out to dry, the three weary travelers treated themselves to the most luxurious appointment of all—a large, tiled, steaming bath.

"The Romans aren't the only ones who know how to bathe," said the fat proprietor as the men eased themselves one by one into the cleansing flood. "I've even an Archimedes screw, cast of a single piece of ceramic, by which I fill the cauldron that heats the water. I'm building a raised rainwater cistern to do the same thing."

"Very good," Merlin replied by way of dismissal. He waved his hand, gesturing the balding fellow toward the tiled archway from the baths. "Very good. Thank you."

The proprietor seemed put out until he discovered a pair of silver coins in his grip, as though set there by magic. He bowed his thanks and stepped from the small, vaporous chamber.

Merlin groaned in ecstasy as heat seeped into his old joints. Hot mist circled through his tattered white hair. "Ahhhh, I do miss the Romans."

Ulfius settled into the square pool across from him. His back came to rest against woad-dyed tiles. "Yes, I *do* miss the Romans."

"Did you know, they did not cook at home—they feared fire," Merlin said. "So they ate out, or the patricians did. They had a saying, 'If the day has treated you well, order two glasses of wine, one for yourself and one for humanity. Wait long enough, and humanity will sit down beside you.' "

Arthur sat slowly in the hot flow, the third generation in this trinity of men. The mists of the bath ghosted dreamily across his eyes. "How did you meet the Mistress of the Mists, Grandfather?"

Merlin sighed. He took a deep breath and smiled. "It was over a century ago—"

"Over a century," hissed Ulfius softly.

"Hush," Arthur said. "I want to hear this."

"I was fleeing Wotan and his hordes. They came in dragon ships, like those at Barrow on the Humber. They came to slay me and take my god-killing great sword. They were Northmen—tall, stout, blond, and angry. Ice cracks their brains up there. Ice and too much fresh air. And the pickled fish they eat. Riding about those icy seas in open boats with a bunch of hairy Saxons, eating fish gelatin and drinking their own urine—it is no wonder whenever they land, they go berserk and kill and pillage and rape. If it weren't for Saxon ale, those blue-eyed and red-faced monsters would have overrun the whole world. If it weren't for Saxon ale and the beauties of Asgard, I could condemn the whole group to perdition. . . . They have some comely maids too—"

Ulfius let his hands drop in a despondent splash. "Arthur, you should be learning real history, not this drivel—"

"It's not drivel!" Arthur interrupted angrily. "It *is* real history. It is Grandfather's history."

"It's madness. He would have to be a hundred fifty years old—"

"And why not?" Arthur said. "You've seen his magic. You've seen him fly and change into a dragon and drive off Saxons and talk to stumps. Why couldn't he be a hundred fifty years old? Why not fifteen hundred years old? Why madness? Why not history?" His eyes flared. "Now, hush." He turned back toward Merlin. "What happened next?"

Merlin glanced patiently between his two companions to make certain they were finished. Sighing, he leaned back into the candent pool and said, "I landed on the eastern shore of Britannia, just north of where Blythburg is now. I was half a day ahead of my pursuers, thanks to having slain the east wind. I climbed the shore and fled amid the weeds. I went into town only to find more Saxons, High Germans enlisted by the Romans to defend the eastern marches against their own countrymen. They had been Saxons a hundred years before, but were now as Roman as anyone else. I warned them of the coming invasion. They sent runners to the seashore to check for ships and, sure enough, the horizon was black with them. An alert went up. Signal fires were lit. Riders carried the news to muster. Farmer Saxons laid down their hoes and shovels and shucked their yeoman's clothes, dragging out spathas and legionnaire armor.

"They detained me for questioning, which I allowed. They would need help in the fight. When they tried to take my sword, though, I shrunk myself and it away from their hands and ran. The Saxons landed. The Roman Germans were not powerful enough to repel them. Wotan fought against them. The Tetragrammaton did not fight for them. I sneaked out among them to provide what aid I could. It was not enough."

His gaze grew faraway. "I know you think war is glorious, Arthur, but it is not. There is little glory in bodies cut in half. It is not even butchery. It's not a clean slice to the neck or a killing hammer blow. There is no clean gutting, no decorous and beautiful fallen. In death, men lose dominion over their bowels. The fetor of battle is the smell of shit, and then of rot. And during and after battle, there are hosts of men halfway dead and halfway alive. They cry piteously to be dragged to one margin or the other, to be saved or killed. Living men missing half their bodies and losing more each moment to the creeping work of gangrene. Dying men with bodies whole but for a single slender stab to the gut, enough to kill slowly but certainly. It is seeing them, speaking to them, bearing water to them, clutching their hands as inexpert men with axes or saws or torches do their best to stop the spread of death—that is war. The moment's glory is followed by decades of torment and regret. That is war." Merlin stared down into the turbid pool where the three men rested.

"This, Arthur," said Ulfius quietly, "this is history."

The young man looked chastened. "But how did you meet the mistress?"

Merlin waggled his head. "Well, we lost. We lost in the east, and I fled. I fled the Saxons and the Roman Germans and the horrors of war. I headed west. It was a mad flight. Alone, delirious, desperate, starving, I traveled across Britannia. I cannot tell you much of that time. Dark dreams tormented me. I awoke to find only darker realities. I ran as far as I could, until the sounds of battle lingered only in my mind, though there they were deafening. At last, as thin and dry as a twig, withered and lost in that verge between living and dying, I collapsed beside a pool where I had stooped to drink.

"I awoke. I know not how long had passed. The lake was steaming, like this pool where we sit. Its waters were clear to thirty feet, and dark, deep—beautiful. There was an isle at the center of it. It seemed ever-changing, once a tall tor where stood a Roman abbey, then a gentle slope on which apple trees grew in wild and fragrant groves. I had fallen so that my mouth was in the water, and beside my mouth, my hands. In one of my hands, I clutched the hilt of the damned sword that had caused all this harm.

"And a woman arose from the steaming flood. She asked of me my name, and I told it. I asked of her her name, and she said she was Brigid, divine queen of Britons, and Mistress of the Mists. She asked me what misadventure had brought me to her shores, and I told her: this cursed, god-killing sword. I told her of Wotan and how he coveted the blade. She said, 'Yes, he covets it. Originally, it was most common. Then you reforged it to be excalibur,' which in her tongue means 'without peer.' She said Wotan wanted the sword because he knew it was the destiny of this sword to kill him. It had killed many gods before and would kill many gods in future. I said I would be rid of the cursed thing if only I knew where to secrete it that Wotan would never find it. She said, 'Though this blade cannot forever be hid from Wotan, and though it will one day slay even me, I will keep it here for you. I will keep it and hide it away from Wotan's eyes until the one comes who will wield it to unite the land.' "

Merlin shrugged, coming out of his oracular delirium. "So, I gave her the sword. She lifted it," Merlin raised his own dripping arm overhead, "and drifted backward and downward until she was swallowed up by the lake. Only the sword jutted forth. Then, even it was gone."

Amazed and utterly enspelled by the tale, Arthur said, "And this is the woman we are going to go see? This divine queen? This goddess?"

With a gentle nod, Merlin said, "Yes. And Glastonbury is on the way."

Ulfius heaved a snort. "Well, yes—I approve. We'll go to Glastonbury tomorrow, if only to show you it is no misty Avalon, but a real place with a real abbey. It is not even an island, but a peninsula, and this lovely lake is no more than a shallow swamp." Ulfius crossed arms over his chest. "Yes, Arthur. Tomorrow you will see. Tomorrow we go to Glastonbury."

18

The Gates of History

Midday next, Ulfius felt his assessment was borne out. After following the Harrow Way near to Cadbury, the three riders had headed north on a thin dirt road cleared and maintained by the monks of Glastonbury. The path led along gently rolling hills where scrappy forests vied with sheep-shorn grasslands. In time, woodlands and swales gave way to a wide, sloping trough, the valley of the River Brue. The trail sank down along the northern bank of the river. Its flow was wide and shallow. Cattails and reeds clogged the edges. The only clear water slid blackly in the midst of the marsh. After a few leagues along the channel, the Brue spilled into a wide, circular slough surrounding a low tor. The hills around the spot were merely weedy mounds. The water was a shallow wetland filled with lily pads and algae. The isle of Glastonbury looked like nothing more than a rumpled felt hat. An abbey crouched on the southwest edge of the thing, and a path from it led out across a palisaded ridge that narrowly linked the peninsula to dry ground.

"See?" Ulfius asked. His horse snorted sarcastically. "Not an island at all. And your lovely lake is a mosquito-infested swamp. Mistress of the Muck is not so grand a title."

Arthur glanced with timid appraisal at Merlin.

The old man sat his horse like a sack of grain. He gazed bleakly forward. "You are certain this is Glastonbury?"

"Oh, absolutely," Ulfius replied. His horse turned an anxious circle, champing and stamping. "That small rill is the Ponter's Ball. Those palisades there—those were put up by the priests. If we approached the gate, we'd see a few of them coming out to question us, to bar the way. Do you see?

Your mistress and your sword and your war with Wotan is all an illusion. None of it happened."

Merlin dismounted. The reins of his steed sagged limply to the ground. He took a few staggering steps off the dirt path. The grassy verge dropped swiftly away to a wetlands. "But it was different a hundred years ago—"

"You weren't alive a hundred years ago, Merlin," Ulfius objected. "You dreamed the whole thing. You've lived your whole life in delirium. If only you could recognize that, could shut away all this impossible fancy, you could slough off this madness and live your final years out placidly—"

"Don't be so cruel," Arthur said as he dismounted to follow his grandfather.

"I'm not being cruel," Ulfius said. "It is cruel to humor him, to believe in all his ludicrous stories—battles with gods, people turning into mulberry bushes, portals to the Otherworld, centuries-old lunatics with swamp-water girlfriends and gigantic swords. The purpose of this trip is to teach Arthur what he needs to know to fulfill his dest—his potential, not to boggle him with empty nonsense."

Merlin tromped into the water. Algae clung to his bedraggled riding cloak. Cloth wicked water up his legs. "This was different. The water was deep and clear and misty. The isle was wooded in apple trees. The hills about were secluding."

A gentle pair of hands laid hold of Merlin's arm. "Come back now, Grandfather. There's still a long ride ahead of us today."

The old man turned bleary eyes on Arthur. "It was here, Arthur. You must believe me." He wandered deeper into the slough, dragging Arthur along with him.

"You were never here, Merlin," Ulfius interrupted. "You were never aboard a dragon ship. You never fought Wotan. You never visited Asgard. You never turned an old girlfriend into a cow. You never fought titans. None of your stories have ever happened."

"Enough, Ulfius," Arthur insisted as he struggled to keep Merlin from going deeper. "Grandfather is only trying to find out who he is."

"I'll tell you who he is," Ulfius replied. "He's a right lunatic! But that doesn't matter. What matters is who you are, Arthur."

Merlin stopped. He stood waist deep among reeds. Arthur clung to his arms, as if bracing a man who stood at the edge of a precipice. The old man lingered there, breathing slowly and staring into the bleak reality that underlay his fantasy. He closed his eyes and quietly said, "He's right, Arthur."

"What?"

"He's right," Merlin said. His shoulders slumped in resignation. "If I did not stand here, I did not give Brigid the god-killing sword. And if I did not give it to her, perhaps I never had such a blade at all. Perhaps all of it is a lie—an elaborate, fantastical lie meant to disguise the fact that, in truth, I am only an old, mad beggar."

"No," Arthur said, shaking his head. "You are no beggar. You are my grandfather."

Merlin cast a miserable look at Ulfius, seated on his impatient steed.

Ulfius's features softened. "You're not *just* a beggar. You do have power, Merlin."

"I still believe the stories," Arthur said. "Even if you don't, Grandfather, I believe in them. I believe in the Mistress of the Mists and in Excalibur and in all of it."

Ulfius dropped his gaze sadly.

"I believe in your battles with Wotan, and I believe there is a new king coming to unite the land."

Ulfius raised his eyes to study young Arthur.

The boy—at fourteen, he was not truly a man—was suddenly transfigured there in the afternoon sun. He seemed a young and gleaming Apollo. His hair was golden. His riding cloak streamed radiance. His armor shone brilliantly.

Merlin also was transfigured. No longer the bedraggled lunatic, he seemed suddenly the wise lantern bearer. The reeds around them glimmered like glowing raiment.

But it was not the reeds that shone like gold. It was the water itself. And no longer did Merlin and Arthur stand *in* the water, but *upon* it. Sunlight played across the deep lake.

Only where mists rose warmly from the flood was the beaming sun obscured, and then only to be turned into flowing curtains of light. These shining veils billowed gently across the lake and half hid the isle at the center of it. No rumpled felt hat, the tor was larger, taller, and somehow, much farther away. Its dark bulk was glazed with white apple blossoms, and a cool breath of air from across the lake bore the sweet scent of them to Ulfius. Apples and deep water and mystery . . .

Ulfius struggled to gabble out an observation, but his tongue could only lie in awe between his teeth.

Then, in the midst of the misty veils, there was a figure. As radiant as Arthur and Merlin had seemed, this creature was dazzling beyond description. She was stately in flowing robes. In one upraised hand, she held a great torch—no, not a torch. It was a sword. It was the great, god-killing sword. Across the water, she came. She did not walk, but floated. Her feet hung just above the moiling waves.

Ulfius realized only then that what he had mistaken for the sun was, in fact, She.

As the woman approached, Merlin and Arthur dropped to their knees and bowed their faces to the lapping waves. Light intensified. The island was unseeable beyond it. Soon, sky and lake too were burned away, until there was only the glorious lady.

Ulfius buried his face in his hands for the bald glow of her. Through the narrow spaces between his fingers, he saw what came next.

The woman reached Merlin and Arthur. Serene and stately, she lowered the great sword toward the bowed boy. She could have cloven him in half with the thing. It descended like hard lightning.

"Caladvwlch," she said gently. The air thrummed with her warm voice. "Excalibur."

She touched the blade to each of Arthur's shoulders. Lifting it, hilt uppermost and point toward Arthur's back, she sheathed the sword in a dazzling, jewel-encrusted scabbard.

"Rhiannon," she intoned.

Then sword and scabbard, Excalibur and Rhiannon, came flashing down. There was a crack of thunder, and the woman was gone.

In sudden darkness, Ulfius fell from the saddle. He clutched his eyes, wondering if he would ever see again. "Saint Paul, preserve me," he muttered into the iron grass.

There came a watery sound ahead. Lying like a craven worm, Ulfius lifted his gaze toward it.

There, in the red-jagged afterimage of his vision, he saw two dark figures toiling up from the swamp. They reached the bank and hurried toward him. Arthur and Merlin. Their boots sloshed as they came. Their clothes were mucky to the waist. Black seed pods—no, leeches—clung to their cloaks.

"Are you all right, Ulfius?" Arthur asked, gripping his shoulders and rolling him over.

Ulfius groaned. He stared out toward the tor. All was as it had been before—cattails and reeds instead of sacred waters. Breathless, he said, "I just . . . I just had a—"

"A delusion?" Merlin asked capriciously.

"Yes," Ulfius confirmed as he struggled up to his elbows. "It felt real enough, but it was a delusion. I am a sensible man, and what just seemed to happen was not sensible at all. Swamps don't turn into lakes. Suns don't turn into women. Boys don't receive their rites of arms from sword-toting goddesses—"

Arthur and Merlin traded ironic glances. Then the boy reached over his shoulder and hauled hard, drawing from its scabbard a great sword. He said simply, "Excalibur!"

Ulfius saw no more, too busy fainting.

Two days hence, Ulfius led his companions on a high, narrow road in the western extremity of Britannia.

Solemn at last, young Arthur rode between Ulfius and Merlin. He wore Excalibur in Rhiannon on his back. Over the cantering hooves of his horse, he listened intently to Grandfather.

"And the scabbard will prevent its wearer from bleeding,

so keep it ever with you—" Merlin's manias had only been heightened by the appearance of Excalibur and Rhiannon. He was drawn to them, staring at them longingly, hands trembling to hold them. In fearful speeches such as this, he provided Arthur instruction on the care and use of Rhiannon and Excalibur. "Scabbard and sword, both, are not merely enchanted, but holy."

Arthur nodded gravely. His young shoulders were square beneath the weight of the blade.

"Excalibur has been called the Sword of the Spirit, and Rhiannon has been called the Spirit of the Land. The sword is the male part, you see, made to kill. The scabbard is the female part, made to heal. Sword and scabbard are like unto the king and his divine consort—he who rules by she who empowers. Do not let sword or scabbard be taken from you, nor let them be separated—"

"I will not," Arthur affirmed.

"Nor will blade or scabbard rust or tarnish. This is part of their holy composition. They are not plated, as is the case with spathas. They are pure, solid metal, of an essence unseen beneath the stars. They are immune to corruption. Not so their wielder. Though they will fight for you and heal you, bring you victory, it is you who must put them to the right use. It is you who must wield them for good—"

The first sign of uncertainty crossed Arthur's face. "But why me, out of all time? Why am I the one to bear this blade?"

Ulfius responded. "The answer to that question lies just ahead."

He pointed down the peninsula road. The hills, which had formed low triangles on either side of the curving gravel track, fell away. The sea of green grasses led to a true sea, vast and gray-blue, moiling beyond the rocky cliffs. Salty winds poured up from the sea and swept across the lands. Straight ahead, sea cliffs fell away on either side of the road. The path led out to a prominence overlooking the ocean. A castle perched there, magnificent and black amid silver air and tossing water.

"Tintagel," Ulfius said. "The answer to your question, Arthur, lies there." He urged his mount from a canter into a full gallop and leaned across the creature's neck.

Staring after him in surprise, Arthur turned a quizzical look at Merlin.

The old mage dipped his head. "He is right." With that, Merlin lit out after Ulfius.

Shrugging, Arthur followed. The three riders sent a dust cloud up like a long pennant in the air. The rocky shores converged to either side. Soon, they were on a thin causeway that led to a gatehouse—the very gatehouse where Uther and Merlin and Ulfius had arrived. In the noonday light, the spot was not the black bulwark it had been in that long-ago midnight.

At the portcullis, Ulfius reined in his stamping steed. Merlin pulled up beside him, and Arthur completed the company moments later.

"These are dark days for such impetuous arrivals," bowmen atop the tower called down to them. "Who is it that rides with such dispatch toward our gates?"

Ulfius drew a deep breath and called out in a strident, happy voice. "Tell the duchess that it is her onetime chamberlain, Ulfius, and her onetime mage, Merlin, and a young man she met for mere moments fourteen years ago. Someone she longs to see."

"That is quite a lot to shout," said the man on the wall.

"Tell her Ulfius has returned to fulfill his vow."

As the cry went up, Arthur nudged his horse up alongside Ulfius's. He leaned toward his mentor and whispered, "What is this about? I know no one in Dumnonia. I have never even heard of this duchess."

Ulfius's smile was rueful. "Oh, you do know her, Arthur. You know her in the dark mind where dead truths reside. And though you may not have heard of the duchess of Dumnonia, you surely know her by her former title, Queen Igraine."

No sooner had these words left Ulfius's lips than portcullis chains rattled in their casings. The massive grille of oak and iron slid upward. Beyond, the drawbridge to Tintagel Castle began its clattering descent. Black wedges of wood shone against the forbidding curtain wall of the castle. The bridge angled magnificently outward and settled into its fittings.

From the far end of that bridge walked a woman. In her gossamer gowns and rich robes, she seemed a mortal version of Brigid. A small golden diadem crowned her silver hair, and her eyes shone with the care of a woman who had lost much—two husbands, one child, and a whole nation.

So sad and regal was her gaze that Arthur slid from his saddle and knelt there on the causeway. Ulfius and Merlin did likewise. They would receive this woman as they had received Brigid herself.

The duchess approached the kneeling men. She brought with her a scent that was warm and fragrant, like bread on a hearth. But her words were weary, perhaps even fearful. "How could you come back, Ulfius, after all this time?"

Head bowed, the chamberlain said, "Duchess, forgive me. These are perilous days. I have stayed away only to fulfill my vow to you."

The woman lifted her eyes toward Arthur. Trembling tears shone in them. "And have you fulfilled your vow?"

"Yes, Duchess," Ulfius said. "He is the finest young man I have ever known, well taught, well trained, well mannered. And he is beautiful, as you can see."

Arthur raised his face to peer at the poor, tortured woman. His gaze seemed only to bring more tears from her.

"And does he know me? Does he know who I am?"

"Yes, Duchess," Arthur said quickly. "You were once queen beside Uther."

Bleakly, Igraine shook her head. She daubed streaming eyes. "How could you come back, Ulfius? How could you?"

It was Merlin who answered. His gaze shimmered with joy. "He will know who you are and who he is, Igraine. He will come to know you."

Igraine's hand clutched Ulfius's shoulder before she moved on to touch Merlin likewise. And last, she came to Arthur.

He knelt there with Excalibur and Rhiannon upon his back.

She did not touch the sword, or the lad. Staring into the young, strong face, she studied his features. There was Uther in the line of his jaw and the intensity of the boy's silver eyes, but his other features were more graceful, almost elfin.

"Welcome to Tintagel, Arthur," she said sadly. "Welcome home, my son."

19

Tintagel

Of course Arthur was shocked by the revelation of his true parentage. The boy who ardently believed Merlin's mad past could not believe his own. Every evidence was marshaled. Diaries, lineages, likenesses, Uther's decrees, Igraine's memories. . . . Still, Arthur could not believe.

He pretended to, if only to mollify the sorrowing duchess. Ulfius saw through the pretense and plied only the harder. The afternoon was torment. Words tangled around Arthur's head in ceaseless discord. Was this what it was like in Merlin's mind? Nothing made sense anymore. Arthur was no longer who he had always been. Nor was he the glowing prince Ulfius styled him. Arthur was neither. He was nothing. His whole life had been a lie. The louder Ulfius ranted, the more Arthur was certain of it. He was nothing.

By evening the fragrance of roast duck drifted from the kitchens. Merlin's eyes lit with hunger. Ulfius's attention drifted toward the banquet table. The downpour of proofs slowed to a trickle. Igraine left to find her daughter. This was Arthur's chance.

He excused himself to visit the garderobes. It was the only place where they might leave him alone. Arthur sought out a jakes on the ground floor, one with a window propped open for air. It felt wonderful to scrabble through that window—unprincely behavior. He felt like his old self.

Winning free of the tight casement, he stumbled out onto the shake roof of a shed. Night swathed him. Sea winds slapped his face. The cold scent of brine felt bracing after drawing-room air. For the first time in hours, Arthur's mind was clear.

"I've got to get away. I've got to get away."

The courtyard below was deserted. Igraine had few retainers left. The castle was haunted with the ghost of its past grandeur. It would be an easy thing to navigate the bailey and get to someplace beyond the reach of all this—this lunacy.

Thrushes snapped up crumbs of pie crust from the kitchen windowsill. Crickets sang in the overgrown castle gardens. The distant clack of a soldier's feet came from the wall. A horse whickered in the stables.

The stables. A lantern glowed dimly there.

Shucking his formal clothes, Arthur stripped to camise, trousers, and bare feet. He tousled his hair and rubbed a bit of grit from the shed roof onto his cheek. "They'll not recognize me now," he murmured gladly to himself. Without regalia, he was, after all, as common as a stable boy.

Bundling his clothes atop the shed roof, Arthur dropped down into the courtyard. The ground, once hard-packed from daily foot-traffic, bristled with thorny weeds. Arthur tiptoed among the stalks. In some places, the yard seemed a Caledonian plain, tall thistles everywhere. Barbarism. The place was sinking back into savagery.

"And Ulfius wants me to believe this is *my* castle?"

Arthur neared the stables. They, at least, seemed well tended. Yellow thatch lay thick on the roof. Every window had a shutter, and only a little light leaked out. Best of all, the stable doorway was clear of thistles. Hobbling into the lantern light, Arthur paused to pick a burr from the arch of his foot.

"Barbarism."

A shushing sound came from within the stable—a broad

brush on a horse's flank. Arthur stalked cautiously toward the doorway and peered within.

Past rows of stalls, he glimpsed a beautiful young woman. Her black hair ran in intricate braids to the middle of her back. Her face was the color of milk. Wide brown eyes, a delicate nose, and fulsome lips—she was the loveliest creature Arthur had ever seen. She made her homespun shift seem finest samite, her mud-stained skirt a gown of gold. There was strength in her arm as she drew the brush across the flank of the beast, but her sure-handed ease made the work a graceful dance.

Arthur was drawn to her. Before he knew it, he was inside the stable and halfway to her.

At the sound of his footsteps, the young woman looked up.

Arthur froze. His eyes grew wide. She was his height, but he was more muscular. There was a mature wisdom in her eyes, and oh, what eyes!

"Who are you?" she asked.

Arthur yammered, "I'm—I, ah . . . I'm new—"

The young woman continued brushing the horse. "New? Since when has there been coin for someone new?"

"Oh," Arthur said, blinking, "they aren't paying me—"

"Aren't paying you? Are you a slave?"

"No. No. I'm a freeman," Arthur improvised, trying to devise a plausible lie. "It's just that, well, my father is a farmer, and I don't want to be a farmer, and so I thought— that is, the duchess said if I helped out in the stable, I could train to be an armsman—"

"An armsman," the woman murmured. "Just what we need. Another armsman."

Puffing out his chest after the successful lie, Arthur moved closer. "Yes, I'd say so. Your garrison is nearly empty. You've got more thistles out there than soldiers."

"That's the way I prefer it."

He was very near her now. She had a sweet smell, the scent of sage. "The castle is going back to the wild."

"What's wrong with the wild?"

"What's wrong with armsmen?" he countered.

She stopped brushing the horse. Only in that moment did Arthur realize it was his own bay that she tended. The young woman crooked a finger at him and said, "Come closer, armsman. Come look at this."

Gladly Arthur moved closer.

She lifted the mare's tail. "Look."

Arthur blushed.

"You don't even know what you're looking at, do you?"

"I have a guess—"

"This mare is pregnant." She dropped the creature's tail again. "She's pregnant, and an armsman rode her all the way here from Chertsey. Rode her hard. He had no idea, or he didn't care. That's what's wrong with armsmen."

Arthur's blush only deepened. "Well, when I'm an armsman, I won't make that mistake. I mean, after you've shown me what to look for—"

The woman crossed her arms over her chest. "What did you say your name is?"

"I didn't say, but my name is Ar—Artemis."

"Well, Artemis, you don't just look," she said. "The eyes deceive. Eyes reveal appearances, not essences. You have to use every sense, some you don't even know you have. Can you imagine riding this beast for a hundred leagues and never sensing she was pregnant? I can't touch her without feeling the power of life in her." The young woman grabbed Arthur's hand and set it on the point of the horse's hip. "Don't you feel that feverish heat, that holy fire?"

Arthur did, but not from horse. "You said your name was—?"

"I didn't," she replied, "but it is Morgan."

"Morgan," Arthur repeated, nodding. The name was pleasant on his tongue.

Morgan stared at his hand, vague suspicion in her eyes. She let go. "If you're here to help, you might get to work." She nodded toward a corner where a manure shovel leaned beside a bucket.

Arthur retrieved them. "When is she due? The mare, I mean."

"It will be months, yet," Morgan answered, continuing to brush down the horse. "The signs are obvious, but nobody pays attention anymore. Fertility used to be the magic of the land. Midwives used to be village elders. Those who brought life into the world once ruled the world. Now its only those who take life away. Armsmen."

Topping off the bucket, Arthur said, "Where did you learn all this?"

"I've studied," she responded immediately. "Mostly on my own, but there are a few others who remember the old ways, who dare to practice them in this age of killing."

"Witchery," Arthur said in sudden realization.

Morgan looked up. "That word once was not a curse. Neither was sex a filthy word. All that has changed."

Leaving the full bucket, Arthur sidled up toward her. "It doesn't have to have changed."

Morgan distractedly stared at the mare's flank. "Yes. Everything has to change. But that doesn't mean we can't change it back."

"Precisely," Arthur said gently. He ran a finger along her jaw.

The brush paused in her hand. "What are you doing, Artemis?"

"Changing things back."

He leaned inward. His lips touched hers. She didn't pull away. The kiss bore that same feverish vitality he had sensed before. A thrill moved through him. The moment would have lasted longer, but he swooned dizzily back.

Morgan was equally affected. "What was that?"

Arthur smiled through his blush. "Witchery. Fertility. What was that filthy word you used—sex?"

She shook her head. "No. This isn't right. You're so young. And you don't seem to realize who I am."

Grinning, Arthur replied, "You're right. I've never heard of you. But I'm equally sure you don't know who I am."

Morgan's lips quirked impishly. "Then, who are you?"

"Well, you might not believe this—I have a hard time believing it myself—but this castle that has gone to seed, it's actually my castle."

"What are you talking about?"

"I'm Queen Igraine's long-lost son. I'm Prince Arthur."

His cheek suddenly blazed with feverish heat, and he was spinning aside before he realized he'd been slapped.

"You bastard. I've spent all my life hating you, and now I have another reason to."

Crouching away from her, Arthur look up in shock. "What? What?"

Morgan flung her hand out toward the mare. "This is your horse, isn't it?"

Arthur's brow furrowed in confusion. "Who are you?"

"I'm Morgan! I'm Igraine's daughter! I'm your sister!"

That last word struck him more brutally than the slap. Arthur staggered backward toward the stable door.

"Your father killed my father and raped my mother," Morgan hissed, "and you have all the lines of Uther in you. I see them now. I smell Uther in you, I taste him in you." She spat into the straw. "You stand for everything I hate. You stand for death and sterility. You plan to be king, to subject this land to your will. But you will not dominate me, Arthur. I will not be your subject. And while I live, death will not rule Britannia—"

Arthur heard no more, fleeing out into the reeling night. He plunged blindly away. Thistles rose like armsmen around him. They clawed him, tore him, flung him down. He fell to his side and curled into a ball. His feet bled feverish vitality into the ragged earth.

Morgan disappeared from Castle Tintagel that night. Search parties scoured the castle and the peninsular rock beyond. Arthur, with feet salved and bandaged, joined them. Every armsman and page and cook in the castle sought her—even Duchess Igraine. They let loose the castle hounds, though the curs only added to the confusion with their mindless baying.

Merlin's spells—the best hope for tracking the young woman—proved worthless.

"She is using a kind of magic I know little about," Merlin said bleakly.

Dawn came. The search moved to the lands beyond the peninsula. It continued again into night. At last, Igraine ordered her folk back to Tintagel.

"If Morgan does not wish to be found, she will not be found," the duchess said. "In one day, I have gained a son and lost a daughter."

She flees us. She flees the dogs and the men she calls dogs. Away from mother and Tintagel, from murdered father and murderer not-father. The oak boughs will be her mother's arms, the angry skies her father's eyes. She hides in the one from the other. She hides and flees.

Back in time she goes. Roman roads turn to cart paths to foot paths to deer trails. Fields of corn turn to meadows to clear-cuts to virgin forests. She flees back before the spatha and scutum, before the conquering Christ and the conquering Caesar. She hides among the Celtic deeps. No, not simply hides. She plumbs them, seeking power.

There she is—moon-skinned and lambent, her feet folded among the oak roots and holly boughs wreathing her hair. She sits, and upon her virginal lap she holds the feet of a king. His feet are folded among her legs as her feet among the oak roots. It is an ancient image of power, she the virginal and ever fertile land, and he the rod of law empowered by that land. Together, they rule. Two souls entwined but never touching, desirous but forever chaste, equal in power— man and woman—but forever apart.

No, this is not Morgan I see. This wreathed and oak-folded creature is Tuatha Dé Danann. She is born fey and placed into a human cradle. She is raised to be the chaste bride of the king. Her feet remain among the oaks only if she remains virgin pure—Tuatha untainted by man. Betrothed of Arthur— I remember now that piteous night in the deluge—her name is Guinevere. Deep in the power of the land is Guinevere. She will make a great king of a young man. They will rule together in chaste joy.

But deeper in the power of the land is Morgan. She flees back past the Tuatha Dé. She flees before the faerie folk to Albion, to the deeper magic of titans and gods.

There she is, bone-skinned and lambent. Her feet are not folded among roots, but are themselves roots. Six legs she has, and three bodies, and three heads. She is the weird— maiden, mother, crone—female trinity that encompasses all heaven and earth, all living and dying. She conceives the king in her womb, she suckles the king at her breast, she buries the king among roses. More ancient than the coequal foot-holder of the Tuatha Dé Danann, Morgan seeks not mortal power, but immortal. She will be no queen, but divine consort. She will be the weird—maiden of the king, mother of the king, mourner of the king. Her power lies not in chastity but in fecundity. And with that power, she will strike down my Arthur. She will slay her own brother. I have found her, but I cannot reach her. In the arms of the oak she hides.

Oh, Morgan, you have fled so far. I fear most when you return.

Merlin sat between merlons on Tintagel's south wall. He had repaired the rampart himself, transforming crumbling rock to solid granite.

It pleased him to aid in the castle's renovation. In the months they had remained at Tintagel, Merlin had repaired the whole of the curtain wall, had revitalized the graying thatch upon many a roof, had grown new panes of glass to fill out the battered rose window of the great hall, and had even cobbled the lanes with a spell that enlarged pebbles to stones. His aid had not been entirely architectural. He'd put on fireworks shows in nearby villages to enlist armsmen for the garrison. He'd enchanted the arrows of the castle hunts- man to assure better and more plentiful venison in the castle larders. He'd even tuned the howling of the hounds. Now beneath a full moon, the throaty cries formed rough songs.

Arthur had meanwhile worked similar improvements. Just now, his Farmers Corps, as he jokingly called them, practiced weapons in the bailey below Merlin. Three months ago, these villeins had never hefted anything more deadly than a scythe. They'd had to use their scythes to clear the courtyard of Caledonian thistles before they could even begin work with wooden swords. With Arthur's diligent instruction, the thirty-some farmers became impressive at fighting dummies. This was considered a good start since the average dummy was smarter than the average Saxon. Another few months of instruction, and these villeins would be the corps of a new private army for the young prince. Even now, they looked damned good, hacking away at padded posts.

The young prince, on the other hand, left something to be desired. Arthur practiced just below Merlin, in a ring surrounded by hay bales, lest anyone get hurt. Though the boy was adept at waggling any typical sword, Excalibur was anything but typical. Six feet long, weighted to fall like a mallet, enspelled to kill gods—this was an unwieldy weapon. Arthur looked awful wielding it.

The young prince stood in his ring of hay bales, the great sword gleaming before him. Arthur was stripped to the waist. Sweat covered his muscular frame from towhead to toes. Excalibur wavered weightily in his two-handed grip. It seemed a pernicious caber, poised to topple.

"You can't be afraid of it, Arthur," Ulfius instructed. The chamberlain stood beside the towering castellan, Brastias. Together the men oversaw the revitalization of the garrison, and Arthur was their mutual project. Ulfius scratched his graying hair. "Let your *foes* be afraid of your sword."

Determination flattened Arthur's lips into a grim line. He tried an experimental swing. The blade was meant to skim the top of a hay bale, neatly trimming the stalks that jutted from it. Instead, Excalibur buried itself in the block, severed the twine that bound the thing together, and sent hay bursting in a flurry all around.

Ulfius flung his arms up in frustration. "The sword is too

heavy, Arthur. Perhaps when you are fifteen. Perhaps when you are sixteen—"

"Or twenty-six," Brastias rumbled unhelpfully.

"No!" Arthur interrupted stormily. "I train with Excalibur now. This is my sword, the key to my destiny. I must learn to use it."

To himself on the wall, Merlin said, "Good for you, my lad. Good for you."

Ulfius nodded, having expected the response. "Then keep your weight lower. Think of this sword more as a lance. The lance gets its power from the weight behind it. You've got to keep a lot of weight behind Excalibur, or it will have no power. Try it again. Show me a low stance. Imagine a straight line of force from your ankle, through your hip, to your wrists. Drive from the ground."

Arthur complied, and the glimmering great sword swept through a steady, lethal arc before him.

"Good! Good!" Ulfius shouted. "Better than cleaving hay bales."

Merlin nodded happily. "Better, indeed."

Someone approached him on the wall—Duchess Igraine. The winds of early autumn tugged playfully at her cloak, but her face was grave, as it had been since Arthur's arrival. "Hello, Merlin."

The mage bowed in the crenel. "Good day, Duchess."

She flapped a sealed sheaf of paper in her hand. "The messenger arrived. There is another parcel for Arthur. A page from Ector. A half page from Kay. What seems like a Pauline epistle from his mother . . ."

Without taking his eyes off the perilous one-man combat below, Merlin said offhandedly, "Arthur's epistles to her are just as voluminous."

Igraine gave a sigh, like the coo of a mourning dove. Merlin glanced up at her. The care lines had only deepened since their arrival. The woman had known much grief. In the face of it, she was having to become Arthur's mother all over again.

"He is homesick," Igraine said, watching Arthur jab the

great sword clumsily at a bale. "He loves his mother very much."

Merlin smiled. "Have you noticed that he is also coming to think of Tintagel as home, and of you as mother?"

Igraine looked away, her eyes as fragile as glass ornaments. "It is unkind to tease a hopeful soul."

"Yes, I know," Merlin said. "I have had hopes dashed too. But I do not tease. Imagine one of your long talks with Arthur. I have seen you two sit for hours by the great room fire and speak of Uther and Gorlois. Imagine one of your talks written out on paper. Would the sheaf be any less thick than this note from Diana?"

A smile trembled at the edges of the woman's mouth. "Here I am with Arthur at Tintagel, jealous of words on a page. Off in Chertsey is Diana, jealous of words face-to-face. Is it a blessing or a curse for a boy to have two mothers?"

"Both, I daresay," Merlin replied. "Especially for the mothers."

Further speculation was cut short by a stroke of Excalibur that nearly cut short Arthur. The young prince stumbled aside, lost his grip of the great sword, and landed in the dirt next to the clanging thing. Dust puffed up around him. Arthur lay unmoving on his face.

"Oh, gods, is he hurt?" Igraine muttered, clenching her hands.

"Only his pride."

Arthur lifted himself slowly. Dirt clung to his belly and face. He shook his head. "Maybe you're right, Ulfius. Maybe Excalibur can wait till I'm older. Who needs a god-killing sword to fight men? Maybe you're right, Ulfius."

Merlin stood, his face painted in outrage. " 'Maybe you're right, Ulfius'? Did you hear what you just said, Arthur? 'Maybe you're right, Ulfius'?"

Teeth rimmed in dirt, Arthur grinned up at Grandfather.

Merlin stepped from the wall and descended through air in a drifting line down toward the practice grounds. "Ulfius? Right?"

"What's so ridiculous about that?" Ulfius wanted to know.

"This," Merlin replied, lighting beside Arthur and snatching up Excalibur. "This tells me you are wrong." He held the beaming, beautiful blade up before him. Sunlight danced in the mirror edges of the thing. "Excalibur is everything. It is the gift of the Mistress of the Mists. It is the sword for the one who will drive Wotan from the land. Excalibur—if you will remember, Ulfius—proved that everything I said about Avalon and Asgard and dragon ships was true."

Ulfius glared at the mage. The Farmers Corps had one by one ceased their practice to gawk. Feeling conspicuous, the chamberlain said, "What does any of that have to do with whether Arthur practices with Excalibur or not?"

"Of course he must practice with it! Excalibur is Arthur's future, just as it is my past."

It was the young prince who spoke next. "Yes, Grandfather. I believe all of that. If only we knew more about its past, perhaps we'd know more about my future. Who forged this sword and why? Who first wielded it? And how did you come by it?"

Merlin did not respond immediately. He stood there, holding Excalibur. The sun-bright blade gleamed in his old hands, showing finger bones within flesh. Merlin's grip only tightened. His eyes slid closed. He drew a deep breath, like a man poised to submerge himself in cold and deep water.

Arthur waited, watching. Ulfius and Brastias watched too. Igraine picked her way down the wall stairs.

Merlin's lips trembled. Foam flecked them. His whole being shook. Between grinding teeth, he said, "Bright . . . blinding . . . too deep . . . too deep."

"Grandfather!" Arthur gasped, lunging toward him. He was too late.

Merlin fell. He flopped against the hay bales. He thrashed mindlessly like a landed fish. Excalibur sliced into his convulsing hands. Blood ran down the blade in lines and sanguine veils. Merlin's eyes flipped open. Only wet whiteness showed beneath. He shuddered, biting his own tongue.

Arthur knelt to help him, but Merlin riled free of his grip.

Between wrenching spasms, the old man croaked. "Too deep . . . too deep . . ."

Brastias pried the man's mouth open and shoved a rag between clattering teeth. He struggled to peel Merlin's fingers from Excalibur. It was no good. The old man's grip was implacable. Blood gushed from his hand and boiled away in pink vapor.

Brastias backed away.

Ulfius flung a bucket of water on the writhing figure. It only turned dust to mud.

Then, as suddenly as the convulsion had begun, it ended. Merlin flopped to stillness. Gory hands fell away from the blade. Excalibur dropped in the dirt.

Arthur crouched fearfully above Grandfather and yanked the rag from his tattered mouth. "He's still breathing," the young man panted excitedly. "That's good."

"Yes," croaked the voice of Merlin. His eyes opened, bloodshot and sleepy. "That is good."

"Grandfather!" Arthur said with a relieved laugh. "What new madness is this?"

Merlin shook his head. "Not a new madness, Arthur. An old one. A very old one."

20

The Sword in the Anvil and Stone

The spring roads were barely navigable. Wagons became hopelessly mired. Horses were mantled in mud from hooves to hocks. Rain fell in sullen fits on travelers' backs. Even bandits sensibly stayed indoors.

Arthur was not known for sensibility. His mare clomped along on heavy hooves, her foal doing its best to step in the wide divots she left. And it wasn't just the horses who had to struggle along. Anyone who dismounted for a moment in the brush returned with feet of clay. Ulfius's boots were mortared in their stirrups. Merlin's travel cloak was stiff and dun colored from a series of recent falls. The twenty armsmen from the Tintagel garrison griped incessantly about the mud. They had hoped not to march until midsummer.

Arthur had hoped to remain at Tintagel as well, but bleak news had come from Chertsey. Three separate kings claimed sovereignty over the Midmarch, and a levy of Ector's troops was required by each. The duke refused, and fielded a contingent to back up his refusal. It had been a near thing, but now there was one fewer tyrant in the Midmarch. Though he won the battle, Ector needed more troops, and Tintagel had them. He also needed Arthur and Merlin and Ulfius. Igraine understood. Tintagel was now one of the best-defended sites in Britannia. She willingly sent the reinforcements, but sadly bid her son good-bye. Arthur was saddened too.

As he rode the London-Cadbury road toward Chertsey, Arthur saw that Ector was not alone in his troubles. All of Britannia was disintegrating. Villages erected palisades, towns built walls, fortresses dug moats. . . . Those who didn't fortify ended in smoldering ruin by the roadside. The living, breathing country left by the Romans had expired. Britannia was falling into decay—decay and mud.

"I cannot wait for a hot bath," Arthur hissed, using a stick to scrape clean the shoulder of his mare.

"You'll not have to wait much longer," Ulfius said, standing in the saddle. "Chertsey lies just beyond that brake of alder."

Heart leaping in his chest, Arthur stood as well. "Anyone game for a mud race?"

Without waiting for a response, he set heels to his horse. She bounded. Hooves pulled from the sucking road. The mare ambled forward in a sliding, drunken gait. Mud splashed form her frogs and pasted itself to the trotting foal.

One hunk of muck struck Ulfius in the cheek. "All right, that's it," he growled and lit out afterward.

The spray from his mount was worse than that from Ar-

thur's. Pent-up armsmen received the brunt of it. They kicked
their steeds to gallop. A brown gale trailed them all. Ladled
with filth, the company charged up the road to Chertsey Castle.

A welcoming horn blew from the walls. Arthur hadn't
heard a more beautiful sound in years.

Slewing sloppily, Arthur's mare gained the drawbridge.
The foal happily clomped onto clear wood. A caravan of
horseflesh and armsmen followed as Arthur reined in before
the rising portcullis.

Ector, Diana, and Kay waited beyond. Joy and fear,
amusement and revulsion warred across their faces.

The young prince won his feet free of the clogged stirrups
and dismounted. After a few panting breaths, he clumped
toward his foster family.

Ector grinned stupidly, tears welling in his eyes. Kay wore
an amused look, muscled arms folded across his chest. But
Diana—she who had written so many long and heartfelt letters to her foster son—Diana was withdrawn inside herself.
Beneath an elegant coif, her eyes were guarded. She wore
finery, as though she were meeting not a son but a king. And
then, most telling of all, Diana dropped to her knee before
the muddy young man and bowed her head.

"Oh, no!" Arthur said, laughing. "This is not how I want
to meet you, Mother."

He took her hand, lifted her, and wrapped her in a muddy
embrace.

Tears flowing truly now, Ector smothered his son in a bear
hug.

For some moments, Arthur was happily buried in that tearful grapple. Once the clench broke, he said, "I may be the
heir to Uther Pendragon, but here in Chertsey, I will always
be your son."

"Glad to hear it," said Kay. He walked jauntily toward
Arthur. "And you'll always be my kid brother. But you'll
get no hugs from me until you've had a bath. You're a
mess."

Arthur grinned an apology. "The road's a mess."

"The country's a mess," Ector said with sudden sobriety.

Arthur nodded. "Well, Father, we'll see what we can do about that."

"Ah, yes," Kay said with a flash of jealousy. "Invincible Arthur and his invincible sword. So, this is Excalibur." He reached out to touch the bejeweled scabbard, and then drew forth Excalibur. In the gray light, it shone like silver. "Impressive."

"And even more impressive—I've learned to wield it."

Kay's dazzled eyes belied his casual voice. "Have you ever figured out where it came from?"

Arthur hushed his brother and whispered, "That's a sore subject. Every time it comes up, Merlin has a fit."

Kay sheathed the sword and laughed. "I'd like to see that."

"No, you wouldn't," Arthur said. "Trust me."

"Where is the old codger anyway?" Kay asked, peering out at the dripping war band.

Arthur craned his head. "He was right behind us."

The armsmen on the bridge looked back too. They seemed to spot Merlin, for they guided their horses aside to let him pass. Into the opening gap clomped a thing that looked not so much like a rider and horse but a shambling and dejected clod of mud.

"Ah," Arthur said lightly. "Here he comes now."

Diana at last spoke. "Break out the bucket brigade."

She had been joking, but Kay ran off to actualize the plan. Soon, the courtyard was filled with darting armsmen and sloshing buckets, laughter, and mud.

Baths followed, and after baths, a feast. Salt pork, yearling lamb, game hens, pickled beets, loaves of winter wheat, and a barley brew finer than anything in the cellars at Tintagel. Merlin was especially pleased with this final offering, supplementing it with jiggers of Ector's rye spirits.

"There are certain deprivations that make barbarous places truly barbaric," he had commented between draughts.

At the height of the feast, Arthur regaled his family with the story of his adventure at Avalon. A few barrels of ale convinced Ulfius and Merlin to climb onto the great hall's tables and pantomime their parts. Merlin's impersonation of a selkie swimming between Ulfius's legs got everyone laughing. Arthur then enlisted the aid of others—Kay as the young prince, Ector as a series of backward guards, Diana as Brigid and Igraine, both.

After the mud was washed away, after the farce was done and the revelers were heading to their beds, a simple truth hung undeniable in the air of Castle Chertsey.

Arthur was home, and here, he would prepare to be king.

The antlered child is full regaled. The Thames and Brue flow from his eyes, streams beside the cities he will join. Key by key, he has unlocked the chambers of my mind. Into each, his light has pierced. Mad shadows flee to deeper, darker corners. The final key he holds now, largest, without peer— Excalibur.

But when I take that key in hand and slide it gently in the lock that seals the last and deepest, darkest door, there comes a bubbling flood beneath. Another river. Lethe flows and drags me down and drowns and drowns and drowns me.

Arthur was seventeen before he made his bid for the throne. Seventeen was one year older than he had thought necessary, and one year younger than Ulfius had thought practicable. Desperation decided for them both. A number of legitimate kings in the border lands—Lot of Lothian, Fergus More of Dalriada in Scotland, Galem of the Northern Picts, King Carados of Carados, and the barbarian King Aelle of Sussex— were assembling an army, ready to divide up the land among them. If Arthur did not ride now to Canterbury to make his bid, there would be no Britannia left to rule.

Arthur, Merlin, and Ulfius set out in the spring of 504.

Canterbury was a beautiful spot. The city resided between the toiling channel and the green fields of the Thames Valley. Among the first Roman conquests, Canterbury had enjoyed an influx of rich gentry and coin-bearing soldiers. They hauled in their wake massive works of limestone and marble. Arched entries, pillared porticoes, grand stairways, baths, markets, public ovens, and all of it positioned patiently along stone boulevards. Here and there, one could make out the chiseled letters DVROVERNVM CANTIACORVM, the Roman name for Canterbury.

Ulfius, Arthur, and Merlin rode down the Durovernum High Road. Even on the outskirts of Canterbury, the buildings of timber and brick were fashioned in imperial style, with stuccos that made rubble walls seem grand. Tile roofs far outnumbered thatch. There was a southern gentility to the sea air, warm in the noontime sun. The Britons walking the streets were shaved and well accoutered in long linen tunics, leather belts, trousers, and boots with puttees. They looked at the bearded and hide-cloaked outlanders with a discomfort that bordered on suspicion.

"You must remember," Ulfius said as he pulled off the deer-pelt outer cloak he wore, "that to these folk, beards and barbarian dress mean Saxons. They've been fighting off the invaders for a hundred years. Were it not for the garrisons here, Canterbury would have fallen."

Arthur similarly folded the stoat-trimmed cloak he wore. He self-consciously scratched the downy blond beard that crossed his chin, wondering if he himself looked too furry.

For his part, Merlin neither shucked his savage cloak nor lamented his scrofulous beard. He was watchful and uncomfortable. He sniffed the air, as though he smelled a skunk. "It's not just the garrison that guards this place." A huff came from within his silvery beard. "It's Tetragrammaton. His power here is absolute, and he does not welcome company.

"Tetragrammaton?" Arthur asked. "Who is he?"

Ulfius cantered up alongside the young prince and said conspiratorially, "*The* Tetragrammaton is J-H-V-H—Jehovah. It is a word used by Jews who do not wish to sully the name of God," he glanced at Merlin, "and by Pagans who fear to invoke him."

Merlin ignored the jibe. "Wotan fears him, and rightly so. Tetragrammaton has killed other gods before."

"Yes," Ulfius seemed to agree. "Military might, Roman history, barbarian fears, and seat for the bishop of Britannia—Canterbury is the place to make your bid for the throne, Arthur."

The young man nodded, nervously quiet.

"And the Christchurch Basilica is the perfect venue—at the heart of Canterbury, between the marketplace and the military grounds." Ulfius patted the saddlebags behind him, stuffed with scrolls and parchments. "On the steps of the basilica, I shall give my series of speeches. Any who listen will not be able to doubt your lineage, Arthur."

At last, the young prince spoke. His voice was pensive, his hands tight on the reins. "I do not think it will be so easy as that, Ulfius. This throne will not be won by words, but by the sword."

"Yes," said Merlin, sitting up and staring at Excalibur, riding on Arthur's back in Rhiannon. "Yes, by the sword."

Ulfius waved them off. "A throne gained by the sword must forever be maintained by the sword. No. Let birthright elevate you to the seat that awaits."

Arthur gave Merlin a long look. The old mage shook his head gently. A wink beneath his linty brows and a hitch of one corner of the mage's mustache assured Arthur that Merlin had a plan of his own.

In companionable silence, the three rode on into town. Wooden fences gave way to rubble-work revetments, and they to cut-stone walls and murals in fresco. Street-level buildings gained second and third stories. Instead of farm carts and donkeys, there were chariots and horse teams. The British rabble diminished, and Roman-born gentry moved at ease among the smooth streets. The Durovernum High Road opened out like a river flowing into a large lake. Three-storied shops and houses along that grand way drew back like canyon walls.

Along one side of the way, the porticoed garrison house fronted the parade grounds and barracks of the army of Canterbury. This would be the destination of the Chertsey and

Tintagel contingents, journeying even now eastward for the jousts.

Beyond the garrison house, a broad marketplace spread. Bright-colored tents shone in the still air of noon, and beneath them bustled buyers and sellers. The sweet scent of bread came from open ovens, and casks of wine and ale hemmed in tables where diners took their midday meal.

On the other side of the high road, the grand, round Christchurch Basilica stood. It was a great domed building with transepts pointing toward the four corners of the globe. The western transept opened in a trinity of archways, for Father, Son, and Holy Ghost, and above them hovered a cruciform window in limestone. The dome itself was massive, held aloft by fat gray drums beside each transept. The whole structure perched on a small rise, at the top of twelve steps.

Ulfius looked with appreciation at the patio before the looming structure. "The perfect site," he said to himself. Urging his horse toward a tie-up, Ulfius dismounted. Even before Arthur and Merlin came up alongside him, he was digging in his saddlebags and gingerly pulling forth his speeches.

Merlin stared dubiously from beneath white brows. "Don't you suppose you should get the bishop's permission before using his church as a pulpit?"

The warrior waved away the suggestion. "Once he hears what I have to say, he will be unable to deny me the right to speak."

Arthur and Merlin sighed in unison, less irritated than sad.

Arthur suggested, "Before we start giving speeches, let's find someplace to stay."

"Lodgings?" Ulfius asked. "I imagine we will be asked to stay in the royal garrison, or even the basilica itself."

"The lad and I will take in the market," Merlin said. His eyes lit. "Perhaps we'll find something to eat." Taking the young prince in his arm, Merlin led him away from Ulfius.

The warrior gave an affable grin and a wink over the pile of parchments. "I'll send someone for you when the crowd is roused to a patriotic frenzy."

Turning, Merlin whispered to Arthur, "And he thinks me mad."

An easy smile came to the young man. "Poor Ulfius. He's too rational. He expects the rest of us to be just as level-headed. But you can't legislate a king into being."

"Yes," Merlin agreed. "Logic has little to do with politics."

Together, they strolled across the paving cobbles toward the marketplace. The smells and sounds of the place flowed out around them. Bright-dyed scarves in saffron and red fluttered on poles. In an adjacent stall, sapphires and kobold beads gleamed in wooden trays. There were rugs from the land of the Aethiopians, horses from the desert tribes of Ishmael, slaves from Germany and the far-off shores of the Hamites, and spices from the Celestial Empire.

Arthur was amazed. His hands moved among the items, as though by touching them he could touch the distant lands.

Merlin took in the smell of the market like a man breathing the fragrance of his beloved. At one point, he caught the aroma of hot olive oil and drew it deep into his lungs. His feet seemed to take root.

Meanwhile, Arthur discovered a pair of tinkers working out of either end of a single box wagon. The man at one end reached into the vehicle and received platefuls of fresh chicken meat, which he skewered and hung for sale above a small fire. The man at the other end reached into the wagon to receive trays covered with the bones of saints. He had all twenty-eight of Saint Peter's finger bones, which sold out twice an hour.

In the distance, Arthur heard a whining sound, like the high keen of an insect swarm. He turned about to see that Ulfius had begun his oratory. Thinking himself some Pericles, the warrior stood with one leg before him. He gesticulated into the air. No one gathered. A pair of beggars moved to a more populous spot.

Arthur smiled ruefully. Poor Ulfius.

The next stall was a smithy. The shed was a large and permanent structure with two interior forges and a pair of massive anvils. A third forge stood in the open air of the courtyard, its anvil mounted on a large rock. Mauls of all description hung along the soot-blackened walls. The man who animated them was as burly, blackened, and burn-scarred as his tools. Just now, he carried a pair of giant tongs in one hand and a coal shovel in the other. He might have seemed thick-skulled, but his work showed a delicate genius. All across one wall hung swords and daggers, gleaming bright. Their blades were straight and solid, their hilts ornate. Bastard swords, spathas, great swords, cutlasses, broad-swords, poniards, stilettos . . .

Merlin bumped up beside Arthur, who stared in amaze-ment at the blades.

The young man said, "So many ways to kill—"

Merlin nodded. "There are other, better uses for swords."

So saying, he reached up to the hilt of Excalibur, riding across Arthur's back. From Rhiannon, he drew forth the long, dazzling blade. Its ringing emergence made passersby stop to stare.

The weapon smith also paused. He hung tongs onto one of the anvil horns, leaned the coal shovel against a stand, and approached, wiping sooty hands on a cloth at his waist.

Merlin held the blade aloft, allowing it to glint in the sun. More folk on the street came to a halt to see that spectacular sword. It seemed to hum in the air, its lines as brilliant and dreamy as sun on water.

"Ever seen the like?" Merlin asked the weapon smith. He spoke loudly enough that anyone nearby could have heard. "An enchanted blade. A holy blade." The words had their effect. A crowd gathered behind Merlin.

Arthur gave him a nervous, beseeching gaze.

The weapon smith arrived and extended meaty hands, soot lining the creases of each finger. "May I?"

Arthur shook his head in objection, but Merlin surrendered the sword.

The weapon smith sighted along the edges of the blade. He turned it over. Holding the thing in only one hand, he took a swing with it. The sword executed a lovely arc, its metal singing. A reluctant smile appeared at the corner of the smith's mouth. He swung Excalibur again in a series of impressive passes designed to disarm multiple opponents. Sunlight flashed in amazing array across canvas tents and tinker wagons and the great basilica.

The crowd grew.

Arthur watched it all with sick dread, sweat prickling his brow.

"Beautiful," the weapon smith said, walking back to return the blade. "You are right. I have never seen the like. This is a priceless blade. Who is the maker?"

"The gods made this blade," Merlin replied simply. "It is not just priceless, it is holy. This blade will save Britannia."

A murmur moved through the crowd.

The weapon smith tilted his head. "I don't know about holy swords. You would have to ask the bishop—"

"Destroy it," Merlin said blankly.

"No!" Arthur protested, but Merlin's gentle hand quieted him.

The weapon smith looked between the two. "The lad is right. It would be a sin to destroy a blade such as this."

"Destroy it," Merlin repeated. "I will grant you a hundred gold ducats if you can destroy it."

A querulous look crossed the smith's face. "What is this about? Why would you offer me a fortune to destroy this priceless weapon?"

"I'm offering it to you because you cannot destroy the sword. It is more than priceless. It is holy. This sword will save Britannia. You will prove it by trying to destroy it."

Mouth pressed in a grim line, the weapon smith took one last, longing look at Excalibur. He walked to his tool bench and pulled out a diamond-tipped awl. Returning to stand before Merlin and Arthur, the smith held up Excalibur and drew the diamond awl across its flat. A look of sadness filled his face. "There, it is marred."

"It is not," Merlin corrected.

The smith blinked. He looked at the blade. It shone with the same incorruptible gleam as before, not a mark on it. The smith drew the diamond awl across it again. Still, no scratch appeared. "That's not possible. I use this to mark metal—any metal—but there isn't a mark—"

Nostrils flaring, the smith strode to his outdoor forge, chucked the blade in so that it was swallowed to the hilt, and pumped the bellows. Red coals flared within. The smith's eyes also glared. The stillness around the shop deepened even as the crowd redoubled. At the back of the group, folk strained to see. The smith yanked the sword from the forge, slapped it down atop the anvil, and brought a maul thundering down on it. The hammer head reverberated in his hand and jangled free. The sword rang with a bell tone, but neither bent nor broke.

Something else broke, though—the maul struck the smith's foot. He yelped, dropped Excalibur, and hopped miserably. "What sort of blasted metal—?"

"It isn't even hot," Merlin advised, seeing the blade fall atop loose straw. "You can touch it and not be burned."

A thrill went through the crowd. At its back appeared a personage accustomed to being the center of crowds, the high bishop of Canterbury. He was amused by this loud display. Not so the man standing beside him, a certain warrior whose speech had been preempted.

The weapon smith gingerly touched the sword. "You're right. It's not hot."

"Destroy it," Merlin repeated. "Destroy it, collect a hundred golden ducats, and prove that this sword is an ordinary blade. But if you cannot, believe that this holy weapon will save Britannia, and us all."

The whole crowd heard—merchants and gentry, slaves and serfs, warriors and clergy, the bishop and Ulfius. They all heard, and leaned in excited anticipation as the smith did his worst.

He set the tip in a vise and hauled brutally on the hilt. The blade did not so much as bend. More effort only snapped the vise from its mounting and sent it clattering to the cobbles. Next, the smith battered those self-same cobbles with strokes from the blade. It neither dented nor dulled, solid as ever. Each stroke sounded like a chime and unnerved the sweating smith. He next balanced the blade, tip and handle, on a pair of bricks and compelled a plow horse to stand on the center of it. The horse did, and lunged a couple times for effect.

Amazement swept in hoots through the crowd. The bishop himself clapped excitedly when the smith held aloft a pristine sword.

Done in with fatigue, the burly man concluded his attempts by bashing the blade against anything in sight, all to no avail. With each musical stroke, the crowd's cheering grew louder, and the smith's labors grew more desperate, more exhausted.

Merlin strode into the midst of the display and snatched Excalibur from the kitten-weak man. He held it aloft. "Behold, people of Canterbury, of Britannia. This is Excalibur, a blade of old—holy and enchanted. It will save our land. It will unite our people. It will guide us to the rightful king of Britons."

With that, he hauled back on the blade and sent it lancing into the anvil atop the stone. Excalibur sank through oiled iron as if into water, and impaled both metal and rock.

"Whoever can draw this sword from this anvil and stone will be king of Britannia!"

21

Arthur, the King

Merlin and Arthur sat on a sunlit balcony.

To one side, the marketplace bustled. To the other, the garrison parade grounds thronged with warriors at tournament. Straight ahead towered Christchurch Basilica, backdrop to Ulfius's perorations. He seemed a tiny gnat beating his wings against a gale. No one heeded his message of hope. The thousands in the square waited in long lines to draw the true hope of the future—Excalibur.

Merlin watched the blade. It had a dreaming power. It forever captured the eye, drew the hand, possessed the heart. When intussuscepted in its scabbard, the sword's power was completed and contained. United, Excalibur and Rhiannon held their aching glory between them. Separated, they longed for each other. They beamed into the cold distances and drew all folk into their radiance.

Even then, Arthur clutched Rhiannon to his chest. He stared feverishly toward its distant mate. "Why this, Grandfather?" he asked for the fourth time. "Why this?"

"Britannia must see. They must be drawn to the sword and its bearer." The old man's voice was faraway and sad. "Even your family and comrades vie for the blade. Kay and Ector, both, have tried to pull it, and failed. But they have felt its power. They will swear to the one who draws it."

Arthur turned eager eyes on Merlin. "Let me go down, then, Merlin. Let me draw it now. Why must I wait?"

"They still arrive, Arthur. Your friends from Dumnonia are not here yet. You could not win the kingship without them. And others—friends and enemies. They come to the sword. They must all try and fail before you pull the blade."

Arthur sat back in the seat and kicked his feet up on the rail around the balcony. His legs jiggled with nervous energy. "I don't know why I am so eager. It will not be easy to rule. It will not be easy to ascend that throne and stay there. I will have to fight."

"Yes," Merlin agreed. "But you will fight with me beside you, and your foster father and brother, your mothers and Brigid, Rhiannon and Excalibur—"

"Tell me about the sword, Merlin," Arthur said, dropping his feet flat against the balcony. "Tell me. How can I fight with it if I know nothing of its origins?"

Merlin eased back in his seat. These were deadly questions. Merlin knew it, and Arthur knew it too. Excalibur's beginnings lay entwined with Merlin's own beginnings—a mystery with a poisonous heart.

"I'm sorry, Grandfather," the young man said. He scratched his downy beard and sighed. "I'm just all pent up.

I'm just—I'm just going mad with this waiting—"

Going mad with this waiting—

"No, Arthur. You are right." Merlin's voice was infinitely heavy. "You must know, at whatever cost. You must know about the sword, and I must know too."

The mage turned his thoughts to interior reaches.

Before Merlin tumbled a black and forgetful river. The ancients called it Lethe. It separated life from death.

On its near shore lay the rankled fields of Albion—a fearsome wonderland of talking stumps and laurel-leaf maidens and purple Pendragons.

On the far shore lay nothing at all, a wasteland of bones and rot. All deadly things dwelled there, awaiting those who dared cross the Lethe.

To cross that hateful tide was to die. To ride it was to be borne down into the welling depths, where bobbed the flotsam of past selves.

Merlin took a breath of bitter mist. It stung his nose and prickled across his brain, numbing it like rye spirits. He looked upstream. The river stretched into tangled eternities. He looked downstream. It plunged into deep black caverns. Down there lay endless waterfalls, boiling cauldrons, oceans that lapped ebony shores. Down there lay the secrets of Excalibur.

There was a little boat tied up by the wash. It would be just enough to hold Merlin. He slid aboard the craft and lifted the paddle from its braces. With it, he pushed away from the shore and into the hungry current.

The tide carried him toward a yawning cave mouth. Its throat roared with descending water. Merlin and his tiny boat drifted into the stony maw. A ribbed ceiling slid past. Light failed. Currents quickened.

Down he went, and down.

•   •   •

"It was long ago, Arthur," Merlin said in oracular tones. *"Before I came to Saxony or Asgard. It was before I came to Britannia. More than a century ago. I was very young then. No, not young. New. I was very new. Even the Christ himself was not quite four hundred years old then."*

Merlin's boat bounded down the flood. There was mad reason in those convoluted passages, smooth concavities like auricles and ventricles. In looming walls, more shadow than material, he saw figures: Roman soldiers in phalanx, casting spears. Buildings buckling and crumbling under some obscenely powerful explosion. Scribes fleeing, their robes trailing fire. The banners of Constantine.

"I was near the capital of the empire. In a city with many people, many soldiers."

Among these mercurial images there came a man, a bearded maniac. His hair stood from his head in wild rage. Foam and blood flecked his mouth. His lips were tattered by raging teeth. The man's frame, once muscular and broad, was now wasted by starvation. Pox covered his skin. Skin barely covered bones. And no clothing covered skin or bone. Fabric burned away to nothing.

"I was truly mad then."

In withered fury, the man stalked the streets. His eyes rolled wildly. Where they lighted, death in Gorgon stone followed. He raged endlessly, rehearsing nonsensical offenses. Each vicious word emerged and became a rag soaked in Greek fire, igniting anything it touched. And when he chose to shriek, the banshee keen deafened any who heard. A killing stench rolled in poisonous green cloud all about him. Birds that crossed into it fell from the skies. Beggars who couldn't escape his shambling approach slumped dead before him. His mere presence soured oil and rotted meat and changed wine to blood. But his touch, it was most powerful of all. Anything that entered his grasp was transmuted from substance to essence. His bare feet fused sand to glass and limestone to marble. His hands clutched coal into diamonds, transformed olives into entire trees, and raised the dead to shambling life.

"I moved through the city like a living cyclone. Wherever I went, death followed. They tried to kill me. They tried, but could not."

A whole battalion surrounded him. Their spears pierced him. The wooden shafts sprouted leaves and roots. He tore them out of his belly and slew his attackers with the Evil Eye.

They lured him into a blind alley and sealed off the end, then flung jars of Greek fire down on him. Flames rolled inward until they struck his skin. Then, transformed from material fire to essential fire, the blaze arced back outward. It blasted away stone and mortar. It turned flesh to ash. It turned bone to meal. A ruse meant to slay the madman killed hundreds of citizens, instead.

"I would not leave. I was searching for something, for revenge. I was searching for the god-killing Sword of the Spirit—"

"Excalibur," Arthur whispered.

That single word brought with it the young prince and all the uncoiling decades. Merlin reeled.

The shadows on the cave wall disappeared in utter blackness. The tiny boat tumbled through the cascading Lethe. Waves

surged over gunwales. The inexorable tide dragged boat and
madman both down into a maelstrom. Merlin flailed in the
spinning torrents. Stone walls battered head and ribs and
hips. Hands clawed bellies of sliding stone. His lungs burned.
At last, he drew in the stinging, awful, forgetful flood. He
was drowning. The last air from his lungs bubbled bloodily
forth. He thrashed his head.

The vision was gone.

All was lost.

Even his body was no longer his. It convulsed uncontrol-
lably. His shrieks were only gurgles. He was dying.

But down through the loud chaos of it all came a single
silver thread. Merlin latched onto it and clung, battered and
hopeless. The line pulled him up, out of endless black water
and toward light and air thousands of feet above.

The silver thread spoke to him, saying softly again and
again, "It's all right, Grandfather. It's all right."

Months later, Merlin sat nervously in the Saints' Garden.

It was a small bower replete with curious little statues.
The shortcomings of the British sculptor were mercifully
masked by creeping ivy and leaf shadows. Saint Paul was
here, freshly fallen from his horse and seeming Laocoön for
all the vines that snaked around him. Saint Thomas was
nearby, jabbing a finger in Christ's side—doubters in their
moment of greatest doubt.

Merlin could empathize. He could have been quite at home
in this overgrown space except that the temple of Tetragrammaton loomed to one side. Merlin feared the Christian deity
as much as he feared Wotan. Even so, here he sat, not a
stone's throw from the ornate door that led into Tetragrammaton's temple.

Arthur and Ulfius had just passed through that door, walking beneath a tympanum that depicted Saint Jerome. Even
now, they met with the high bishop, seeking Tetragrammaton's blessing of Arthur's rule.

Merlin felt betrayed. His plans had proceeded well. All

summer, nobles from every corner of Britannia had flocked
to Canterbury. Petty kings, dukes, counts, viscounts,
horsemen, and freemen had arrived to try their hand at pulling the fabulous blade from its entrapment. None had succeeded, but all had felt the power of the sword. All felt its
draw. When at last Arthur pulled the sword, they would
swear fealty to him. They would make him king. There was
no need to gain the Church's sanction. There was no need
to invite Tetragrammaton to share Arthur's throne.

"It is a grave turn," whispered a voice in Merlin's ear. It
seemed a mere pattering of leaves. It would have to be. Aside
from statues, Merlin was alone.

"Loki," he breathed in realization, gripping the sides of
his head and crumpling forward. "Always you come at my
darkest hour."

The suggestion of a smirk came to the lips of Saint Constantine. "When else will you listen to me?" In languid flapping, the words formed. "What are we to do about this?
Tetragrammaton is no friend to either of us."

"What are *we* to do?" Merlin echoed. "Arthur's ascension
is none of your concern."

A chill came to Loki's voice, frost on yet-green leaves.
"You are mistaken, my friend. Your future king is very much
my concern."

Merlin was in no mood for banter, especially with phantasms. "I dreamed Arthur before he was conceived. I arranged his conception. I brought him into being, reared him,
taught him. And I shall set him on the throne, without Tetragrammaton and without you."

"You forget, my friend," Loki replied silkily, "I brokered
the bargain that lifted the curse from Arthur's head. I saved
his life and brought Guinevere into being. She will be the
power of his throne. I inspired you to fight for Uther and
save the land from the Saxons, that Arthur might rule it. You
and I together—we are making Arthur king."

"There is no *we*, Loki," Merlin said, vexed. The god
seemed all around him—twisting the lips of Saint Stephen,
poisoning the pen of Saint Jerome, painting a mustache on

Saint Mary—but it was all delusion. "There is no *we* because you are a figment of my mad mind. You come only in the darkest hour because only then do the bars of reason bend enough to release you from your cage. And I know why you have come. It is not because of Arthur. It is because I am unlocking the deepest, darkest door of my madness—the place you call home. And when that door swings wide and truth pours in like the breaking dawn, you and all the other shadows of madness will be dispersed forever. You come not because you fear Tetragrammaton, but because you fear me."

A laugh answered that, a laugh devoid of pleasure. It shivered through leaf and vine to twist in roots below. "Oh, how wrong you are, Merlin."

"Am I?"

"You truly believe you visited Asgard, battled Wotan, fled with your precious Excalibur—but you do not believe that Loki followed you from those high halls?"

That thought sent a chill through Merlin. "If you are real, why do you appear only to me? Why has no one else in Britannia met the great Loki?"

"I do appear to others, old man," Loki replied, "and soon, in solid form. My power grows. It grows with every Saxon born here, with every Saxon who lands on these shores. It grows as Arthur's power grows, as Guinevere's power grows. Power is the dividend paid to the king-maker, and I am the king-maker. Remember that, Merlin—I am making Arthur, and I can unmake him. For every Guinevere, there is a Morgan. . . ."

The truth of Loki's words came suddenly clear to Merlin. He stood, trembling. "Do not threaten me, Loki. Do not threaten Arthur."

"You think you have this all arranged? You think the sword in the anvil and stone will make your boy a king? Well, Merlin, boys are impatient things. Perhaps I could prove my reality to you by making Arthur draw the sword too soon. . . ."

"Begone, Loki!" Merlin roared. "I will unlock the darkness where you dwell and scour it with blazing truth. Begone forever!"

Saint Jerome smiled mockingly in his tympanum. "You do that, Merlin. Unlock your deepest madness. Let the blazing truth shine in. It will not destroy me. It will destroy you."

No sooner had those words been spoken than the transept doors opened. Out stepped Arthur and Ulfius. Both beamed gladly.

"There you are, Merlin," Ulfius said. "I hope your wait was as pleasant as our meeting with the high bishop."

Glassy-eyed, Merlin could only nod.

"The church is endorsing me!" Arthur said, bounding down the steps to his grandfather and wrapping him in a glad embrace. "They are going to call me the Chosen of God."

In the youth's strong grasp, Merlin felt weak.

Ulfius smugly rolled a set of parchments. "The bishop was impressed by Arthur's lineage, his grasp of doctrine, his virtue—"

"And I promised not to tax the Church," Arthur added excitedly. "Isn't that grand! I can ascend the throne with you on one side and God on the other!"

Merlin nodded numbly. "Grand, yes. Grand."

Autumn had cycled by while the best and brightest of Britannia tried their hands at drawing the sword in the anvil and stone. None succeeded. The line of waiting men still stretched halfway around the basilica. Many had even returned for multiple attempts.

Only Arthur was denied the chance, and all because of Grandfather.

The young prince stood on the balcony and yanked at his hair. "I can't stand it any longer! I'm mad with waiting. I can't bear watching another unwashed idiot haul on Excalibur!"

Merlin tried to soothe him. "It is not time yet. Do not do this, Arthur. Everyone else must try first, or it will mean war. Do not rush this thing, or there will be bloody mayhem."

"Bloody mayhem sounds pretty good right now," Arthur muttered, striding toward the door.

"Don't draw it! I'm warning you!"

"Who made you God?" Arthur slammed the door and pounded down the stairs. He muttered angrily, "He probably thinks I'm going to the smithy. Let him think it! Let him gather some spell to stop me!" Arthur emerged from the stairway and turned toward the garrison grounds.

Cheers rose ahead, but not for him. Tournament battles had quite naturally arranged themselves among the armsmen who'd failed to draw the sword. They took out their frustration in fights and feasts and trysts. Even those avenues were closed to Arthur. Ector and Diana forbade him to enter the jousts, lest some errant stroke slay the heir of Uther.

"They'll change their minds. They'd better."

Arthur strode to the Chertsey pavilion. The blue and white banners of Ector's heraldry slapped him lightly in the face as he entered. On one side of the tent, a row of cots held the bruised and battered warriors of house Chertsey. On the other side ran a long table where breakfasted the hale and healthy warriors. By day's end, most of them would have crossed over. In the back of the pavilion, behind hanging curtains, were the private chambers of the man who administered all this mayhem.

Arthur marched between moaning casualties and chomping eaters, straight back to his foster father's chambers. He abruptly threw back the curtain, set hands on his hips, and declared, "I want in on the fun!"

The words were no sooner out of his mouth than he realized Ector still lay abed, Diana lay with him, and they hadn't exactly been sleeping. The two rolled apart, pulled linens up about their necks, and glared. Their initial shock at the interruption crumbled into giggles.

Arthur was infuriated. "Stop laughing! Thanks to Ulfius and Merlin, everyone is laughing at me. I'm sick of it! I want to fight. I want to enter the joust lists, and the sword duels, and the group melees—"

Diana's face was sweetly troubled beneath rumpled silver

hair. "These are just games, Arthur, dangerous games. You are meant for greater things. You are meant to be king. You cannot risk yourself—"

"I can and I will!" Arthur said. "I have been inducted into the rights of sword and horse. I am an equal warrior to Kay, and he fights every day. He is your own flesh and blood, and you let him fight! Why won't you let me?"

"Son, son," Ector said, "you're only seventeen. Most of these fighters are men. Most of them weigh twice as much as you. Most of them have fought in real battles and killed real men—"

"Just my point," Arthur said. "Isn't it better for me to fight mock battles before I fight real ones? If I am going to be king, I will have to fight."

Diana said, "Ulfius and Merlin think they've worked out a way you won't have to—"

"Nonsense! Nonsense!" Arthur raged. "These petty kings don't care what my lineage is. They don't care who is endorsed by what god. They'll submit only to someone who can beat them. I have to fight. I will never be king unless I fight."

A look of resignation crossed their faces. Arthur could see this was a difficult moment for them. Their hands had clutched him tightly for seventeen years, and now he was prying those hands loose.

"Find a sword," Ector said at last. "Find a sword, and I'll add you to the lists."

Jubilant, Arthur whirled about and headed for the flap. Before passing through, he said, "Thank you, Father. Thank you, Mother. You won't regret it. They won't be laughing at me any longer."

Plunging through, Arthur ran headlong into a squire, got tangled up with the boy, and sprawled in a heap on the floor of the tent. There was a fresh batch of laughter from the tables and cots.

The loudest guffaws came from a new arrival among the wounded. "Wait, wait!" Kay cried from the pallet where he lay. "Give the cot to my brother. He is more wounded than

I." Peals of merriment answered. Kay, bloody in disheveled armor, led the chorus. An especially deep cut crossed his left shoulder. A sword had severed plate and mail, skin and muscle, leaving an agonizing wound. The hoarse grate of Kay's voice bespoke the pain. With each jag of laughter, sweat and tears streamed down his face. His hand trembled on his sword, beside him on the pallet. "You're lucky you fought only a squire."

Arthur climbed up through the storm of derision. He fought his way past varlets and squires, busy unlacing Kay's armor and gingerly sliding off pieces of it. At last beside his brother, Arthur said, "What happened? Who beat you?"

"Beat me?" Kay gasped out with nervous laughter. "I won!"

"But your arm—" Arthur said, cringing as varlets dragged the severed armor over the grisly joint. "You'll not be fighting for weeks."

"Ah, but what a fight it was, Arthur. Glorious!"

A happy glow filled Arthur's eyes. "Yes. And since you won't be fighting for a few weeks, how about lending me your sword?"

Kay's eyes rolled in exquisite pain as jiggers of spirits were poured over his shoulder. He bucked on the cot. His teeth clenched tightly against the onrush of agony. Then, quieting, he sighed out, "Sure, Arthur. Take it. Take the sword." He weakly lifted his hand from the blade.

Triumphant, Arthur drew out the sword and held it high. "Behold, Arthur of Chertsey!"

Hilarity filled the tent. Kay pounded his fist on the bed.

Arthur looked up, astonished to see that the blade was broken. He brandished little more than a long dagger with an impressive hilt.

Varlets wrestled Kay, struggling to get bandages on his shoulder despite the convulsions of mirth. All around, the wounded and the well fed shrieked in glee.

Arthur tossed the sword hilt to the ground and stalked out.

Horse laughter followed him as he went. He was furious. He felt as though he could set the grass on fire with each angry stomp of his feet. The jeers of his family and the cheers of the crowds melded together into a single maddening keen. The bright morning became a crimson haze. The fairgrounds collapsed into a fiery tunnel. Arthur was dimly aware of great black steeds thundering along jousting lanes beside him; of crowds ranked in stands of rough-sawn ash; of luffing banners and snapping pennants and tilting lances. But these meant nothing. There was no other person in his world. There was only one thing at all—

Excalibur.

Go find yourself a sword. . . .

"I know just where to find myself a sword" growled Arthur. His eyes narrowed, and his teeth clenched. "I know just where."

A black stallion and a bay charger converged beside him. Lances struck shields, slid off to impact breastplates, cracked, splintered, and exploded into millions of wood fragments. The two impaled riders fell from their saddles. One was fouled. His weight dragged his horse into the lane poles. A tangle of black meat and red blood rolled, shrieking, through the smashed pole. The mangled stallion struck the bay and broke its legs. It thrashed to ground. A cloud of dust enveloped the two masses.

The screams of dying horses and dying men shot through the air. They merged with the cheers of the crowd.

Arthur marched obliviously onward. "Think they can keep me from competing—" He passed from the tournament grounds, out beyond the garrison building, and into the market square courtyard. "Think they can make me the jester rather than the king—" Dogged and implacable in anger, Arthur stomped straight for the sword in the anvil and stone.

To one side, a small crowd stood, dutifully listening to the high bishop droning on about the benefits of having a God-blessed king. Ulfius nudged his way up beside the man, tugged the sleeve of his chasuble, and whispered something. The high bishop peered out myopically from under his shock of tonsured hair. He shouted to the crowd, "There! There is the young prince! There is Arthur, son of Uther, heir apparent, warrior extraordinaire, friend of the Church, Chosen of God! Behold! Turn around and see! That man there. The angry-looking one! Hoi, Arthur! Hoi! Look this way. Show the people your noble face."

"Give me a broken sword and think it a joke," he groused to himself. "Think my whole plight a joke—think it's easy to be son of a dead king and grandson of an old lunatic—think they can plan my whole life for me, tell me when I can sit and stand—think I'm going to be that sort of a king, well I'm not!" He lifted his eyes and shouted. "I'm not!"

The crowd around the high bishop followed Arthur. Ulfius and the priests went with them. Even folk from the jousting grounds flooded onto the square.

Arthur walked along the line of folk waiting to make a try at the sword. They stared at him, this angry young squire, much spoken of but little believed. He'd been gazed at like that for months. Now he stared back. Now he met every eye, his own focus intense and piercing. One by one, they looked down.

"Too soon," came a feverish voice beside him. He knew it to be Merlin, matching his stride. "Too soon. There will be war. Kingship cannot be grasped too soon. Loki put you up to this, didn't he? He was in Ector's tent, wasn't he, masquerading as someone else? Don't draw it, Arthur. There will be war."

Without turning to face him, Arthur said, "Yes. There will be war, Grandfather. And I will have this sword to wage it."

"And you will have me beside you," the old man pledged quietly.

Other voices spoke now. Those who had spent a year asking, "Why doesn't he draw the blade?" now murmured in hushed excitement, "He's going to draw the blade. He's going to draw it!"

Currently, an overmuscled Caledonian hauled on the hilt. His boot was planted on the stone and his meaty torso struggled to drag the thing heavenward. The Hebridean Hercules could not budge the blade. A roar broke from his straining lips, and a hiss after that. Then the Caledonian glimpsed young Arthur striding purposefully toward him. Hands trembling and sweaty, the man backed away.

Excalibur called all men, but Arthur, it answered. Arthur it reflected, it desired.

He halted just beside the anvil. Excalibur gleamed before him. It shone with expectation—promising, hopeful, glowing in the presence of its beloved.

Arthur reached out. Goose flesh spread up his arm and across his body. Fingers slid around the hilt and wrapped tightly. He might have prayed in that moment, had he known whom to invoke. Instead, Arthur took a deep breath. The distant din of the marketplace grew silent.

"Excalibur!" Arthur cried, and hauled hard on the hilt.

With a flash like lighting, the sword slid from the anvil and stone and leaped into the sky. The silence of the previous moment deepened. Everyone in the marketplace heard Ulfius speak the final words of his long-planned speech.

"Britannia, behold your king—Arthur!"

Then they all went to their knees. First, the Hebridean Hercules knelt. Next, Merlin dropped down, and the line of waiting warriors. In a great wave, thousands of knees kissed the cobbles. They all dropped—Ulfius and the high bishop, the folk flooding up from the festival grounds, even Kay, who had spent the afternoon gambling in an alehouse. . . . Ector and Diana emerged from their tent to stare into the weird silence.

"He found a sword," Ector said wryly.

Diana's reply was drowned out by a wave of chanting voices.

"King Arthur! King Arthur! King Arthur!"

Arthur's foster parents joined the chant. In moments, it became a deafening shout.

"King Arthur! King Arthur! King Arthur!"

22

Coronation at Caerleon

*A*cclaimed in Canterbury in eastern Britannia, Arthur would be crowned in Caerleon in the west.

The ancient city stood on the edge of Celtic Dyfed, in a firth that joined the midcountry with the Eire Sea. The Romans, in their time, had called the city Isca Silurum, but it was founded long before them. The Celts had arrived at the spot centuries before Caesar and established their city atop a faerìe mound. It was a beautiful spot. The high hill overlooked the wide, clear River Leon. On the far shore, dense forests ran with harts and wolves. On the near shore stood wide plains rich in grain.

Deep history surrounded Caerleon, and deeper legend. Myth would have it that ten thousand Celts had died battling the Tuatha Dé Danann who ruled the hill. When the battles were done, the Celts designed to remain in Caerleon forever. They raised a series of earthwork embankments around the city, topped them with palisades, and enclosed the rest in an inner wall of stone. Rock by rock, they piled jetties out into the Leon to provide defensible harbor to boats from as far away as Iberia and Saxony. Though these defenses fortified the city against human invaders, the Tuatha Dé Danann were all but human. Deep within the tumulus, their catacombs and petraglyphs remained. Fey folk seeped up from the earth like water from saturated ground. They could not be driven from their ancestral home. Nor could the human conquerors. More wars raged through the city. Another ten thousand died. At last, hope came unexpectedly.

Stories told that King Ricford of the Celts one night fell into a well. The currents dragged him down into the tumulus. There, Princess Rhia among the Tuatha Dé Danann witnessed his plight and dove into the waters, dragging him to safety. She nursed him there, and brought him back to health. Rhia knew the elder fey would seek to slay him, but she tricked them, claiming the man had saved her from capture. They feasted the Celtic king and treated with him for peace. He welcomed the offer, on condition that Rhia would serve as his foot-holder and queen.

From that time to the present, Caerleon had been a place where kings were made. It would be no different for Arthur. Ulfius and Merlin had arranged the coronation for spring in Caerleon. Word went out to every noble and petty king in the land, requiring them to attend a parade of fealty. And now, at long last, they had come.

From his lofted chambers in the tower of Castle Caerleon, Arthur watched the kings, their entourages, and their personal retainers arrive. Already, the grassy plains were filled to overflowing with tent camps and cook fires. Forests had shrunk slightly from all the scavenged wood. Arthur studied the encampments, staring along the north road. On horseback, more waves of supplicant kings arrived.

"They seem as much armies as noble retainers," Arthur said as he pulled down the white cuff of his sleeve.

"That's what they are," Ulfius said. The warrior wore his best dress suit. A Pendragon tabard covered a brassy breastplate and tunic of white. He strode to Arthur's side. "But they are your armies, now—or will be after tonight's parade of fealty. It is just as I said—it was merely a matter of reason and right that you should hold this crown. If you had declared war, those armies would have been arrayed against you, not for you."

"The day is not done," Merlin said.

Unlike his comrade, Merlin chose to stay in the shadows. He had been morose since Canterbury. The mage had begun to relapse into his old ways—lost between dream and truth, spending long days in dark incoherence. He whispered incessantly about Tetragrammaton and Loki, saying they plotted against the king. His talk tonight was more of the same.

"Arthur, you must keep Excalibur ever with you, and in

Rhiannon at all times. Your power is greatest when they are together. Do not draw your sword except in direst need, and do not ever be separated from the scabbard. No matter what they say or how they smile, there will be many after your blood today. Without Rhiannon, they might have it."

"Gloom and doom," Ulfius said. He waved a dismissive hand behind him. "Merlin, don't ruin this day. You needn't cast the dark specters of your mind on the bright hopes of the boy—"

"The king," Arthur corrected. "I am eighteen now, Ulfius. I am well versed in Latin and Greek, Gaelic and Saxon. I know my sums and geometries. I am a horse soldier of the highest order, a foot soldier trained in hand-to-hand combat, owner of a god-killing sword and a man-saving scabbard, and heir to the Pendragon." He smiled a rueful sideways grin and gestured expansively to the crowded plains. "Please, do not call me 'the boy' today, or surely I will be slain by my gathered nation."

Ulfius bowed in genuine respect. "Of course, my king. Of course, King Arthur."

"By divine right, by inheritance of the blood and prowess of the Pendragon, by the acclaim of the sword Excalibur, by the joyous will of the people, by the strength of the land, by the approval of the great wizard Merlin, by the sanction of the Church, and by my own sanction as high bishop of all Britannia," the bishop intoned that night in the throne room of Caerleon, "do I hereby declare you to be Arthur Pendragon, king of Britons!"

The bishop lowered a golden diadem, encrusted with brilliant gems of every color, upon the bowed head of the kneeling king.

A hush moved through the watching throng—dukes and counts, princes and kings, noble warriors and footmen, all in splendid attire. They filled the floor of the vaulted space. Their breath rose in ghosts in the cool air of the springtime dusk. Ermine and sable, cashmere and samite, gold and silver—nobles gleamed in the gathering night.

The young king rose. He seemed drawn upward by the crown. His eyes met the clear and joyous gaze of the bishop.

With reverent step, the king strode toward his throne. It was a glorious seat of black-stained oak, high backed and appointed in red velvet. Ornate and ancient, the thing had once held the Caesar himself, and before him the heroes of Dyfed, and before them, the fabled fey kings of the Tuatha Dé Danann. To the throne's left stood Ulfius, the even-handed warrior who had trained the young king. To the throne's right stood Merlin, the odd-headed mage whose mere presence frightened would-be rebels. Between them, Arthur stepped onto the throne dais. His cape dragged regally across the floor. He turned and sank slowly into the seat.

Arthur looked out upon the vast and expectant multitude. There might have been a great cheer then, except that his power was yet incomplete.

A new figure approached, a maiden in white. She was a graceful creature, as young and stunning as the king himself. A devotee of the Pagan powers of the land, the priestess came to the base of the throne. Arthur had never seen so beautiful a woman. Not even his half-sister Morgan could compare to this one. Long brown hair, radiant skin, deep brown eyes. . . . Though no one else was allowed to sit in the presence of the king, this woman sat at the base of the throne. She was the power of the land, the virgin foot-holder.

Arthur consciously slowed his breaths as the priestess slipped his shoe from his right foot. She lifted it into her hands, and set the foot in her lap. This was an act not of submission but of empowerment. Only when his foot was couched in lap of the woman, grounded in the power of the land, was Arthur truly king.

Then the cheers were immediate and deafening.

"Long live Arthur! Long live the king!"

•   •   •

Merlin stood beside the great black throne.

His presence in the shadow of Arthur was as potent as the presence of Excalibur at the young king's back. With sword and sorcerer, Church and land, Arthur could not but be king. Even so, Merlin was present in body only. His spirit wandered interior spaces.

Dream and delirium occupied these days. Words spoken to him drooled nonsensically from the lips of the speakers. Images of half-remembered and unreal things flashed through his mind. For the past year, Merlin had dwelt hard beside the Lethe. He stared through forgetful mists toward the twisting figures on the far shore. He had ventured often into the cave of memory where lay the truth of Excalibur, of himself. He had emerged each time with a battered head and a gnawed tongue.

Even as the throng cheered Arthur, Merlin braced himself in a standing swoon. The very air pulsed with unholy life. Limestone walls breathed slowly in and out. Banners swung on black hammer beams. The very carpet transformed into a blood-red river, flowing down from the seat of Arthur and spreading among the nobles there.

It was a premonition, Merlin knew. It was a vision of the coming war, created by Loki and flowing down from the throne of Arthur. The young king would need Merlin most in that hour, whenever it came. Lying beside the numb and madding spray of the turbid Lethe, Merlin wondered if he would be fit to rise and fight that desperate fight.

Then, something reached up from the very rock beneath Castle Caerleon—not something, but Something—a Presence more real than any of the creatures gathered before the throne. Faintly through the mists of Lethe, Merlin felt a being with many hands and one mind take hold of his feet. He was rooted in place, an old oak tree, alive but unable to move. An essence like sap coursed up into him. Strong tendrils insinuated themselves through his muscles. They wrapped around his leg bones and pelvis and ribs. He was transfixed on a network of lines, as though the ancient leys of the land had been traced across his being.

The Presence spoke. *Why are you here, Merlin?* The voice was multifarious, arising from a thousand throats. It was as strident as the pipes of Eire, as strange as druid song. They were the fey. They were the banished spirits of the old titans and fairies and gods that had once dwelt here, dwelt still in the depths of the land. *Why are you here?*

Power wormed up Merlin's neck and around his troubled mind. Slim fingers slid along the outer edge of his eyeballs. He could hardly form the response. It was only one word, but a sufficient answer. "Arthur."

There was something like dark humor in the tangled tendrils reaching through him. *Why do you dabble with human kings, Merlin?*

The reply to that was as difficult as the first thought had been. "Arthur."

But you, Merlin, the Voice insisted, *you are one of us.*

Merlin clenched his hands into tight fists. He flexed every muscle across his being, squeezing the network of tendrils out of him, back toward the floor. "I am not!"

In that final moment before the Presence released him, it spoke wryly. *You will see. You are one of us, or Arthur is lost.* Then it was gone. It fled away like blood from a severed limb.

Merlin entered a true swoon then. He crumpled to his knees, his hands clutching the young king's throne. Arthur glanced over toward him. Merlin's eyes, rheumy and lost in dark visions, met his, and the old man said simply, "Arthur—"

It was a supreme moment. In the midst of roaring ovations, in the literal crowning instant of Arthur's rise, the man who had been Grandfather and mentor to him fell to his knees in obeisance. The crowd's shouts dropped away to nothing. All ears strained to hear the word from the old man's mouth. It was simply a name, the king's name, spoken with such grave feeling that others in the crowd grew faint.

"Arthur—"

Ulfius stepped from his position beside the throne. "Be-

hold, people of Caerleon, people of Britannia. Behold how
the great wizard worships his king. Come forth, people of
Arthur. Bow before him and do fealty." So saying, Ulfius
himself dropped to one knee beside the throne. In emulation
of Merlin's posture, the warrior clutched the arm of the
throne, bowed his head, and said, "Arthur—"

When he lifted his eyes, he saw that the king did not
acknowledge his gesture. Instead, Arthur's eyes were on
Merlin. The old man trembled. Tears welled in his eyes. He
slumped, boneless, beside the throne.

"Grandfather," Arthur said in sudden concern. "Merlin!"

Ulfius rose. Anger shot through him. This was to be Arthur's moment. This was to secure his throne. To remain
awake for one hour—was it too much to require of the man?
Circling the front of the dais, Ulfius saw that Merlin's state
was worse than usual. Behind his mask of beard and wild
hair, the man's face was ashen. No breath stirred his lungs.
Not a twitch came to those ceaselessly moving fingers.

He lay now in the arms of the priestess foot-holder. She
had moved quickly to catch the falling mage. Daughter of
King Lodegrance of Cameliard, the woman stroked silver
hair away from Merlin's face. She seemed the Virgin holding
the ragged and lifeless Man hauled down from the cross.

Ulfius stared a question at her.

Grim-lipped, the priestess shook her head.

Ulfius nodded.

Arthur gazed in disbelief and horror.

Ulfius gestured armsmen in to bear the mage away. Three
men arrived, wrapped their arms gently about the still figure,
and hauled him into the air. The daughter of Cameliard went
with them. Meanwhile, Ulfius turned to address the murmurous throng. "Come forward, now. Come forward and declare your fealty before the new king!"

As nobles filed into the center aisle, Arthur pulled Ulfius's
sleeve. "What are you doing? What about Grandfather? How
can I receive the nation now?"

"You must," replied Ulfius without a moment's pause.

"You must. Either you become king now, or you never will be king—"

"But, without Merlin—"

"Without Merlin, you are still king. Without Merlin, you still have Excalibur and Rhiannon. Without him you are still the son of Uther Pendragon."

The king's eyes were watery. A tightening of his lower lids held the tears in. Miserable resolve hardened his jaw. "You will send messengers to the healing room, to find out what is happening?"

"Yes," Ulfius promised. "Yes, King Arthur."

Turning around, Ulfius descended the dais, solemnly greeted the first folk lined up there, and asked their names. With elaborate decorum, he addressed the king. "Your Highness, I present Duke Antonius and Duchess Isabelle of Dyfed, our hosts this evening."

Immediately, the duke dropped to one knee and dipped his gray head. "My king!"

The duchess—old and prim and with a grandeur that made her courtly manner utterly reverent—ascended the dais and knelt in the place where the young woman had been. She took Arthur's foot in her own hands, saying, "My king."

Ulfius nodded approvingly, and introduced the next noble couple.

23

Excalibur Born

Merlin walked the labyrinths of dream.
　　Stone walls mazed away around corners.
Windows hung black and empty.
He was naked.
Eyes in distant rooms watched him.
Swords in distant hands waited.

Now and again, a hail of black shafts entered the street where he stood, only to be flash-burned away to nothing. The smell of them was strong in the air, like campfires and lightning. It was that more than anything else—the smell—that told him these were true memories, not delusions.

Insignias of late Roman design were etched into cornerstones and walls and archways, but this place was not Rome. The mosaics in kobold blue and argent and saffron confessed that much. The olive-skinned folk, with their black hair and watchful brown eyes, confirmed it. But they were here in force, the Romans—their shafts soared in flocks down over him. Their leather tasses disappeared around corners. Their sandals, their tunics, their spathas all spoke of Rome, here in the east.

Byzantium—or, what is it called now, Constantinople? No, not so great a city as that. But large, all the same, this place, and eastern, and held by Rome—

Merlin staggered up the street. He could do little else. The mind that remembered it all was not the same as the mind that had lived it all, the shattered consciousness. Then, it had only been step, step, step, step, though now it was walking, staggering. Then, it had only been instinctual roving, like a dog on a scent trail. It was a quest for revenge, a search for the destroyer, the Great Foe. Merlin had wandered the streets for days, seeking. And this day, he sensed his prey near to hand, close and dangerous before him.

He stalked up a rankling road. A two-story house stood at the peak. Roof beams jutted from a block-and-mortar facade. Deep-set windows kept out the harsh sun of summer. As Merlin approached, burlap curtains burst into flame. Their burning tatters revealed a starkly furnished room beyond.

The inhabitant of the place appeared, staring in shock. He was middle-aged and bearded. Sackcloth draped him. Ink blackened his fingers. His back was bent, eyes glassy and myopic. Seeing the famed madman approach, he turned as if to dash up the stairs and fetch something, thought better of it, and fled out a back door. Wood barked against stony walls. Feet sounded on gravel in the alley.

It did not matter. Merlin was not after the man. He did not hate the man—this craven ascetic with girls dancing through his brain—he hated the man's work.

Merlin stepped to the front door. Wood went to cinders before him. Black smoke coursed across the ceiling. He stepped into the room. It was cleanly kept, walls of painted mud, stone floors, a crude pitcher of gray clay, a pair of sandals, and a cot. This last flared in his presence. Canvas luffed with heat. It split. Wooden members cracked and fell away. The sandals burned too. Even the paint on the walls darkened. More smoke spread across the ceiling, seeking escape. Much of it spilled up the stairwell.

Merlin followed. What he wanted lay up there. What he hated—the aggregate foe that had made him a madman. Taking the steps two at a time, he reached the upper chamber.

It was a crowded space—a slanted desk, a writing chair, a stand for inks and quills, shelves loaded with old parchments and papyrus, lexicons and bound books, piles of plain paper. Every luxury in the man's life was lavished on his scribbles. The desk was surrounded with scrolls. Inks filled small stained pots on the windowsill. There were needles and thread for stitching folios; knives and sheers for cutting them, and neat piles of vellum. A number of books lay open on the table's surface. They, and all other inflammables in the room, went up in immediate smoke.

All but one book. At the center of the desk, a thick volume of vellum lay open. Though wreathed in flames, the book did not burn. Merlin approached.

This was the killing thing. This was the murderous book that had brought him to mad ruin. And, worst of all, the monstrous message of his destroyer was written in his own native tongue. It seared into his eyes as his fiery presence destroyed the room all around:

nam et si sunt qui dicantur dii sive in caelo sive in terra
siquidem sunt dii multi et domini multi nobis tamen unus Deus
Pater ex quo omnia et nos in illum et unus Dominus Jesus
Christus per quem omnia et nos per ipsum

Growling in rage, Merlin gripped the edges of the fat volume in his hands and slammed it closed. The report was a thunder stroke. A flaming wind surged off the pages. It blasted up through the burning roof and sent charred beams into the street. Still, the book would not burn.

Merlin yanked it from the desktop and clutched it to his breast. His flesh grew red-hot, a man made of embers instead of skin. Sunlike, he burned, wrapped in holocaustal flame.

But not the cursed book.

Merlin had slain titans. He had wooed nymphs. He had fought beside champions. He had drunk nectar and feasted upon ambrosia, had scaled the highest mountains and plumbed the deeps of the oceans, only to be undone by this single book.

And then it was no longer a book. Somewhere in the storm of fire, in the desperate and shuddering hands that clutched the volume, it had begun to transform. Page melded to page. Vellum became once again vital skin and reshaped itself. Only, instead of flesh, it was silver—quicksilver. It lengthened into a shaft of lightning.

It was a fine blade, a great sword like those borne by Vandals and Visigoths. But it was unlike them as well. There never had been a blade like this before—

"Though originally it was most common, it was reforged to be peerless."

The words came from another place and time, a far-future place, but they rang true. The Latin word for common book was vulgata. The Tuatha word for peerless sword was excalibur.

"Excalibur has been called the Sword of the Spirit . . . and the Sword of the Spirit is the Word of God."

Lifting the blade overhead, Merlin released a fearful cry. "Excalibur!"

"Do not fear, Mage Merlin," said a gentle voice. "Excalibur is safe with the king."

The room that had once burned now melted away. Delusion died. Merlin breathed the air of Britannia.

In place of soot-caked ruins, he lay in an opulent couch. The scribe's room gave way to an antechamber. And instead of fear-eyed Jerome, he stared into the beautiful face of a young woman.

"What . . . What has happened?" he gasped.

Dark-haired and gentle, the priestess fondly stroked his whiskers. "You were overcome in your display of fealty, Mage Merlin."

He blinked, struggling to reassemble his mind from the fragmented flotsam that jostled through his head. "You know me," he said at length, "but I haven't the honor—"

"I am king's foot-holder. I am the daughter of King Cameliard of Lodegrance," said the young lady. "My name is Guinevere."

The man who next ascended the dais was grave of aspect. Eyes like chips of obsidian glinted darkly beneath gray-streaked brows. His nose was as prominent and craggy as a Pictish standing stone, and a peppered beard curled neatly about his broad jaw. The red robe on his back was trimmed in white ermine and lined with sable, and the crown he wore was twice the size and four times the weight of Arthur's own. But instead of ornamental armor, he wore a battle-scarred breastplate, skirt of tasses, and chain trousers. His right gauntlet rested on a sword that was a plain and brutal thing, the sort that Caledonians used to shatter the legs of charging horses. It was the equal in size and heft of Excalibur. His left gauntlet held the reposing fingers of his wife. In gossamer white silks and veils, with hair piled high in silver combs and a silver buckler in the Saxon style across her waist, the woman was a beautiful vision.

"Shall I announce you?" asked Ulfius of the man, meanwhile directing the woman toward the vacant foot-holding spot.

The man pulled his wife back to his arm and said, "You

shall not. I will announce us." He strode straight-away up to the foot of the throne and stood, glowering.

Behind him shouldered two more kings, these without women on their arms. Ulfius recognized them as King Carados of Carados and King Fergus More of Dalriada in Caledonia. Like their predecessor, they wore battle armor. Gauntlets gripped the hilts of great swords. Behind them followed a fourth ruler, the gigantic Saxon King Aelle of Sussex. His belt and helm were hefty ironwork with florid touches matching those in the brooches and belt bucklers worn by the woman.

"A conspiracy," hissed Ulfius to himself. "A military rebellion." Intent on warning Arthur, he hurried up the dais beside the newly arrived contingent. He was too late.

The man in the ermine robe stood unbending before Arthur, and spoke to him in vulgar informality. "Do you recognize this woman, Arthur?" His hand lifted briefly from his sword hilt and gestured to the lady on his arm.

Ignoring the effrontery of their approach, Arthur studied the lady's face. There was something familiar about her elfin nose, her wide brown eyes, the small point of her chin, even the graceful carriage of her neck and shoulders. Still, he was quite sure he had never seen her face. "Honored woman, I fear I do not know you."

"Of course you do not," the man snapped. His voice was loud enough and sharp enough in timbre that the whole room listened to the exchange. "This is Morgause, my wife, daughter to Queen Igraine. Of course you do not recognize her. This would only be your sister."

Arthur's eyes intensified in thought. Instead of the dread the man had hoped to evoke, the young king's face showed happiness. "Mother told me of you, Half-sister. I have met Morgan, but not you. And she told me of your husband, the glorious King Lot of Lothian. Welcome to my coronation!"

King Lot bowed his head before he realized what he had done. "We owe fealty and honor to the true son of Uther by Queen Igraine—were there a true son. Your mother spoke to you of Morgause, but why did she never speak to Morgause of you?"

"I have proofs," interrupted Ulfius, "elaborate and well-demonstrated proofs of the lineage of this man, traced back through Uther and Constantine and even to Caesar himself!"

A derisive laugh came from the king. "Every man in this room and every pig in his holdings can be traced back to Caesar. It means nothing—"

"What of Excalibur?" Ulfius replied. "What of the Sword of the Spirit, and the contest with anvil and stone?"

"I was never allowed a try at the sword," Lot replied. "Nor these men with me. None of the eleven outlying kings were given the chance to draw the sword."

Arthur stood from his throne. His eyes were fixed, immovable, on those of Lot. His young jaw was set in a grim line. Reaching to his back, Arthur drew Excalibur from Rhiannon. The blade hummed in a sudden violent arc. It jabbed down toward Lot.

Roaring in fury, Lot hauled Morgause back from the king. He ripped his own great sword from its scabbard. The bronzed steel was too slow. Lot's sword was still clearing its sheath as Excalibur found its mark. The holy sword sparked in brutal penetration, and sank deep.

A roar of indrawn breath dropped away to silence. The crowd saw—

Excalibur's hilt jutted from the marble floor. It glowed with an alluring light that illuminated Arthur as though he were a saint of old. On the battle armor and swords of the four kings, the light cast a greedy glow. The rulers were at once repelled by and drawn to the radiant weapon. Lot watched it with particular hunger. He held Morgause protectively behind him.

"You may have your chance now, Lot," Arthur said regally. "You and the kings with you. And I will bear this sword personally to the kingdoms of all the outer kings to allow them a chance to draw it. I and my armies will go to them to let them try—and to receive their fealty should they fail."

Lot's gaze darkened. He did not look at the king, focusing on the sword. "I will not submit to this charade of yours. Since when have the kings of this land been determined by hunks of metal in rock? The contest is a vile creation of the vile mage you keep in your pocket. I will not touch the sword and thereby fall beneath the spell laid on all these others. Nor will I bow to a usurper whelp!"

Ulfius growled beneath his breath. "Do not oppose this man, Lot. He is the true king. He bears the true sword. He is sponsored by the greatest wizard who every lived. He has Church and nation behind him—"

"Kingship is not determined by stones and anvils. It is determined by war. And by war, you, Arthur, shall be proven," Lot said. He sheathed his great sword and turned on his heel. The iron ridge of his battle boots scratched a half circle in the floor as he pivoted. Leading the company of rebel kings, he marched down the central aisle of the great hall.

The fealty line parted to let these militants pass. One, and then another of the nobles joined the retreating company.

"Rally them," Ulfius hissed to Arthur. "Rally them, or you will lose them all!"

Arthur cupped a hand to his mouth and shouted, "Go in health, Lot of Lothian. And health to any who dares march with you!"

Without turning, Lot answered in a violent voice, "You would do well to look after your health as well, pretender."

Two more kings added themselves to the growing contingent of defectors.

A moan of dread passed among those gathered. It was the sound of a creature that realizes it is about to be torn in pieces. War, like a black-armored foe, rose palpably in their midst. The silvery shine of state was dimmed by a premonition of battery and blood.

Two more kings followed the rebels.

A divine light flashed before the crowd. Down-turned heads lifted. Metal slid from stone with a sharp shout—an Otherworld call to arms. Before them all stood a vision: Arthur, young and beautiful in his kingly raiment, muscled and noble, eyes flashing like stars, and above his head, suspended as though the very radiance of God, hung Excalibur. The claims of Lot melted away in that holy light. The word "pretender" rang like tin in their ears. This could not be a false ruler. This could be only the true king.

"I bear Excalibur. I am warrior of the people. I am chosen of the Church. I am favored of the mage Merlin. I am King Arthur of Britannia!"

The ovation that answered him was deafening. The line of fealty, which once had faltered on the verge of disintegration, now reformed. Young and old were emboldened by the vision of their king and the unanimity of their nation. The luster of armor returned. Kohl-painted eyes shed their hopelessness and sparkled again. The specter of war shrugged off its funereal aspect and clothed itself in panoply.

24

The Dark Secret of the Sword

*A*rthur strode purposefully into the sickroom where Merlin lay.

The old mage was still weak, his eyes rheumy and swimming with visions. He clutched at the cushions around him as though he feared falling from the feather bed. His clothes had been pulled straight, and his white hair and beard combed gently by the priestess who tended him. As Arthur knelt at the bedside and clasped Merlin's hand, the young king could not keep his attentions from straying to the woman.

So lovely her features, so gentle her manner, so powerful her presence . . . she seemed a living locus of the land.

Tearing his thoughts away from her, Arthur stared into the

weary face of his mentor, his friend. "Grandfather—how do you fare?"

A weak smile moved across the man's lips. "Well enough, Arthur." He coughed miserably. "The question is; how do you fare?"

"Well enough," Arthur replied. "I have the fealty of twenty-five petty kings and fifty-three noble houses. I am king of Britannia."

"What of the others?" asked Merlin. "What of the eleven?"

Arthur's bright visage dimmed slightly. "I go to discuss that matter presently."

"A council of war, yes," Merlin said, coughing violently. "This is the damned hand of Loki at work."

The young woman's face looked troubled.

"Loki? Don't worry about Loki, Grandfather. Right is on our side," Arthur said, all the while staring levelly into the eyes of the woman. "Right and the people and the Church—"

"Yes, the Church—more than you know," Merlin growled in sudden pique. "Damn them all! Loki and Tetragrammaton and the Tuatha Dé! Is every god of every pantheon grasping after you, Arthur?"

A blush crossed the priestess's cheeks.

Merlin clutched her hand in sudden apology. "Forgive me, my dear—"

"What are you talking about, Grandfather?" Arthur asked.

Merlin struggled to his elbows, and the woman deftly placed pillows behind his back. "There is grave news, Arthur. I have seen the origin of Excalibur. The vision almost slew me, but I know the dark secret of the sword."

Arthur's eyes lit up. "Tell me, Grandfather. Tell me! It will make all the difference in the council of war."

"No, you are not to tell the council. This matter must be kept in darkness. Only we three shall know."

"We three?" Arthur asked, puzzled.

Merlin squeezed the woman's hand. "This one has drawn me back from death. She has held my hand and saved me. She knows already, for she heard my ravings. And I foresee that she will be your greatest ally, Arthur." He smiled weakly at the priestess. "Votive of the land, daughter of Lodegrance, heir to the slumbering might of the Tuatha Dé Danann—this is Guinevere."

The woman dipped her head in a graceful bow.

"Guinevere," Arthur whispered in awe. He bowed to her as well. "You cradled my foot—"

"Yes," she said quietly.

"She channels great power, Arthur," Merlin said gravely. "How I wish all your power came through her. But there is also the cursed blade." His mood soured. "Oh, why did I put that god-killing thing in your hands!"

"Speak, Grandfather! Tell me of the forging of Excalibur."

Merlin drew a calming breath. "There was a time, two centuries ago, when the followers of the Nazarene were at war one with another. They had broken into petty kingdoms, just as Britannia has. The Gnostics fought the Arians, who fought the Coptics, who fought the Manicheans, who fought the Donatists, who fought the Catholics. Bishops warred with bishops. Popes warred with popes. Even the first Constantine with his Nicene Creed could not end the struggles, just as our Constantine III could not unify Britannia. They flailed for the hand of the divine, and when they laid hold of air only, they dreamed the divine hand into their own. Such is the fate of all who strive for revelation."

"I remember these lessons, Grandfather," Arthur replied. "In 381, Emperor Theodosius made Christianity the state religion of Rome and forbade Pagan rites."

A jag of agony swept over Merlin's face. He bucked. Guinevere took hold of one of the man's hands, and Arthur the other. A calming energy seemed to flow between the two, through Merlin. His muscles eased. With a ragged sigh, he settled back in among the pillows.

"Yes. I taught you well. But even Theodosius and the pope could not put an end to the battles. The hand of Tetragrammaton did not reach down to them.

"Instead, revelation came in slow and gentle measure to one good monk, alone and starving and flagellating himself.

He was a great lover of books, you see, and had long harbored a passion for the Pagan stories of Homer and Ovid and Virgil, as well as the Hebrew scriptures and the Christian gospels. He became convinced that his desire for the former things was corrupt, evil—and he put away from himself his great library to focus solely on the words of Tetragrammaton." Merlin looked bitter at this turn in the story. "It was a great loss, a great sacrifice, and Jerome—for that was his name—was plagued with thoughts of licentious Jupiter and his succession of lovers. No mater how he tried to shut from his mind the Pagan things, always they returned to him, in the guise of dancing girls." Merlin laughed sadly, and tears filled his eyes. "It was quite a trick to play on a monk."

Guinevere and Arthur only clung to the delirious man.

"And so, Jerome determined to learn Hebrew—the arduous task would occupy his mind and be pleasing to jealous Tetragrammaton. Already, Jerome knew Latin and Greek, of course. And having learned Hebrew, he invented another arduous task—to translate all of the Hebrew and Christian scriptures into Latin." A grave shadow of memory passed over Merlin's teary eyes.

He suddenly reeled, as though struck in the face by an invisible fist. "Jerome did so. He made even the language of Jupiter serve Tetragrammaton. Already, Rome belonged to Tetragrammaton, and now Latin did, as well. It was a bitter, killing thing . . ."

Arthur shook his head, wondering at Merlin's vehemence.

"Jerome had just completed the first version of his translation by the time I had hunted him down. I hated that book, that Latin Bible—what his later works would reproduce as the *Vulgate*. I hated it, and I hunted it down and lay hold of it—"

Arthur was incredulous. "You . . . you touched the original *Vulgate*?"

"More than that, Arthur," Merlin said feverishly. "In those days, I did not simply touch anything. My mere presence burned away whatever would burn. Sight of me slew beggars and kings. Nothing could stand before me, so awful was my power. I did not simply touch things. But the *Vulgate* would not burn. I willed it into oblivion, but the book would not be obliterated. So, I seized it. And in my hands, it transfigured. It went from substance to essence. The greatest weapon of Tetragrammaton became the greatest killing thing I have ever held. In my grasp, the *Vulgate* transformed . . . from word . . . to sword."

Arthur's gaze was horrified, wandering the blankets.

"At your back, my king—like the weighty crucifix of Christ himself—you bear the Sword of the Spirit. You carry Tetragrammaton's god-killing word."

Arthur's eyes grew wide. Letting go the old man's hand, he staggered to his feet. Arthur wavered there for a moment. Then, reaching over his should, he numbly clasped the hilt of Excalibur and drew it forth.

The blade glowed in the darkness of the antechamber. Its cold light made Guinevere seem a statue, a figure of Greek beauty. It cast a sepulchral hue over Merlin.

Arthur peered intently at the blade. "It is the Sword of the Spirit, as you have called it, the Word of God. It is the power of God made manifest." He stepped back from the bed and made a few swings of the blade in the air. "No wonder Wotan coveted it. No wonder he called it a god-killing sword. He knew the jealousy of the God of Israel, of the God of the Christians. He knew that in the hands of another, this sword could kill him."

"Yes," Merlin confirmed. His eyes were drawn to the blade even as he cringed away from it. "And Brigid knew it too. She said it would kill her one day. One day it will kill all gods that oppose Tetragrammaton. But Brigid kept it safe until Wotan threatened at the shores. Then she gave it to you, Arthur—the man who could slay Wotan."

Arthur seemed suddenly weak. His hands trembled on the hilt of Excalibur. His knees folded beneath him. He managed to sheath the blade before collapsing beside the bed.

"This is the fate you see for me, Grandfather?" he asked, panting. "To kill a god?"

Merlin nodded. "Yes, Arthur. But it is worse than that.

You kill one god at the behest of another. You slay Wotan only so that Tetragrammaton may better pull your strings."

Closing his eyes in dread, Arthur slumped onto Merlin's knees. The king was suddenly only an eighteen-year-old boy. His shoulders, broad though they were, could not possibly bear such weight.

Merlin drew trembling fingers through Arthur's hair. "I have brought you to this, Arthur. My madness. I thought I dreamed you. I thought I created you, shaped you so that one day you might save me. But I am a mere man. A madman. A pawn of gods. Tetragrammaton, Loki, even the Tuatha Dé—I have been their pawn, and have made you their pawn too."

Arthur wept quietly into the blankets. "It is though I am Judas, destined by one god to bring another god down to death." Arthur lifted his teary face. "It is too much, Grandfather. It is too much. Ulfius and Ector have taught me to fight men, but no one has taught me to fight gods!"

The old mage's eyes were faraway. "Now you see the destroying secret at the heart of Excalibur. Now you see at what peril the truth comes to light."

Arthur's gaze was bleary. "However will I bear it?"

The answer came not from Merlin, but from Guinevere. Her hand laid hold of his. Her touch was warm. The power that once had coursed from her through Merlin now channeled directly into the young king.

"You need not be a pawn, Arthur," she said. "I will stand with you. We will bear the blasts of gods on all sides, empowered by all, but beholden to none. We will choose our own way, Arthur. We will make a land where no god rules supreme, and all gods live. Use Excalibur to carve out such a kingdom, and I will bring forth the sleeping power of the land to make that kingdom thrive. Together, we will make a place as has never been before on the ravaged earth."

Arthur hung on her words. He drew in the scent of her. Courage came with it.

"Yes, Guinevere. I see it now. I see this heavenly city brought down to earth. We will build it, you and I. Yes."

His jaw hardened in sudden resolve. "I will bear it, Grandfather. I will bear this unbearable weight." Arthur rose, still holding Guinevere's hand. "We will bear it."

At last, hope glimmered in Merlin's hopeless gaze. "Yes. You will."

King Arthur took a deep breath, and the events of the last hours cascaded down around him. "But before I fight gods, I must fight men. Forgive me Grandfather, Guinevere. I must go now to my council of war. When you have regained your strength, Merlin, come join the council." The king looked to Guinevere, bowed before her, and kissed her hand. "And, beautiful priestess, come with him. I need your strength as much as he does."

At last, he let go her fingers. Turning, he strode from the room.

Merlin and Guinevere watched him go.

The priestess shook her head and said quietly, "He is so beautiful and young. He is so precious and vulnerable. But he is strong, as well. Stronger than even you believe, Merlin. He can bear that sword. I have seen it."

"If anyone can bear that sword, it is Arthur." Mustering his will, Merlin rolled to sit on the bed. He heaved an anguished sigh and braced himself on trembling arms.

Guinevere moved to his side. "Wait, you are too weak for the king's war council."

Pushing away her gentle hand, Merlin struggled to his feet. He clutched the staff standing beside his sickbed. "It is not to his war council that we go, but to another. Arthur alone can save us, perhaps, but in this hour, you and I alone can save Arthur."

So saying, the mad mage Merlin swept his cloak out around Guinevere. He grasped her in its dark folds and whisked her into the deepening night.

The edges of reality swam away. Sight lines folded about themselves and disappeared. Only blackness remained. In that blackness hung Merlin and Guinevere. For a moment, only they two existed.

Then figures impressed themselves on the night—wedges of light like welts rising. Here, they formed into a pile of wood, wreathed in flames. There, they took the semblance of legs crossed beneath hunched bellies. A ring of attentive faces surrounded Merlin and Guinevere—surrounded not them, but the man who stood on the opposite side of the fire—Lot of Lothian.

The rebel king gestured upward, his fingers rising among sparks and floating embers. Firelight brightened the angry arches of his eyes. It imparted heat to his words. "This pretender, this lowland bastard, unproved in battle, untried in the affairs of state, a mere boy—likely a mere virgin—this sword-pulling and robe-wearing and magic-leaning child. He dares to rise to command our fealty? He, who has not led an army or taken a fortification or even brokered a peace—he wants to take hold of all this isle by fiat? No conquering Caesar, no campaigning Constantine, not even a Vortigern, let alone an Uther. This lad—"

"This lad—" interrupted Merlin, now full-formed beside the bonfire. All eyes turned with shock toward him. Their gaze bore Merlin down. The bedraggled mage leaned heavily on Guinevere. "This lad does not so much want this isle, but must take it. He takes it to save it from falling to shards on the floor. No one can stop the hammer of Wotan descending on us. No one can stop it, but this lad—this man, this *warrior* with his holy sword and his armies and his church and nation and mage—yes, his mage—he can withstand that hammer blow! He does not want this isle, but he must take it. And you must take him, or be destroyed!"

King Lot stalked around the fire toward Merlin. The man's face was demon-bright. "Withstand the hammer blow? You cannot stand yourself, master mage. Only by this little woman, here, do you stand. If the mighty Merlin cannot stand, how stands the straw man he has built up? And if Arthur can withstand the blow of Wotan's hammer, why does he fear me, fear me enough to send a dotard to plead for peace?"

Merlin began a grumbling response, but a racking cough caught it short.

Guinevere flung back the cloak and stood boldly forth. "Arthur does not plead for peace," she said. "He does not plead for anything. He warns you to submit. He forbids you to deny. He promises your damnation should you refuse. Swear your fealty, or die!"

The ring of faces became a ring of blades. Steel hissed out all around Merlin and Guinevere.

Lot's sword was foremost among them. He advanced. The defiance in his eyes had deepened to hate. The king lofted his blade and brought it hacking down across Merlin. The other swords converged.

Even as steel bit through fabric, Merlin wrapped his cloak again about Guinevere and growled an arcane command. Those scores of blades became a school of darting trout, and they swam away. Darkness swept over them.

They reappeared in a distant place, in a very different council of war. No cold canopy of night. No surrounding army. No swords painted the color of fire. Instead of dark-browed warriors in battered armor, here were gathered elegant nobles.

At table sat Ulfius, Ector, Igraine, Kay, and forty others sworn to the king. At the head of the table stood Arthur.

Arthur rested one foot on the great chair meant for him and leaned over a map. "Here, Lot's armies are encamped, and there, the King of Carados, and there the other rebels." He gestured expansively to a swath of forest atop a ridge. It lay between Castle Caerleon and the rebel troops. A ravine lay just beyond the forest. Only the Dyfed main road bridged the ravine.

"Here is their greatest asset. This damned ditch. As long as they linger on the other side of this and we on our side, they do not need a castle, and a castle does us no good."

All eyes turned as Merlin and Guinevere took solid form

beside Arthur. The mage was weak. He clasped Guinevere's arm to remain upright.

"Now, Arthur. You must muster your forces and charge, now, while the rebels are in disarray."

Arthur turned. He grasped Merlin's arms and helped Guinevere ease the man into the chair. The king's hand touched the maiden's, and again that strange energy moved between them.

"What has happened to you? I said not to come until you were well—"

Merlin gasped for breath, unable to respond.

Guinevere broke in. "We went to see King Lot. We went to warn him from his treacherous course. He would not submit. So, we inflamed his anger in hopes that fury would burn away his well-laid plans. It did. He tried to kill us. Merlin whisked us away at the last, but these spells he casts—they draw the life out of him."

"Attack now," Merlin repeated, disheveled in his manifold robes. "Attack now. I will join you when I can."

For a solitary moment, Arthur stared into the face of the weary mage. Then he whispered. "Rest, Grandfather. I will see you once this battle is done, and then we will both be well."

Merlin grasped Arthur's arm. "Keep Rhiannon ever with you. Do not wield Excalibur until you are most sorely pressed. Pray to the God of the sword for success."

"You will be my success," Arthur assured.

A rueful darkness passed across the man's face. "Do not pray to me, Arthur. My day is done now forever."

25

In the Traitors' Camp

*A*rthur vaulted into the saddle of his black charger. Like
a fiendish incarnation of the night, the beast stomped
the cobbles of the bailey.

Around him, a thousand more horsemen climbed into their
saddles. Two hundred riders from Chertsey were there, and
two hundred from Tintagel in Dumnonia. Caerleon's own
blackguard of three hundred fifty made up the bulk of the
forces under Arthur's immediate command, with ten petty
kings and their ranks providing the final two hundred fifty
mounted warriors. Beyond the walls of Castle Caerleon, another five hundred loyalist horsemen and one thousand infantry readied their own attacks. Four great kings and six
petty ones quietly mustered forces in their encampments.

Despite their varied livery, each warrior loyal to Arthur
wore on his helm a sash of gold satin, an emblem torn from
the king's best robes of state.

"My power, my will, rides with each man this night," Arthur had said in the council meeting. He had torn his robe
down the middle and stepped from it, "and let this be the
sign of it. When this battle is won, when the rebel kings are
cowed into submission, let each man return to the throne of
Arthur and surrender his gold sash, that a new, splendid robe
be sewn from strands of individual heroism and devotion!"

And so, it was done.

A total mounted corps of two thousand would converge
from three directions on the broad encampments of the rebel
kings. Arthur, Ulfius, Ector, and Kay rode in the vanguard.
They would strike first, slay quickly, and receive the brunt
of the counterattack. Then, Brastias would thunder down
from the meadow road into the flank of Lot's forces and hew

inward. A third contingent, anvil to Arthur's hammer, would surge up behind the rebels and cut off escape. Even so, these three divisions, totaling two thousand, were only a third the fighters in Lot's army. Arthur's forces would need their every advantage.

Snatching up a torch, Arthur lifted the fire high and cried, "Britons, friends, true-hearts, all. Since my father's fall, we have fought ceaselessly and for nothing, beset on all sides by a tide of evil, incapable of stemming the flood. The bravery of every man was wasted on the bravery of every other. Brother fought brother, Briton fought Briton. Tonight, though, we band together. Tonight, we stem the tide of evil. Tonight we ride down out of darkness to disperse darkness, and light will dawn on a new Britannia. Dawn will come, bathed in hope, brighter than a dream, all from the dark work we do tonight.

"Come, Britons! Fight with me!"

A roar went up from the men. The walls of the bailey caught up the shout and sent it wheeling into the heavens.

Arthur waved the torch, gathering Ulfius to his right, Ector to his left, and Kay behind him. Each snatched up a torch of his own. "Stay near to me."

"You stay near to us," Ector said, concern in his voice.

"Yes, Brother. Keep between our swords."

Arthur smiled fondly. "I may be son and brother to you, but to Britannia, I am king. You will stay near me. The light of our fires will guide the men—these lights and the staring moon. Let Lot think the thunder of hooves comes from but a small parley company, with king and retainers in the lead. We will break from the forest road into the heart of the camp and be hundreds among them before any has sense to draw sword."

He signaled for the castle gates to rise. With loud report, they ascended.

Ulfius studied the seated king. "What is this new blade you bear? Why not draw Excalibur? Let the people see it lead."

"I lead," Arthur reminded, "not my sword. Excalibur will

do battle when the time is right." So saying, he drove heels into his charger's sides. The beast leaped eagerly toward the yawning gates. Arthur thundered through the space.

Ulfius was ready for the quick departure. He kicked his mount to a gallop and matched Arthur's speed. Torch fire rattled angrily overhead. Ulfius hunched over the pelting steed. Ector gained the king's left flank. Kay came with him. Horsemen filled the arched passage behind. Hoof reports crowded the air. Muscular and sinuous, Arthur's cavalry rushed out beneath the starry heavens.

Arthur charged down the Dyfed main road. Stones gave way to gravel, to mud, and last of all to trampled, dewy grass. Out across the Caerleon Valley they rode, amid eroded hills that gave into the chill black river. Ahead, the road topped a rise and delved into a primeval forest. Black with night, the forest lay like a thick quilt on the rill. The charger raced up the road. Torchlight cast the shadows of horses in a centipede around them. Ring mail and breastplate flashed beneath the roiling light. Cloaks fluttered behind the four riders. Strips of gold satin streamed from their helms.

"Stay tight!" Arthur signaled above his shoulder.

He led the contingent over the ridgetop and into the vast forest. His torch splashed orange light against oak trunks and weeping boles of elm.

Ahead, at the eaves of the forest, a lantern bobbed uncertainly. Its bearer held the light high in the dark, his face straining to see. Eyes grew wide in alarm. The lantern dropped to the ground and lit the soles of retreating boots.

"They know we are coming," Ulfius shouted.

"Yes, but they do not know how fast," Arthur replied.

He kicked his mount to full gallop. The tattered flames around his torch almost failed to hold on.

Ulfius, Ector, and Kay paced him. The main column charged as well. This was the moment of greatest jeopardy. Here, in the moonless night, if a single steed stumbled, all those behind would tread upon it and fall. Even so, Arthur's pace only redoubled.

The tiny snick of arrows came from either side of the road.

Arthur and his company passed by unharmed, but behind them, men and horses shrieked as the shafts sank into them.

"A trap?" Ulfius shouted.

"It no longer matters," Arthur replied.

His horse vaulted over the guttering lamp left by the sentry. He broke free of the forest. There, in the swale before him, a vast army camped—six thousand strong amid tents glowing with candle and flame.

Already, the sentry had reached the camp. Already, warriors stumbled, half-dressed, from their tents. Some struggled futilely to haul saddle and halter from their gear, only to stop, drop leather, and draw steel.

Arthur's horse ate up the ground between him and the first such warrior. At full gallop, he rode down the man. Hooves bore him under. Arthur held to the horse with legs only, torch in one hand and sword in the other. The second warrior he met was torn in half by the king's sword. The horse barged through a tent, trampling two more.

A pair of warriors rose up before him.

Keeping the first at bay with his whirling torch, Arthur smashed steel on steel with the other. Blades raked together. Arthur drove his beast forward, backing the man against a tent's outer wall. A thrust of Arthur's blade brought a fountain of blood from the rebel's eye. He sprawled onto the canvas.

Arthur's torch flung back the other man's sword. Another swipe lit his cape. Burning cloth caught hold of Arthur's torch and wrenched it from his hand. In flames, the rebel tumbled onto the tent. It became a pyre for him and his comrade.

Arthur turned, triumphant. Only then did he see his own forces, mired in battle hundreds of feet behind him.

Ulfius and Ector each fought two men from horseback. Kay's horse, struck from under him, lay kicking as he fought onward. All held aloft their torches and peered hopelessly into the dark to find their king.

Backlit by the burning tent, Arthur signaled them, but they did not see.

He turned his mount, only to face a wall of Lot's infantry, closing in with swords.

Ulfius reined his steed in a stomping circle. His spatha cut a wide swath around him. It hewed Lot's men like a scythe reaping grass—except that grass does not scream. And with each scream, more rebels poured from the tents. Meanwhile, the advance of loyal horsemen had slowed to a trickle.

"Where are the rest?" Ulfius cried out.

"Mired," Ector shouted back. He was huge beside his fallen mount. Rebels lay in a bulwark before him, paying pound for pound in human flesh for the horseflesh they had killed. From one of these foes, Ector had wrested a sword. He paired it with his own gladius for tandem attacks. Two Lothians met simultaneous ends before he could draw breath to continue. "Each horse that falls blocks five more."

"And the arrows keep coming. Crossfire," Kay roared nearby, also fighting afoot. He had dropped his torch to allow him two hands on the great sword he swung.

"You two," Ulfius ordered, "find three other unhorsed warriors. Lead them back to the woods and clear out the archers."

Ector finished one foe and took on another. "And leave your numbers diminished here?"

"Clear out the forest, and we'll have plenty of horsemen," Ulfius replied. "I'll take the rest deeper."

"Deeper?" Ector asked.

"Arthur is ahead there, somewhere." Ulfius drove heels into the sides of his mount and waved a torch to rally the others. "To me!"

His steed clambered forward through a wave of rebel infantry. Barded shoulders bore many down. Ulfius's spatha cut through more. The surge of riders in his wake plunged through the rebel line. With only the light of that single torch, orange across desperate eyes and savage helms, they fought past an overwhelming foe.

Ulfius's steed was as much a fighter as he. It used hooves

and flanks and even the violent strike of forehead and pole. It kicked embers from smoldering fires into the charging rebels. It churned tents under its stomping feet. It shrieked in ears and sent men recoiling from its demonic charge.

Twenty horsemen made their way through a welling tide of rebels. Half-armored, half-dressed, half-armed, and on foot, the Lothians could not stand against them.

"Yes, but what good is any of it," Ulfius wondered through gritted and bloodied teeth, "if the king we fight for is dead?"

Arthur was battered and weary in the midst of the rebel army, but alive.

That first mob had cut his horse from beneath him and spilled him to the ground. Scrappy and quick, Arthur had scrambled from the tumbling creature and dashed among the host. There, with dagger and stealth, he made silent work of eight men before the others tracked him down. In the dark confusion, they could not seize him. He tossed dirt in the eyes of any who came too near. He hurled gravel straight overhead so that the descending volley would make each man whirl in fright and slay his comrades. They did so with alacrity. The wall of rebels was soon no more than a field of dead.

Arthur, at last unable to hide in the crowd, faced down the final three warriors.

They surrounded him, three blades to one, and often won through with stunning, bruising attacks. Arthur would have been minced thrice to bone had it not been for the quiet magic of Rhiannon. The scabbard stitched up whatever wounds the attackers landed. Triumphant cries had come with the first successful strikes. Now, the men fought in wary dismay. Arthur repaid blow for blow, himself never tiring or succumbing. Blood hung in red rags across the rebels, but Arthur's armor was clean.

One great sword broke through Arthur's defenses and clove hauberk, shoulder plate, and muscle down to grate across bone. The blade yanked free, but Arthur still stood.

There came no fountain of gore, no staggering and gurgling.

The warrior hissed, "What sort of deviltry . . . ?"

"Merlin." Arthur's laughter rang in his helm. "He has cast a spell over us. . . . We shall never bleed. . . . We shall never fall."

Palpable dread shivered through them all. Their swords converged, but with less heart behind them.

Arthur smiled grimly as he batted them back. "And the high bishop likewise. . . . Any rebel slain unrepentant . . . shall be struck from the Lamb's Book . . . and consigned to the devil and his angels."

"Lies!" shouted one of the men. He lunged inward, taking the bait.

Arthur was ready. He stepped aside. The man over-balanced. As he staggered past, Arthur drew his sword across the man's helm straps, slicing them and opening the rebel's throat. " 'Timete eum qui postquam . . . occiderit habet potestatem . . . mittere in gehennam!' " Arthur growled.

"He's casting a spell!" one of the other two shouted.

"He's summoning Satan!" the other replied.

They turned and fled into the raging night.

Arthur hissed. He flung back his visor and dragged the draping sweat from his brow. All around him, the dead and dying lay. Beyond the gasping ring of them, tents burned and men ran and horses shrieked and reared. Campfires cast scimitars of light over rushing figures. Moonlight set cold shards of ice across disheveled hair. Lot's men struggled toward the mounted warriors at the head of the camp. In the half-light, it was horse not livery that marked out which side was which.

The fact that Arthur was on foot made him virtually invisible.

"Invisible, and impervious to sword strokes," Arthur mused breathlessly. To return to the fore would be pointless, now. To continue on, though, to reach the fire where the traitors had met, to face down Lot himself—"Perhaps this war will be concluded tonight."

Shaking off his fatigue, Arthur gazed across the encampment. The highest ground lay to the north, above a small brook. The tents there were more commodious than those below. The fires had been stoked since the attack. That was where Lot would be.

"Watch after your own health, King Lot of Lothian."

Though the council fire burned bright against the roaring night, Lot did not remain beside it. He stood in the shadowy lee of his personal pavilion, fixing dark-trained eyes on the battle. The line was barely holding. Some thousand of the infantry had roused and armed themselves and reached the conflict. More were on the way every moment. Meanwhile, Arthur's heavy cavalry poured mercilessly down from the forested main road. Runners reported that the archers in the woods were dead, to a man. Worse, a line of mounted warriors stretched back to the castle.

"A thousand mounted troops," Lot growled. "Has he put every bootblack on a swayback mare and sent it out to fight?" He had not expected such a quick or awful attack from Arthur. It was bold and brilliant. There was more to this boy than met the eye. And these were only the cavalry. What if he had infantry lined up too?

"Your Highness, King Lot," came a voice in the night. A panting messenger knelt in obeisance before the king. "I have news from the rear."

"Speak," Lot commanded.

"Fergus More of Dalriada, Galem of the Northern Picts, and King Aelle of Sussex have each handily escaped the attack. Their reinforcements are expected any moment. Your men and Carados of Carados should soon gain their aid."

Lot looked out toward the north end of the road. "Yes. Even now, our allies arrive."

There, to the northeast, a new contingent of infantry marched. They moved rapidly, a gigantic millipede. Without pause, the column slithered from the road and out through the camp. They slashed tent cords and set fire to canvas.

Swords flashed in the night, and sleepy soldiers fell, half-garbed, in sloppy piles.

"Betrayed!" the runner gasped.

"No," spat Lot. "Not betrayed. Those aren't our allies. They are Arthur's. Go. Sound the alert. Order a counterattack in the northeast."

The runner blinked young eyes in the bald moonlight. "Will we prevail tonight?"

Lot struck him on the face, and sent the messenger sprawling. "In this camp alone we have twice their forces. When Carados and Aelle and Galem arrive, we'll have triple their numbers. Now, go!"

Even as the runner clambered to his feet and fled off through the embattled camp, Lot strode from the shadow of his pavilion to the stables. He found his horse. It was saddled, barded, and ready for battle. The beast stomped impatiently as the king pulled the reins from the post. He mounted and turned the white creature around.

Arthur would be down there, in the thick of the fighting. He would be down there, and with his glorious sword, would be as obvious as a firefly. It would take but a single good stroke to slay him atop his horse and bring all this nonsense to an end—and bring the sword Excalibur into King Lot's hands.

Kicking his steed to a gallop, Lot said, "Death is coming for you, young prince."

Arthur had an easy enough march from the middle of the encampment to the base of the hill where Lot's pavilion stood. Mayhem and darkness covered his trail. The pavilion itself was no better protected. All the armsmen had flocked to the fight. Despite a blazing bonfire, not a soul occupied the grounds. Not even Lot.

Arthur cursed under his breath. Still, if this were the king's pavilion, there would be arms and armor within—things that would melt well on a bonfire. And, there would be maps and war plans, registers listing units and commanders, information about stores of arms and food. Though he had hoped to face down Lot himself in this space, to lay hold of such critical information would be almost as great a boon.

Dragging off his Pendragon tabard and unlacing his royal helm, Arthur ran fingers through his sweat-tousled hair. The quickest and darkest approach lay just ahead, up the steep embankment to the corner peg of Lot's pavilion. A quick knife cut to the canvas and he would be within. Leaving helm and tabard where he dropped them, Arthur clambered up the rubble-strewn slope. He clawed his way to the base of the tent. Drawing a dagger from his side, he punched it into the tent wall and drew downward. With a final look behind him, Arthur slid into the darksome space.

One person *did* remain in the pavilion . . .

A tremendous force struck Arthur on the back. He sprawled to his face amid pillows. He tried to flip over, but his attacker was too forceful. A powerful hand grasped one gauntlet and thrust it up behind his shoulder blades. Arthur groaned as he wriggled his hand out of the war glove. One-handed, he pushed himself from the floor. A foot caught him square in the back, and he fell again. Then, there came a wrenching motion. Something round-edged and wooden struck him in the head.

Arthur went black.

26

Merlin and the Death of a God

Ulfius and his force had pushed past the main battle and into the center of the encampment. With hooves and blades they made their way.

A small contingent of rebels had broken away from the main force to engage them, but the rebels were on foot, without a commander or orders. They fought desperately, trying to keep the loyalists from reaching King Lot. They needn't have.

King Lot came to them. He rode a white horse that flashed boldly. He gathered warriors to him as he came. Lot drew these men as Excalibur had, a vision of purpose and victory. By the time Lot and his private force had reached the invaders, rebels outnumbered loyalists.

"Break through to the king!" Ulfius shouted, leveling his blade above the tossing mane of his mount.

As if inspired by this command, the creature reared. It brought its fore hooves cracking down on the heads of two rebels. The beast bounded into the space they vacated. A pair of horsemen shouldered up beside Ulfius's mount and cut through the lines.

Eager for the fight, Lot kicked his steed forward. The horsemen converged at a canter. Sword met sword, conveyed on the might of the war steeds. For their part, the war horses barged and shrieked and bit. Black horse and white boxed head to head, their eyes blood-red in the light of dying fires.

Aback them, king and warrior traded blows. Spatha crashed with great sword, the former light and deft, the latter heavy and devastating.

Lot brought his blade hammering down. Ulfius caught the thing with the edge of his sword. Sparks rained from skittering metal. The great sword grated near the spatha's pommel. Ulfius used the added leverage to fling the point away and jab inward. The tip of the spatha slashed open Lot's tabard, but stopped at the hauberk beneath.

"You fight well, for so young a king," Lot allowed.

Within his helm, Ulfius smiled. *Let him think this is his showdown with Arthur. Let him tire himself until all his reserves are spent, and then Arthur can come to finish the job.* Raising his voice slightly so as to sound like the young king, Ulfius replied, "You are finished, King Lot. Even now, loyalists march from northeast and northwest upon your camp. Surrender, and save yourself and your men."

"Never!" Lot shouted. He underlined the refusal with a violent sweep of his blade.

Ulfius lofted his own sword. His horse barreled into the

white steed. A shout came as edge struck flat. The unsteady weight of the beasts threw Lot's sword off its mark. Deflected, it struck the barded rump of Ulfius's mount. Angered, the beast gave a mulish kick that tore a rent in the haunch of the white horse.

Lot growled, struggling to pull his blade back for another attack. While it was trapped, Ulfius chopped viciously at the laces holding the king's helmet in place. Three leather thongs burst open. Ulfius levered his sword upward to fling the king's helmet off.

A surge of rebel cavalry swept up suddenly around them. The sheer press of horseflesh and steel forced Ulfius back.

Reeling, Lot dragged his great sword up beside him. "Surrender, Arthur!" he called to his retreating foe. "Even now, the armies of the five join my one army. And more come."

In a thicket of dancing swords, Ulfius struggled to hear the king.

Lot raged, "These riders slew your northeastern army. Your northwestern will die too. Surrender, Arthur! Save yourself. Save your men!"

Just before the vicious fray pushed Ulfius beyond the reach of words, he shouted. "I am not Arthur! And Arthur will never surrender. Never."

Then there was no more time for words. All was steel. Ulfius's band of thirty had shrunk to twenty, and they were hard pressed by a corps of more than fifty. Hemmed all around, the loyalists made a ragged retreat toward the main body of the fight.

As they withdrew over tents and trampled campfires, Ulfius saw King Lot, sitting his bloodied horse in dread stillness. He had flipped the visor from his face and looked out dispassionately over the battle. A satisfied smile crossed the king's lips.

Between sword strokes, Ulfius saw why. Most of Arthur's cavalry had been cut from their horses. They now fought desperately on foot. To the northeast, Arthur's infantry had turned about to meet an onslaught of greater numbers pouring down the main road. They were retreating toward the backs of the main battle, and soon would be fighting on two fronts. The army of the northwest was similarly engaged, though already whole segments of the loyalist line were collapsing or turning to flee.

Astride his white horse, King Lot of Lothian leaned his head back and laughed heartily.

Ulfius continued his grim sword work, slashing the arm from one opponent only to have two more ride in to take his place. Blades jabbed past his defenses. They ate away at tabard and ring mail and breastplate, all.

"Arthur," he rasped out, suddenly uncertain. "Arthur, do you yet live?"

Bloodied and exhausted, a messenger trundled into the antechamber where lay Merlin Magus, the last hope of Britannia.

The mad mage languished in a fitful coma. The covers about him were torn in disarray. Here and there, small coils of smoke rose toward the dark vault above. Embroidered pillows smoldered beneath ragged white hair. There would have been a full-fledged fire among silken veils but that Guinevere sat beside the bed and doused flames with a pitcher, cups, and a basin.

The messenger stood only waist high. Dwarf, he was called—Spawn of the Fey. Despite his height, Dagonet had learned to ride a full-sized horse and wield a dagger as though it were a sword. He'd been in the thick of battle when Ulfius chose him to take back the message.

Dagonet strode to the bedside and clutched Merlin's robes. He shook the man. "Awake, Merlin," he hissed. "Awake."

Guinevere leaned close. "He has not awakened since Arthur charged into battle."

The dwarf looked up, eyes intense beneath a shock of black hair. "I bring urgent news of the battle. News from Ulfius."

A decision formed in Guinevere's worried eyes. She leaned down to Merlin, clutched his shoulders, and whispered gently into his ear. "Wake up, Grandfather. There is news of Arthur. Wake up."

Like a swimmer rising through a deep black pool, Merlin held his breath, clutched his arms to his sides, and arched his neck upward. Even his tattered, smoldering robes seem to ripple with the streaming flood.

"He is struggling against nightmares," Guinevere said.

In time, Merlin's rigid stillness softened. He hungrily gasped air and thrashed against Guinevere's hold.

She did not release him, speaking soothingly into his ear. Despite her efforts, five little blue flames leapt up from the tiptoes of his left foot.

Wide-eyed, Dagonet backed away.

"Yes, Merlin, yes. Guinevere is here," she said quietly. "Breathe a little. Just breathe a little. Everything will be all right."

"In fact," the dwarf interrupted, "the news I bear would indicate otherwise."

Merlin ceased his struggles. The fire left his toes. He opened his eyes and blinked a silent thanks to Guinevere. In a ragged voice, he asked, "What news?"

The dwarf cleared his throat. "Ulfius and his forces are hard-pressed. When I was dispatched, he was being pushed back toward the ravine. In the northeast and northwest, the armies of our allies have been routed. And, worst of all, Arthur is missing."

Merlin sat bolt upright. Though the flame was gone from his feet, blue fire snapped and danced between his eyelashes. "He has been captured!"

Dagonet bowed politely. "We do not know his fate."

"He *has* been captured," Merlin repeated with certainty. He trembled as though he could feel the cold bite of shackles on his own arms and legs.

"If this is his fate," Dagonet replied solemnly, "then we know the fate of the rest of us, as well."

The flames in Merlin's gaze went from kobold blue to a sickly green. "Yes . . . the fate of the rest of us." He stared beseechingly into Guinevere's eyes. "We almost arose, didn't we, my dear? We went from mad heaths to Castle Caerleon. My dreamy deliriums became for a time true. But only for a time. The child of Uther, a child of trickery and illusion, became for some moments the true king of Britannia. But if he is gone, now—if my grandson, my Arthur is gone—" He lapsed into gibbering. His fingers moved in manic little convulsions on his lap. "Arthur . . . my Arthur . . ."

"He is missing, Merlin," Guinevere said in a quiet and urgent voice, "perhaps captured. But until we know, we must fight for him."

The old man reached his hands out imploringly. Green flame arced finger to finger. "I cannot fight . . . I cannot even stay awake . . . too weak to stand . . . but in dreams. . . ."

A stern light crossed her face. "Then fight in dreams, Merlin. Fight in your dreams. It was there that you found Excalibur, and there that you found Arthur. Fight in your dreams, Merlin, and find yourself."

He shook his head with the fury of a terrier shaking a rat. "Too deep . . . too dark . . . it almost slew me."

"If you do not find yourself," Guinevere said flatly, "we are all dead anyway."

Merlin plunged back into the deeps. It took only a moment. There was no watery journey. There was no cave wall dancing with shadows. Now, there was only a deep shaft, conformed to his very figure. He plunged.

And then he struck bottom.

The scripture-sword. I hold it in my hands, the god-killing blade that is to be called Excalibur. I hold it in my hands, in that burning room where Jerome translated it.

Paint smolders on mud walls. Windowsills stream smoke into the air. The bright sky shines overhead through a disintegrating roof.

I turn. The blade is beautiful and white-hot. It is the glorious weapon of God the persecutor, JHVH the killer. And now it is mine. With this sword, I can never be killed. With it, I can slay the legions that chased me from Rome, from my own home. With it, I can return in glory, can reclaim the empire, the kingdom lost to me.

Constantine had done it. The emperor had called the warring bishops to Nicaea, and the Nicene Creed became an assassin's dagger in the hands of JHVH. With it, JHVH killed Diana and Athena, Apollo and Venus, Mercury and Mars. With it, JHVH slew the whole pantheon and flung their bodies from Olympus and took it over as his own. He won the legions of Rome, turned the naiad pools into baptismals and the dryad trees into crosses. JHVH took up residence in the hearts and dreams and prayers of the people. No longer did folk think to entertain gods unawares, but angels. No longer did they eat ambrosia but unleavened bread, nor drink nectar but the Blood of Christ. Constantine had been the worldly ruler who had gained JHVH his heavenly throne.

And then Emperor Theodosius had assured the new kingdom. He outlawed the former gods. Not even a pinch of incense anymore. The puny Creed had been a mere dagger. The laws of Theodosius had been a spatha.

But JHVH was greedy. He sought a greater weapon yet, and Jerome had fashioned it for him. It was a book complied of half a hundred books and translated into the empire's tongue: Latin. The Nicene Creed had been but a dagger, but the Vulgate would be a great sword.

And now, the sword is mine.

Dazzled by the beautiful blade, I hold it before me. I descend the smoky stairway. Walls burst into flame. I feel their enraged heat. It is a purifying blaze. The stairs curve and open outward into a blackened room. I cross beneath dissolving joists and between slumping walls. I reach the doorway and emerge into the cobbled street.

There, a legion awaits me. Spears raised high, they block all escape. They hold their curved scutum shields in a wall before and atop their phalanxes. And, in their midst, Jerome stands.

Thin and angry in the robes of an ascetic, he shouts, "Slay

him! Slay this demon. He has destroyed the word of God!
Slay this son of Satan!"

"Son of Satan!" I roar. "Son of Satan? I am not Satan!
You, of all people, should know me, Jerome—Latin scholar
Jerome!"

The man stares in open-mouthed amazement. With imploring eyes, he considers my bearded and glorious visage,
my figure robed in light, sword uplifted.

"You are the one who finally killed me," I shout. "You
and your book!"

"Jupiter!" Jerome gasps in realization. He crumples to
his knees before me, before the fallen god. "Jupiter!"

The legionnaires quaver.

"Yes," I say, "it is I, Jove!"

As I speak the words, the burning house slumps to ground
behind me. Cinder and flame leap outward in a rolling corona.

Yes, it is I. Jupiter. I, who had been the king of the Roman
heart and mind, who had been dreamed from Hadrian's wall
to the halls of Osiris, from the Hindoo lands to watery Atlantis. And now I am dreamed in none of them. Now, only in the
mind of a few scholars does Jupiter live on. To all other men,
I am a dead god. To all others, I have fallen from divinity to
mad humanity, have gone from being the king of all creation
to being its most pitiable creature. I know just now who I have
been. It is a single lucid moment in a storm of madness, but I
will use it to regain all I have lost.

"Jerome, you know me," I say. "You know what I was,
what has been stolen from me."

The monk bows prostrate before my blazing presence. The
legion holds its ground, spears lifted high and eyes fierce
within the cave of their scutum shields.

"Tell them to lower their pilums and shields. Tell their
commander to obey me."

Jerome stares. Terror flits across his gaze like so many
dancing girls.

"Only through Constantine did Jehovah conquer. Only
through your work can the conquest of Jehovah be complete.

But through you, I can have a Constantine. I can return to my empire. Fight for me, Jerome. Tell them to lay down their spears and shields."

A deep sadness steals through Jerome. I can sense it. But the sadness is not enough. Amid fond memories of Ovid and Virgil, there lurks a new terror of all things Pagan. Jerome loves Jupiter and his children, loves the stories of antiquity, but he also fears his God. He fears JHVH.

"Slay him! Slay this demon son of Satan!"

Pilums fill the air. They converge, hundreds of them. The first onslaught melts right away, iron heads from wooden shafts. The second burns and bursts in flashing flutters of flame. The third, though—the third wave breaks through the incinerating aura around me.

I swing my great sword in an arc and smash aside many of the spears. A few crack past my guard. Molten metal slams into me.

The pain is unbearable, maddening. It tears through me. All hope of a return to empire drains away. Sanity's last drop goes with it. The old madness wells up—the old rabid madness. I shriek as iron dribbles from gaping holes in my deathless flesh.

The sound sends Jerome fleeing like a hind.

I charge after him. The legion blocks my way. More pilums fly, more fall aside. The twenty nearest men in the phalanx die in my aura. Thirty more fall with my strides. And then it is only killing forever.

The fallen god was gone, and only the mad mage remained.

Guinevere clung tightly to Merlin. The fires that had been jetting from fingers and toes erupted from every pore. They filled the room. She clutched to him even as flame engulfed her. Only her Tuatha blood saved her.

Dagonet was less lucky. The blast of flame flung him against the wall. He hung there, pinned by fire. He opened his mouth to scream. The sound was rammed back down. Unholy tongues darted through him. Slowly sliding down the wall, Dagonet riled. By the time he struck the floor, the dwarf rolled in exquisite pain there.

He shrieked. And then he laughed. The sound was the same. Shrieking and laughing. He riled in ticklish torment. Blazing madness infused him. Divine lunacy. The idiot mantle that had draped Merlin all these years was flung off to envelop and smother the hapless dwarf. It transformed him.

And Dagonet writhed on the floor, giggling in mortal agony.

27

When Kings and Gods Awake

*A*rthur awoke to a naked candle flame. His hands were bound behind him by samite scarves. Candlelight flitted across a canvas roof, luffing in night breezes. Despite the pillow, his head ached with throbbing fury. The sound of it was like the distant roar of war, of horse hooves and dying men—

Then, he remembered.

Arthur tried to sit up, but was bound to the bed. His captor had been thorough. But samite scarves? These seemed hardly the restraints used by an armsman. These were more the tools of a woman—

From the shadows, Queen Morgause moved toward him. Her face was cold and severe. Lines of worry etched her eyes. Her cheeks and temples were sunken. She reached the bedside, seated herself, and gazed at him.

Arthur realized she was considering his elfin nose and silvery eyes, the lines of his mouth, the shock of tousled hair. They were not just his features, they were hers.

"Sister," he said.

Her hand seemed a darting dove, but it struck his cheek

like a falcon. Words formed on her lips, but did not manage to work themselves forth.

Wincing, Arthur turned back toward the woman. "It is true, Morgause. I am your half-brother. Your mother is my mother."

Morgause rose to pace. Quiet fury filled her eyes.

"And our mother wants me to be king."

Morgause wrung her hands. Knuckles stood out from her white flesh.

"Her forces fight for me, even now. Destroy me, and you destroy her."

"Half-brother," Morgause spat. "You are my *half*-brother. Your father killed mine."

Arthur's eyes darkened. "Yes. If the stories are true, my father's army killed your father. Perhaps this moment was foretold in that. Perhaps Igraine is cursed to have every member of her family kill every other member—"

That comment visibly nettled Morgause. "I could have killed you already—"

"But instead, you'll let your husband do the dirty work," Arthur countered.

She whirled savagely on him. "What else can I do? You are my foe—"

"I am your brother—your mother's son."

"You are my husband's foe. If I release you, you would only kill him."

"If you release me, Sister," Arthur replied solemnly, "on my honor I swear never to slay your husband—and to command the same of all who fight for me."

Morgause paused. Her hands twisted in agitation at her sides. She drew a deep breath and snatched up a long, curved blade.

"Listen to me, Morgause—"

"Shut up. I've made up my mind."

She lifted the dagger. A cruel light gleamed in her eyes. Fingers tightened around the hilt. Summoning her nerve, she brought the thing slashing down.

Arthur felt the knife sink between chest and arm and cut downward. Steel sliced through sinew, and silken bands fell away. She cut the scarves around his ankles. He was free.

"Know this, though, King Arthur—you have another sister, a sister younger than I, who hates you singularly for what you are and what you did to our father."

"Yes," Arthur said, sitting up and rubbing his sore wrists. "I have met Morgan."

"She is powerful, Arthur, and grows more powerful each year. She will not suffer you to sit the throne of this country. Run afoul of her, and all you have won and all you will build will be destroyed."

The dream had become reality. Delusion transformed into truth. The delirious mage was transfigured into something wholly other.

Merlin rose from the burning bed. He ascended in the cruciform image of the God who had destroyed him. Light arced from his flesh. His beard and hair and brows were bleached white as lightning. His eyes, like blue scoops of sky, were windows into an immense soul. His tattered robes burned until they were as bright as the sun.

And all the while, Guinevere clung to him. But for her tenacity, she would have been hurled across the room as had Dagonet. Clenched lips and eyelids shut out the divine glory. She held to Merlin as a daughter clings to her father in the face of a raging gale.

But now the gale spent itself. Storms of light softened to a mere beaming glow. Merlin's feet slid down to touch ground amid the ashes of the bed. He gently peeled her fingers from his robes.

"I must go now, child. I must go fight for Arthur, while some of my radiance remains." He lifted her face, beautiful in its gleam. "If it weren't for you, I would never have fought through the madness to clutch the truth. If you weren't holding my hand, I would not have had the courage to remember this dismembered self."

Guinevere clasped his hand. "Then, take me with you. This is not Rome, great Jupiter. This is Britannia. And here, men do not rule unless the land grants them power. I am Tuatha Dé Danann. I have held Arthur's foot, and held your hand, and empowered you both. Now, take me with you."

A wise smile came to Merlin's lips. His cerulean eyes were full of laughter. "Yes, this is not Rome. And neither am I great Jupiter. He is dead and gone. I am only the fleshly husk left behind. I am glad you will come with me, for I have need of your power. To save Arthur, I will need to seem the god I once was." He reached down and regally grasped her about the waist.

She clung to him again, though not as a child. Guinevere seemed now an Athena, goddess of wisdom, beautiful in her divine raiment, and born full-formed from the mind of Jove.

They rose. A high window on one wall was black with night. Merlin and Guinevere drifted through it and out under the warring heavens.

Behind them, a scabby dwarf lifted himself from the ashes. He capered across the ruined chamber.

Dagonet had been transformed too. His hair stood like thistledown across his head. His armor and livery had peeled back into wild flourishes, the costume of a jester. His legs and arms, always strong, now had a preternatural power. Most telltale of all, his eyes gleamed the same cerulean blue as Merlin's.

Lunatic giggles bubbled from his lips as he vaulted head over heels. In a single bound, he reached the high window. Catching a foothold, he sprung again, a human locust. Above the dark castle he soared in the chill air of night, and grasped hold of Guinevere's raiment.

There, he swung, his mad laughter pealing out over the black hills.

Arthur clambered out the very slit he had cut in the side of Lot's pavilion. His feet, numb from the scarves, got tangled. He spilled facedown in the dirt. It tasted wonderful. It was the taste of freedom.

Morgause had granted him freedom and life, had even returned to him his holy sword and scabbard. "Sweet sister," Arthur whispered in thanks.

Arthur turned and gazed down the ragged hillside. The battle was faraway, half a league, at least. It looked to be a desperate fight. Fires illuminated Lot's warriors in their thousands. Arthur made out the bleary faces of his own men, pressed horribly in a slow retreat. Most ominous of all, though, were the dark mounds of dead.

"I need a horse," Arthur told himself. "A horse, or all of Britannia is lost."

He gazed out alongside Lot's pavilion to see a covered stable. Rubbing the knot his sister had given him, Arthur reminded himself the value of caution. He stole along the dark wall of the tent, peered across an empty commons, and marked the distance to the stable. Taking a deep breath, he ran.

Wind blew through his hair—he no longer had a helmet, a golden ribbon, or his Pendragon tabard. "They will know me by Excalibur," he muttered.

Arthur reached the corral and fetched up beside a rail fence. There was no guard. Every man was busy in battle.

Five fine horses circled uneasily in the yard. Two bays, a roan, a piebald, and a majestic white horse. Arthur had ridden a black steed into battle, hoping it would be cloaked in the night. Now, he sought to be seen.

There was no time for a saddle. As it was, these northern lords did not use stirrups anyway, and their saddles were little good for mounted fighting. Arthur grabbed a harness, climbed the fence, and stalked slowly across the dung-strewn corral. Though the other horses shied from him, he locked eyes immediately with the white steed and spoke to it in gentle words of command.

"I am King Arthur, beautiful beast. I have need of your help. I have need of your fleet hooves and your bright pelt. Will you bear me into battle?"

The beast held its ground, one fore-hoof scooping out a trench of earth.

Arthur moved up placidly beside it and took its mane in one hand. He patted the creature softly. "When they see the noble steed I ride, they cannot but know that I am king."

The creature nodded its head twice before allowing the halter and bit to be slid into place. Arthur vaulted to its back. Powerful and impatient beneath him, the horse cantered in a quick circle.

Only then did Arthur realize he had forgotten to open the gate. He started to slide off, but his steed broke into a sudden gallop. Arthur clung tightly to the reins and hunkered down beside a wildfire mane. The horse leaped. It seemed to float above the fence. At last, it came to ground again, beyond. It snorted, kicking dust from the road.

"You want to be king more than I do," Arthur remarked.

With only the slightest pressure on the creature's flanks, he sent it charging down the main road. To either side, empty tents luffed in the black breezes of night. At full gallop, Arthur charged for the front lines.

He drew Excalibur. It leapt from Rhiannon with an exultant shout. Its gleam shone like the morning star rising above a benighted battle. Even as Arthur drew the sword, it drew him. Like the tallest oak in a grove, the uplifted blade called down lightning. Power coursed through his arm—more than power, it was pure fury, pure battle fury. No longer crouched beside the straining white neck of his mount, Arthur held Excalibur aloft and gave out a war cry.

Just before him, a determined knot of loyalists held their ground at the head of the road. They knew that to lose that spot would be to lose the battle. Lot's host had swept in around the group and pressed them on all sides. Cut off, this embattled twenty fought not only for a scrap of land, but for their very lives. Every last one of them had lost his horse. Some had shattered swords and had to wrench fresh blades from the hands of the dead. All fought onward with a grim determination. Blood speckled the gold strips on their helms.

Arthur thundered toward this group. His best soldiers would be there—Ulfius and Ector, Kay and Brastias. Shrieking like a Saxon berserker, he reached the fray at full gallop.

Excalibur cleaved a rebel horseman clean in half. The white horse breasted among rebel cavalry. Arthur hacked them furiously as he went. Caught unawares, they tumbled from their saddles. Lot's folk fell back. An avenue opened straight into the beleaguered host. Chopping, Arthur rode through the midst. Blood boiled away from Excalibur, leaving it clean.

Voices rose above the din of battle.

"It's King Arthur!

"That's the holy sword! That's Excalibur!"

In moments, he was among his own folk. His mount reared, and he lifted Excalibur high.

"God fights for him. He cannot die!"

"Even his horse—a lightning flash!"

Arthur patted the steed in appreciation and shouted, "Surrender, all of you! Declare your fealty to me and quit the field! I will slay none who surrender now. I will take away no lands from those who swear to me. Surrender!"

The battle raged on, heedless, though the crowd parted a second time. A new figure fought forward atop a white horse. King Lot was mantled in blood from wrists to breastbone. His armor was battered, his livery cut to ribbons. His staved helmet hung limply from half-severed laces. Even his horse was sorely wounded, but he fought on.

"This horse ridden by Arthur—it is mine!" Lot shouted breathlessly as he hewed loyalists. "He sits a beast that is not his . . . and a throne that is not his. . . . He is no king, but a horse thief!"

Ulfius declared through bloodied teeth. "You are the pretender!"

"He is king by right," Ector shouted above his ringing blade. "Surrender!"

Lot rode up directly before Arthur. Footmen fell back, lest they be trampled by the horses. And the two kings, young and old, stared each other down.

Excalibur gleamed coldly, poised to strike. It made Arthur seem an alabaster statue. "Surrender."

Lot's own sword waited across his lap. He glowed red with torches and exertion and blood. Beneath the creases of his beetled brow, his eyes were implacable. He nudged his horse forward until it locked necks with Arthur's steed. The two creatures—stable mates—nibbled each other fondly.

A sneer on his lip, Lot said, "You are the traitor, not I." His sword thrust suddenly from the hip, slicing open the neck of Arthur's mount.

Red life gushed from the creature's severed throat. It opened its mouth to scream but had no breath. Eyes rolling in piteous terror, it went down, dumping the king.

Mantled in gore, Arthur clambered to his feet.

"Here is my fealty!" Lot cried and plunged his great sword down through Arthur's neck. The blade sank halfway to the hilt, its sanguine edge forcing Arthur's chin back. "Here is another soul for Satan!"

The battle stilled.

Arthur staggered back, taking the great sword with him.

Lot struggled to hold on, but was yanked from the saddle. He landed atop the slain horse and lost hold of his sword.

Both kings had fallen. . . .

Arthur whirled sickly. He reached his free hand up, grasped the hilt of the sword that impaled him, and drew it slowly forth. It emerged cleanly, no blood spilling from the wound. It scraped clear of his collarbone. Muscle and skin knit themselves together behind it.

Steady at last, Arthur held aloft Lot's blade. "You forget, God fights on my side." He flung the rebel's sword back to him. "I will not kill you, Lot. I have sworn an oath. But my men will kill your men. Surrender to me, or they will die."

All around, warriors craned to hear the next words.

"Better that they die!" Lot hurled himself at Arthur.

Excalibur met Lot's blade and bashed it back. Arthur followed his block with a whirling stroke. It carved the space Lot had occupied a moment before.

Staggering back, the rebel king planted his foot and lunged again. Steel rang on steel.

With the shout of metal came the resumed shout of men. Ulfius, Ector, and Kay surged up beside Arthur to guard his flanks. They laid in like woodsmen felling trees. A wall of swords sprang up around the twenty-some others. Bathed in the glow of darting Excalibur, loyalists rallied to hold back the overwhelming tide of rebels.

Lot charged Arthur. Their weapons ground against each other. They locked together, trembling.

"How many of your friends will you kill for this dream, Arthur?" hissed Lot in his face. "You cannot win, now. . . . We hold the field. . . . We outnumber you five times. And you will not kill me." He shifted his stance, stepping back as Excalibur arced down by his flank. "Surrender to me, or your friends will die."

Between sword blows, Arthur saw that Lot spoke the truth. His corps of twenty had shrunk to fifteen. The circle tightened. And the rest of his forces were already in full retreat through the woodlands.

A series of feints and lunges threw the rebel king back, and Arthur shouted, "Bow to the will of God and the sword of kings—"

Parrying quickly, Lot growled, "I will not bow to Excalibur unless it bows me."

"You cannot kill me, Lot—you have seen that. Nor can I kill you. But our stalemate slays nations—"

Lot lunged. His sword sliced across Arthur's breastplate, cutting loose the straps that held Rhiannon. Even as the scabbard slid free to clatter to the ground, Lot followed up the attack with a quick jab. The tip of his sword plunged through chain and plate both, drawing blood.

Arthur staggered back, his hand catching up a gush of gore. He stooped to snatch Rhiannon from the ground.

Lot took the opportunity to strike again. His sword sank deeply into Arthur's side. He pressed the attack, and Arthur staggered back, tumbling over his fallen horse.

Lot stooped and lifted the ornate scabbard. He stared appreciatively at it. "So this is the secret to God's favor? This enchanted scabbard guards you? And without it? Without it, what are you, Arthur?" He climbed over the dead horse and swung a brutal downward stroke.

Arthur rolled away. The blade clove the back of the beast. "You are only a boy. And with it, what am I? Invincible!

With this scabbard I can kill you and gain Excalibur, and then *I* will be king!" He stalked toward Arthur, whose face was pale with blood loss. Lot raised his sword overhead for the killing blow.

"What will you be then, Arthur? You will be nothing at all."

"No! He will be king!" came an imperious cry upon the wind.

The voice brought with it a glorious and terrible dawn.

The sun rose above the forest. It shone upon loyalists retreating there. They stopped, heartened.

Advancing rebels stopped as well and gazed upward in horror.

This was no natural sun. It was a supernatural orb.

At its center was an old man who seemed the Ancient of Days, the light of the New Jerusalem, the Light of the World. Or perhaps he was Lugh, the bright-shining one, or Belatucadrus of the north. Some there would even have described this figure as Jupiter of old. But it did not matter by what name he was called. This was a god manifest. And in his arms there was a goddess—the sacral virgin, the Virgin Mother, Mebd of Eire.

God and goddess both proclaimed Arthur king.

"Fall to your knees!" they called angrily. *"Fall to your knees and receive your king!"*

In a single rush of armor and cloth, the living warriors dropped in obeisance among the dead. Even men already sworn to Arthur fell to their faces in worship. The quick and the dead were indistinguishable, all prostrate before the shimmering form. The carnage seemed complete.

Lot did not bow. Emboldened by the holy scabbard in his hand, he kept his feet.

Arthur lay below, dying. It was enough.

The rebel king stole backward, taking Rhiannon. Tying it nervously around him, Lot grabbed the reins of his rearing horse. Bloody fingers clutched the traces. He clambered to its back and stared one final moment at the approaching gods.

Then, brutally kicking the beast, Lot turned it. The horse stomped and whirled, trampling soldiers. Leaping, it lit out fearfully along the road.

In moments, horse and rider had fled beyond the hills, in shadows cast by the coming gods.

Merlin almost pursued Lot. Had he truly been Jupiter of old, Merlin could have plucked the rebel king from the saddle and taken back Rhiannon and cursed his issue to the tenth generation. But Merlin was only Merlin. It had taken all his strength to blaze away the madness in his soul, and now his power was waning. The vast glamour that enveloped him and Guinevere had its true power in the minds of men. It had ended a bloody battle, had sent warriors to their faces, and had driven away a rebel king. But to try to save Rhiannon now would be to lose Arthur. To lose all.

Merlin let Lot flee—Lot and anyone else with the will to. There would be another day to fight them. Instead, he floated down, a dimming star, and lighted on the battlefield beside his dying grandson.

Guinevere slipped from Merlin's grasp and knelt at the king's side. She drew a glowing corner of her raiment up to stanch the flow of the king's blood.

"Arthur," Merlin said quietly, "Arthur. You have won."

Pale in Guinevere's arms, the young king gazed up into Merlin's face. "Grandfather . . . what has become of you?"

"I remembered who I was, Arthur."

"God Almighty?"

The glowing figure laughed. "No. Not the Tetragrammaton. I am no living god, but a faint reflection of my former self—Jupiter of old."

Arthur's smile was sweet through trembling lips. "This is the maddest of all your dreams, Grandfather. And it has turned out to be the truth."

Nodding, Merlin said, "Mad truths are the hardest to grasp."

"I have become a king, and you have become a god. We

came of age together, Grandfather." Arthur's skin was suddenly the color of ivory. He reached a wan hand outward. "But I fear I will have been king only a day."

Guinevere laid her hands on the vast laceration in his side. Her touch was warm. Vitality poured from her fingers. "You will live, Arthur. Rhiannon's power is my power as well. A land cannot live unless it can heal." Slowly, the wound began to knit.

Arthur laid his bloodied hands on hers. "Don't spend all your strength on me, dear Guinevere. There are many men in need here."

The earth all around was strewn with bodies. Many were dead. Others were merely slain in worship.

A single figure moved in that multitude. He bounded energetically among the soldiers, scampering and dancing. The scrofulous little man leaped from back to back like a frog crossing river stones. All the while, he sang a song.

> "When gods are hid in madmen's rags
>   And kings are hid in boyish clothes,
> When Lot revolts and fights and brags
>   And slays the lad he loathes,
> When truth is coin for any man
>   And Dagonet the rogue's
> An oracle, O heed, for when he nags
>   He utters sweetest oaths!"

"Who is that craven figure?" Arthur asked.

Merlin shook his head. "I myself do not know. He was a warrior and messenger when first he came to me. I fear, though, that my madness has maddened him."

Arthur rolled his eyes wearily at the jeering little man. "It is well to know my court will not be all too sane."

Epilogue

*A*nd so, I learned who I had been. The past made a king out of Arthur, and it made a god out of me. Still, it is not enough to be a king. One must be a good king. And it is not enough to be a god. One must be a good god.

Upon a pallet, amid his cheering countrymen, King Arthur was borne back to Castle Caerleon. Guinevere held his hand all the way. She held my hand too. Yes, I knew who I had been, but that revelation made my old legs only shakier. She was a strong and wise lass, and I needed her hand now more than ever. Guinevere was the one who would make a great king of Arthur, and her steady faith would help make a good god of me.

The madness was gone. Delirium and dream had cleared away. They left me standing on a fearsome threshold. I knew now who I had been, and wondered keenly who I was to become. . . .

BOOK TWO

Immortality

For Aidan
my red-headed child of fey

Prologue

It was a perilous time. We all knew it. Arthur had worn his crown only hours before he had to lead his first battle. He was nearly slain in that battle. The most vicious stroke cut away his holy scabbard Rhiannon, which had the power to heal him.

Lot now had the scabbard, and fled north with it, and Arthur lay sorely wounded.

I was nearly slain as well—not in battle but in delirium.

I fought my way through the forests of my madness only to discover a single killing truth at their heart. It lurked there like an old and vicious dragon. It almost slew me. In truth, I was no mad mage at all. I was a fallen god. I had been slain by the God of Excalibur, by the Sword of the Spirit itself—the Word of God. I had fallen to earth from a great height, from the cloudy realms of Olympus. The fall had made me mad.

What man wouldn't be, who was left a naked and craven beggar, when once he had been Almighty Jove?

Arthur had been king for only hours when he fought his first battle. I had been a god for only moments when I fought mine. Were it not for Guinevere, priestess of healing and power of the land, both Arthur and I would have perished in the next days. Even with Guinevere, we had no assurance we would survive the battles before us.

Lot was routed, but not defeated. Britannia lay in tatters, aching to be built into something whole and grand. Arthur and I dared to oppose Lot and his armies. We dared even to dream of a glorious new nation, and at the heart of that nation, the city of Camelot. In the coming months and years, we might well be defeated by rebels and Saxons, and if not them, by our own dreams.

It was a perilous time indeed. The future was anything but sure for a risen king and a fallen god. . . .

28

Of Kings and Fools

King Arthur Pendragon and his retinue climbed the
steep and grassy embankment. Evening stretched
overhead, from the black east to the gloaming west. Below,
on the Portabello road, the armies of the Pendragon marched
in grim file.

Arthur's ascent was hard. The dewy grass was as long and
stringy as an old woman's hair. There were no cattle to graze
these hills—too near the reivers of Annandale and Lothian.
Blades of grass clutched at the king's boots and putties as
he reached the crest of the rise. Before him lay folded low-
lands, across which ran a long low black wall.

"We've reached it," Arthur said wearily. He drew back the
patchwork coat of gold he had donned for the climb. It had
been pieced from the auric ribbons worn by his troops that
first night of the campaign. It was worn by King Arthur this
last night. "Hadrian's Wall. We've reached it at last."

"Yes." Ulfius came up beside him, panting. The warrior
was fifty now, and for a year he had shouldered command
of Arthur's multifarious army. It wore on him. "Yes. The
wall. We cannot hope to drive them farther north . . . not with
this army of ours. The men are tired, Arthur. We've succeeded this far only because Lot hasn't opposed us. . . . But
beyond that wall is Lothian, and Saxon Bernicia. Lot has had
a year in Traprian Law to mass for another strike. . . . We've
driven him from Britannia. That will have to be enough, for
now."

"Yes," Arthur said, exhausted. "I am sick to death of war.
The men are too." He leaned on the shoulder of his stepbrother Kay. "What say you, Brother?"

Blond and muscular, Kay retained his enthusiasm for battle. Still, he preferred bright tournaments to dark marches. "I'd be willing to press on right through Caledonia, and ship for Orkney and the Hebrides, if you'd ordered it."

Arthur snorted in amusement. "So says the Seneschal of all Britannia. Haven't I already given you enough land, Brother?"

"More than enough," Ulfius said. "The trick will be holding it." He pointed ahead. "That shelf beside the wall would be broad enough for an encampment, with good views of the road and the lands around. We can fortify there, set up a permanent garrison."

"Yes," the king said. "A good camp for the night, and a good fortification for the coming months. But we will need more men if we are to keep them back much longer—"

The king's observation was interrupted by a sudden shimmering in the air. Out of the red gloaming, a gray-garbed figure took form. He spoke even before his being solidified. "Ban of Benwick and Bors of Gaul are similarly pressed, across the Channel—"

"Merlin," Arthur said in fond relief.

"And an alliance with them could provide a large enough army for you and them both," Merlin finished. He still seemed half shadow, though his eyes glowed like candles in the dusk.

"An alliance. It is an idea with merit," Ulfius agreed.

"And speaking of alliances," Merlin said with a quirked smile, "I have brought your greatest ally up from the healing caravan." He drew back his tattered travel cloak, revealing Guinevere.

The Tuatha priestess was ever beautiful, whether in court gown or in the white robes of a battlefield healer. She gleamed especially this night among dark and weary soldiers.

Arthur held his hands out to her. "I am sick to death of war, and when I see you, my dear, I remember there is much more than war." He received her into his cloak of gold. She was warm, and her hair had the scent of wind in dry leaves. "Every time I see you, I see the heavenly kingdom brought down to earth—"

"The New Jerusalem?" Ulfius wondered aloud.

"Asgard more likely," Kay put in.

"Olympus would be better still," Merlin whispered dreamily.

Guinevere smiled at her friends. "What of glorious Avalon?"

"Oh, our city will be all of those rolled into one," Arthur said, sweeping Guinevere into a Lydian serenade there on the darkling hill. His feet, so used to trudging, were suddenly light. His cloak seemed a signal fire on the height. "A place where mortals and immortals will mingle, where no god will rule supreme but all will be welcome—gods and fey and men—"

"Camelot," Guinevere said.

Arthur nodded. "Camelot."

An impatient look crossed Ulfius's face. "Well, dream of your glorious city these nights, Arthur, but there is yet a waking war to win—"

"Once the wall is secure, I'll send you to Benwick and Gaul to secure more troops," Arthur said, continuing his courtly dance.

Merlin suggested, "Perhaps I should go to Avalon to determine what divine troops might aid us."

"Excellent idea," Arthur replied. He stared into Guinevere's fey eyes. "And ask their advice on building Camelot." He executed a rapid turn-step. "Oh, and Merlin, what news of Rhiannon? Can you sense where the scabbard is kept?"

The candle glow of Merlin's eyes died. "No. Lot has hidden it well. It is swathed in ancient magics, older than mine." His face was utterly dark. "This is the work of Lot's sister-in-law, your half-sister—Morgan Le Fey."

Morgan Le Fey stood in the gloaming garden of Traprian Law.

Since her arrival at the castle, the garden had thrived. Gone were the ordered and sterile beds, once planted with species of rose and lily from Rome. They were beautiful blooms, yes, but emblems of Caesar and Christ—and they had not taken to the peat and murk of Lothian. Now, the place was a fertile riot of wildflowers, and most prominent of all, the voracious thistle. Purple flower, green stem, white thorn— beauty, fecundity, and ferocity. Yes, the garden had thrived. It was beginning to feel like home.

Morgan's wandering footsteps led her to the centerpiece of the garden.

The white-marble statue of the Holy Virgin now bore new adornments. A fat vine of poison oak spiraled patiently up Mary's once-pristine flesh. Morgan had brought that ivy from the deeps of a sacred grove, had planted and nurtured it and guided its seeking tendrils. It had grown with preternatural eagerness, constricting about the Virgin. Lot had objected, of course, complaining his sister-in-law had turned Mary into Eve, seduced by the Serpent. Morgan had only laughed. Let the man think what he would. This poison oak vine was no serpent. It was the wizened crone to Mary's virgin maiden. And one more planting had completed the triune weird— mistletoe, the fertile and parasitic mother. This was ancient magic, rooted in the female divinities of the earth, older than Tuatha priestesses and fallen Roman gods.

Yes, Morgan sensed the truth of Merlin's past. She had grown powerful in the old ways. Her garden weird was a bit of magic even Merlin could not penetrate.

In the Virgin's embrace rested Rhiannon, the holy scabbard. Its tip was poised in the stony fold between Mary's chaste feet. Its bejeweled edge rose to one shoulder. Poison oak wrapped it tightly, and mistletoe cloaked it from any eye that did not know to look. Most important of all, though, the ancient magic of the triune goddess hid it away from the eyes even of gods.

Far behind Morgan, Lot entered the garden. He was heavy-footed and blunt in this gentle space. He seemed to think the thistles weeds. He would not enter the garden at all except for his prize, his holy scabbard. Thrice a day he fretfully checked it, making certain it remained.

Morgan knew the warrior-king approached, but he could

not have guessed her presence, there in the darkness. Not until he rounded the bend.

"Morgan!" he cried out in startlement. He clutched his chest and stalled a moment. Then, growling, he advanced, "It's no wonder you witches have fallen from favor, with all your skulking about in the dark."

A humorless smile crossed her face. "You are all too happy to benefit from the powers of this witch—"

"Only because Arthur has a warlock," Lot said, stopping to stand beside the statue. He crossed arms over his chest. His eyes glinted beneath peppered brows. "You are certain this is enough to blind his roving eye?"

"More than enough," Morgan replied. "Of course, if you doubt, you could remove the scabbard and see how long it takes Merlin to arrive—"

"No, no," Lot said hastily. "The time is not yet. The army is not yet ready. I have tens of thousands mustering, from Deira and Bernicia and Sussex as well the British and Pictish lands. When they are poised, we shall march." He glanced at her. His hard eyes seemed to trace the family lines in her features. "But then, I shall want you along. I do believe in your dark arts, Morgan, as much as I may despise them—"

"The scabbard itself comes from those dark arts," Morgan reminded. "It formed itself out of ancient sacrifices of blade and gem. It formed itself around Excalibur to guard the world from the killing thing. Believe what you will, Lot, but you survive only at the sufferance of the goddesses you despise."

"You misunderstand," Lot assured apologetically. "I am thankful for your aid—"

"I do none of this for you, nor for my sister. I do this *against* Arthur. You and he are too similar, Lot. Had I any notion you could actually defeat and replace Arthur, I would not aid you," Morgan said darkly.

Lot was astonished. "The land needs a king—"

"Not a king like you. Not a king like Arthur."

"Then perhaps one of my sons—Gawain, or Gaheris, Agravain, Gareth—"

"None of them. The land needs a king as of old—a human

consort of the goddess. You and your sons are unworthy. You are meant only to occupy Arthur until such a king can be born."

Shaking his head in irritation, Lot said, "You may know witchcraft, Morgan, but I know statecraft. And war. Kings are made, not born—"

"All things are born, Lot of Lothian," Morgan replied, "and the true king of the isle will be born—of me."

Wreathed in holly with feet folded in the oak, how strong-seeming you are, sweet Guinevere. And yet, when my mind's eye draws back, I see the oak in which you are rooted, that great powerful ancient gnarled thing—how it dwarfs you. I see how you are tiny and ephemeral against its vast bulk, how you might be but a perfectly green leaf that will wither and die when autumn winds blow. And, worse, I draw back again and see a semblance in this great and powerful and ancient tree where your feet are folded. And the semblance is that of the greater power, of Morgan Le Fey.

"Why do I get all the rotten jobs?" muttered Ulfius under his breath.

He rode his horse at full gallop across the meadowlands of Gaul. To his right, the seasoned warrior Brastias sat tall in his saddle, lance couched and eyes watchful. Dagonet was less well prepared. He claimed to have kin in Gaul, though Ulfius thought it more likely he had kin *with* gall. Arthur had sent him merely to get the little imp out of Castle Caerleon. Just now, Dagonet stood on the back of his charging beast, clinging to the reins and waving gaily to farmers scything wheat.

Ulfius growled, "Sit down, you lunatic!"

"We lunatics must stand, that all might behold our moony mistress!" the fool proclaimed, shoving down his waistband.

Ulfius did not look. Instead, he focused intently on the

road ahead. Despite the idiot's antics, this was serious business—and deadly. These rolling hillsides were the realm of King Claudas, sworn foe of Bors and Ban. The trespass was unavoidable. The ship from Britannia had landed at Quentovic in the north, and there was no other route to Benwick in the midcountry. Knowing their peril, Ulfius had kept to deer paths through the woods whenever possible and pastures and fence lines when not. The riverbed to the west, though, had steadily pressed them toward the road. Now, forced to ride it, Ulfius led them at a gallop.

The reason for all this haste appeared now at the head of the lane. Between dense brakes of forest, eight horsemen rode with measured tread into view. Their helmets bore orange plumes. Their livery and barding were orange and black—the heraldry of Claudas. They spotted the three galloping foreigners and cantered easily toward them.

"I feared this moment would come," Ulfius muttered.

The captain of the crew cantered a length ahead of the company. He held up a black gauntlet and signaled for Ulfius and his companions to halt their horses. Clearly, he was accustomed to being obeyed.

"Level lances!" Ulfius shouted as he pulled his shield up beside him. "Full tilt!"

Brastias nodded. He and Ulfius hoisted their lances and tilted them down to bear on Claudas's men.

For his part, Dagonet stood in the saddle, whistling.

Above the lilting tune and the thunder of horse hooves, a growled curse came from the Frankish captain. He flipped his visor into place, lowered his own lance, and kicked his mount into the charge. His comrades did likewise.

"Eight lancers to three!" Ulfius roared angrily.

"Eight to two," corrected Brastias.

Dagonet's song continued.

"Stop whistling!" Brastias shouted.

"Arm yourself!" Ulfius ordered.

Dagonet did neither.

Ulfius and Brastias crouched behind their shields. Lances

sped to the attack. The horses bent their necks in angry charge.

Behind and between them, the idiot stood in his saddle. His bell-covered cap waved in the wind.

The storm of hooves and horseflesh converged. Leveled lances jagged together like lightning bolts.

Ulfius ducked at the last. The captain's weapon, meant for his head, whirled through empty air over one shoulder. Even as the captain bolted past, Ulfius caught the lance of a second rider on his shield. The blow almost knocked the shield from his hand. Tearing the Pendragon insignia, the lance scraped free.

It nearly shot through Dagonet's waist. The dexterous dwarf leaped up from the saddle, and the weapon passed harmlessly beneath him.

Ulfius's own lance at last connected. A black-armored armsman caught the blow in his gut. The lance punched through breastplate, muscle, and viscera. Shrieking, the man was flung from his mount. The splintered lance jutted from his side. He tumbled for a moment in air before ending in a heap on the ground.

Brastias's lance was making similar work of another armsman. It caught on the foe's shield and flung it away, along with its bearer. With the shriven nub of the lance, Brastias knocked another rider from his horse. The hilt spun away. Defenseless, Brastias hunkered down beside his horse's mane and charged outward.

Ulfius, beside him, did likewise.

As his companions cleared the foe, Dagonet still pranced horseback in their midst. A lance rudely vaulted up from Claudas's men and nearly ended Dagonet's performance. He executed a sharp flip to avoid it and took a moment to lift his hat and waggle his tongue.

He shouldn't have. The last lance caught his upraised hat. Instead of letting go, Dagonet held onto it and dropped his horse's reins. The resultant flight was inevitable. Dagonet hung for a fascinating heartbeat amid the charging group of Claudas's armsmen.

The ground intervened. Packed dirt stole his feet, and he tumbled. During the third revolution, he realized just how fast these horses had been going. During the thirteenth, he realized he hadn't previously realized just how fast they had been going, but did so now. Somewhere around twenty-one, he no longer cared how fast they had been going, concerned then only with how slow and solid was the fence post he hit. He sprawled in a disheveled heap there.

Claudas's men were skilled cavalry. The five that had remained mounted rode right up around Dagonet, pulled their swords, and impressed upon him the importance of lying still. Dagonet was just now capable of little else.

"Who are you?" growled the captain in the Gaulish tongue. He flung back his visor for a better look.

Dagonet blinked up through clouds of pain and dust. He answered with the most imposing name he could imagine. "I am Arthur, king of Britannia!"

The armsmen laughed, lifting their visors to behold the runty king.

Their captain was less amused. "The Britons are ruled by a misshapen turd?"

"Ah, you have heard of me!" Dagonet replied. He crawled achingly to his feet. Brushing the dust from particolored pantaloons, he declared, "Yes. It is I, King Arthur!" With this proclamation, he thrust high a four-inch-long dagger.

The laughter ceased as the warriors watched for some trick. "What is that?" hissed the captain.

"Excalibur!" Dagonet declared. "The king-maker. The fabled blade of Britons! This sword has won countless battles."

"Countless battles?" joked one of the warriors. "Only if you fought carrots!"

Dagonet gave a frown and looked the blade over. "Wait a minute. This isn't Excalibur." He felt along his waistband and drew an even smaller knife. "Ha Ha! Excalibur! God-Killer!"

"Britons must have very small gods," gibed another.

"Britons must have very small everything," added a third.

The captain's horse stomped closer. "Surrender now, impostor, or die."

"Excalibur!" shouted Dagonet, drawing a third and even smaller blade.

Despite the captain's irritation, his men laughed heartily.

Dagonet smiled and began juggling the three knives. They sparkled in their tumbling orbits.

The armsmen watched, amused. One whistled. A couple of others even sheathed their swords and started clapping in time to the knife throws. Dagonet sped up his handwork, and the clapping kept pace.

"There is but one trick to juggling knives," he said pleasantly. "Keeping your eyes on the tips."

In a sudden flurry, the knives leaped outward. Three armsmen shouted in shock and clutched their faces. The bloody handles of the blades shuddered in eye sockets. As one, they slumped dead from their horses.

The captain raised his blade to slay Dagonet.

The dwarf cringed back, but could not escape the descending sword.

Steel ripped through armor and into flesh and bone and finally heart.

But it wasn't Dagonet's heart, or the captain's steel. It was Ulfius's sword carving into the captain's side. Ulfius and Brastias had wheeled about and returned at full gallop, the sound of their approach drowned out by clapping armsmen. Now, both men grimly drew their swords from Claudas's dead men.

They stared balefully at the fool.

Dagonet beamed back at them. "An excellent afternoon!"

"Why you little—!"

"Genius?" Dagonet supplied. "Look, ye—I single-handedly killed three armsmen, while each of you killed but two. And I rounded up these five horses as a gift for Ban and Bors. If you're quick, you might each catch a horse and a half to add to the group." He stretched painfully. "Just watch me, lads. I'll teach you how to fight."

"For the Love of Christ!"

"You needn't thank or repay me. I'd prefer to keep you in my debt."

29

Merlin in Avalon

Merlin rode to Avalon. He could have flown, but he didn't have time for whimsy anymore. He didn't have time for madness and dreams.

It had been quite a revelation. His lunacy had arisen not from human but divine frailty. He had been a god. He was a dead god. He had been slain when his nation had been slain—first by Visigoths and Vandals, and then by Constantine and Constantinople, and last by Creed and *Vulgate* and an emperor who dared to call himself Theodosius—God's gift. Perhaps JHVH's gift, but not Jove's. Jove had died when his former folk stopped dreaming of him. He fell. He became mortal and insane. Only his own dreams kept him from disappearing utterly.

Now, he had no time for dreams, only for reality. The lunacy that had governed his former days infested the fool Dagonet, and all the childish joy had gone with it. Merlin was left with a stern realization of what he had been, of the predation of gods upon each other, and of the likelihood that the God of the sword would one day slay every deity of Britannia.

So, he rode. He wore his old riding cloak. A floppy hat covered his streaming hair and beard. The lance couch bore his gnarled staff. Packs on the horse's rump carried the fetishes and fancies of his magic.

He headed for the Otherworld, where time flowed in violent jags. Mortals who ventured there were often stranded in far centuries or reduced to ash the moment they returned. The Otherworld was a place of gods and heroes, numinous spirits and the dead. Merlin was none of these—a stranger in the halls of time.

He laughed darkly. "And I, who once slew Chronos, titan keeper of time, should fear now to tread the labyrinth of time?"

Slew Chronos . . . he too had killed the gods who had come before. The divine history of the world was as bloody and hopeless as the human one. Arthur was working to mend human history, with his dreamy city and his reign of peace. Perhaps Merlin could do the same with divine history. Perhaps Arthur's city—what was he calling it, Camelot?—could be a haven for both man and god.

The road led out of a forest of glittering beech trees and down onto the Glastonbury plains. It was an old British path, wide enough for a single cart but not a Roman chariot. Its dust was as much marked by the passage of bare feet as it was by the wheels of any conveyance. The hooves of Merlin's horse flung up puffs of dirt in his wake. The steed pelted down the hillside.

Below lay the lake of Avalon, steaming in morning sunlight. This was not the mean marsh that Ulfius had led them to nearly a decade before. This was not the tor where stood the Christian abbey. That locale greeted any mortal man who sought out the material Glastonbury. But Merlin sought Avalon, and he found it.

The lake itself was deep and black. Ghosts of mist rose from it and coiled in the shadow of the surrounding hills. The fog played tricks with sunlight, making the lake seem betimes a limitless sea, and betimes but a murky pool. Beyond the misty margins towered Avalon.

The isle was broad and weird. Apple trees whitened its slopes. Despite the autumnal chill in the air, these trees bore the verdant livery of spring. In frigid January, they might even dangle fruit. Stories told of many a starving wanderer who glimpsed that sight and strode out across the frozen waters to reach it, only to disappear forever. No one passed into Avalon without the leave of the Mistress of the Mists, Brigid. It was her audience that Merlin sought.

The dirt path gave way to an old road. River stones had been its base, six inches down, upon which had grown and died generations of lichens and mosses and, eventually, a tender-bladed grass that was like walking on thick carpet. Of its own accord, the horse slowed its pace to a gentle trot and seemed to drop its hooves only reluctantly on the ground.

Wildflowers crowded up beside the road and craned their heads to see who had come to Avalon. Merlin drew a deep breath, accepting their welcome, and exhaled gratefully. The flowers seemed to draw in his scent as well. Merlin smiled. To flowers, bad breath smelled as sweet as life. That was the sensation of entering Avalon—leaving a world where all things fought one another and entering one where the exhalations of one creature were the glad inhalations of another.

The path opened along the lake's verge. Green banks wrapped a curving black shore. Veils of steam waved slowly above the water.

Merlin halted his horse and dismounted. He unbuckled its harness, slipped it from the creature's head, and hung it from the saddle. The horse dropped its muzzle greedily to the clover there. Merlin meanwhile approached the mirror verge of the lake and inhaled once more.

Lifting his arms, he called out an invocation.

"Holy Brigid, Mistress of the Mists, your servant Merlin has come, seeking audience."

His words strode out across the waters. They were caught up in dancing mist and swept away. There came no response from the dark and distant isle except, perhaps, a breeze that shivered among apple trees.

"It is I, who brought you the sword Excalibur. It is I, who brought you the boy Arthur, who now is king—"

"It is you—" came a voice from nowhere and everywhere, the mellifluous tones of a woman, serene and powerful. "— and it is not you. You have changed, humble Merlin."

The shrug began with the mage's white eyebrows and traveled to his shoulders. "We all change."

A deep sigh moved across the waters. "Not this way. I do not perceive a difference in you outwardly, or even in your essence, but there is a difference—"

"I know what I am, at last," Merlin said softly. "The madness is gone, for the nonce."

The waters parted. Black and clear, they rolled back. From their frothing midst rose a glorious figure. Sculpted of living water, Brigid was at once fluid and solid. Her eyes were as black as the lake. Her robes were gossamer cloth of mist. Her limbs were supple in glimmering light. The lake closed up behind her. She approached across the water. With every step, she solidified. Dark water took on the tone and hue of flesh. Mist wove into a silken gown. Hair flowed blackly back from her high, clear brow. Though she had emerged near the center of the wide lake, it took her only three steps to reach the shore. And once she stood beside Merlin, she seemed only a noble lady in flowing garb.

"I had once seen Venus arrive that way," Merlin remarked.

A coy smile danced onto Brigid's face. "I know. I thought you might enjoy it."

"You know?" Merlin began.

"I could sense who you were when first you arrived, over a century ago," Brigid said gently. "And what your sword was. No doubt Wotan could sense it as well. Not even madness could cloak who you were, and only Rhiannon could cloak the identity of the sword."

Merlin's eyes lowered. He blinked toward the grass at his feet. "I fear the scabbard has been captured."

"I sensed that, as well," Brigid said. "While it and Excalibur are apart, the country cannot be whole, and Excalibur will draw Wotan, as it has before."

"Yes," Merlin replied. "Yes. Even now, Arthur has sent to Kings Ban and Bors in Benwick and Gaul, hoping for armies to take back the scabbard." He lifted his head. "But Arthur is not only a king of war. He seeks to build a peaceful nation. He seeks your aid and the aid of all creatures, mortal and immortal. I have come here hoping we might call a convocation of the divinities of Britannia. . . ."

Brigid took the man's measure. Her eyes moving fondly over his aged figure. "It is right that Jove should seek to assemble a pantheon."

A wry look entered Merlin's eye. "But I've misplaced Olympus and was wondering if I might borrow your holy mountain?"

Brigid looked back toward the towering isle, haloed in golden mists in the morning sun. "We prefer the term *sídh*. You have known much about us, Merlin Magus, but now you are one of us. The Otherworld, only glimpsed by you before, has become your native land. You have been born into a new world and must learn to breathe rarer air."

Merlin went to one knee before the goddess. He clutched her hands. "I am not one of you, not any longer. I am only what may become of any of you, should Arthur fail."

Her smile was dazzling. "You are a sweet creature, Merlin Magus." And her aspect transformed before him. Gossamer garments became brown homespun, her hair became a concealing hood, and wood and wicker wove themselves into a cross hanging about her neck. "Some of us have learned how to survive the sweeping purge of the old gods. I, for one, am known by the followers of the Christ as Saint Brigid." Her ascetic aspect melted back into her former appearance, and she lifted Merlin to his feet. "And you need not be a dead god forever, Jove."

Rising to the pressure of her hands, Merlin said, "Let us first fight the wars at hand and build us a place where gods and mortals can live together in peace. Then we will worry about my fate."

"I expected no less," Brigid replied.

And they were moving. Though their feet remained still, the pair of them drifted across the misty lake of Avalon. The ghosts of fog had paused in their dance—frozen in time. The apple trees had ceased their sighing sway. Even the waves on that black lake were still.

"This is the easiest path across," Brigid said. "The leybridge. To step on this highway is to step from the fabric of time. The power of particles is subsumed here in the power of the whole. All the tiny motes surrender their pull upon each other, so that walls of solid stone are passable. The material of our being sifts right past the material of all else. The beaming rays of heat and cold go tepid on this highway, that we can stand in fire and not be burned and in ice and not be frozen. Even the hourglass of time repents its monotonous trickle. We may journey from Dumnonia to Orkney and back in the space between heartbeats."

Merlin watched it all in wonder. His magic had not played with time, but only with matter, only with semblances and forms. This was new and glorious.

The pair approached a flock of geese hanging in startled flight above the water. One bird passed harmlessly through Merlin's chest. He looked back across the mirror waters to see the bird, unchanged. His own horse stood with one foreleg lifted and head bent back to snap at a biting fly. That single beast, caught in its temporal struggles, became an image of Arthur and his kingdom—of all mortals, caught in time.

Merlin's attention was dragged forward by the approaching shore of Avalon. Just as the lake had been wider than it seemed from the far bank, so too the isle was larger, more spread out, and brighter. Pebbles in dove gray and moss green formed a wide sweeping shore. Higher up lay a reedy sward in dusty blue, and beyond it, the apple trees in white bloom. They rose up a rangy slope to the far distance, where the climes grew too cool for trees. Scrub and grass clung there until the sere heights, which had none of the gentle roundness of the rest of the isle. The pinnacle of the tor was jagged, carved only by wind, rain, ice, and the hands of titans.

"It is an Olympus," Merlin said, "though from the shore it seems only a large hill."

"Avalon is farther away than it looks," Brigid says. "Most mortals can never see it at all, and even those who do see it from worlds distant."

Then all distance was removed. Brigid and Merlin slid sideways into the rising land. Pebbles and embankments of humus gave no more resistance than the goose had. They waded in the land until it reached their chests. Reeds flashed through their heads. Their very eyes skimmed the surface of the soil as if it were a waterline. Then they were plunged in deep darkness. If it weren't for the warm grip of Brigid's hand on Merlin's, he would have felt he was drowning in the land. Stone and clay, sand and dust poured through his being as they glided forward.

"Aeneas has just such an underworld journey," Merlin muttered to comfort himself.

"Otherworld," came Brigid's voice in gentle correction. "This is the realm of the Tuatha Dé Danann, former rulers of these isles. They seem almost human—your own Guinevere is Tuatha born. There are other fey here as well—titans like those you once slew, spirits of air and water, elves and dwarves, brownies and bogeys. Everywhere, they live below the bright world they abandoned. Even in Avalon, where they roam freely, their true homes are beneath the mountain. They have made the measureless caverns of Avalon a home as they once had made the face of the world."

"It is Olympus, removed only farther from mortal wars," Merlin supposed.

"They will not be altogether welcoming of you, Merlin, save that you are my guest. Nor will they be all too eager to let us convene your meeting. They do not want to share their halls with the heroes who slew them and sent them to ground," warned Brigid. "It is quite a task you have set yourself."

Merlin laughed heavily. "When they hear my fate—who I once was and who I have become—they will listen, at least. And when they hear of Arthur's Camelot, where once again they will walk in the mortal world, they will perhaps welcome me."

A smile filled Brigid's voice. "So, Arthur would make a city that is Samhain year round?" She laughed. "Perhaps you will dissuade him once you see the realm of the Tuatha Dé Danann beneath Avalon."

With that, the darkness fell away. Brigid and Merlin drifted into the world beneath the tor.

30

The Eternal City

A green mountainside tumbled away below the dangling feet of Merlin and Brigid. It dropped in steppes down to a lapping and beautiful sea. All around the dappled water, steep rock cliffs rose to flowered hillsides. Above them were budding forests, and these in turn gave way to high tolls of lichen-laced stone. There, on craggy aeries, eagles made their nests.

Other figures—some avian, some human or bestial, and others a mix of all three—coursed through skies and lands and seas. The forests danced with the movement of dryads. Brownies busily tended blossoms, wove vines, and sung in choruses of wind and leaf. The meadowlands were criss-crossed with footpaths where elven folk moved lithely among blooms. Lantern light showed fitfully in caves that honeycombed rocky cliff faces. In the water, gigantic creatures moved. Leviathans swam with smooth mass. Spike-backed sea serpents and schools of fish darted in silver flash beneath the waves. But, most amazing of all, at one end of the vast sea, a broad and silvery cascade poured down out of the illimitable sky.

"All of this beneath Glastonbury Tor?" Merlin wondered aloud as they slid out over the broad sea.

"All of this *through* Glastonbury Tor," replied Brigid. "All of this and much more." She gestured toward the center of the sea.

A churning mound of bubbles disturbed the surface. Gazing down through the water, past coiling columns of air, Merlin glimpsed a great rent at the bottom of the basin. Through it, sea water poured in a vast cascade.

"Where does it go?"

"To the world of the Fir Bholgs," Brigid said quietly. "This land you see is the realm of the Tuatha Dé Danann, who were driven out by the Celts and Britons. Beneath it is the realm of the Fir Bholgs, who were driven out by the Tuatha Dé Danann, and beneath it, the realm of the Fomorians, who were driven out by the Fir Bholgs."

"How deep does this world go?"

"As deeply as belief goes. Farther back than history. Farther back than story. The sídh extends down to the first creatures that were believed and prayed by the first folk on this isle. And each lower level was driven out by the one above— old gods killed by the new. Even now, the druids and filids and seers that drove out the Tuatha Dé Danann are seeking entry into the Otherworld, among us."

"Beautiful," said Merlin breathlessly. "Endless."

"Not endless," replied Brigid sadly. "When all the divine creatures of the Glastonbury plain were driven to this place, it seemed very small indeed. But a haven is a haven."

"That is what Arthur and I seek to build aboveground," Merlin said. "That is why I have come. Where could we best meet?"

A broad smile broke across her face. "The city of Avalon." She quickened her pace, drawing Merlin on through the streaming air. They rounded a great prominence of stone and glimpsed the golden city.

Atop a tall gray plateau, Avalon gleamed. Impossibly thin towers edged the corners of the curtain wall, which fell straight down a thousand feet to the sea. Aerial ports provided entry to the red-winged creatures swarming above the city. Within the walls, ivy-covered spires and thatched roofs gleamed in green glow.

"Our city of Avalon is composed of all the cities destroyed when the Britons invaded—those cities and our dreams of what those cities had been. The Fir Bholgs' lands center on

Dun Aonghusa, their last great fortress against the Tuatha
Dé. The Fomorian lands have a sacred cavern where Balor
of the Baleful Eye resides. All these cities are connected
through a central sacred circle. It is there that I now take
you."

The two whirled up the long cliff wall below Avalon.
Selkies and merefolk splashed on the rocky shores. Cave
spirits dwelled among rock sparrows, starlings, and thrushes.
Welkin sylphs whirled in a dance all around them. Brigid
and Merlin rose out of their midst to the high-piled wall.
Elven guards on the bartizans bowed their heads in welcoming deference to Brigid. She led her guest up over the battlements, and Merlin felt a thick curtain of magical might
sweep up around him. It plucked at his riding cloak, his very
flesh. Sorcery clawed over him, and he realized it could rend
him into pieces. In moments, though, the spell's talons softened into gentle fingers that withdrew from him.

"A haven must be guarded," Brigid said simply.

Over the rooftops they flew. These were of the old style—
poles piled in living grasses that grew a thick thatch. Sheep
grazed atop the rooftops, and leaped building to building in
their scattered herds, or crossed thin archways of fieldstone.
The skyline seemed a field of grassy hummocks, more a pasture than a city. Where there were not green rooftops, hanging gardens opened to the golden light. Ivy and mosses
covered every wall. It seemed almost as though this great
city had been abandoned to the rampant reclamation of nature—

Except that the grassy lanes thronged with folk. The Tuatha Dé Danann were there. They all had Guinevere's lithe
beauty. Not entirely elfin, not entirely human, they dwelled
in the Otherworld remnants of their former lives. Bards sang
ancient songs in languages not heard in the world above
since the British invaders swept the land. Yeomen trudged
up streets, hauling carts filled with whatever grains they had
borne in their final hours. Soldiers manned their posts, sellers
hawked their wares, buyers plunked down bags of coin that,

next morning, would appear in the same place they had that morning.

"It is dream-time here for any mortal creature," Brigid said sadly. "When we gods withdrew, we let those few who still believed come with us. They help us, you see—for we live only in the dreams of the people. But mortals cannot live well in dreams. They need true walls, not walls of fancy. They need the inevitable and inescapable approach of death to order their lives in forward ways. Remove that, and they are trapped in the cycles of mind and memory and obsession. Some live mere moments, over and over. Others are capable of sustaining days or weeks or—a few—even months at a time, but none can live truly."

"Captives," Merlin observed.

"Yes, of their own thoughts and of our need. All that we have here is the imagined relic of our past glory, and were it not for the mortals, the Tuatha Dé Danann, we would not have even that. In return, we grant them eternal life, and keep them as contented and comfortable as we can. It is a heaven, and a haven—or the best we can provide."

Merlin gazed thoughtfully down at the quiet bustle below.

A young man leaned against an ivy-covered post. He lurched to stand when a young woman emerged from a nearby shop. The lad smoothed his tunic and brushed an errant leaf from his trousers before giving the woman a gentle bow. She carefully stepped around him, trying to keep her fullered tunic out of reach. He followed for some moments, speaking excitedly to her. Even as she quickened her pace, his entreaties grew louder and more hopeful.

A butterfly happened along a grassy roofline and descended to land on his shoulder. The man turned, startled, and shrugged the creature away. In a flash of purple and green, the butterfly took to the air. The young man, dazzled, chased the retreating creature. He gestured no less emphatically or hopelessly to the bug than he had to the woman. She was altogether forgotten.

"Yes, I remember living in such fragments of mind. I remember that life—at once absurd and meaningful."

"Here is the spot, just ahead," Brigid said.

Below them, at the heart of the city, lay a great amphitheater. Carved of concentric rings of granite, the space had a dizzy aspect from aloft. The central circle was a high platform, surrounded by twenty descending tiers. At the base of the twentieth tier, a broad ring of deep blue water stood. On the opposite edge of that watery verge, the tiers rose outward again, the fortieth of which was at street level. The resultant structure seemed a great bowl, with a sacrificial altar at its center.

"The amphitheater is modeled on the sacred cauldron. It gathers and channels power. It is a place of sacrifice, the point of union between the worlds of humanity and divinity." So saying, Brigid alighted on the center platform. Her trailing robes pooled on gray stone all around her. "It is powerful enough to gather the divine forces of this sídh, and others throughout the land."

Merlin set foot to ground. He eased down from his toes and released a sigh. A sardonic laugh came from him. "Strange that the sky-god of the Roman empire should be so happy to stand on solid ground."

An ironic look answered from Brigid. "Not exactly solid." She tapped a foot on the round tier beneath their feet. Its essence changed, rock dissolving away into scintillating motes of energy.

Merlin's feet felt the same vibrant pulse he had sensed in passing through the barrier over the city. It was like standing on fingers struggling vainly to grasp. Worse, though, was the sight of that shimmering space. Chaotic figures cavorted through the darkness: faces forming and contorting and dissolving, snakes devouring one another in roiling beds, shadows of men with spiked clubs, fangs and hackles, horrors manifest.

"What is this?" Merlin asked.

"A dreaming pool," Brigid answered. "Dreams are fluid, chaotic, powerful, volatile. They can move a man or an army. They can nourish, entertain, refresh, and drown any who venture into them. This dreaming pool touches on all the old gods here within this *sídh*, and all gods in any *sídh* throughout the isles. It is connected to the conduit of ley lines that crosses the land. When transformed from stone to chaos, the dreaming pool allows those divine creatures to enter Avalon."

Merlin looked all the more eager to skip away from the clawing platform. "What if one comes through when we are standing here?"

Brigid smiled serenely. "I have opened the door, but not yet summoned them." She took his hand and led him from the dais. Together, they descended three tiers and turned. Brigid lifted her arms in invocation and spoke a single word. "Rhiannon."

"Rhiannon?" Merlin echoed.

"It is the name of the goddess-queen and wronged mother," Brigid responded. "Her son Pryderi was stolen from her when he was newborn, and she was accused of his disappearance. She is rather like your Igraine. Rhiannon did not survive the coming of Christianity, though her name is still a word of power—and a name for powerful things."

There was no more time for explanations. A tremendous rumbling noise came from the center of the amphitheater. The tier beneath Brigid and Arthur trembled. The dream pool boiled. From the rolling surface, something red and enormous jagged upward.

The creature was gargantuan, a great column of muscle. It was only just visible through a cloak of darkness. Scaly and mantled in a leathery crest, the giant serpent prepared to strike. Its jowls opened to reveal rows of dagger teeth. Baleful eyes fixed on Brigid, and a pair of horns arched downward in irritation.

"You called me from the hunt, Brigid," hissed the serpent furiously. "This had better be important."

"Were it not," assured Brigid, "I would not have invited such as you to Avalon. Now, clear the path."

Giving a last long hiss, the red worm vaulted in a terrifying arc overhead. Its obscuring envelope went with it.

Merlin winced involuntarily back from the massive creature. Brigid stood placidly as its venous hide slid past.

The serpent plunged into the ringing pool, coiled through it, and climbed out on the far side. With a final snap of its tail, it transformed into a woman with skin and cloak of red. The deep darkness remained about her, swathing her from sight.

"What is that black aura that envelops her?" Merlin asked Brigid.

"It is mystery—the armor of the gods. When this theater is filled, it will be as dark as a pit."

More creatures emerged from the dream pool, each dragging along a swath of murk. There were dog-headed warriors, a pair of shrieking storm crows, a brilliantly glowing figure that resembled Apollo reborn ("that is Lugh, Shining One," Brigid said) astride a beautiful white steed, three women bearing bread and apples in baskets, a red-armored woman with three raven heads ("Badbh Battle-Crow, goddess of warfare and death"), a man all in red with a staff topped by a skull, swarms of glinting pixies, a pair of loping wolves, two men in the brown robes of ascetics ("those are Saints Patrick and Germanus, who brought Christianity among us"), a warrior in mirror-bright armor, a huntress with a gleaming bow and quivers, a watery dragon that could barely drag itself from the portal . . . All of these and many more arrived, paying a moment's heed to Brigid—some with hatred, some with fondness, some with worship. Whether on foot or fin or wing, they moved out from the dreaming pool and took up places along the ringing amphitheater. Already, the vast place was filling up with a strange and powerful menagerie. Mystery cast a deep twilight.

Then emerged from the dreaming pool the most fearsome guest of all. Robed and bearded, with eyes like lightning, he could be none other than Wotan.

31

When Gods Plan War

*W*otan, sky-god of the Saxons, had a grandeur none of the others had possessed. White hair and beard mantled his grim features. Shimmering robes of gray draped his powerful figure. He clutched a golden staff in his hand. Wotan's eyes narrowed as he gazed out across the throng. The two storm crows that had already emerged let out a unison shriek and winged through the air to land on Wotan's shoulders. So, too, the pair of greater wolves loped up to their master.

"Ah, yes, the crows Hugin and Munin," hissed Merlin to Brigid. "I remember them from my stay in Asgard—and from their spying missions since then. The wolves are named Geri and Freki. All-seeing and rapacious. This is a god to beware."

"And yet, a god of the land, of the Saxon lands in the east," said Brigid evenly.

By Wotan's side appeared a capering figure in black, hair jagging madly from his head and eyes blinking frenetically. Whip-thin, he wore a black leather cloak and leggings.

Merlin was stunned. "Loki," he whispered to Brigid. "Yes. Loki. I had once thought him only a figment of my madness—"

"It was what he wished. You were a force of chaos, and he fed off your mind."

Loki seemed to hear their guarded words. He smiled, a grin like a dagger collection—and sketched a bow.

Merlin only nodded stiffly in response.

The muscular lightning god Thor appeared behind Loki, a great hammer on his shoulder. Next came the mother of gods, Frigga; war-god, Tyr; giant wolf, Fenris; giant brothers, Fafner and Fasolt; dwarven chiefs, Alberich and Mime; Rhine maidens; Valkyrie—all gathered around Wotan like an army around their embattled general.

The sky-god of Saxons stared levelly at Brigid. He spoke in the savage tongue of his people. The thrumming air transformed mortal language into immortal thought. "You have opened the wrong door, Brigid."

The goddess shrugged. "Perhaps. But like Pandora before me, I have opened the wrong door in order to bring hope into the world."

Loki struck a narrow cane on the ground. From the point of impact, a slender rainbow issued. It arced out over the dark moat and broadened into a multicolored path. With a sardonic flourish, Loki stepped back to allow his master to proceed across this miniature replica of Bifrost, the rainbow bridge that connected the mortal world to Asgard.

With utter solemnity, Wotan held out his arm for his wife, Frigga, to take. They strode in stately array onto the bridge. In their wake went bearded and burly Thor, son of Wotan, and the rest of the assemblage.

Merlin turned to Brigid and murmured, "One would think they ruled this land."

A reply came from above. Hugin winged down on black pinions to squawk, "We will. We will."

Merlin paid no heed.

Wotan was watching him sharply. There was much in the Saxon god's eyes—old animosity and new fear. Wotan had hosted Merlin in his own palace, tried to trick him out of his sword, to kill him. . . . Excalibur still haunted Wotan's eyes.

It was at that moment that Loki's bridge of light, loaded with the dignified gods of Saxony, displayed its signal virtue. A great wind rushed up from the rainbow bands, blowing the robes and gowns of the gods up and over their heads.

As Wotan and Frigga and Thor wrestled uncooperative garments, Loki fell to gaunt knees and pounded the floor in laughter. Mouth gaping, the god indulged a glee akin to fury. Black hair stood on end all across his head. The folds of his black waistcoat bristled like the hackles of a hyena.

A flash of lightning from Thor's hammer struck the trickster. He was pinioned on leaping energy. Then, cloth and flesh turned into ash that sifted to the ground.

Merlin reeled back. Across his eyes glowed the afterimage of Loki, crucified in lightning. Now, there was only a drifting dust cloud. "Dead?" he gasped out to Brigid.

She shook her head placidly as the rest of Wotan's entourage continued to the dark outer rings of the amphitheater. "No, these are mere semblances of the gods themselves—public faces, if you will. These powers are here in form but not in essence. None can be killed."

"None but I," Merlin reminded her.

Brigid gave him a genuine smile and flung her hand out toward the pool of dreams. The crawling chaos ceased. Energy solidified to stone. "Any who would kill you would have to answer to me."

Taking her hand, Merlin squeezed his thanks. He ascended the dais and turned slowly about. Darkness filled the amphitheater. From that darkness, eyes watched—silent, attentive. Some looked questioning, some resentful, some hateful.

"I am Merlin," he said. His eyes sparkled beneath aggressive brows. He drew a rumpled cap back from his white mane. "Many of you have heard of me, as I have heard of you. A few of you even know me in my truer semblance."

He spun around and lifted the edges of his robe winglike. His figure blurred into a white, spinning top. Fire erupted, brighter even than the lightning of Thor. The cyclone rose on the dais and spread outward in a blinding spectacle. Then the arms of the tempest curved out over the water and faded.

In the midst of the dissipating storm stood a new figure—twice Merlin's height, thrice his brawn, half his age, but centuries older. He was a man at the pinnacle of his physical prowess, so perfectly sculpted in sinew and bone as to seem a statue. Even his white raiment was more alabaster than cloth. His eyes raked outward with a beaming brilliance that was near impossible to bear.

"This is how I appeared for ages upon ages—to Greeks and Romans—and how I was when slain. For me there was no underworld to which I could retreat. There was no pocket of believers who still pinched their incense to Jupiter, lord of the gods. I did not fall to a point halfway between divinity and mortality. I fell completely and became human."

His diminishment had begun. He shrank inward. Light faded. Muscles that had once been adamantine became withered flesh. The dark, small, decrepit figure of Merlin reappeared.

"You know all too well how the new gods slay the old, how old dreams fade and die. The very layers of Avalon confess it. This haven in which you dwell is as much a prison as a paradise. To walk these streets and be dreamed by captive souls is not true life. Worse—a new God comes, one who will not allow you even this measure of life. I know, for he is the God who slew me."

A rumble of disbelief and dread moved through the amphitheater.

"You needn't take my word for it. Among us are two saints of this very God, two who brought him to these isles—Patrick and Germanus."

The murk parted to show them. Patrick was gray-haired and thin in his regal robes. Germanus was stout and black-haired. He was tonsured and dressed in a simple shift of sackcloth.

Patrick stepped forward. His voice had the lilt of his green isle. "Merlin speaks the truth. Our God took Rome for his own, and the whole of the empire, and Byzantium, as well. He took Eire, and will take all of Britannia. Even now there is a man dreamed of who shall be called Aidan—Saint Aidan, who will do for Britannia what I did for Eire."

That statement was a declaration of war to some. Actual growls came from the more bestial members of the caucus.

"And will he suffer the rest of us to remain?" Merlin asked.

Patrick smiled kindly and shook his head with regret. "Not gladly. He is a jealous God. He slays any deities he encounters."

The Red Woman spoke, her face emerging in the spiny

crest of her serpent form. "And what of you, Patrick? How is it you live?"

The contemplation on Patrick's face deepened. "We are not considered separate gods. Folk dream of us, pray to us, invoke us, seek our guiding hand, but we are only human souls serving the one God." He cast a glance at Brigid. "Indeed, our own Brigid is cannily becoming a saint, that she might escape the coming holocaust." He grew solemn. "It is not a salvation open to many, though. If history proves right, most of you will become nothing at all, or at best demons. Such has already happened to Baal, Beelzebub, and Pan. Such has also happened to Jupiter, slain outright."

"This God must be mighty, indeed, to slay great Jupiter," said Badbh, her three raven heads squawking in unison.

"Not so powerful as to slay me, though," said a new voice. The speaker stood forth, a warrior in magnificent red armor, with a sword perpetually dripping blood and eyes like twin flames. "Do you remember me, Jupiter?"

Merlin blinked at the speaker. "I do not."

"I am Mars Smertrius," replied the warrior, "god of war."

"The Mars I knew had no second name," Merlin replied.

"It is no more a change than the addition of Saint to Brigid," Mars said. "In war, I have proven myself to a new people, and so have survived."

A sardonic look crossed Merlin's face. "Have you survived? Do you any longer walk the lands above? Do you any longer march at the head of human armies? And, when this new God comes, will you survive? He does not make war with blades. He makes war with belief. He changes dreams. He destroys gods with words."

An angry murmur moved among the group.

"But I've come to you with hope. There is a new king in Britannia. He wields the very words of this new God, transformed into a righteous sword, Excalibur. He wields also the scabbard Rhiannon, fashioned by the powers of Avalon. Just as King Arthur draws power from gods old and new, he wishes to make a place for all gods, all heroes. He wishes to build a glorious city where you might walk the earth and breathe the air and mingle among mortals, once more."

Merlin whirled again, his robes fanning outward. Another light awoke in the center of his being. It rose from spinning robes and into the air far above his head. Sparks leapt from the blaze in a looping orbit before diving back down into the midst of it. Smoke coalesced into a broad cluster of hills. Atop them formed shimmering towers and walls. Motes of light outlined high-vaulted halls, octagonal towers, arches, wandering lanes, gargoyles, temples, a cathedral, and even an open-air stone ring.

The ethereal city shone splendidly in the midst of the company. Its light penetrated even the murk of mystery. The faces of gods and heroes were alight with it.

Merlin slowed his spinning and, breathless, stopped to stand beneath the spectral city. "It is this vision of Arthur's that has brought me here."

"How is Arthur to build this vision," asked the immortal hero Cú Chulainn, "even with the help of the fallen Jupiter?"

"He cannot with my help alone," Merlin replied, "but with your help? I ask you to rally behind this mortal king, that we all might live and prosper. Divided, we will be destroyed by the God of Patrick and Germanus. United, we can make a living haven for us all, god and hero and mortal."

"I am no builder," Cú Chulainn said, lifting high his sword. "I am a warrior."

"Arthur needs warriors as well," Merlin said. "Even now, King Lot of Lothian rallies folk in the north to destroy the young king and his dreams of Camelot. I ask you to aid his armies. Fight for him, and for Camelot."

The Saxon high-god stood forth, defiance flaring in his clenched teeth. "Who is this King Arthur with his god-killing sword? Who is this fallen god who wishes to build a new domain? What wages will he pay to those who ally themselves to him, who work to build his glorious city?"

Angry remembrance filled Merlin's face. "Your Asgard was built by giants—".

"It is a trap," Wotan continued. Even as he did, the vision that hovered gloriously over Merlin's head faded into drifting plumes of smoke. "He calls us here to fight for him and to build for him until he can lure us all into a trap that even we cannot escape. And there, one by one, he will corner us and slay us with his god-killing sword!"

"No!" This time it was Brigid who spoke. "Jove-Merlin speaks the truth. I have seen Arthur. I have granted him Excalibur, for he is the king who will unite the land. I have granted him Rhiannon. The land itself has chosen him. Ally with him and be welcomed in peace. Battle him and be destroyed by the God to come. If you battle Arthur, you battle destiny itself."

"Then I will battle him and destiny," declared Wotan furiously. "You, Brigid, Mistress of the Mists—so it was you who hid Excalibur from me all these decades. And you granted a god-killing blade to a mortal man. And, of course you ally with Merlin and Arthur, with Patrick and Germanus. Your place in the Christian pantheon is already assured!"

The crows Hugin and Munin circled his head in a flurry, and the wolves Geri and Freki circled his feet. His robes went from gray to crimson, and his eyes did likewise. He stomped his foot, creating a new rainbow bridge from his feet across to the dais.

"We will not join you, Jove. We will not submit to your vile trickery. We will fight you and your king on every battlefield across this land. You no longer need fear the God of the sword, for by the time this Aidan arrives, Britannia will already be mine."

With that, Wotan took the arm of Frigga and strode militantly onto the rainbow bridge. Thor shouldered his hammer, and the rest of the Saxon pantheon followed.

"Know that you are the enemies of Britannia," Brigid called to them as they crossed. "Know that you have declared war on all the rest of us."

Wotan's step did not slacken. "Not all of you." He gestured behind him.

There, from the darkness many of the gods and heroes stood to follow. The Red Woman and the dog warriors were first among them. The Highland Banshee and the eternal champion of Orkney went too. Cavorting purple imps filled the air in an impatient flock above Wotan, just out of reach of the snapping beaks of Hugin and Munin. The beautiful faerie Lhiannan Shee from the Isle of Man joined the dissenters. Raven-headed Badbh, selkies and kelpies, ogres, bugbears, bodachans, and many others flocked across the bridge.

Wotan reached the dais and struck his foot on it. The stone became once again the dreaming pool, filled with writhing figures and contorted faces. Before stepping into it, Wotan said, "You have come to enslave us, Jove, to make yourself a new Olympus from which you might reign. But many of us have escaped your spell. You have come to assure your place in peace, but have succeeded only in assuring your place in war."

With that, the Saxon god stepped into the dreaming pool and sank away. All the other followed. Dreams swirled in around them and dissolved their beings. The rainbow bridge disintegrated behind them, streaming down into the moat in oozy lines of color. The dreaming pool solidified once more.

Merlin and Brigid were left standing there amid a half-full amphitheater. Patrick and Germanus remained. Lugh, "Shining One" of the Eire pantheon, and his champion Cú Chulainn also was there. Mars Smertrius, the Tuatha Dé Danann, the kimouli faeries, sprites and brownies, Seelie hounds, and hundreds more had stayed to fight for Merlin, for Arthur.

The king of the Tuatha Dé Danann, a stately creature in shimmering robes, said, "I cannot speak for the Christian saints or the high gods or the heroes among men. But I do speak for all the fey and all the land. Know this, Merlin. We join you not because of any words of yours. We join you because of the one who holds Arthur's foot."

Merlin smiled. "Yes, beloved Guinevere."

"Without her, there is no king."

"Together, they will rule," Merlin said quietly. "Arthur and Guinevere, world and Otherworld. They rule together."

•   •   •

Atop another sídh we will fight, a tumulus of ghosts. We will fight Wotan and his host. Grave spells and ravaging monsters and looming titans.

I see the battle that will be my last. I am slain there, on that haunted hill. My ashes dance in the wind. Wotan burns me away to nothing—

Why, when I was mad, my visions were all full of hope, and now that I am sane, they are all full of despair?

32

Strange Bedfellows

*A*rthur awoke shouting obscenities into the night. He couldn't escape. A gigantic fist clutched around him. The sinews of that hand were implacable and cold. They bit like iron—muscles harder than bone and bone harder than steel. Arthur thrashed, but the titan's grip grew only more powerful.

Except that it wasn't a giant who held him. It was a god. It was Wotan.

The Great Saxon clutched Arthur in an inexhaustible fist. Another hand rummaged impatiently through the dark—and another hand, and another. Gigantic and shadowy, the god probed every corner of the chamber. His mind meanwhile coiled and recoiled like a seeking snake.

It was here here it was here and now is gone I felt it but it disappeared the blade was here while Jove was not and could not hide it . . .

Arthur realized only then that he dangled above his own bed in Castle Caerleon. His bedclothes pressed ironlike against his body. Tables and chairs overturned. Tapestries tore into rags and slumped to the floor. Shutters were ripped from windows. Mortar grated in a pelting spray from between rocks in the wall. Slates clattered atop dusty rafters.

Wotan moved, invisible but undeniable, through the royal bedchamber.

Worst of all, though, Arthur gazed down at the rent samite sheets and the mound of feathers that had once been a mattress—and he saw that Excalibur was gone.

The god-killing blade was here I felt the edge of it felt the wound of it it was here and now is gone and without Jove to save it it is gone Arthur hides it . . .

Drawing breath against the unbreakable hold of the god, Arthur growled out, "Yes, Wotan. Yes, I hide the sword. And I wait. I wait for the right moment."

The invisible hands paused in their work.

"I wait for the right moment, when you are most vulnerable."

Only silence answered his words.

"I wait to drive the sword through your heart."

The fist around Arthur tightened until no breath entered him.

You will be in my lands soon, Arthur. You will be among my believers. There, you cannot hide the blade from me. There, Merlin will die, and you just after.

Then, suddenly, the pressure was gone. Arthur dropped out of the air atop his shredded bedding. A final petulant gust rattled through the room. Tearing shutters clean away from the eastern window, Wotan left the royal bedchamber.

Arthur knelt in the ruins of his bed, panting miserably. His head throbbed. Sweat pasted feathers across arms and hands. He trembled. A god had held him, would have slain him but for the missing sword.

The missing sword . . .

Arthur stood. He could hardly get a breath. Excalibur gone? He kept the blade always beside him, even in his bed, lest it be stolen. It had been there, Wotan had felt it, and then it had disappeared.

There was someone else in the room, Arthur suddenly realized. There, in the shadow behind the massive headboard, someone waited and watched. A glint of steel came from that waiting figure.

Arthur backed away. "Who are you?"

"It is gone?" came a woman's voice. "Whatever it was is gone?"

"Who are you?" Arthur repeated insistently.

"It is I, Guinevere," she said, remaining in the shadows.

Arthur's brow beetled, and he stared into the darkness. "Guinevere? Why are you here?"

"A voice," she said quietly. Her tone was haunted. "A voice spoke to me. A voice of the land. It told me come to your bedchamber—"

"Come to my bedchamber?"

"It told me to hide Excalibur in the folds of my robe." She drew back her robe. In the dark bedchamber, the blade gave off a cold glow. She lifted it toward the king. "It told me to save the sword and save the land."

Eyes wide with wonder and relief, Arthur rushed toward her. He caught up the blade from her grasp and held it admiringly before him. It shimmered, beautiful in his feathery fingers. He kissed the blade gratefully. "I thought you were gone."

Gaze shifting from the sword to the woman who had saved it, Arthur swept Guinevere into his arms and kissed her full on the lips.

"Thank you, Guinevere. Thank you. Once again, you have saved this nation."

Her face glowed with a warm light that countered the light of the blade. But there was worry in her eyes. Even as she clung to him with one hand, Guinevere's other hand pressed against his chest, pushing him back. "You know what it is to be a foot-holder?"

Incredulous, Arthur shook his head and laughed. "I'm not talking to a foot-holder. I'm talking to you, Guinevere. I'm talking to a woman—"

"The voice I heard, I heard it because I am a foot-holder, because I am bound to the land," she continued.

"Yes," Arthur said with a wry smile. "And I couldn't be happier." He drew her to him, kissing her again. The touch of her lips was warm and lingering. Desire passed white-hot through that kiss.

Guinevere pushed away again. "You don't understand. If I am bound to a man, I can no longer be bound to the land. If I am bound to humanity, I will cease to be Tuatha Dé Danann. I saved Excalibur, and the land, and my king because I am chaste."

The dawning realization brought sadness to Arthur's eyes. He blinked.

Guinevere's face was warm and bright before him. She smiled sweetly, though her hands lingered on him. "If I choose you," she said, "I lose the land. If I choose the land, I lose you."

A shuddering breath entered Arthur, no more gentle than the gust that carried Wotan away. He hefted Excalibur and gazed appreciatively at its shining perfection. "Thank you, Guinevere, for saving Excalibur and the kingdom." With a final squeeze of her elbow, he released her and turned away. "And for saving me."

It was a weary Ulfius that rode with Brastias, Dagonet, and a brace of Claudas's horses into the valley below Benwick Castle. They had ridden all night. The body count on the farm road had come up one short. Instead of pursuing the survivor and perhaps running afoul of more soldiers, Ulfius had decided to ride hard, through evening and night and morning, to Benwick Castle.

Their horses were exhausted. Brastias slumped low in the saddle. Only Dagonet maintained his vigor. He stood aback his mount, as was his wont, one hand on the reins. The other clutched his heart as he sang:

"I ride, I ride to Ben-a-wick
    And fight to give my foes a lick
    And sing until my friends are sick
    Taloom, Taloom, Talaay!

With greenish bile their boots are slick . . .
Taloom, Taloom, Talaay!"

Sick indeed. The dwarf was intolerable. His wit was as sharp as a meat cudgel, and he wielded it with the same sanguine verve. Already, Ulfius's brain felt bashed into blood pudding.

"Enough! Enough! Enough!" Ulfius insisted, clutching his ears. "We have humored you, tolerated you, ignored you, and requested silence. Now I will demand it. Enough! Silence! Sit down and be still!"

At last, the warrior broke through Dagonet's glib mood. He closed his mouth, harrumphed, and settled down atop his saddle. The horse bounced the little man brutally as it went. Ulfius wondered if this were the reason for Dagonet's odd riding style. Still, the dwarf was in a full-fledged pout. He sullenly sat his horse.

"And sing until my friends are sick . . ." he muttered bitterly.

Ulfius said, "It's not much of a secret flight when you sing at the top of your lungs. It's as though you wanted us to get captured. Our only hope is to travel faster than word of us. Otherwise—"

"Behold, Ulfius," Brastias interrupted, "a war party—perhaps forty horse. They approach from the castle at full gallop!"

"Taloom, Taloom, Talaay . . ."

Half a league up the brown ribbon of road, horsemen rode in tight formation. One hundred sixty hooves churned the dirt, sending dust sloping up into the air. The wind followed on the heels of the company. It bore up the choking cloud into a curved mantle behind the horsemen. Already, Castle Benwick was obscured by it.

Ulfius stood in his saddle and set a hand visorlike on his brow. "They wear the colors of King Ban. But why so many, and why a war party?"

"Perhaps our companion's works precede us," Brastias said with a glance at the dwarf.

"With greenish bile, their boots are slick . . ."

Grimly, Ulfius set a hand on the hilt of his sword. "We cannot outrun them, and even if we could, we would be paying for our own safety at the cost of Arthur's alliance. No, we ride and meet them."

"Taloom, Taloom, Talaay . . ."

The roar of hooves rose with the all-enveloping cloud. Lances that might have glinted in the morning sun shone only gray. The captain pointed a gauntlet toward the invaders. Horsemen trimmed their course, intent on the invaders.

When the distance between them had closed to a thousand paces, Ulfius raised his left hand and signaled for parley. He reined in his horse and motioned his comrades to a halt. Their own dust lingered coyly at the fetlocks of the horses.

The cavalry of Benwick neared. Their golden tabards were clean and straight, drawn down in stern lines across their chests. They rode with precision—Roman-trained forces, not the rabble of Britannia. They wore trim beards, and short-shorn hair clung tightly to their helmeted foreheads. Even the horses' hooves clattered along in unison. The dust cloud behind them loomed up, an aerial mountain. It cast its shadow over Ulfius.

"Will they ignore the sign for parley?" Ulfius wondered aloud.

"Do they have the same sign for parley?" Brastias asked. "Will they simply ride us down where we stand?"

> "And find it's all a cru-el trick,
>   Taloom, Taloom, Talaay!"

The song Ulfius was unable to stop was at last ended by a coughing jag. The mantle of dust swept over the companions. Ulfius and Brastias joined Dagonet, and even the horses were sneezing before the Benwick cavalry captain motioned for a halt.

The captain's horse snapped to a stop. He was well within spear range. The other riders spread out in a semicircle to either side of their captain. They assumed designated positions, as precise as draughts on a game board. Their postures were haughty, their gauntleted hands menacing as they draped reins over their saddle rims.

"I am Ulfius, master of arms of King Arthur," called Ulfius, irritated that the dust had left his voice quiet and tremulous. "I bear a message from my king to your king."

The captain dismounted even as Ulfius was speaking. He patiently and somewhat impudently folded his gauntlets and set them on his horse's saddle. Dragging the helmet from his trim black hair and beard, the man turned to stare appraisingly at Ulfius. "I am not interested in dealing with mere messengers." He spoke in the tongue of the Gauls.

Ulfius was stunned into momentary silence. "Mere messengers—"

"Word of you has already reached us," the man interrupted. His face was a meaty red, but his eyes were the cool blue of ice. "We have many spies in the courts of Claudas, spies that keep message pigeons—"

"Who are you to offer affront to the master of arms of King Arthur?"

"King Ban," the man interrupted impatiently as he strode toward the group.

"No, I am master of arms of *King Arthur*—"

"And I am *King Ban*," said the black-haired man, pointing to a small circlet of gold in his hair, in the fashion of Roman rulers.

Eyes dropping wide, Ulfius quickly dismounted and fell to one knee, his head bowed. "Forgive me, King Ban." He motioned Brastias and Dagonet to bow as well.

The former was already on one knee. The latter was busy working out a rhyme for "Ban."

Ulfius gabbled. "I—I did not know."

King Ban waved away the comment. His eyes gleamed blue. "As I said, word of your arrival has reached us. You slew King Claudas's firstborn son—"

"We did? We did!" Ulfius noted.

"A great boon to us. His son Rorin was more the warmonger than Claudas himself, and a more capable tyrant. Oh, King Claudas will not give up—he has a second son, Dorin, who is not nearly as able—but you have hamstrung him by slaying his firstborn." King Ban strode from Ulfius to Brastias.

Both men forgot their decorum and gaped in amazed disbelief.

Ban's meaty lips formed a stern smile. "And, further, Claudas now has a new foe in King Arthur."

Ulfius stammered, "Well, we are . . . we are pleased . . . if you—"

"I never would have believed it," Ban continued, reaching Dagonet, where he sat astride his horse. "I never would have believed a dwarf could be so powerful a warrior."

Dagonet smiled broadly. It was a toothy expression, the sort that is contagious. Many of the warriors of Benwick leered gladly back at him. Dagonet boasted, "Three in one blow."

"In fact," Ulfius broke in, motioning Dagonet down off his horse, "we slew seven of the eight—"

"And what sword work!" Ban continued, amazed. "The survivor said your great sword Excalibur moved so deftly it seemed three blades, lightning leaping one to the others."

"Actually, King Ban," Ulfius tried to explain, "Excalibur is back in—"

"Where is the blade?" Ban asked Dagonet. "Where do you secrete it? Back in what?"

A lurid gleam came to Dagonet's eyes. "Back in my horse's arse!"

Ban's hand strayed toward the beast's posterior before he stopped and glared at the dwarf. Then, exploding in laughter, he said, "Yes, I am a horse's arse to ask where so precious a weapon be hid!" He laughed again, and his men joined him.

Ulfius smacked himself on the forehead, struggling to rise. He would sort out this confusion.

"Welcome to Benwick, King Arthur!" Ban said, exuberantly clasping Dagonet's arm and shaking it.

Clambering toward Ban, Ulfius said urgently, "Your Highness, forgive my presumption but this—"

"I am deeply honored you yourself have come to seek alliance, Arthur," Ban declared. "I would have turned back any other offer."

Dagonet's grin only deepened. "I personally see everyone," he said with great conviction. He waved an arm dramatically outward.

King Ban laughed again heartily. Dagonet joined him, as did all the horsemen of Benwick.

Only Brastias and Ulfius were silent. Blood abandoned their heads and fled down their necks.

Ban turned toward Ulfius, who was petrified with indecision. "Yes, yes, Ulfius? What impertinence must I forgive?"

Mouth gaping in sudden dread, Ulfius considered his options. If he revealed that this was not Arthur but Arthur's fool, he would make Ban a fool. If he allowed Dagonet his moment of glory, perhaps he could conclude the alliance this very evening.

The honest course led to certain death. The dishonest course led to an uncertain one.

"Forgive my impertinence, Highness," Ulfius said, bowing stiffly and gesturing at the horse's tail, "but I see no sword back here."

That time, even Brastias joined in the laughter.

33

New Friends

Merlin walked the streets of Avalon.

It was a beautiful city—gold-glowing walls, rioting roses, rooftops like verdant hillsides, statuesque inhabitants, apple blossom air, the star sparkle of sprites and fey. . . . It had been nearly a century since Merlin had walked the streets of Asgard and nearly two since he had dwelt serenely on Olympus. It felt good to walk again on divine soil.

Merlin breathed it all in.

Still, he was troubled. He turned his eyes down to the riverstone cobbles at his feet. His hands clasped behind his back. The events at the divine council burdened him. He had come to Avalon to seek immortal allies, and came away with as many immortal foes.

"I heard you were looking for fighting men," came an eager voice at his elbow. The speaker's language was imperial Latin, and his inflection held the sound of home.

Merlin turned.

There beside him in the bustling road stood a young man, short of stature and olive-skinned. He wore the bronze breastplate and greaves of a Roman centurion from the time of Caesar. Instead of a spatha, he carried a short gladius sword and a round parma shield. Equipped for close-order regimental fighting, the man would have been massacred in the barbaric wars Arthur had to fight. He lived here only because some god had need of his belief.

"I have found all the fighting men I need," Merlin replied kindly.

The man's expression fell. He bit his lip in thought. "I'll prove my keep. I've fought in three campaigns already. I know I seem young, but I joined the northern legion at fifteen. Somewhere, I got wounded and separated from my company. If I could just join another regiment heading to battle, I'm sure I could find them."

Merlin placed a dismissive hand on the man's shoulder. "I'm sorry. Your company will be nowhere near our battle. I cannot help you."

Distress flitted beneath the surface of the man's expression, but he put on a grave face. "Thank you, then. May Jove guide you to victory." So saying, the man bowed curtly and marched away through the crowd.

Merlin watched him go, sad wonder flocking around his heart. It was men such as that one, believers in Jove, who had kept him alive all this while.

"Your company is nowhere near either, is it, Jove?" asked a woman's voice.

Again, Merlin turned. This time he could not make out the speaker. He stood in a small courtyard, folk streaming into it on one end and out of it on the other. The homes that surrounded the courtyard were attached one to another, and their rooftops formed a great grassy bowl. At the center of the space, hemmed in by bricks laid in a mossy square, stood a lovely fountain. Its waters quietly shimmered in the golden glow of the place. And from that fountain, the woman's voice spoke again.

"Your court is gone, your Olympian friends, your palace, your nation, your people. You have neither Hera to nag you over your dalliances, nor your dalliances to drag you from Hera."

"Who speaks to me?" Merlin asked flatly.

In answer, the water parted momentarily from the fountain. It drew away in a tender ribbon that coiled in air, forming the lithe figure of a young woman. Lacing liquid outlined legs and arms. Celtic knots coursed across torso and head. Water streamed down in beautiful hair. Lovely in her broad hips and slim waist, she took form before him. She wore an ankle-length tunic, cinched at the waist by a belt of silver gilt, with sandals on her feet. And her smile was welcoming.

"I am Nyneve," she said, a quiet smile on her face and her eyes beaming gently. "I am a naiad from the court of Brigid."

"A young naiad," Merlin replied.

She shook her head in gentle admonition, "Indeed not. Looks deceive. I am older than you, Merlin, older even than the god you once were."

"Then, why the young guise?" asked Merlin.

She walked placidly toward him. "It is a guise, yes, but not a *dis*guise, for I come to you in my true aspect, as a nubile creature, seeking your company." Nyneve reached him and circled slowly around the old man, studying his form. "And I would ask you a similar question, Merlin— why this aged *dis*guise?"

The mage's brow rumpled in thought. "This is no disguise. This is my true form."

Clucking in disapproval, Nyneve tenderly drew her hand along Merlin's white beard. "You fool yourself, Merlin. You are ageless, as I am. You have the power to take whatever form you will, as I do. Why this sexless decrepitude?"

"Because I am sexless and decrepit," answered Merlin testily.

"Sexless, perhaps," Nyneve said, "but hardly decrepit. A decade ago when you came to Avalon to receive the sword Excalibur, you were only a foolhardy boy, the same age as young Arthur. You both were dreamy children, lost in the wishes of a half-imagined world. Since then, you both have grown up. You have put away childhood fancies and seen the truth of who you are."

Stern-eyed, Merlin drew the naiad's hand away from his beard. "Yes, I am no longer a child. Now I am a decrepit old dead god."

Her smile was dazzling. "That is not the way things grow, Merlin. You cannot leap from childhood to dotage. Like it or not, you are now a randy youth, the same age as Arthur. Like it or not, you are Jove of the thousand dalliances."

She reached to him again and touched his white hair. Where her fingertips traced, the dried out strands straightened and grew strong. Their color went from white to auburn brown. They shrank upon his head to form a trim cap of hair. His beard melted away, too. The network of wrinkles and scars across his face straightened and disappeared. Gray pallor gave way to a freckled and healthy blush. Freckles merged into a perennial bronze. Merlin's back straightened, his gnarled hands unfurled, and the tattered ruin of his robes transformed into a clean, straight tunic and sash.

Nyneve gazed delightedly across his transformed figure. "Here is your true aspect, Merlin. As strong and young and nubile as I."

As though batting away a mosquito swarm, Merlin irritably dispelled the image and resumed his old form. "There is no time for dalliance now. Didn't you hear the words of Wotan at the counsel? This is a time of war, war among men and war among gods—"

"Precisely," said Nyneve, wrapping an arm over Merlin's shoulder. Her touch transformed him again, the youthful man peering out beneath the semblance of age. "War is fought by hot-blooded young men, fought for the honor of hot-blooded young women."

"Too much is at stake," Merlin objected, though he breathed in the clean warm scent of her. "The divine alliance, the alliance with Gaul, the fate of Britannia, Arthur's kingship—"

"Alliance and dalliance are but one letter apart." Her fingers twined in aged locks, returning them to their brunett gleam. "Arthur's kingship comes through his union with Guinevere. You know that a man cannot rule Britannia save that he cleave to the land. Why do you think you can rule the sky without cleaving to the sea, Merlin?"

"I do not seek to rule the sky," Merlin said, at last pushing away. His eyelids closed in ache as he won free from her. "I am no longer a god."

"You could be a god again," Nyneve insisted. "I could help you. It is an easy enough thing. You are not a decrepit and sexless old man, Merlin. You are only a bashful adolescent, fearfully pushing away what you really desire."

He grasped her hands, his old self fully returned. Only his fingers were young and strong. Gazing intently into her eyes, he said, "Call it what you will, Nyneve, I am pushing you away."

She drew her hands free. The playful smile on her lips had faded. She blinked soberly at him and cocked her head. "And I had thought you remembered who you were."

Nyneve reached the fountain and stepped within. Her hands wrapped gently about the statue at its center. Already, her fingers were melding with the water.

"I'll give you time. Every boy eventually grows up, Merlin. Every boy."

The great hall of Castle Benwick was a loud and lively place that evening.

King Ban had brought out the very best his huntsmen and larders could offer—salmon and eel; pheasant, goose, and crane; lark and finch and dove; pasties, sweet pies, and savory pies; dried apples, dates, currents, and blackberries; mead, ale, wine, and spirits. King Bors had arrived, bringing with him fine spices—ginger, buckwheat, cumin, licorice, aniseed, and coriander. Both kings brought their noblest retainers, great and wealthy warriors; gluttons and drunkards all.

Ulfius encouraged the drinking, hoping a haze of delirium would help hide the fact that "King Arthur" was a dwarf and a fool.

Even now, Dagonet sat ensconced between Kings Ban and Bors. Before the dwarf were two plates, one piled high with nibbled lark bones and the other with newly arrived eels. Brastias kept delectables coursing down Dagonet's gullet so that undesirable words might not course up.

Meanwhile, Ulfius made himself the master of ale. He kept the true kings' tankards brim-full, and even spiked the royal cask with a whole jeroboam of spirits. Ulfius had tried to keep Dagonet's mug empty. When the dwarf had thrown a tantrum, Ulfius had taken a separate cask, drained half the ale into the pig troughs behind the kitchen, and replaced the missing portion with water from the cistern. He had instructed servants to give "King Arthur" ale only from that cask. The result was perhaps not what Ulfius had intended— the host kings were jocular and talkative, while Dagonet became more bloated and bellicose with each watery tankard.

"Look here," Dagonet said at one point, interrupting a long and almost incoherent account of Bors's doings in Alsace, "what sort of piss-water do you serve me?"

King Bors stopped, mouth gaping. He had the same meaty face as his brother, but hay-blond hair that stood on end at Dagonet's comment.

Ban showed equal astonishment. A small lull came over the conversation.

Dagonet stood on his seat, rising to the level of the other

men, and pointed in declamation at his frothy tankard. "Piss-water! Piss-water!" The crowd went silent.

Ulfius stumbled in, gabbling an explanation. "High praise! Th-that is high praise! In Britannia, our best ales come from a river called the Pizzwalter!"

"Shut up," King Ban said, glaring at Ulfius. "You presume greatly, servant." Turning his drunken gaze on Dagonet, Ban said, "Does our ale not please you?"

"Piss-water!" Dagonet declared, waggling his finger. "It's weaker than a drowned kitten!"

It was Ban's turn to gabble. He could not seem to produce a word, and so chose to fill his mouth with ale from his own tankard. A bitter tear struck his eye as the stuff stung the back of his throat. "It seems to me more leonine than kittenish." He blinked toward Bors, who also took a taste.

Gasping and grimacing, Bors said, "Strong as the Lion of Judah!"

Dagonet took a gulp of his own tankard and, in disgust, spewed the thing in a blond arc out over the table. "I could sooner get drunk on breast milk than this piss!"

Bors and Ban traded sly looks across the indignant figure of the "king." Ban slurred, "That sounds to me like a challenge!"

Dagonet plunked down his tankard, rolled up his sleeves, and clasped the arms of the kings in a hearty shake of agreement. "Bring out the buxom lass, and I'll—"

"No," Bors said. "A contest with us. A drinking contest. The last king standing commands the allied armies in his own battles first. Agreed?"

"Well," Dagonet considered dispiritedly, "I did rather like the buxom lass—"

"Agreed," Ulfius said enthusiastically. "I'll fill the tankards myself."

Leering wolfishly at each other, the Gaulish kings rubbed their hands together and laughed.

Uncertain just what had transpired, Dagonet allowed himself to be swept up in the laughter. Even Ulfius laughed, gladly filling the tankards from two separate casks of royal ale.

34

Armies of Hope Arrive

Night winds howled through dry grass and out over the White Cliffs. The channel seemed not a sea at all, but an abyss, the end of the world.

Merlin stood at the brow of the cliff. Night flowed like ink through his dark robes. Perhaps this was the end of his world.

Lot descended from the north. He and his allies numbered forty thousand. The kings of the north were rich and could offer not only enticing advance pay, but also spoils and land grants in crippled Britannia. Rebels swept south, overwhelming every loyalist stronghold they encountered. Most recently, the hill fort of Bedgrayne had fallen to the tide of destroyers.

Arthur, meantime, had raised an army of only fifteen thousand, and they largely without pay. His force would be no match for the foe, and his god-killing sword was useless against a man who could not bleed. Rhiannon—and Arthur's geis against killing Lot—made the rebel king unvanquishable.

No word came from Gaul.

"The end of the world."

Merlin's peered into implacable blackness. Murmurous and endless, it lurked beyond the white shore.

At last, he glimpsed it. Faint and distant in the black belly of the sea, a promise glimmered. It seemed as though the moon were rising. Rags of dim light shone atop the waves, though the sky remained as black as before.

Hope broke across Merlin's face. "Sails. Ships."

There were hundreds of vessels, each perhaps bearing fifty warriors.

"Ulfius returns. He comes with an armada. He comes with an army."

Merlin danced a jig on the brow of the cliff. His soft boots sent showers of chalk toward the shore below. Perhaps it was not the end of the world.

> "Forever from despair's black heart,
>   If stare ye long, with fierce desire,
>   There comes a ragged, risky hope
>   That brings a thousand rising moons."

"I should have believed my dreams. I should have remembered Arthur is dreamed to be king."

Hugging himself happily, Merlin started out along the cliff's edge. He sought a route down to the white shores below. He could merely have floated down, or vanished and reappeared there, but Ulfius would take time to reach landfall, and the work of climbing would give Merlin the chance to dream awhile.

"I should have believed my dreams."

Dagonet stood in the prow of the ship as it struck sandy ground. The deck heaved. He tumbled out into the black and churning sea.

Grabbing a coil of rope, Ulfius wondered darkly if he should allow the false king to drown.

The vessel bearing Ban and Bors hove up beside and likewise grounded itself. The true kings managed to keep their feet.

Ban cupped hands to his mouth and hollered over the waves, "Your king has fallen! Rescue the king!"

Ulfius stomped irritably fore, brandishing his coil of rope. "I know! I know!"

"Dive in after him! All is lost if Arthur drowns!"

Growling, Ulfius nodded. His own drowning would be a pleasant outcome. He was sick to death of playing chamberlain to a fool, of forever having to pay showy homage to that idiot. "Why do I get all the rotten jobs?"

Slipping the coil onto one shoulder, Ulfius launched into what he expected to be an impressive dive. A retreating wave dragged the vessel back from the sandbar and stole Ulfius's feet. Instead of clearing the prow rail, he landed athwart it. Air burst from him in a sound that mocked his own name. The coil of rope on his shoulder overbalanced him. He toppled overboard. He made one complete revolution before entering the water in a more-or-less dive.

Several things occurred to him in that moment. If the ship had struck ground and the water over the sandbar had retreated, the sea here was perhaps a foot deep. Dagonet could not possibly drown in water a foot deep. Nor could Ulfius dive—

The next thing he knew, Ulfius lay beneath a ring of faces, dark against the black sky. King Ban was explaining the accident. "The servant of King Arthur fell overboard, wounding himself. Arthur, who had already debarked, returned to rescue him. Otherwise, the oaf might have drowned in inches of water—"

Servant . . . fell overboard . . . Arthur . . . debarked . . . to rescue . . . the oaf?

"Arthur debarked?" came another familiar voice, at once rich and craggy.

"Yes."

Dagonet grabbed Ulfius's arms and began pumping them cranelike by his sides.

"King Arthur here," Ban said, "who even now ministers healing to the hapless man. Ulfius has proven himself quite the clumsy lout during his visit."

"King Arthur?" the other replied, and at last Ulfius recognized the voice.

"Merlin," Ulfius gasped in relief. He struggled to continue, his words chopped up by the rigorous ministrations of Dagonet. "Yes, King Arthur. He's—*whoof*—the one pumping my arms. It's hard—*whoof*—to see in the dark—"

Merlin crouched down over him. "Ulfius, you've hit your head—"

Dagonet dropped the poor man's hands and began probing his skull. "Does this hurt?"

"Yes!" Ulfius shouted, grabbing Dagonet's fingers.

"You fool!" Merlin said to Dagonet. "Get your hands off him!"

"Indeed! He is your king!" Ban declared, flinging Ulfius's hands away. "The effrontery!"

"Does this hurt?" Dagonet asked.

Ulfius abruptly sat up, intent on escaping the torturous hands. The throbbing ache in his head redoubled. He collapsed back to the white sands. "Yes, Merlin. Ban speaks of this diminutive man—our great king, our King Arthur here. He performed wondrous feats of glorious—" the next word was almost too galling to produce "—single-handed combat, and Kings Ban and Bors were so honored to have the dwarven king of Britannia come *personally* to their courts, they pledged *immediate alliance.*"

Merlin's eyes were querulous little glints in the night air. "And I thought I was mad. . . ."

"We will follow this little majesty wherever he leads," Bors proclaimed stoutly.

Merlin coughed. "Yes, well, tonight he leads north. The armies of the king's rival, Lot of Lothian, have overrun the hill fort at Bedgrayne, and Arthur has taken the field to turn them back once and for all."

"*Arthur* has take the field?" Bors and Ban asked together.

Merlin stammered, "W-well, yes—that is—Arthur the Less has taken the field. Arthur *the Less*, monarch of much of the south country, and liege to this one, here—"

"Arthur the More," Dagonet proclaimed joyously.

"Arthur the More," Merlin and Ulfius echoed in dour tones.

"You say we march northward, even tonight?" Ban said. "How shall we see? There are no stars, no moon to guide us."

A gleam entered Merlin's eyes. "I will show you a highway that lights itself. More ancient than the Roman roads, and smoother. It is attended by friendly spirits. Your men will be succored and rested and in Bedgrayne this very night."

It was like walking in a dream. The path was razor thin, and yet the armies of Ban and Bors marched twenty abreast, with room on either side.

They had entered the ley-line path in a ring of oaks—what Merlin called a sacred grove. He muttered a few words, and the great oak on one edge of the grove split in half. A red shaft of light passed through its core and out across the landscape. In numerous places, the highway bisected other trees, separating their halves widely.

"Such destruction," Ulfius said, disapproving even in his wonderment.

Merlin clucked. "No destruction. This is an infinitely slender slice from the Otherworld. It cuts through trees and hills, lambs and men without harming them. It freezes them all in time while we walk that way. We will step into this highway near the White Cliffs and, in the same instant, step from it at Bedgrayne."

With an ironically cocked brow, Merlin gestured the army to march between the halves of the oak. Ulfius led the way, keeping Dagonet close by.

Once they strode onto that red-glowing pathway, it began working improvements on them. Scratches from briers knitted gently closed. The liquor of exhaustion slowly leeched from every weary tissue. What remained was an uncommon clarity of mind and eye.

Ulfius saw Britannia as never before. He saw not only the forest but the trees, not only the trees but the rings, and not only the rings but the years alive in those rings. Worms burrowed blindly through history. They consumed the millennial hearts of the most ancient trees, but modern rings lived on. Ulfius glimpsed the lightless insides of bisected cattle, their manifold stomachs caught in moments of constriction. Severed veins and cloven bones gave views into the cores of life. He saw a sliced yeoman asleep on his pallet within a wide-opened hovel. Layer upon layer, the man was like a ringed tree. His species was thousands of years old at the moment of his first breath.

The world seemed a very different place when beheld in the rubefacient light of the swarming fey. It was their magic that created the highway. The saving armies of Ban and Bors were healed and fortified and carried across the land in a river of minute creatures.

Then they stepped from the ley line. It was as quick as that. Suddenly the warm red envelope was gone. They stood in the black dew of a field. On one side, the primeval forest of Bedgrayne loomed. On the other lay an equally ominous sight—a night-encamped army with not a single lamp lit. Only a new-risen moon illuminated the scene.

A horseman on a blustery steed stomped in the midst of the dark tents. The steed's sinew seemed the only solid thing amid flapping canvas. The mount reared and turned. It charged across the glade, straight toward Ulfius, Brastias, Bors, Ban, and the armies of Gaul. In the rider's wake, more forms mobilized. The whole camp came to life. Horses and hauberks boiled in the inky night.

Ulfius called out along the line. "Brace to receive a charge. Infantry to the fore and set pikes! Cavalry, back the footmen!"

There was no more time for orders. With a wild whistle that shivered the bones of Gaul, the rider arrived. He pulled up just before the living palisade of soldiers and polearms. The horse seemed to want to run them down, but the rider hauled hard on the reins. The host behind him came to a pounding halt.

From the height of his steed, the rider shouted down in a hearty voice. "Welcome to Britannia, Ban and Bors. Merlin has told me of your coming, and just in time!"

"King Arthur!" Ulfius cried out in happy realization.

"King Arthur?" Bors wondered, confused.

"King Arthur the Less," Ban clarified.

A broad laugh came from the man on the horse. "Yes, Merlin told me of that too. I welcome back also King Arthur the More, who is called Arthur Pendagonet."

"Pendagonet!" Ban said. "Yes, I have heard of that surname. Pendagonet!"

A waddling figure emerged from the armies of Gaul, trundled past the pikemen, and approached the stallion. With an athletic flip, Dagonet leaped onto the horse's back. He landed facing Arthur.

"Ah, Arthur!" Dagonet cried in joy. "Give us a kiss!"

Ulfius smacked himself on the forehead, creating a sound only slightly quieter than the smack of that ardent kiss.

"Whence do you come, Arthur Less?" asked Bors. "And where are you bound?"

Atop the impatient steed, Arthur said, "I ride from the noble army of the king, fifteen thousand stout hearts and true, marched here fresh this day under cover of faerie allies. Merlin has won for us the help of the wood spirits of Bedgrayne and the water dryads of Sherwood. We have advanced under an ever-shifting curtain of brier and ivy, cloaked in mists rising in ribbons from streams and rivers. The axes of our foes have busted and rusted and fallen from any hand that wields them for firewood. It is well to have forest allies! The deadfall the rebels have gathered for their campfires smokes mightily and spews noxious fumes so that they are all even now griping of raw throats, gritty eyes, and throbbing skulls."

"Is that where you are bound?" asked Bors. "Where *they* are?"

"Yes!" Arthur replied in an excited rush. "Lot's main army has come out to drive west and south across the countryside, over forty thousand of them."

"Forty thousand! Against fifteen thousand?"

"Ah, but now you are here with another ten—"

"That still makes forty thousand to twenty-five thousand—"

"And there are the fey allies, and the deities of the oak—"

"That still makes forty thousand to twenty-five thousand—"

"And I am King Arthur!"

"The Less."

"Yes," Arthur said. "Yes, but that is where I am bound, into the heart of the forty thousand. I have selected a band of one hundred, including myself and Merlin, for a midnight strike against them. We go with fey allies, who can hide us as though we were the wind. We will be in their midst before they rouse from their smoldering fires. Just as the angel of death through the lands of Egypt, we will pass. Each of us will have the blood of ten men on our swords—the ten most defiant men we meet, and no alarm will sound. We will move like the thief in the night, and steal away Lot's best commanders, and make the rest tremble at the coming battle. Merlin will meanwhile terrify them with glamours across the stage of the sky. With valor and cunning, we will whittle our foes to wooden soldiers by morning."

"One hundred against forty thousand?" Bors gabbled.

"My Royal Hiney will hie forth, of course, with this noble band," declared Dagonet dramatically, standing in the saddle.

"Then, of course, I, King Ban of Benwick, will hie mine hence as well!"

"I too, and fifty of my men!" King Bors declared.

"Fifty of mine!" Ban replied.

"And Ulfius of Chertsey, and Brastias of Tintagel," shouted Ulfius.

"Good," Arthur replied. "We will stand down while you settle the most of your men here on this meadow. The forest folk will hide you, sight and sound, as you camp. Then bring your best and brightest here beside me, and I will tell you my plan. We shall ride together into the heart of the foe!"

35

Thieves in the Night

Two hundred strong, Arthur's force advanced in slow silence through the Bedgrayne woods. Horseshoes had been struck from hooves—the tree folk wanted no iron-shod beasts clottering over their roots—and war livery and saddles were left in camp. Only the men were armed and armored. Their mounts were stripped to nature, that they might make their way with the silence of harts. They walked lightly, careful to avoid the faintly glowing rings of mushrooms, the dark sparkle of sacred wells and springs, the oak groves that glimmered with moonlight. Yes, they trampled undergrowth, of course, but in their passing left the fragrant gifts of horses, a payment like gold to the pixies there.

Otherwise as to raiment, the warriors wore the tendrils of the forest—lichens, leaves, vines, and moss. Upon these natural bits of disguise, the faerie folk of Bedgrayne had laid enchantments. Brownies and sprites knew much about hiding in plain sight—the virtues of grays and duns, the sort of humble line and down-turned aspect that deflects eyes. As a result, no one could look directly at the warriors. They seemed almost an army of green men, indistinct from plant and water and air.

Not so the forces of Lot. They had pitched tents right up to the eaves of the woods, unable to clear the tenacious trees—hard as iron. The campfires were few and sooty amid many dark tents. The stench of noxious smoke mixed with spilled wine and spilled suppers, sweat and irritation.

Arthur ordered a halt. The whispered word moved back among the trees like a restless breeze. Bors and Ban pulled up to one side, and Ulfius and Brastias to the other. Dagonet sat before the king.

"Arrogance. Do you see—not even sentries?"

Bors laughed darkly. "We can sweep through the whole army, tent to tent, in silence, cutting throats."

"Not much honor in that," Arthur said. "These are countrymen. We follow the plan: engage only those outside the tents. Let sleeping men lie."

Ban said, "They'll not sleep for long."

"We still have surprise on our side, and the fey, and Merlin, and right," Arthur replied. "Dishonor would only undo us."

Bors spoke, a new regard in his voice. "How is it that a man of such courage and honor and wisdom should be called the Less?"

Arthur struggled with a response and could produce nothing. He said simply, "Dismount." The signal went back among the leaves. "We'll need our steeds on the open field tomorrow. Tonight, we leave them here, in the hands of the forest folk. Ban, Bors, Ulfius, Brastias, go to your divisions. On count of one hundred, we enter and begin the night's grim work."

"God be with us!" Ban said as he dismounted.

"God and gods both," Arthur replied.

In aside to his brother, Bors said, "I've never heard so lunatic a plan as this."

"Oh, no, Brother," Ban replied. "I see its wisdom. In fact, this lesser king seems the more to me. Beside him, Arthur Pendagonet is but a gimpy fool."

A soft count to one hundred began on whispering lips. The five men departed one another, seeking out their separate companies of forty men each. At count of fifty, swords whispered from sheaths. At count of seventy-five, the air was alive with prayers murmured to all the gods dreamed in the Midmarch. And at one hundred they set out, striding from the eaves of the forest toward the first flickering fires amid the tents.

With Excalibur still sheathed, Arthur led his contingent on silent feet. He stepped lightly past a set of tent ropes, between slopes of uneasy canvas, and out beside the smoldering fire.

Men sat on logs and stones beside the blaze. Others lay in drunken stupor beside or half-within their tents. Drowsy words passed among the wakeful folk.

Arthur motioned for his moss-cloaked men to circle the fire, behind the rebels gathered there. It took an exertion of will for Arthur to make out his own warriors. Lot's forces were oblivious. Wan firelight made their faces into orange mosaics. In moments, Arthur had them surrounded.

"Where are you, men of Lot?" Arthur asked in a voice like the haunted whisper of the very night around them.

All around the fire, eyes rose and grew wide. The slumped fighters straightened, listening. Their mouths formed little Os in their faces.

"Where are you, men of Lot?" Arthur repeated. "This is not your land. It does not want you."

A tall warrior just beside Arthur stood and whirled, searching the darkness. Unlike the other rebels there, this man wore a sword at his waist. "Who speaks? Who is there?"

"It is I, King Arthur. It is I, and my sword Excalibur, and my army."

The tall man waved hands before him, inches away from brushing Arthur. "We cannot see you. What sorcery carries your voice hence?"

"No sorcery, but only the land. The land you wrongly claim."

The tall man drew his sword. "How are we to fight you, King Arthur?"

"You cannot fight the land," Arthur declared. Shrugging off the cloak of moss across his shoulders, he drew Excalibur and stood glowing before the smoking fire. "Surrender or die."

"He's a ghost!" declared one of the unarmed men at the fire.

"He's got an army of ghosts," another said.

"How do we fight ghosts?"

Gritting his teeth, the tall man said, "Here's how." He swung furiously.

Flaring brightly in defense of its master, Excalibur leapt into the fray. Steel struck adamantine. Sparks skipped from the tangled blades. The pair parted.

The tall soldier flung his sword in an overhead strike at Arthur. The blow was batted back with a metallic shout.

Excalibur leaped in, skewering the man through the middle.

He staggered back, near to falling into the sullen flames. With a groan, he crumpled to his knees.

Arthur looked down sadly on the gasping man. "Where are you, men of Lot?" He withdrew Excalibur entirely.

The warrior slumped among dust and moldy logs.

Wide-eyed with terror, the other men lifted their hands helplessly in the air. There were eleven of them, unarmed and spooked, sitting paralyzed in the dirt. One red-bearded man ventured irritably, "What's to happen to us? We haven't even our swords—"

Arthur tilted his head in consideration. "You can return to your tents to retrieve them, if you like. You can even awaken your comrades so that they can come out and fight us. But I swear to you, any armed man who emerges from his tent this night will die. I swear to you also, any man who remains in his tent will live to see the morn. We will not enter your tents."

The red-bearded man blinked in uncertainty. "You will allow us to return to our tents without being slain?"

"Yes," Arthur replied, "there to regain your swords and awaken your companions—"

"Or to remain, and live?" the man finished.

"Yes."

"We will not surrender," another man growled.

"I'm not asking for surrender," Arthur said. "I'm asking only for sense. Those who fight me tonight are irredeemably men of Lot, and will die. Those who go to their tents and remember my words—they may well be men of Arthur when this battle is done. Now, enough talk. Back to your tents.

Fight, those who will, and sleep, all the rest."

Stiff with fear, the eleven stood and turned. Hands over their heads, they walked among the shadowy figures that surrounded them. Eyes marked out what might be dim blades, obscured by enchanted foliage. Fingers trembled with the terror of facing this force. Lot's warriors stalked slowly toward canvas feeling their way through the forest of fighters. One by one, the men entered their tents. Whispers ensued within, and fumbling in the dark.

Two rebels returned.

Their war cries were only half formed, their blades half lifted when they were cut down. Heads leaped from necks and tumbled to ground beside sloppily sprawling bodies.

In other tents whispering ensued.

"Would anyone else this night wish to fight the land, to fight King Arthur?" asked the young ruler. No response came. Tent flaps hung loosely. "Then remain within and live to fight us tomorrow." Arthur donned again his mantle of moss and ivy. He merged with the night. Quietly choosing two of his warriors, he posted them as guards. "Any who emerges will die."

Then, signaling the rest, Arthur pressed onward toward the next fire. The tide of enchanted warriors followed him.

All that night, they rolled slowly through the forces of Lot.

It was a quiet invasion.

Arthur's forces were more than invisible. They were grave, almost priestly. Not only had the forest cloaked them, it had invested them with its ethos of subtle and inevitable conquest. The warriors that had whooped excitedly hours before were now shadowy diplomats. Arthur, Bors, Ban, Ulfius, and Brastias all possessed that solemn spirit. Yes, they slew men, sometimes one by one, sometimes in their tens and twenties. But it was sacrifice, not slaughter. They slew men swiftly and silently and sent the rest of Lot's army off to bed. Those slain were Lot's heroes and champions, the officers intent on rallying the men.

Next day, Lot's army would be a fearful rabble.

Even Merlin was inspired to quiet conquest. Instead of painting the skies in images terrible and calamitous, he merely called forth the hidden constellations, reshaping them to terrify the foe. Draco glowed brilliantly overhead. Its draconian figure was enhanced to resemble a Pendragon. He moved Corona Borealis, the crown of the north, until it rested brilliantly on the head of the dragon. And then, with a wry smile, he made Jupiter beam so brightly that it seemed a moon.

Dagonet too had a subtle turn of mind. Instead of vaulting through encampments, taunting Lot's forces into blind rage, Dagonet stole a horse blanket and some dirty tunics from a line where they had been drying. He donned one, arraying the thing so it seemed the dress of a washer woman, and stuffed the others into the bundled blanket. Then, utterly placid, he wandered from fire to fire ahead of the advancing army. He would tap a drowsy soldier on the shoulder and, in a woman's voice, ask, "Where is the ford? I've so much washing to do tonight."

Without waiting for reply, he would wander to the next site. In his wake, men gaped and grumbled about the ill omen.

"The wee washer at the ford!"

"The bean-nighe! The caoineg!"

"Harbinger of death!"

Soon, Arthur's troops came to firesides where no one sat. Fey reported sporadic groups of rebels fleeing northward through the woods. Desertion after desertion—and all because of a dwarf with a bundle of dirty laundry. In the dark, none of Lot's folk seemed to notice that their wee washer had a stubbly beard and breath that could slay an ox.

Dagonet delighted in his silent battle. He couldn't decide whether he preferred to be a banshee or King Arthur of Britannia.

•   •   •

Vision and truth are indistinguishable to me this night. It is lunacy, this shambling army of green men, quiet and deadly in moss, harvesting heads as though they were melons. Arthur flits into and out of being in their midst, glimmering king one moment and less-than-shadow the next. And though Dagonet may truly be the Less, he proves himself the More. He makes specters from banal blankets. And I am as madly engaged. I bring silent terror from spangled skies.

Ah, I should have known you would be here, Loki, in this constellation of truth and phantasm. You allow us this night of killing. It delights you, the sanguine absurdity. But there is more than delight in your winking eye. There is connivance. You let us slay the invaders because you know a greater threat rises for Arthur. Perhaps it comes in tomorrow's battle . . . Perhaps it comes in treachery beyond. . . .

Yes, I see her in your eyes—I see Morgan Le Fey.

Morgan awoke with a start. She sat bolt upright in the darksome tent. A queer sound filled the air. It came not from outside the tent—she'd grown immured to the vulgar noises of soldiers—but from inside.

Rhiannon was singing.

Morgan turned on the reed pallet and squinted toward the scabbard.

It floated, as before, in the center of the space. The spirits of the weirds still coiled about it—maiden, mother, crone—holding it aloft. They rose from a sacred cauldron and danced in joy about Rhiannon, specters warding the scabbard from detection and harm.

But why was the scabbard singing?

Morgan edged across the canvas toward the spot. She had worked this magic herself, a simple but powerful ward. The sacred cauldron was in fact Lot's best helmet, blessed for the task. It bore not only the great feminine powers of the cauldron, but the great masculine powers of the head. Best of all, by gazing into the blood it held, she could scry the mind of the Lothian king.

That was the second part of the spell, blood. Blood was life. When a small sacrifice was placed in the cauldron, a great bounty flowed from it. The tiny seed of the father is sacrificed to the cauldron of the mother to bring forth the bounty of the child. In this case, the sacrifice was one of blood—her own—and it brought the bounty of the ever-watchful weirds. Lot's helmet and Morgan's blood were a potent combination, and the weirds thickly wrapped the scabbard.

Why did Rhiannon sing?

"Excalibur is near," Morgan whispered in dread realization. "Rhiannon sings to Excalibur."

Heart pounding, Morgan knelt before the cauldron. Her raven hair pooled on the canvas floor. Taking the helmet in her hands, she prayed. She felt the coldness of her blood through the battered metal.

She began a chant. The sound moved through her. It warmed the cauldron. It warmed the blood. The weirds quickened their spectral dance. The vapors about the scabbard grew opaque.

Still, Rhiannon sang, longing for Excalibur. The sword and its master approached.

Morgan sang as well, matching her tone to the scabbard's. She sang a prayer to the goddesses.

The holy sheath began to glow. Its gems sent facets of light throughout the tent.

The weirds danced in a cyclone now. Their figures seemed almost fleshly, so thick they were, but still they could not shut out the light of the scabbard.

The helmet grew hot in Morgan's grip. She opened her eyes to see a rim of bubbles forming in the blood. Slowly, it began to boil.

Excalibur would be just outside now. Arthur would be just beyond the tent flaps.

Morgan did not rise, trusting to the old ways.

Rhiannon trembled. Its tone grew piercing. Red steam rose from the boiling blood. The helmet seared Morgan's hands. She shut her eyes to the scorching heat.

There came a sharp sound beyond. A body fell heavily against the tent flaps. There were voices, hushed and efficient.

The helmet began to melt. Giving a small cry, Morgan drew her hands back. Steel folded and blood hissed on the canvas floor. The weirds dissipated. No longer held aloft, Rhiannon plunged. It struck the bloody earth and lay still. Its singing ceased.

Morgan panted, kneeling.

Excalibur was gone. Arthur was gone. Had they lingered a moment longer, sword and scabbard would have called each other with such force that nothing could have kept them apart. Now, the young king and his sword were gone.

So too was Morgan's sacred cauldron, her blood sacrifice, and the weirds that guarded Rhiannon. She would need another cauldron, more blood—and quickly.

Morgan rose from the puddled gore and staggered toward the tent flap. She looked out.

The guard beyond had been slain. He had been a massive man, and honest—trusted by Lot to protect his greatest treasure. Arthur himself must have slain him. What sword other than Excalibur could cleanly cleave off the top of a man's skull? The stroke must have been meant to decapitate him, but the guard ducked at the last. Just above ear and eye, the sword had passed. The brain case was hewn cleanly from the rest.

It was a brutal scene, but there was one saving grace. The severed bowl of the guard's head lay just within reach, pooled with fresh blood . . .

Unknowing, Arthur himself had provided a more powerful cauldron, a more powerful blood sacrifice. How much better a skull than a helmet? How much better the blood of a guardian than that of a witch? With this cauldron, Morgan would see into the mind not only of Lot, but of his army. She would know how things fared in the battles. . . .

"Your own actions bring your own doom, Arthur."

With sanguine reverence, Morgan Le Fey reached for her new cauldron.

36

Death in Bedgrayne

Morning dawned in horror. The terrible nightmare that each rebel had suffered in solitude turned out to be true.

The dead lay, two or three, beside each burned-out fire. Always, they were the bravest fighters, the best men—three hundred fifty-five of them. Most often, they were nobles who fought from horseback, or captains of infantry divisions. Their horses were stolen away too, reins slashed and left on the ground, saddles untouched in the equipment piles, and even shoes struck from hooves.

These nobles and captains were not the only ones lost during that nightmare evening. Guided by the light of beaming Jupiter and a crowned Pendragon, deserters staggered northward through the forest. For every one man slain, there were ten who fled the invisible army of death. They could not fight the land, and so surrendered to it, letting it lead them back toward their faraway homes. The fey folk that had conveyed Arthur into the heart of the camp now conveyed Lot's men outward. Brownies urged them on, bent branches back to form straight avenues, lit dim constellations of mushrooms to direct their feet where the stars overhead were hid.

And for every man who deserted, there remained ten more who wondered why they hadn't. It was craven fear, they decided. They were told to stay in their tents and live, and so stayed and lived—for one more night. It had been a desperate night of cold sweats and moral anguish. When morning came and showed that the angels of death had melted away, men emerged from tents smelling of worry and urine. They had a haunted look, weary to the bone. The word "surrender" murmured among dead coals and ashes. They might have fled even then, in broad daylight, but for their kings.

With a fury unlike that of the invaders, the kings rode among their troops. Lot, Carados, Cradelment, Aelle of Sussex, Fergus More of Dalriada—the eleven rebel kings harangued their dispirited troops. Done up in fine war armor and riding barded horses, they stomped among the tents. Bundles of blazing torches were clutched in their hands, and wherever they went, they savagely shouted up the army.

"Pile that firewood here! Drag those bodies over!"

"Move, you worthless curs—comrades slain while you quivered in your beds!"

"There's a breakfast fire for you! There! Warm yourself by the pyre!"

"Breathe it in, lads. That's the stink of death. That'll be the stink of you lest you draw sword and fight today!"

Lot was most bloody-minded of all. He reached one fire circle where not a single man showed himself. He called into the tents for any cringing worm that remained to emerge for his due. When none did, he charged his stomping stallion atop tent after tent, killing any man within. And when signs of movement came from those tents he had not yet reached, he hurled torches atop them.

"There's your safe tent! There's your cowardice! There's your pyre!"

Lot wheeled his horse and charged to an embankment. He stood in the saddle and shouted, "We are thirty-five thousand! But are we men or worms? If we be worms—thirty-five thousand worms—we are doomed to writhe in flames until our skins are crisp and the man Arthur plucks us up one by one and bites us in two. But if we are men, men like this Arthur, better than he—we will march this day to find our foe and slay him and all those with him. If we are men, then we will fight and prevail and, this day, Britannia will be ours."

From tens of thousands of ragged throats and bloodless lips rose a cheer—a great, hopeful, and angry sound.

●   ●   ●

The distant shout—unholy and bloodthirsty—broke into Arthur's morning repast with his ally kings. From steaming trays of egg and crisp piles of bacon, the kings lifted their eyes and listened. The cry was chilling, yes, but also sad—full of suffering.

Arthur gazed levelly at his allies. The young king's eyes were very old that morning—weighed down with killing. "This ends today. We will slay today so that tomorrow we might heal." He pushed his unfinished plate of eggs away from him across the table. "The land is sick from drinking blood."

Bors watched warily, his blond-bearded jowls working as he chewed. "They still outnumber us by ten thousand. What plan have you for that?"

A dark smile crept onto the king's features. "I plan for them to outnumber us by twenty thousand." He laughed grimly. "I plan to hold your forces in reserve."

"What?" sputtered Ban, yellow bits of egg speckling the table before him.

"There is a narrow meadowland that cuts through Bedgrayne Forest, used to drive sheep through the woods. It is flat, grassy, and verged tightly on both sides by ancient woodlands. At its narrowest point, it will keep them to a hundred horse abreast. We shall station our force at one end of that passage—only fifteen thousand of us. Lot, furious after the night's losses, will throw his thirty-five thousand into that passage. We will meet them there, where the terrain will prevent him from flanking us or bringing all his forces to bear. There, we will fight them, with our woodland allies beside us."

"They will grind through you," Bors said. "At the last, unless you can slay three men to one, they will grind through you."

Despite the sun-bright pavilion that held them that morning, Arthur's aspect grew dark. "Once they are committed, Merlin will convey you by the ley-line highway to appear, ten thousand strong, at their undefended back. *You* will grind through *them*, and slay ten for every one. Merlin will aid you there. The rebels will surrender—let us hope—or we will capture their kings. And remember, no one is to slay Lot. We are sworn to it."

Ban asked, "What if they do not surrender and we do not capture their kings?"

"That is worst of all—and I am grieved to think of it. Then, the rebel armies will feed the grass."

In mirror-bright armor and purple-and-gold Pendragon livery, Arthur rode at the head of an army of fifteen thousand. Ulfius cantered at his side, the royal standard in his lance holder. In his other hand, he wielded a spatha. Behind them rode nearly five hundred noble warriors from across Britannia. Ector and Kay were there, amid a contingent of eighty other riders from Chertsey. Brastias led up a group of sixty riders from Tintagel. Gryfflet of Dyfed and Lucas of Bath had eighty men each, and Caerleon had sent a hundred twenty. Their various panoply made bright spectacle in the early morning light.

Behind them, well rested and caparisoned in clean armor, marched an eager infantry. Pikes glinted in the morning sun. Spathas sent bright wedges of light across the thick foliage to either side of the road. Among them marched five hundred archers from Dyfed and Gwynedd in the west—the best bowmen on the isle. The army of Arthur was small compared to the forces marshaled against them, but they were well armed, well fed, and in fighting trim.

"Ahead, here," Arthur said to Ulfius as they rounded a bend, "you see where the way narrows? That is where we will meet them."

"And soon," Ulfius replied, pointing. "For there, now, is the army of Lot."

Over a rill in the north, rebel infantry and horsemen poured in a dark tide.

Arthur stoically watched them come.

Earlier, he had spotted mounted scouts along the edge of Bedgrayne, and had sent five horsemen to give chase. The peril of their narrow escape had no doubt added urgency to the scouts' report. It was meant to be another umbrage Lot could not to bear. It had worked, drawing him perfectly into this trap. Now, Lot marched his folk southward into a killing strait.

Less than a mile separated the two armies. Through the bee-buzzing air of the meadow, the dress and demeanor of Lot's army was clear. They wore gray and wrinkled livery and bore armor dimmed by dirt and haste. Beneath disheveled hair, their eyes glowered angrily. Sleeplessness and shame ringed their gaze.

"I had hoped for fear, not anger," Arthur commented quietly.

Ulfius blinked toward the advancing army. "There is fear there too," he replied, "only masked by anger. And one wonders whether the anger is directed forward or backward." He pointed to where the standard of Lothian fluttered.

Over the grubby heads of the infantry, other banners shone—the Saxon wolves Geri and Freki for Sussex, a red boar on a green field for Carados, a white ram's skull for Dalriada . . . Eleven kings and their armies stretched out to the forest horizon.

"Call up the archers," Arthur told a mounted messenger. "Send them ahead of us, through that corner of woodlands. Order them to fire when Lot's forces enter range."

Nodding, the young man turned his horse against the tide of the army and cut his way through. Another rider pushed up to take his position. In moments, the divisions from Dyfed and Gwynedd cut through the woods.

"It would be best if you fell back, Arthur," Ulfius said. "Do you see where Lot rides? In the midst of his men?"

Arthur was distracted, watching the archers move rapidly through the dense forest.

Ulfius pressed. "This war is about you, Arthur. If something happens to you in the first charge, then—"

"Then the rest of you won't have to die," Arthur interrupted as his archers assumed their positions and nocked arrows.

Grim-faced, Ulfius shook his head. "You cannot afford to be impetuous."

"I cannot afford not to be impetuous," Arthur replied irritably. "This battle will be won by valor, or not at all. I haven't the resources to be conservative."

"That is how Lot will fight—conservatively," Ulfius said. "In fact, at this point, according to the traditions of engagement, he will likely signal for parley—"

"I doubt that very much," Arthur replied, standing in his saddle.

"You doubt that very much—"

"He's ordered a charge," Arthur said calmly.

A contingent of horsemen five hundred strong swept up before the main body of Lot's force. He was holding more—many more—in reserve. With grim efficiency, these riders formed five lines of charge. Their horses champed and snorted impatiently.

With a distracted air, Arthur said, "They would have had twenty-five hundred had we not freed so many horses last night."

"They are five hundred, and this in the first charges," Ulfius replied. "Had we stolen the horses instead of freeing them, we could have had twenty-five hundred mounted troops. As it is, we can receive only one set of charges, and then our infantry will be exposed to lines of heavy horse."

In the distance, Lot signaled the first charge. Heels dug into horseflesh. Whickers and snorts came from the line. Mounts bent their necks to the charge and drove off hind legs. Forehooves sank to earth and flung up great divots of it. The drone of marching armies gave way to the rising thunder of a cavalry charge. Like a great tide of muscle, they swept toward Arthur's units.

"The glades were glad to have the horses," Arthur said quietly.

"Countercharge?" asked Ulfius urgently. "Order a countercharge."

Arthur pursed his lips and shook his head.

Bowstrings twanged from the forest verges. Shafts rose up,

white against luffing leaves and cerulean sky. They hailed down along the charging line. The pang of steel on steel rattled through the air. Shafts thrummed into flesh. Riders fell. Horses shrieked and ran on, feathers jutting from shoulders and flanks. Perhaps twenty-five riders from the line of one hundred went down. Seventy-five continued onward.

"Now a countercharge," Ulfius suggested, eyes widening as the horsemen converged. "Now."

Arthur shook his head. "Epona, specifically, was grateful for the horses. She spoke to the Tuatha Dé Danann, who spoke to the redcaps, who spoke to the meadow conies—"

"What are you talking about?"

Suddenly, as though struck by invisible lances, half the line of charging horses shrieked and flipped over. They crashed down atop their riders. Some men were thrown free and ended in broken ruin before the line of charge. Most, though, became only armored pulps of meat and gristle beneath their dying steeds.

"What?" gasped Ulfius. "Otherworld pikemen?"

"Rabbit holes," Arthur replied easily. "They have been digging all night."

A few more riders went down in the next moments, and the momentum of those who did not was broken. The survivors slowed, picking their way across the treacherous ground. More arrows hailed down in their midst. Reinforcements rode up to replace those who had fallen and moved gingerly across the space. Once they had navigated it, they reformed their line and continued the charge.

One hundred heavy horse plunged toward Arthur's lines.

"What new salvation, then?" Ulfius asked. "Poisonous spiders? Giant crows? Mad pigs?"

"Charge!" Arthur shouted, leveling his own lance before him. His heels drove against the sides of his mount, and he pulled away from the marching company.

"Charge!" Ulfius echoed. His horse broke into a gallop, lurching up beside Arthur's. "Charge! Charge!"

The rest of the cavalry broke into a charge. At first merely an amorphous mass of thundering horseflesh, the first hundred of the noble warriors formed themselves into a great, arching line. They surged across the meadowlands. Grass clumps flew behind their hooves. Bees drew lazy orange circles around their rushing forms. Shoulders and stifles riled beneath immaculate barding. Iron shoes flung back the world. Lances like slivers of the sky tilted down and soared levelly toward the foe.

The lines converged. The ground vanished. Horses loomed impossibly large. Then there was no sky, no forest, no ground, but only the vast thrashing collision of horseflesh and steel.

Arthur's lance drove straight through a man's midsection, bucking him up out of the saddle to tangle in traces and slump over the horse's rump. Arthur released the fouled lance and drew Excalibur, swinging it in a great arc overhead. He brought the blade down on another foe. It clove through ring and plate, both, laying open the man's chest from shoulder to heart. He slumped, grisly, to the ground. Arthur drove up past him and smashed aside another man's swing.

Swords sang as they struck each other. Blade called to blade.

Scraping free of Excalibur, a foe's blade darted in beneath Arthur's guard. It struck him in the hauberk, severing links of chain but not laying bare his flesh. Another lunge punched through the bronze plate on Arthur's chest and stuck there.

He roared. Excalibur plunged down and cracked the spatha. The sword broke in two. The tip remained in Arthur's belly. The riven hilt came away in the shaking hand of his foe.

Arthur gave no time for wonder. He ran the god-killing blade up beneath the warrior's visor. Arthur drew it forth as his opponent tumbled from the saddle. Only then did the young king take time to yank the sword tip from his own stomach. It, too, was covered in blood.

"Rhiannon," he growled, seeing his gauntlet painted in red. "I need Rhiannon." He lifted his eyes to the standard of King Lot, and drove forward.

• • •

Groans of dread and the clottering of nervous hooves filled the gigantic army of Lot. The king himself stood in his saddle and shaded his flinty eyes. "What is happening? My eyes are thick. Tell me, what is happening?"

His standard bearer, a squat, pathetic creature unfit to bear arms, vaulted to stand aback his horse and gaze dramatically outward. "Oye, King. It's like staring into the wrong end of a donkey."

"Specifics! Tell me specifics!"

"Well, now—" the scrofulous fellow paused to scratch a place usually inaccessible to anyone sitting a horse "—there's a horse of ours down, kicking up dirt, broken bones jutting, and there's a rider of ours who's looking for his right arm, gone missing—"

"Not that specific! Tell me, what is happening!"

"I'll not tell thee, but sing it:

"King Arthur pretends to the throne of the land
But does not pretend with his battling band
Unless half our horsemen are just playing dead
The very half, fearfully lying abed,
Allowed him to take away two thousand head,
And lay there with hind halves in hand!"

"Who are you?" Lot roared, savagely ripping the standard pole from the dwarf. "A spy?"

Giving a lunatic grin, the fool waved a stumpy hand and said, "Forgive me, sire. I must have the wrong king." With a lash of his reins, he flung his horse into a gallop. He never sat in the saddle, riding with one hand raised behind him like some equestrian acrobat.

Eyes burning red, Lot gabbled after the man. A tremor of fury moved through the king. "Charge!" Lot drove iron heels into the flanks of his steed and surged forward.

"What of the archers?" a captain shouted.

"I'll kill the archers myself! Charge!"

"What of the horse-killing ground?"
"CHARGE! CHARGE! CHARGE!"

Merlin stood at the issue of the ley-line highway. His arms were lifted high, holding open the vale of magic. From a razor-thin fold of Otherworld power, the very human armies of Ban and Bors marched.

They had crossed the primeval Bedgrayne in the space of a breath, ten thousand troops—eight hundred of them mounted—through the literal heart of a millennial forest. There had been no sacred grove to provide entrance onto the ley-line highway. Merlin had had to beg the dryads and sylphs of the southern Bedgrayne to hold the way open. Now, eight leagues north and on the farther banks of the Sherwood River, there was a whole different set of woodland spirits—fearful and flighty. It was only by promising protection against their vengeful mistress that Merlin convinced the pixies and brownies to open the way.

King Bors brought up the rear of the company. He reined in and turned a contemplative look on Merlin. The king's blond brows crawled with faerie fire. Red motes powdered the nostrils and flanks of the warhorse he rode. "You are a strange one, Merlin Magus!"

An irritably cocked eyebrow was all the response Merlin provided.

"A Pagan, a witch, a powerful filid, condemned with all sorcerers to Gehenna—and yet here you are, Moses beside the Red Sea, holding open the way for the armies of a Christian king. You fight for a god who condemns you."

"I fight for no god at all," Merlin replied in a half growl, "but for Arthur, for my grandson." So saying, he brought his upraised hands clapping thunderously together. The ley-line highway slammed shut, cutting off the tip of the horse's tail.

The king's eyes grew wide within his helm. He stared back where the highway had sliced through hills and tree trunks and deer. Now, only the muddy Sherwood River and the impassable Bedgrayne Forest stood behind them.

"Well, whatever reason you fight, Merlin Magus, I am glad you fight on my side." Not wanting to risk further exchange, Bors trotted his horse up the riverbank toward the assembling army.

Merlin rubbed aching arms and started up the rutted bank—except that his feet wouldn't move. They were rooted to earth as firmly as any oak. Something underground clutched him.

It was magic, as red and implacably powerful as the ley-line road itself. This power was different, though, not impersonal but intentional. There was a mind within that tingling, paralyzing flood of energy. It rose up through Merlin, taking over legs and torso and arms. When that mind reached his brain, it spoke to him.

So, the wood spirits gave you passage into my land?

Merlin could not move, but he could think. Have we met?

I know you, Jove, the sinuous voice said. *I know you from the meeting at Avalon. But you do not know me. I am the Red Serpent of Nottinghill. Had you known me, you would not have come.*

Merlin tried to sound casual. Ah, an ally of Wotan.

I ally to no one. This is not Wotan's land, but mine. Were he to come here, he would be kitten weak, as are you, Jove. The creature's tone grew sly. *In a way, I am grateful for this little war of yours. It brings armies of men for me to feast upon. Armies of men, and even a few gods. . . .*

Then he could not even think. All was agony.

The Red Serpent of Nottinghill coiled about his innards, consuming him from the inside out.

37

The Horrible Press

*A*rthur reared his mount in the hellish fight.

The main body of Lot's army had crashed into the front, compressing it. There was no longer room to swing a blade, nor to draw elbows back to stab, nor even to see beyond the crowd of men and steel and horseflesh.

Arthur had grimly carved a line of sight by cleaving helms, but always another man surged forward to fight where the last died. Sky disappeared beneath spathas, darting and glimmering like swarming dragonflies. Ground disappeared beneath dead, lying three-deep. The fallen stole the feet of the living. Blood rained down, and souls twisted up.

"Ector! Ector!" Arthur shouted, rearing his steed again above the horrible press. The horse's hooves spun like deadly clubs, cracking the brain of a man who stabbed for its belly. "Ector!" Arthur's foster father had been beside him only moments ago, but had been struck from the saddle. "Ector!"

As the horse dropped down again, Arthur glimpsed Ector's livery. He bulled his steed toward it.

Excalibur danced in hoary fury, a scythe through a field of men. The adamantine weapon cracked through two swords raised against it and clove the heads of the men who wielded them. They fell aside, revealing the scrap of livery Arthur had seen.

It was only barding. King Cradelment rode Ector's horse!

Roaring in rage, Arthur charged his steed straight for the horseman. He brought Excalibur screaming down. Gleaming with the righteous fury of God, the blade sliced through helm and skull and brain and on down through neck and lung and heart until it clove even the horse's head. Without a moment to scream, warrior and mount both went down.

Beyond stood an astonished Ector. "That was my horse, Son!"

Arthur laughed in relief and shouldered up beside the bloodied fighter. He clasped the man's free hand and hauled him up. Arthur meanwhile dropped off the steed. "Here, take mine!"

Yanked into the saddle, Ector started to protest, but there was no time. The battle crashed over them, and Arthur was gone in the bloody fight.

Ban and Bors marched their horses side by side in the vanguard of the army. Had this been Gaul, they would not have led the charge. Had this been a day earlier, they would not have led. But there was something about stealing through the enemy camp last night, offering sleep or death to any they encountered, walking the earth like the faerie folk do—like the *gods* do!—that inspired them. Arthur the So-called Less had an aura about him, the shine of destiny. Or perhaps it was the shine of sorcery.

Even as his steed cantered along between the arms of the forest, Ban wondered about that strange wizard. He had not even moved after delivering the army across the Sherwood. A queer fellow, but useful.

"There they are!" Bors shouted, a finger jabbed to fore.

Ahead, within a grassy glade, the back ranks of Lot's huge rabble stood in reserve. There were perhaps ten thousand men in that company, and not a horse among them. Despite distant sounds of battle, they had been lounging against stones and whittling sticks. A few fires sent lazy smoke into the air.

Ten thousand men, packed as tight as blood sausage.

"First ranks, full gallop!" Ban ordered. His steed leaped eagerly into a ground-eating run.

"Lances out!" Bors cried. Where a finger had jutted moments ago, a quivering lance now tilted. All around him, more spears leveled.

A sorcerer was useful, yes, but so was a stout lance—a

weapon that did not put one in jeopardy of Gehenna.

The first few rebels glanced up, their faces visibly going pale. Half-drunk flasks of courage splashed to ground. A warning rose. More faces turned. More eyes opened in wide alarm.

Those nearest the charge knew they could not escape. They snatched up swords and shields and involuntarily retreated amid their clustered comrades. Those farthest away felt no need to retreat, being beyond the terror of the initial attack. They strode forward, further compacting the army. Those in the middle, pressed on both sides—knowing they may be slain when the heavy horse crashed past the first five rows of infantry and knowing they might well make the forest's edge—the lethal stampede began with them.

Ban and Bors saw what was happening. The grins on their meaty faces faded into hard, horrible lines. This would not be warfare. This would be slaughter.

Ban chose his target, a big-hearted Caledonian in a savage kilt, his dull-edged sword lifted hopelessly before him. Setting his lance for that wide heart, Ban wondered how he could ever have forgotten that war and slaughter were one and the same.

As the army of Ban and Bors disappeared over the horizon, Merlin collapsed. He fell beside the chanting Sherwood River.

An Otherworld snake coiled through him. It wrapped his heart in constricting sinews. Though the liver was the sweetest organ of the body, the heart was the sweetest of the soul. The heart and the brain. They were the feast of cannibals, and this snake was a cannibal of gods. It held him, paralyzed, as it slowly feasted on his soul. It dragged his power into its own.

He would die only as the last drop was sucked away.

Merlin remembered this beast now. The coils that slid through his brain were familiar. The crested head. The bonelike spikes . . . it was the Red Woman who had come in serpent guise to Avalon. She had listened to Merlin that day and learned not only that she hated the dead god but also that she desired his power.

"You really are a fool," she said through Merlin's own lips, *"putting a Christian king on the throne of Britannia."*

Merlin could not reply, not even in thought.

"I know you believe that Arthur is no Christian, that only his sword is. But men have a way of following their swords. And you were a fool to come into my lands, where I am supreme." She let Merlin's hand slump away from his chest, flaccid fingers splashing into the gentle tide of the Sherwood.

Something grasped those fingers, another power.

Merlin felt it even in numb absentia.

The Red Woman tried to pull his hand away, but the grasp was too strong.

A voice came from the flood. *"And you are a fool, Red Woman. You trespass in my realm now."*

With an irresistible surge, Merlin was yanked into the gurgling river. Cold brown water enveloped him. He was dragged down into the murk.

The Red Woman thrashed fearfully within him.

His hands clawed mossy stones. His legs kicked. His neck strained toward the surface, toward air.

The force in the river could not be denied. It bore him down, impossibly deep.

In that chill place, his hot breath could no longer abide. It burst forth in a red flash of bubbles that rose away and were gone.

Still afoot, Arthur carved a path through the ravening foe. He fought lionlike. Arthur was the king of Caerleon, City of the Lion, and would fight like one.

Already he had come to the aid of Gryfflet, also on foot and battling four attackers. The man guarded Lucas, who lay pinned beneath his dead horse. Excalibur split the equine corpse in two. Painted in red, Lucas climbed forth. Side by side, the three men pushed into the rebel host, intent on Lot.

Ulfius joined them, his horse having been cut out from under him. On the way, they ran upon Ector and Kay as well. The battle had turned in their favor.

Arthur was heartened to have these true friends beside him. Five dauntless men at arms and a young king with a divine sword—it was the stuff of legends.

Renewed despite his wounds, Arthur cried, "To Lot, all speed!"

The warriors of Arthur advanced. Their swords flashed in a deadly wedge of steel. Kay skewered a man through the gullet. A coppice blow from Ulfius bashed another to ground. Ector returned a parry with such force his foe spun halfway about and blinded a comrade. Gryfflet used his off hand to flip up a visor and deliver a roundhouse to the nose. Lucas, lately deprived of his own horse, waged a battle to fling down any mounted foe. Their advance was a terrible spectacle, swords grinding the foe to minced meat.

From Arthur's bloodied teeth sluiced a roar that was half fury and half dread.

One man could end it—Lot of Lothian. He fought atop a war stallion ahead. Even from this distance, his eyes flashed like obsidian. His beard was speckled with blood. His black charger was gory to its knees and hocks. It trampled all those in its path.

Lot reached down and hauled aloft a scrofulous dwarf, clutching the poor creature's throat.

Even past constricting fingers, Dagonet's taunting songs continued:

> "Never fear . . . the dreaded Lot,
> Strength is something . . . he has not.
> Arthur comes . . . to draw this Lot
> And quar-ter!"

In a pique of rage, Lot clenched his fist, strangling the dwarf unconscious and flinging him to the gory ground.

Next moment, Lot followed. His saddle slid loose, the severed leather strap striking him in the jaw as he went down.

Clambering to his feet, Lot faced down a bloodied and sweating King Arthur.

The young king's whole figure was sanguine. Only Excalibur was clean. It shone like a wedge of blue sky. Arthur's men at arms advanced beyond Lot, holding back the tide of his army. The northern king was cut off.

"Ah, Lot," said Arthur with a rueful smile. "It is good you carry Rhiannon, for I have a geis with my sister—your wife—not to slay you." With that, Arthur brought Excalibur in a huge descending arc toward Lot's head.

The northern king ducked back and interposed his blade. Adamantine struck steel. Lot locked his blade with Excalibur and turned one shoulder, intent on ripping the sword free. Arthur held on. The men spun once. Arthur won free and stepped back.

Lot seethed, "I have no such geis about you!" He lunged. Excalibur darted to meet the blade—except that the lunge was a feint. Lot circled his sword tip beneath Excalibur and sliced inward. The sword slid into a previous wound on Arthur's hip, deepening it. "And you have no such scabbard."

In the black heart of the Sherwood River, water gushed into Merlin's lungs. Death came with it.

Tasting that cold draught, the Otherworld serpent uncoiled herself from his heart. She cringed in fear, and then swam away.

It was perilous for a god to inhabit a dying mortal.

Merlin remembered no more.

He awoke lying facedown, half out of the river. Water flowed in red tides from his mouth and nostrils. The sun was warm on his drenched back. Cold liquid enveloped his legs and lower body. He was not dead, and better yet, the serpent was gone.

Another voice was speaking, as gentle as the river, as balming as the sun—"must learn, Merlin, which women to wrestle and which not to. It is a common enough error among adolescent boys. As I have said before, that is all you are just now—"

"Nyneve," Merlin gasped out. A gout of blood following the name. He retched the pulpy stuff onto the bank.

"I am honored that the first word you spoke in your return from death is my name."

"Return . . . from death," Merlin echoed raggedly, looking around for the naiad but seeing only the gleaming surface of the river.

"Oh, yes. From death. I had to drown you to get that Red Woman to leave. She is nasty and powerful. Luckily I am just as powerful, and more well disposed."

At last done choking, Merlin pushed himself up to sit and gazed blearily across the placid water. "I'm not sure which is worse . . . her scales, or your cold deeps."

"I am sure her scales only kill. My cold deeps heal. It is from the cold depths that the scabbard Rhiannon came, you know. It was formed of the jewels and swords sacrificed to the Mistress of the Mist, thrown into the lake as offering to her—just as Excalibur was thrown as an offering to her. By the healing power of the deeps, the scabbard Rhiannon was formed around Excalibur. It heals the blade and the wearer of the blade. It makes them whole and complete. So too the cold deeps of this river have restored your soul, drawn away by the Red Woman." Nyneve laughed within the thronging waters. "You really must learn which women to wrestle and which not to."

"Show yourself, Nyneve," Merlin said quietly. "I want to see you."

The glassy surface of the waters gathered and mounded up. The waves wove together. Like a waterspout rising, she took form. Lithe legs, enfolding robes, a knot-work girdle in silver, a torc overlaid in stone of kobold blue, and then her young, bright, beautiful face.

"Come to me," Merlin beckoned.

Even as his hand gestured her forward, its aspect changed. Leathery skin softened and smoothed, gnarled knuckles grew slender and young once again. The transformation traveled up his arms, knitting within them the sinews of youth. White beard and hair retreated, folds and wrinkles smoothed, the sunken pallor of age bloomed into pink health. He was young again.

"You see?" Nyneve asked, advancing toward him atop the waves. "You are but an adolescent boy now."

He took her hand as she reached the shore and brought her down beside him. There, in thanks and not a little desire, he kissed her.

Lot was a nonpareil swordsman. His great sword darted with the tireless speed of a hummingbird and sought the sanguine roses on Arthur's shoulder and flank and hip.

Arthur reeled. He had lost much blood. His army was advancing around him, pushing back the armies of the north, but all of it would be for naught if this man slew him. Weary, slick with his own blood, Arthur hurled Excalibur in another overhead arc that would have slain a lesser man.

Lot merely stepped aside. As Excalibur plunged into ground, the man rammed his sword forcefully up into Arthur's severed hauberk. The blade punched through the broad plate to stab into his gut.

Arthur staggered back. He lurched, trying to pull free of Lot's sword, but the man only rammed it deeper.

"You cannot win, Arthur," Lot growled. "You are nearly dead already."

Arthur clasped his foe's sword in a gauntleted hand, preventing it from cutting deeper. "If I do not win," he gasped, "then the land bleeds and dies—as it has since my father's death . . . as I do even now."

"Then it dies!" Lot said. He gritted his teeth and thrust brutally. The sword stabbed deep into Arthur.

Eyes wide and rimmed in blood, Arthur fell to his knees. He sat back on his heels. As his face went white, he stared in amazement at his foe. "I was not supposed to die. . . ."

Into the storm of black hatred that had raged across Lot's

eyes came a glimmer of pity. "All of us are supposed to die, Arthur. All of us are supposed to die."

Sucking in one last breath, Arthur screamed, "No!"

He let go the bloody sword that impaled him and, two hands on Excalibur, swung the blade overhand. Lightning-swift and heavy as thunder, Excalibur fell.

Lot cringed.

Adamantine struck steel and sliced it as though it were mere paper.

Lot staggered back. The god-killing blade could have cut him in half, but instead it had only severed his sword.

Arthur drew the gory blade from his belly. A fresh gush of blood followed it. He threw the severed sword aside and bit his lip, white for lack of blood. Then Arthur—son of Uther and king of Britannia—rose from the pool of his own fleeing life.

Staring at that ghastly youth, impossibly alive, Lot said, "Haven't you the sense to die? Excalibur cannot heal you."

"A sword . . . cannot make a man king," Arthur whispered as he stalked forward. "Nor can a sword . . . unmake a man . . . who is king."

With final fury, Arthur charged his foe.

Lot stumbled backward, falling atop a slain horse. He lifted his hands before him. "You would slay an unarmed man?"

"Give me Rhiannon," Arthur growled.

"No," Lot said. "You will be dead in a moment, and I will have even Excalibur."

"Give me Rhiannon."

"No," Lot said, smiling through blood. "I will not. And while I bear it, you cannot kill me."

"Whether or not you bear it, I cannot kill you," Arthur replied. "I have sworn a geis. But by withholding it, you can kill me."

Lot laughed, a raking sound. "I do not even have your scabbard, Arthur. Your force was too puny to challenge mine, and I would not risk losing that treasure. It is nearby, of course, should I require it—hidden and guarded by men and magic. You could have slain me at any moment. You could slay me right now."

The bloodless tip of Excalibur wavered before the throat of King Lot of Lothian. Then Arthur slumped down beside him. Together, they leaned on the dead horse.

"Then you have slain me, truly."

Incredulous, Lot stared at the young king. "So, you will not kill me?"

"No," Arthur replied simply.

Lot laughed again—a bleak and despairing sound.

The din of battle grew distant behind the two kings. Arthur's forces were sweeping the field.

Lot said, "I have slain you, and you have slain my army. Your army lives on without a king, and I live on without an army."

Arthur's eyes were closing in death. "Then, take them, Lot. Britannia must have a king. The killing must end. The land must be healed. Take my army and be king of Britannia."

Ruefully, Lot shook his head. "What sort of man are you, King Arthur?"

Arthur's eyes stared out past blood-speckled cheeks. "I was a good man. Remember that, Lot. I was a good man. Now, say you will take my army."

Lot hissed miserably. "I would take them, but they would not take me. Not even with Excalibur in hand. They will kill me—you know this—and quarter me and pike my head."

Arthur shut his eyes. "Then all is lost. If I die, so do you. And if we die, Britannia dies."

"If you live, I live?"

"I have sworn it," Arthur said.

A new light came into Lot's eyes. He blinked, seeming to see Arthur for the first time.

"A man who learns of swords would be a fool not to learn of stanching wounds." He set to work, ripping cloth from his own, unbloodied tabard. "You were a good man, Arthur, yes. And if I can keep you alive a few moments more, you will be yet a good man—and perhaps a great king."

"Guinevere," Arthur replied as though in delirium. "Merlin will bring her. She will heal me."

"Better yet, I will summon the scabbard to do it. Its sorcerous protections are bound to me—my helmet become a cauldron—"

"Oh, no, Lot," Morgan said, shaking her black hair above the bloody cauldron. "I will not bring your prize. Not to heal Arthur. Not to surrender it to him."

She released a long sigh that billowed out and tangled with the spinning figures of the weirds. They held Rhiannon aloft—maiden, mother, and crone—they uplifted the scabbard and warded it. Rising from the severed brain case and blood of the guardian, their power was great indeed.

"You have not fulfilled our bargain, Lot," Morgan said flatly. "You were to fight Arthur until the true king could be conceived. Now, I will take your scabbard and find another warrior-king. He will not only detain Arthur until my son is ready to ascend the throne; he will slay the King of Britons, that my child may accede."

So saying, Morgan reached through the coiling spirits of the weirds and laid hold of Rhiannon. With the same motion, she stepped gently into the brain case of her guard.

Up, out of the blood sacrifice, the weirds redoubled their whirling dance. They engulfed the woman and the scabbard. They swept them up.

In moments, Morgan Le Fey and Rhiannon were gone. Only the luffing tent and the bloody bowl remained.

38

The Foundations of the World

The blood of Bedgrayne soaked into the soil and rose again in russet shoots. Time did not wash it away. The earth did not forget. Time merely drew the blood of individuals into the great cauldron of the land and transformed it into the blood of nations. The earth did not obliterate the dead, but garbed their toothy cairns in soft blankets of moss. The men of Dumnonia and Lothian lay side by side beneath stones and greenery, no longer foes but brothers. That dark, desperate hour was transfigured into the birth struggle of a united Britannia.

A year later on the other side of the nation, it was evident. The battleground of Bedgrayne lingered in stately shadows behind the bright fields of Cadbury.

Arthur rode at the head of the royal procession. A rampant Pendragon emblazoned his tabard. Standards flapped to either side. The regalia of his office accoutered him—a scepter in his arm, a knotted torc about his throat, a crown upon his young head, and of course, Excalibur on his back. Samite and cashmere hid the scars of Bedgrayne, and there was no hint of pain or fear in his demeanor. For Arthur, this was a day of glory.

Guinevere rode beside him. She was the true power of his throne. She had healed his mortal wounds at Bedgrayne, just as she had saved him and the royal mage before. Arthur loved her—that much was clear—but the people loved Guinevere even more. There had been talk of a Tuatha betrothal, of dirty dealings among Merlin and the Saxon god of chaos, though no confirmation came from Guinevere or Arthur. None was needed. All Britannia sensed these two would rule together.

Ranked all around them were noble retainers. Ulfius and Brastias each bore a Pendragon standard. Ector and Kay flanked them, and Gryfflet and Lucas rode thereafter. Even the sons of Lot had joined the royal retinue. There were Gareth and Gaheris, Agravain and Gawain, brave fighters and honest men. They formed a broad V, within which capered the tireless Dagonet:

> "A king so great, of such renown
> That he'd been tossed from every town,
> Rode up a hill he called a down
> And built him a capital there!
> Oh, who will toss him from that town?
> He built him a capital there!"

Ban and Bors, riding behind the capering fool, had taken quite well the news that they had allied with the wrong King Arthur. The true king had fulfilled his proxy's promises, and now there was peace on both sides of the Channel.

After Ban and Bors came a great assemblage of petty kings and nobles from across the land. Most important of all was King Lot of Lothian. No longer the livery of the enemy, Lot's red-white-and-black tabard now bore above his coat of arms the Pendragon. In that single emblem, the land was healed. If the blood of Bedgrayne had enriched the earth and the dead had become brothers with their foes, it was this one man who demonstrated that the living could also find peace. He and most of his allies had sworn fealty to Arthur—all but Aelle of Saxony.

The army of Britannia accompanied the procession. Pike men and cavalry flanked them, protecting the king, his court, and their regalia. Other warriors had doffed their armor to lend a hand at the rear of the procession. There, horse teams and log relays conveyed the giant cornerstones of Arthur's new city—Camelot.

Such a procession, replete with pipes and fifes and drums, did not fail to attract the folk of Britannia. A great crowd flocked to the parade. Nobles rode shy and slim-legged horses. Villeins drove braces of market-bound oxen. Bondsmen carried packs behind their strolling masters. Slaves labored beneath impossible loads. Idiots and tinkers begged and cajoled. There were also children of all classes who are, despite class, children. The folk flocked to see what grand occasion brought the king of all Britannia to a lonely road in Cadbury.

That road was not lonely much longer. Soon it was to be twice as crowded.

Many in the multitude noticed the impossibly thin wall of red that sliced through the hilly countryside and angled down toward the road. Those who had marched the ley-line highway to and through Bedgrayne would never forget the look of it, or the preternatural feel of it. Neck hairs rose in anticipation.

Even through the glimmering air of morning, faint figures were visible on the red highway. Some appeared human, marching along in stately parade. At their sides and near their feet moved other creatures—wolves, stoats, harts, hounds—and overhead scores of falcons and ravens. All around them swirled clouds of tiny creatures that glittered in the air. There were stranger shapes too—what seemed to be walking trees, and stoop-shouldered ogres, ember-eyed fox-men, and a gigantic creature that made even the marching oaks seem like scrub bushes.

Human foot soldiers craned to see around horsemen. Everyone wondered what would happen when the parade of mortals intersected the parade of immortals.

Arthur and Guinevere rode their horses into the curtain of red light. Suddenly beside them appeared Merlin, mounted on a great white stag. Arthur did not rein in his horse, nor the queer-eyed mage his mount. They only continued on, side by side, at a companionable canter.

"Hello, Grandfather."

"Hello, my king. It is a beautiful morning."

"Perfect for the birth of our new city."

Another voice came behind them, mellifluous tones like

the sound of water. "So, these are the friends you have been telling me of, Merlin?"

Turning, Merlin nodded toward the woman who rode a hart behind him. He gestured outward behind Arthur. "Dear Brigid, this is Ulfius, and this Brastias. Here is Ector, Kay, Gryfflet, Lucas, Gawain, Gaheris, Agravain, Gareth, King Ban, and King Bors. . . . Gentles, this is Brigid, goddess of Avalon and Mistress of the Mists."

A muffled reply came from the amazed retinue. Only Ban could muster a response, "You look so like a saint I saw depicted in Iona—and her name was Brigid, as well."

A knowing smile crossed the shimmering face of the goddess. Her hand demurely rose from her lap to draw a coral comb from her hair. "Perhaps a sister—"

There was no more time for exchanges. More faerie folk were emerging from the red highway and merging with the mortal company. They were there, and yet were not there—fey flesh was never entirely solid in daylight, and it shimmered like a mirage. It was easier to see the fey folk from the corners of one's eyes. To look directly toward them was not to see them at all.

Nyneve was there, lovely in a gown of water lilies. A brooding red warrior followed behind her, and a creature that had no real body, but seemed an animate and ever-changing shadow. A pack of Seelie hounds appeared, long-legged and short shorn with pelts that gleamed like quicksilver. A very different pack came next—hobgoblins. No taller than mushrooms and with the same pale cast of skin, they clambered over each other in an eager game of multiple leap-frog. Though close kin to the diminutive folk, the next creature to emerge was a stooped and shambling mountain of a thing, a hag hid beneath a great greasy cap of gray hair. All of them—the horses of Epona, the great serpents, the leafy-faced green men, the solemn bluecaps, quarreling redcaps, and prankish thrummy caps, the barguests, boggarts, and bugbears, the elves, brownies, pixies, and sprites—fell in line beside the human host.

Each new arrival occasioned a fresh wave of amazement

or dread. The kings busily glared down any who would dare offer affront to these Otherworld emissaries. But even the kings could little resist rubbing their eyes and blinking. The faerie folk were there—it was no doubt—en masse at midday, and half a year away from Samhain when they were known to wander the world.

"They are friends of our king," the soldiers whispered nervously among themselves. "They are our allies."

Even that was not assurance enough when the first titan appeared. Like a mountain forming out of thin air, the massive man abruptly took shape. His feet were as large as Saxon dragon ships and bound in leather sandals from some unimaginably enormous beast. His legs were broader than the fattest oaks in Britannia. Knees like knobby cairns, thighs like stone towers, loins uncouthly and inadequately garbed in a half mile of tattered wool. His torso and back were so high up as to blend into the bright sky, and in gargantuan arms he clutched an equally gargantuan stone, twenty men high and ten men across. And then, one of those huge feet of his stepped.

The road trembled. Horses shied. Men cringed back.

"Friends of our king. Allies of ours!"

The titan paused, looking down on the mortals. His eyes were smoky gray and infinitely weary, infinitely sad. Turning away in disinterest, he plodded onward.

"He seems harmless enough—"

And then another titan appeared, and a third, and a fourth. Each bore an enormous slab of stone, up from the Otherworld.

Before the mortal host could break and flee, a voice of command came from ahead, cast outward by the magic of Merlin. "Welcome, my friends! Come gather here. Come gather beside the borning city of Camelot."

The host looked up to see Arthur, dismounted and standing at the peak of a high hill nearby. Guinevere was with him. She held his hand in a gesture both affectionate and empowering. Already, the royal retinue had left their horses to graze. Dignitaries stood arrayed around the king and priestess.

Among them were gods and goddesses, saints and spirits, wolves and doves. Arthur spoke again.

"Come, gather. All are welcome, Christian and Pagan, mortal and immortal, Briton and Pict, Caledonian and Jute, king, noble, freeman, bondsman, and slave. This is your city—not the city of Arthur, but the city of Britannia."

These words seemed to hearten the human throng. To the soldiers, they were orders. To the rabble, they were promised privilege.

Among the faerie folk, though, these words awoke only fear. Any mortal man who would claim dominion over the Otherworld was a dangerous creature. . . .

Brigid spoke to them. Those who approached heard her in their own languages. "Great ones, great and ancient titans from the world before, come forward. You have brought stones from that world, from the foundations of our own world. I have asked it of you, and you have done it. Arthur has asked it of you—great stones to be laid as thresholds for this city's gates. With these stones in place, you shall ever be welcome in the city of Camelot. This plot of land, here among the hills of Cadbury, shall be a city between the world and the Otherworld. Within its walls, mortal and immortal will mingle in peace."

Heartened by her address, the seven titans strode ponderously up the hillside. Once they reached the top, Brigid directed them toward the corners of the large plateau. There, each titan hoisted high the massive stone he bore.

As terrible as the titans had seemed when stooped beneath the weight of the megaliths, they were all the more horrible now. Their knuckles scraped the cloud bottoms. Each one of the stones they hoisted overhead could have slain the whole human host below. Next moment, it seemed that was what the giants intended.

With a world-splitting howl, the seven titans hurled their stones downward.

Each impacted the world with a tremendous tremor. The human host fell, shrieking. Grasslands rippled with the impacts. Forests shuddered violently.

Seven great pillars of dust went up. One enveloped each titan. For a moment they were hidden from view. The mortals cowered below, staring up to the billowing columns as though glimpsing the end of the world.

But then, the earth stopped shaking. A breeze wandered innocently across the plateau and teased away the dust pillars. The titans were revealed.

They seemed enormous statues. Dust stood in dry piles across their shoulders and eyebrows, lending them a sinister aspect. The megaliths they had hurled down lay firmly embedded in the earth at their feet. Their empty hands seemed poised to begin scooping up mortals and crushing them.

That was almost the end of Camelot. One glimpse of those glowering monsters, welcome at any hour into the new city, almost shattered the will of the human company. Words failed Arthur and Brigid, both. Even Merlin could not imagine what to say.

One of the titan's sneezed. Halfway between a wheeze and a growl, the sudden blast of air sent dust jetting comically from the great beast. Dirt sifted from miserable shoulders. Gargantuan legs swooned. The creature ran one vast arm beneath its nose. It blinked out through circling clouds of dust.

Arthur was the first one to laugh. The sound spread from him to his retinue, to Brigid and Nyneve and Merlin. Brastias let out a guffaw, and Kay a belly laugh. Ector and Ulfius joined in. The happy sound coursed down among the folk cringing on the hillside. It flowed over the Roman road and back into the reaches of the ley-line highway. In moments, the welling hilarity was louder than the earthquakes had been.

Gazing out at this strange scene, the phlegmy titan made another swipe at his nose. He spoke something in the ancient tongue of his race. Perhaps it was a curse. Perhaps it was a solemn oath. It might have been anything, but to the people below, it seemed he had distinctly said, *"Bless me."*

The roar only redoubled. Arthur had buckled to his knees, clutching his gut. Brastias was rolling on his back like a happy dog. Only Dagonet did not laugh. The little man stared petulantly at the vast company. He put hands on his hips and stomped, as though he could put an end to it all simply by insisting.

39

Of Cities and Temples

After that, the titans had real difficulty keeping the mortals at bay. Folk crowded right up beside them. They were like men swarmed with mice. Some of the more adventurous filids and tinkers set up their entertainments on the very feet of the giants.

Dagonet led them, singing extemporized songs:

"Upon the mighty titan's toe
I sing a tale of joy and woe
Of Arthur above and Brigid below,
It's better on top, ye know, ye know!
It's better on top, ye know!"

Arthur and Brigid managed to ignore the insinuations in Dagonet's song. The trouble came when the titan on whose feet Dagonet danced started dancing, himself. The dwarf's crowd ran shrieking in terror.

Accustomed to such responses, Dagonet only redoubled his efforts.

"The longest sword that e'er was swung
In Arthur's belt is handsome hung
And Brigid's scabbard seeks his tongue
Of metal. Deep ye go, ye go!
It's better on top, ye know, ye know!
It's better on top, ye know!"

Brigid might have bridled at that one, except that she was busy in the site of the city. She had brought with her a beautifully hammered cauldron of bronze and set it in the center of the grassy space. A parade of naiads bore jars of water from Avalon and poured them into the cauldron. A small hole at the center of the cauldron dribbled this water down onto the earth, where it sank, seeking its kind. Snaking down past grasses and topsoil, clay, sand, and shale, the water plumbed to the earth's bloodstream. In time, water as pure and holy as Avalon's bubbled back up into the cauldron.

It widened and sank into the ground, growing to a great fountain. A bronze statue formed in the center of that flood, three women seated in a triangle with backs together. One held a baby, another a loaf of bread, and a third a basket overflowing with fruits and grains. The jetting waters of the fountain formed a dome of spray and mist that enveloped these three mysterious figures.

"This fountain brings the bounty of Britannia to Camelot. Its waters will flow cold and pure and plentiful while all is right in the court of Arthur. All are welcome here to drink, to bathe, to be refreshed."

Brigid strode across the watery trough and through the dome of spray. Among the Bounteous Weirds, as the people were already calling them, the goddess gathered a set of six bronze goblets, one beside each foot of the women. She deposited them in a fold of her robe and carried them out beyond the flood. Before the end of the day, each of those cups became another, smaller fountain, one for each of the main districts of the city, as she and Merlin had laid it out.

Camelot was beginning to look like a city. Tents for workers and soldiers rose in meandering neighborhoods. Already, the massive cornerstones hauled hence on wagons were seated on the foundation stones brought by the titans. More huge blocks arrived each hour. Gangs dug with amazing speed. Their shovel strokes punctuated the songs they sang. The footings for the wall grew even as folk clambered over them into the grassy spaces within.

Warriors and workers emerged from their tent neighborhoods and thirstily visited the gleaming Fountains of Brigid. Some even said the water for their noon meals became milk, and the water for their evening meals became wine.

The grandest and busiest complex of pavilions belonged to King Arthur. A vast and particolored tent rose, becoming Arthur's throne room. It was positioned atop another megalith, flung down by a titan. The stone completed Arthur's invitation to emissaries from the Otherworld. They were welcomed not only through the gates of the city, but also to the very throne of the king. Upon a natural dais at one end of the tent, Arthur's throne stood. It was a specially built seat, wide enough for two.

The evening revels began with a procession to the throne of Arthur and Guinevere. Thousands of folk crowded either side of the tent and the grassy expanse beyond. Through the throng, Arthur and his retinue—mortal and immortal—processed.

The king was crowned, the implements of his regalia were presented to him, and an ermine mantle of state was laid across his shoulders. He assumed the throne.

Guinevere came to him in white raiment. The hush that had accompanied Arthur's movements became an absolute silence at the appearance of Guinevere. She already seemed his queen. On her slim shoulders, she bore the hope and love of world and Otherworld both, beloved of the people and of the fey. Her steps were regal. Only when she had ritually taken his feet into her lap did that silence end in a joyous ovation.

Rising, Guinevere sat beside the king.

As though invoked by the cheers, a line of Otherworld nobility slowly took shape in the aisle that led to the dais. The father-god Daghda, the war-god Oghma, and the god of light Lugh led the contingent of Tuatha Dé Danann. They and their people were lithe, tall, and pale of feature. As a gift of devotion, they brought the misshapen and gigantic head of a Fomorian, claiming it to be the nephew of Balor of the Baleful Eye.

In their lilting tongue, Daghda spoke for them all: "Arthur, mortal king of Britons and Guinevere, child of the Tuatha Dé, we pledge our alliance with you, to live with your folk in peace, and to fight beside your folk in war. The ancient powers of Eire and Western Britannia are friends to the throne of Arthur and Guinevere."

"And we, and all our subjects, are friends to you, Great Daghda," Arthur pledged, smiling and bowing slightly in his seat.

So went the pledges of devotion. Saints Patrick and Germanus came, bringing promises of alliance from the Church and the communion of saints. Mars Smertrius and Cú Chulainn pledged their aid in any battles that might come. Arawn, master of the Otherworld, offered his help in recovering Rhiannon. Pryderi, the son of the true Rhiannon, swore his assistance in recovering the scabbard and spoke of having, like Arthur, been removed from his parents as an infant. The kimouli faeries, sprites, and brownies held a beautiful aerial promenade as they came to the throne. Silent and glimmering like mercury, the Seelie hounds trotted across the floor, nosed about, and were gone.

While this unearthly company of gnat-creatures and silvery dogs filled the pavilion, Arthur spoke quietly to Guinevere. "I have been thinking, my dear."

She lifted her eyes gently toward him and smiled. "Yes, my king?"

"Call me Arthur. I want us to be equals in all things."

A sadness flitted behind the smile in her eyes. "Yes, Arthur."

"You are the power of this throne. I could not rule without you. I would not."

"Yes, Arthur."

"And, yet, there is more to it than power, Guinevere." He made a polite nod to a bodachan that had brought a plate of eels to lay beside the other gifts. "When I place my foot in your lap, I not only receive the land's strength, I receive yours. I want to be the most virtuous and just man I can be. I want to be worthy of you."

Guinevere turned her eyes downward. "How can you speak of being worthy?"

"I would rather be a worthy man, and your husband, than be king of Britannia," Arthur whispered in sudden conviction.

Guinevere sucked in a startled breath. As a family of Tuatha nobles approached the throne, she lifted her gaze. "You cannot. You must rule Britannia. There will be no peace without you."

"Peace for everyone else," Arthur said. "But *I* will have no peace without *you.*" A contingent of selkies came, sliding and frolicking on their sea-lion bellies across the floor. They shifted form to befurred fey folk, who bowed before Arthur. The king nodded to them pleasantly. To Guinevere, he said, "Don't you understand? I'm asking you to marry me."

She paused in her response. "We are betrothed, I know. It is a deal made at my very birth. But I cannot. I cannot put my own desires above those of the land."

Desperation playing across his face, Arthur said, "It will be a chaste union. You will remain a virgin. I will not touch you. Only—be my wife."

Again, without pause. "I cannot."

Something plagued Arthur. Merlin knew it from the moment he had bowed before the young king.

"Jove-Merlin," he said, announcing himself, "now and forever your servant."

Arthur stared bitterly toward the entrance of the pavilion, toward the back of the long line. It seemed he could not bear to sit there any longer. He only wished to be out in the cool deep night. Even Guinevere looked exhausted. She held onto him, yes, but no longer with both her hands. Her head was downturned, and she little heeded the words of the old man.

"It has been a long road to this joyous moment," Merlin prodded.

"Thank you, Merlin," Arthur said preemptively. He waved, dismissing the old mage and gesturing the next supplicant forward.

Merlin gaped in troubled amazement at this treatment and failed to step out of the way. A pair of ash-dryads nudged him aside.

"You do not want to anger the sisters of the wood," came a quiet voice in Merlin's ear. Nyneve. Her mellifluous tone was unmistakable. Her hands were warm and silken. "And you need not keep *me* waiting."

"Something is wrong with Arthur," Merlin protested.

The woman pulled him around in her irresistible grasp. She stared deeply into his eyes.

Merlin said, "Look at him. He acts as though he has been defeated, his city razed to the ground."

"In a way, it has been," Nyneve said. She twined Merlin's hair around her finger. "He has asked her, and she has said no."

"Asked her?" Merlin replied. "Asked her what?"

"Come away with me," Nyneve said. "The night is cool and deep, and I am done with public spectacle."

"But Arthur—"

"Arthur will be here in the morning," Nyneve interrupted.

She wrapped an implacable arm about the old man's waist and ushered him brusquely past craning rows of nobility. A flash of warm canvas, and they were out beneath the starry heavens.

Nyneve gestured to the brightest presence in that moonless sky. "Arthur will be here, but Jupiter will not be."

Merlin gazed at that brilliant planet. A sweet, sad chill swept through him. It had always been his, the celestial anchor of his soul. He once knew intuitively where the object was in the heavens at any time of day. Now, even emerging from a tent, he could be surprised by it.

"Where are we going?" he asked.

"Somewhere," Nyneve replied cryptically. She took hold of Merlin's hand, and suddenly they were flying.

The sensation was unlike any Merlin remembered. He had

flown before, but to fly by way of spells was to move in a prickly cocoon of magic. He had also flown as a bird, a swan with great surges of white wings and long sloping glides. Then, the buffeting wind was as solid as rolling ground. This was different. This was like floating. The night air was cold, but it did not tear at him, nor did the weighty world claw to drag him down. Nyneve and he moved with the ease of fish through water.

From this height, the land seemed a great tapestry. The tent-camp of Camelot was merely an ornate brooch arrayed on it. The Roman road formed a slim line cutting straight alongside Camelot and outward. It met the geometrical stitchery of small country lanes and streams. Glades were patches of embroidery. Ancient forests were impenetrable brocade. Soft and dark and deep, Britannia slid away beneath them. In moments, Camelot disappeared behind a rankling ridge.

"What sort of magic is this?" Merlin asked.

"We are floating on the ley-line currents. They flow like rivers, you know, toward places of deep magic."

"That is why all feels so still," Merlin decided.

"Yes. We move at the pace of the magical flow about us— like drifting on a breeze."

"And where does this magic flow lead?"

"Here," Nyneve said, gesturing downward.

The site was physically unremarkable. It was a gradual slope in the midst of the Salisbury plain. The hills around it were low and unimpressive. The few scraps of woodland were narrow and sheep-bitten. Physically, there could have been little to recommend the site. Metaphysically, though, it was a place of confluence. In the darksome air, no fewer than thirty separate ley lines crossed. Their razor-thin curtains converged on the center of the slope, forming a crimson starburst. The Otherworld glow rivaled even the staring eye of Jupiter above.

"Why this spot? What happened here to align these pathways?" Merlin asked.

"Mere geometry. It is an accidental crossing, lying on the

path from one sacred site to another. This is the junction point of energies from Iceland to Brittany, from Eire to Essex," Nyneve said. "Were we to build a temple here to the gods of the land, we could draw them to this spot, enlist even greater powers to build your city."

Merlin's eyes glowed with the red curtains of light as he descended toward their center. His hair began to tease out and stand on end. Even the grasses of the swale aligned to the highways. "A pantheon. We could build a pantheon like the one in Rome—"

"British deities are fearful of enclosed sanctuaries. Oak groves and circles of sacred stone are more welcoming," Nyneve said as she set foot to ground.

Merlin landed beside her. "You cannot simply grow a sacred grove or quarry sacred stone—"

"No, but there is a place I know in Eire where lies a toppled henge of stone. It was built millennia ago by the Tuatha Dé Danann and thrown down by the Celts when they arrived. It lies still, moss-covered, on just such a plain. If we bear the stones hence, we can rebuild the henge, and Arthur can build his city."

The light from Merlin's eyes had filled his whole being. Aged strands of hair were weaving themselves together into young, strong locks. Magic smoothed wrinkles into resilient skin. Even his back straightened.

He took Nyneve's other hand and drew her to him. "You do know the best spots in the woods, don't you?"

The din of festival rang distantly from the royal tent. Even here, on the foundations of the curtain wall, Arthur could not escape the noise. He hunched and flung stone chips into the nighttime grasses.

"She said no," he growled, hurling a handful of rocks. "She said no."

"Who said no?"

Arthur startled, standing and turning.

A woman stood there. Her long braids of black hair were

draped in a veil that crossed demurely over her mouth. She was young and beautiful. Her skin was as pale as bone. There was something vaguely familiar about her. Perhaps she had been in the parade of fealty. He sensed magic at work—somehow this woman had crossed the open spaces between the royal pavilion and the wall without alerting him. Perhaps she was Tuatha Dé, like his own Guinevere.

"Who are you?"

"I am a Briton," the woman said softly. "And you are king of Britannia." She moved toward Arthur, making not a sound. "I wanted to speak with you about your kingdom."

Arthur turned and sat on the foundation stone. "Tomorrow. There will be time to talk tomorrow."

The woman sat down beside him. "I know you think you are making a kingdom where all gods, all faiths, will be welcomed. But you cannot carve out such a place with a god-killing sword."

Arthur reflexively reached for Excalibur, finding it in its place on his back. "What do you know of the sword?"

"I know it is the instrument of the Christian God." She shivered, whether from cold or dread, and nestled in beside Arthur. "And the Christian God will suffer no others. He will kill all the gods—even your beloved Merlin, if Wotan does not kill him first."

"I am the one who wields the sword," Arthur said. "I say whom it slays."

"You don't understand. Christ is a spiritual Caesar. He conquers. He makes the citizens of other realms his own. Christ was born in a land Caesar had stolen from his people, and now Christ has stolen Rome from Caesar. Wherever he goes, he conquers."

Arthur waved away the woman's thoughts. "I am in no mood to discuss theology."

"I know," said the woman, sliding an arm about his waist. "I know. You grieve your foot-holder. Your . . . virgin foot-holder." She began quietly to laugh.

"What?" Arthur shouted, pulling away and suddenly angry. Only then, rounding on her, did he see how truly beau-

tiful the woman was—elfin and enticing. Her lips were broad
and red, her eyes as wide and deep as the night. "What do
you know of it?"

The woman rose and approached him with gentle footsteps. "I know there are other ways for a king to harness the
powers of the land. There are other priestesses not burdened
by a vow of chastity." She slid her small, warm hands once
again around his waist.

Arthur did not pull away. Her fingers were hot. His sides
were also. Anger and desire were mixed all together.

"A king cannot afford to close himself to any source of
power," she said, twining about him. "To any connection to
the land . . ."

Her lips too were hot.

The priestess was exquisite. Her very flesh emanated magic.
Every touch was pregnant with power. Such pleasures could
not be wrong—or could be only wrong. Arthur's ecstasy
prevented him from knowing which. . . .

Or knowing whom . . .

In the deeps of night, Morgan Le Fey crept away from her
brother. Life was already awakening in her, and death in
Arthur.

40

The Three-Headed God

The next morning dawned bright and cold. An uncommon hoarfrost covered the grass. It lay in crackling mats
across the pavilion roofs and made the tent poles run with
cool water. The weather was strange for early summer. It
seemed a shadow had cast its pall across the new city.

Even the young king was dour this morning. He had risen

with the sun, as befitted the monarch of a rising nation, but his spirits had remained abed. Hands clasped behind his back and eyes cast downward, he strode alone along the wall's foundations. As he reached each titan stone, he stopped, crossed arms over his chest, and stared out over the rolling hills of Cadbury. Grasses that had stood tall in the blushing summer now bristled with white. They were beautiful in the morning, but would collapse once their icy backbones melted.

Arthur empathized. He had claimed the sword in the stone and anvil, had drawn to him half of the nation and conquered the other half. He had planned and founded this new city and received courts both earthly and heavenly. His every dream was coming into being all around him . . . but how like the tender grass, too green and tall before the promise of summer was real?

"She said no," he muttered again to himself.

Guinevere was the foundation stone. She was the power of the land. All his dreams were only airy visions until they rested on her. But she was far more than that. Pure and powerful, brave, bright, and beautiful . . .

Arthur was in love. He would have given up Camelot and the kingdom and even Excalibur if he could have had her. But, no. He had the trappings of majesty without the truth of it.

Slumping to sit on the rock, he set elbows on his knees and clutched his head, devoid of the weighty crown. "What am I to do?"

"There is plenty," came a kindly voice at his shoulder.

Arthur glanced over to see Merlin in his tattered travel cloak, his old face cherubic within its mantle of white hair.

"The first caravan of wood will be arriving before noon, and with it joiners and carpenters. And when they arrive, we can expect the sylvan courts to protest. I've worked out an arrangement whereby we will cease our logging and sawing operations if the sylvan fey will promise to grow whatever wooden structures we require—"

Arthur gave Merlin a patient smile, and he snorted, shaking his head. "She said no, Grandfather. Guinevere said no."

A wistful look crossed Merlin's features. He stared out at the frosty fields. "Chastity is the root of her power, Arthur. You must understand that. I too said no last night, and it took every bit of will in me to do so." He growled playfully. "A damned fine woman."

"I asked her to marry me," Arthur said. "A chaste marriage, that her power might remain in her, but we might always be together."

Merlin said ruefully, "All this is my doing, and Loki's— a mad arrangement. You were betrothed from birth, and marriage seems inevitable, but it is a strange sort of marriage to cling forever to a woman you can never have."

"Strange, yes, but I could be content. I would make myself content. I love her, Merlin." Arthur stood, pacing toward the edge of the stone slab. "Our chastity would only make our love purer, loftier."

"Chastity has destroyed more than a few monks—"

"I'm talking about pure love, love that is not debased by lust!" Arthur continued emphatically. "It's the sort of love that should be practiced by all great men toward all great women. By all kings and noble warriors—"

"It certainly would put warriors in a mood to kill."

Ignoring the interruption, Arthur barged onward. "The warriors I have around me, the folk who will defend this great city and kingdom, must cleave to a higher standard. There should be a code for mounted warriors, to love chastely from afar, to fight for justice, to rescue the oppressed, to champion the weak, to remain pure in war and love—that's the code of cavalry—"

"Chivalry would be a better term," Merlin muttered.

Arthur's eyes swirled with star glow. "Yes, chivalry. And the men who attain this high honor, who embody this chaste love, they should have a special name. They are, after all, a special priesthood of warriors. Perhaps they should be called priests—"

"How about 'knights' instead," Merlin jabbed, adding under his breath "the Saxon word for 'little boys.' "

"Knights, yes," Arthur said, utterly serious. He nodded in satisfaction. "Knights of chivalry."

The young king shook his head and swatted away bedeviled thoughts. "What am I talking about? More lunatic fancies. More airy delusions." He stomped on the stone beneath them. "It's Guinevere, Merlin. Without her, I will drift away. It makes me crazy to be away from her. It makes me do stupid things."

Merlin laughed. The sound was almost a cough. "What stupid things? It makes you skulk along the foundations in the light of morn, blathering about noble warriors—ah, yes, lad, very stupid."

Fire blazed suddenly in Arthur's eyes. The rest of his face was thrown into shadow. "I skulked these foundations last night too, only I wasn't alone. There was a Pagan priestess, not of the sort that Guinevere is—a priestess of the dark powers beneath the earth. She came to me. She offered me another connection to the land. And I took it."

Merlin's expression grew grave. "You must learn which women to wrestle and which not to—" His eyes suddenly rolled in their sockets. His knees buckled. The old man swooned.

Arthur caught him. "What is it, Grandfather? What is happening?"

Merlin could not answer. He crumpled like a struck tent.

Oh, Morgan, you have swum the blood tides to a broad and fertile land. You ascend now. Sanguine brine runs from you. Soon you will be dry, and will bear as richly as the land where you dwell.

You are transforming. The seed of kings germinates in you. No longer the maiden, you are becoming the mother.

Why had I not foreseen this? Guinevere shall forever be the maiden. Chastity is her power. But you, you must ascend through the triune goddess. Your power encompasses chastity and fecundity and sterility, all. You have made Arthur a mortal consort of divinity, have invoked the ancient magic

*of kings and goddesses. The child you bear—he is to be king
in the old way. Mordred will be his name.*

*Morgan, you have swum the blood tides to a broad and
fertile land. There, you bear a king who will sail those tides
again . . . who will return to slay his father.*

"Grandfather! Grandfather! Awaken."

Merlin's eyes flickered open. Blue morning gleamed in
them. Tears glistened.

"Ah, you have returned." Arthur breathed in relief. "You
haven't collapsed like that since—"

"She was your sister, Arthur—"

"Who was my sister?"

"The woman last night. She was Morgan Le Fey. She was
disguised in magic so that you would not know."

Arthur was pale against the morning sky. "No. It cannot
be—"

"You have sired an evil that could slay you—"

"It cannot be—"

"It cannot be, and yet, it is!"

Arthur bowed his head bleakly. "Then all the more, I will
embrace this chaste love. All the more, I will beseech Guinevere to marry me."

"I have considered your proposal," Merlin whispered into the
fountain at the center of Camelot, "and my answer is yes."

He drew his head back from the playful waters. His beard
dripped a little. The tiny drops were swallowed in the welling
tide that progressed out from the Bountiful Weirds. Water
chanted quietly, but he did not hear the sensual voice he
listened for.

"Come now, dear Nyneve, I know you hear. I know you
watch for me from rivers and lakes and pools, just as I watch
for you. I know you are listening," Merlin said. All around,
workers passed, paying little heed to the lunatic at the fountain. He dragged a finger playfully across the rolling surface

of the water. His beard draped the flood. "I said, my answer is yes."

There came a tug on the end of his beard. An insistent hand lay hold of him. His head plunged into the swirling pool. He felt a kiss, sweet and passionate, and heard a voice. "You are growing up, then, Merlin," Nyneve said. "At last, not a boy, but a man."

Wide eyes flooding with crisp spring water, Merlin gabbled something. Bubbles poured from his mouth and nose. The watery hand released him. He hauled his head up out of the water and stared at the fountain.

"Not *that* . . . proposition," Merlin gasped, shooting water from his nose. Rivulets coursed down his tattered travel robes.

Workers halted to gaze at the spectacle.

Dripping, Merlin realized he and Arthur were equal fools. He lowered his voice and leaned inward.

Nyneve's face formed, beautiful and ever-changing in the water's surface.

Rueful, the old man said, "I meant the proposition to build the henge of stone."

A watery hand emerged to pat Merlin's cheek. "You are full of delays, Merlin. Methinks you will be a child forever." Wrapping fingers in his beard, she yanked him bodily into the fountain.

With a great splash, he was swallowed up. Water closed over him.

Nyneve dragged him down, impossibly deep. "Let's be off to Eire."

Together, they tumbled through the cold veins of the earth. There was a rushing vitality to moving this way. It was not like drifting in the warm wash of the ley-line stream. These uneven passages shouted and pummeled. Many channels gave out into Otherworld lakes and seas, but the naiad avoided them, heading to the Eire sea.

Within its briny depths, Nyneve dragged Merlin past deep benthos. Luminous creatures drifted above—leviathans and the ghosts of drowned seamen.

They reached Eire. Even belowground the land was different from Britannia—greener and wetter. The channels led to realms of twisted Fomorians, to underground shores of the Tuatha Dé Danann. It was an epic and ancient land. Streams tasted deeply of peat and dark waters. Rocks had been worn to glassy smoothness. Music filled the very stones of the place—a sound of water fifes and haunted hollows.

Merlin and Nyneve emerged in a green meadow stream below a vast moor.

Tattered and sodden, the old mage rose from the brook. He shivered in the morning light.

Nyneve took form beside him. Once a creature of water, she turned to flesh and fabric, a regal woman in a long gray gown. She looked him up and down. "You know, you can change your appearance. You might as well be dry."

"I might as well be young too," Merlin said, wringing out his sleeve, "as you have so often suggested. But I'm happier this way."

A broad sweep of forest hemmed in the moor on one side. On the other, a rocky ridge jutted. Atop that flat ridge lay the tumbled megaliths spoken of by Nyneve. They seemed the bones of a giant, barely clad in mossy flesh and abandoned by spirit utterly.

"This is the henge that will build our Camelot?" Merlin asked. "Tumbledown, moss-eaten, forgotten?"

"Stones are only strengthened by time," Nyneve said. "But there is another despoiler here, one with which we must reckon if we are to take this henge."

Merlin's eyes narrowed. "I sense it, too—a different smell aboveground than beneath. It is a new smell, of metal and men."

"The God of your sword has taken this land, just as Arthur has taken Britannia. It is his intolerant sword you sense. The threat of him is still new in the air." Nyneve's arms were stiff with an edge of fear. "He is the despoiler. One of his victims has taken up residence among these stones."

Bowing before her, Merlin gestured toward the low ridge and the pile of titan bones. "Lead on."

They climbed a ragged way up from the stream to the moor, and from the moor to the rocky ridge. The sun rose as they went. Merlin's robes steamed across his shoulders.

Soon, they reached the megaliths. The stones lay in an untidy pile, forming triangular caves beneath. From one such cave came an incessant chatter—the muttering of a man lost in madness.

"This brings back memories," Merlin said. "He may be powerful. Dangerous."

Nyneve shook her head gravely. "No. Not powerful or dangerous. Only pathetic. Pitiable. Locals avoid this spot, and missionaries consider it a domain of the devil. Patrick himself called it the dolman-gate to Hades. You see, the creature who dwells here is a three-headed thing, like Cerebus."

"Three heads, and each one mad—" Merlin said in sad amazement.

"No, in fact, each is sane. Only together do they make a madman."

"How did they come to such a tortured existence?"

"Before the Christ, these three were crafter titans—one a blacksmith, one a wright, and one a jewel-cutter. They worked together to create fantastical weapons. The blacksmith titan, Goibhniu, forged a great lance-head that always struck its mark. The wright, Luchta, worked a lance shaft that would fly endlessly until it reached its target. The jewel-worker, Creidhne, set the whole with gold and silver inlay and diamonds that would return the weapon to the hand of its owner. With weapons such as these, Lugh Shining One and the Tuatha Dé Danann drove the Fomorians below."

"They defeated the under demons only to be defeated by the Christ," Merlin said.

"Yes. The titans were triune then, and these stones were their temple, their spiritual workshop—anvils, benches, tables, all. Their temple was destroyed, their worshipers were converted, and they fell, just as you did. They became mortal. Goibhniu, Luchta, and Creidhne now share a single diminutive body, a single pair of small hands. They bicker over who should be given charge of the body, but none relents to the others. As a result, they spend most of their days in paralysis and arguing. Even if one god can gain control, he must ply his craft with no tools or materials, all the while listening to the rants of the other two. They cannot agree. The blacksmith wants strong hands, the wright callused hands, and the goldsmith delicate hands. Therein lies the madness."

Merlin's features darkened. "The longer you speak, Nyneve, the more certain I am that this *is* a gate to Hades."

"Come," Nyneve said. "Arthur has need of artisans to build his city."

They rounded an edge of stone and stared toward the muttering sounds. There, crouched beside a pile of leaves, squatted a tiny little man. His slim shoulders were overcrowded with heads. The first was black-haired and young, a face burly and blunt, with tiny white scars where errant sparks had alighted. The middle head was brown-haired and middle-aged, with a brow as lined and smooth as planed planking. The third was white-haired and slim. His eyes were pinched at the corners from squinting at gems. The threesome did not notice the new arrivals, their mouths engaged even then in a muttered squabble:

"Either of you had the least concept of exactitude," the white-haired Creidhne was saying, "you would realize we cannot buy tools when we have no money—"

"You're the silversmith," growled Goibhniu. "Make some money!"

"And I can't mold silver I do not have, and in any case I do not make money, but jewelry—"

"Which is why," broke in Luchta, "until we have silver or iron, I should have control. We have wood, and plenty of it. If I had only a day, I could fashion something—a stepstool, or a small box—something we could take to market and sell."

"Or any subtlety at all, you might remember we have three heads and that buyers are suspicious of stools and boxes made by men with three heads—"

"I'll put a bag over each of you," barked Goibhniu, "and charge a copper to have a look."

"And at least ask a silver since I could do something with a silver, though we've not even one bag, let alone two—"

Merlin stepped forward. "Hail, good men. I seek the services of a smith, and a wright, and a jewel-worker. Have I come to the right place?"

"An invader!" Goibhniu hissed. "I'll wring his neck!"

"And afterward you could check his pockets for some silver—"

Luchta blurted, "Wait! Perhaps he needs a stool or a box."

Climbing slowly across the tumbled stones, Merlin shook his head ruefully. "I do not need a stool or a box, but something more on the order of a great, jewel-encrusted palace, with a thousand gates in iron and hammer-beam vaults like overturned galleys. Someone had told me that the only craftsmen who could build me such a place would be here."

"Someone told you right!" Goibhniu shouted.

"Doesn't matter how glorious the commission unless there is gold to keep as well as gold to fashion—"

Luchta enthused, "We have wood enough for twenty such vaults."

Merlin smiled. "Excellent. And I have gold in plenty, for retainer."

He opened the folds of his travel cloak, sweeping the edge of it outward like a pair of wings. In place of feathers, the fabric shimmered in gold coins. The morning sun leaped from the metal and played across the eyes of the three gods. Mouths that never ceased yammering fell open and stayed open. Even their tonsils glowed golden in reflected promise.

Closing the cape again, Merlin said, "Of course, you will need to come to the work site."

"No good," Goibhniu barked. "My anvil is here."

"Though in disrepair, my workbench is here, too, and I cannot possibly fashion gold without it—"

"It would be impossible without our shop space and tools."

Nyneve approached Merlin. "You will be provided tools, and we can move your anvil and workbenches to the site. In fact, we will clean them and set them up for you."

"Impossible," Goibhniu replied. "I can't work with these two."

"Must admit our limited number of hands and limitless number of arguments make unlikely any productive outcome—"

Luchta agreed, "It is very difficult."

"Well," Merlin said, "I have never known a master workman to labor more than eight hours each day, and would ask no more of each of you. If we devise a rotational, each of you can have the body and the workshop to yourself for eight hours, while the other two rest."

"And if two hands are not enough for you, we will provide you with many more—apprentices, as any master craftsman should have," Nyneve added. "Each of you will have a hundred hands to direct and marshal—some of them the hands of titans."

For the first time in nearly a century, the rubble mound was silent. Hope and fear warred across the three faces. For a moment, the three fallen gods had lost their separate minds and found an accord.

Goibhniu broke the silence, speaking for them all. "You can't move these stones."

"Never were lifted except by the hands of gods and only by the hands of the killer of gods were they cast down—"

"It does seem," Luchta admitted, "without block and tackle and an army of men, we are out of luck."

Nyneve smiled knowingly and swept her hand gently outward. Watery sounds came from the triangular cave where the threesome huddled. All three heads came about, and their common body backed suspiciously from the cave. It did so just in time. A spring had risen beneath one tilted megalith and was eating away the ground. Grinding massively against adjacent stones, the slab slid downward. Then, with a sudden boom, it dropped flat to the ground.

The three-headed man leaped back again, babbling. "You trying to kill us?" "And in unmitigated gall to come and undermine the abode of another—" "Our mound! You've ruined our mound!"

Nyneve said simply, "I ruined your mound, but I am fixing your workshop."

Even as she spoke, the loosened stone floated up on a gush of water and began to glide across the rocky ridge, toward the moor and the streams beyond.

"I am moving your workshop, stone by stone. You can come and be rebuilt with it, or you can remain here, without even the refuse of your former life to dwell in."

She climbed gracefully onto another fallen stone, which even then floated like a great barge after its mate.

Goibhniu, Luchta, and Creidhne watched in pale-faced dread as their old life of comfortable madness drifted inexorably away.

Moved by pity, Merlin strode down beside the shivering figure. He reached out his hand. "Come with us. Come back into the light of the world. Jove invites you. Nyneve invites you. Arthur invites you."

Three sets of eyes turned from the disintegrating cairn toward Merlin. Then, moved in common by three separate minds, a single slim hand reached out to take Merlin's.

41

To Build a Nation

Ulfius strode among the foundation trenches for Arthur's palace.

Men toiled there, bent backs sweaty and sprinkled with brown earth. Teams of mules hauled away carts filled with the mounded stuff. Other teams brought foundation stones, dragged across rolling logs. Fresh workers arrived at the south end of the trench and filed in, digging their way along. From the north end, men filed out. Their shovels were borne back by light-footed boys. New arrivals took hold of handles not even cooled from the previous worker.

Those liberated for a time from the trenches rose to wash and drink in the nearby fountain of the Bountiful Weirds. The water bore away grit and sweat both. Mud coursed down into the earth, and clear, pure water bubbled forth to take its place. With elbows on knees and heads bent downward, men rested on the verge. As they sat, their backs gradually straightened and their eyes reacquainted themselves with bright grass and sky. Their lifted noses drew in the savor of venison roasting beside the mess pavilion.

"So unlike Uther's army," Ulfius said, shaking his head in happy astonishment. Even in the back-breaking labor of foundation-digging, Arthur had organized his folk humanely. It was as much courtly promenade as gang work.

Ulfius's mood sagged as he glanced at the sheet in his hand—a list of Arthur's most highly favored warriors. Perhaps in this list, Arthur's humane organization had reached its level of absurdity. "Knights" sworn to live by a code of "chivalry"? What armsman would abandon his homeland to come sit in a castle and talk about virtue? Surely not the next one on the list.

"Kay," Ulfius read quietly as he stalked along the line in the trench. "He should be just ahead."

A mop of blond hair flashed between the walls of dirt. Muscular shoulders labored under a combination of sweat, dirt, and tan that brought the water girls to him a bit more often than to the others.

Ulfius approached over mounds of loose dirt. Reaching Kay's side, he crouched down. "Hello, Kay."

He was answered with a shovelful of soil, which struck Ulfius's tabard and pattered across his paper.

"Oh, hello, Ulfius," Kay said affably. He plunged his shovel point in the ground at his feet and leaned on the handle. "What brings the likes of you to the trenches?"

"Arthur sends me," Ulfius began.

Kay shook his head sardonically. "That's how I got here too. When I agreed to be Seneschal of Britannia, I didn't think that meant digging all of her ditches myself."

Ulfius lifted a blistered hand. "I did my digging this morning. Arthur has enough foresight to assign the morning shift to those unlikely to have tavern headaches." He gestured with that same hand toward the trench. "You'd better keep going. The fellow behind you is catching up."

Shooting a glance over his shoulder, Kay begrudgingly set his shovel to work. Between shovelfuls, he said, "So, what other job does Arthur want to assign me?"

"A job, a responsibility, and an honor," Ulfius said. He began reading from the page before him. " 'King Arthur of Britannia invites you, Kay of Chertsey, to join his permanent garrison here at Camelot. Should you accept this invitation, you will be among a select corps of mounted warriors to be known hereafter as knights of chivalry'—"

"Shivery?" Kay asked midscoop. "Shivery nights?"

"Chivalry," Ulfius corrected. "It comes from the same word as 'cavalry.' It means 'horsemanship'."

"Nighttime horsemanship?" Kay asked.

"Knights—it is a new word, a Saxon word. It means 'servant.' "

"Servants of horses?" Kay protested jokingly.

"Will you let me finish?" Ulfius asked. " 'The knights will be chosen from among the greatest mounted warriors, noblemen all, to ride for Arthur. Each knight will swear an oath of chivalry, to defend the weak, to fight for justice, to love chastely—' "

"To *what*?" Kay asked, planting his shovel truly this time.

Ulfius scowled. " '—To love chastely, to fight for Britannia and King Arthur—' "

Kay shook his head vigorously. "To chase lovelies, maybe, but to love chastely?"

Ulfius rolled up the page he had brought and said, "I don't know exactly what is meant by that bit. Perhaps it means celibacy, perhaps it means that each man will champion and defend women without requiring the . . . traditional . . . reimbursements."

"I'll not swear to horses and swear off women—"

"Well," Ulfius said in exasperation, "I don't know all the specifics. I've delivered your invitation to join the knights of chivalry. If you have other questions, you can bring them up with Arthur."

"Yes," Kay spat irritably. "Once I get the grit out from under my nails and am bathed and beautiful, I'll go have a talk with my high and mighty brother—"

"You needn't wait," Ulfius responded, gesturing with a smile. "The king is the man digging behind you."

While men and mules labored on the hills of Cadbury, a miracle took place on the Salisbury plain.

Merlin stood on the north-south ley line that crossed the hillside. Beside him, Nyneve stood on the east-west line. The winds of evening coursed over tall grasses and caught their robes, entwining them together. From the tangle of fabric came a trio of muffled protests.

With a supreme effort of cooperation, the triune god joined their wills to lift a hand and fling back the robes. White hair, brown, and black gleamed in the sunset light. The god's three heads occupied the east-by-southeast, southeast, and south-by-southeast ley lines.

"This grassy nowhere?" Goibhniu asked. "This is to be our temple?"

"A truly out-of-the-way location for what is to be a temple of great significance in the power of this island—"

"I don't see much in the way of timber," Luchta added.

Another breeze—this one the capricious conjuration of Merlin—flung the robes around the threesome again.

Nyneve winked her thanks. She was too busy with her own conjuration to worry about wind. By the time Goibhniu, Luchta, and Creidhne won free again, the power of her spell was undeniable.

A low rumble shook the ground. The very earth trembled. The grasses rattled no longer with wind, but with earthquake.

The three-headed god ceased their squabbles and gaped. Before them, the ground was rising. It swelled. Grasses canted oddly sideways. A mound formed. It was long and perfectly circular, rising from the ground in a broad ring around Nyneve. Here and there, cracks jagged across the top and sides of the mound. Water gushed from these crevices and jetted into the air. The streams washed away hunks of earth, revealing vast slabs of rock beneath.

"The temple," Goibhniu said. "They're raising our temple."

The rumbling only increased, and with it the spray of water. Long dolmens cleared the shivering grasses and continued skyward. Beneath them, other megaliths pressed, vertical posts to the horizontal lentils. It seemed a vast circle of doorways. The converging ley lines poured their power into the stones.

"Seems after further consideration to be just the right situation for a temple meant to create from raw materials a material culture—"

The dolmens towered all around now. Their bases rose into the last light of day. A courtyard, stone by stone, forced itself upward through the field. Clay sloughed from the grand stones, and sand sifted downward. The rumbling ceased. Stillness settled.

Goibhniu muttered in disbelief. "They did it. They restored our workshop."

"Amazed to stand once again surrounded by the temple we once occupied—"

"Yes, that's our temple, our workshop," Luchta said. "That's the stone henge."

Kay tapped his foot impatiently and stared at the ceiling of the royal pavilion. "Where is Arthur?"

It had been galling enough to spend hours washing and drying his finest tabard, polishing his dress armor, bathing in the chilly fountain, teasing every speck of dirt from his fingernails, shaving and trimming and combing and lacing—all of it without aid of a squire. Kay's squire had, after all, become king. But now to stand amid three hundred other "knights of chivalry" and wait for an hour for that same kid-brother king to arrive—that was intolerable.

"I'm about to walk out of here," Kay hissed.

"Oh, I'll not," said his conversational companion, Andronius of Canterbury. He was paunchy and greasy, with a face that shone like polished armor. "This is likely a test. A knight of chivalry must be patient and long-suffering—all that nonsense. I imagine our king is simply testing us."

Kay lifted his eyes above the greasy fellow, hoping to glimpse his father, or Ulfius, or even one of the sons of Lot. Almost anyone would make more pleasant company than Andronius.

"I'll give him another few minutes, and then I'm leaving," Kay said.

"You've got it easy. You're his brother. He has to let you in. Folk like me have to be expert swordsmen and horsemen, powerfully built, patient, long-suffering—all that nonsense."

If Andronius said the word "nonsense" once more, Kay would test the man's knowledge of fisticuffs.

"Just a load of nonsense—"

Kay was rearing back for the blow when Ulfius staggered into the tent. The chamberlain was battered and bloodied. He fell to his knees, gasping.

Polite murmurs died to silence.

Into that hush, Ulfius gasped one word that carried to the back of the tent. "Dragons!" He fell to his face, unmoving.

"Dragons?" Andronius muttered. "What nonsense?"

Kay bolted from the stunned throng. He reached Ulfius and turned him over. Three deep gashes crossed the chamberlain's face, as though from three claws. In one cut, the man's cheekbone showed whitely.

"Ulfius! No!" Kay checked for breath. There was none. He pulled back Ulfius's collar piece to check for a pulse. The vein was lacerated, dribbling its last blood. "No! No!" Kay scooped up the corpse in his arms and struggled to stand.

Ector arrived, his face despondent. "Is he?"

"Dead," Kay said. The word was the bitterest he had ever said.

A crowd gathered—Gryfflet and Lucas, Gareth, Agravain, Gawain. . . . They stared bleakly.

"He spoke of dragons?" Kay said in disbelief.

"With Wotan about, who knows? But dragons or Saxons— Ulfius must be avenged," Ector said, drawing his sword. It was not his battle blade, only a half-weight ceremonial thing, but Ector clutched it with deadly fury. "He must be avenged!"

Steel whistled angrily from sheaths all around. With shouted oaths, the company pressed for the tent flaps.

Numbly Kay followed. He bore Ulfius along on the flood of horsemen, out onto the nighttime hill.

It was a moonless evening. At first Kay could see nothing in the murk. There was only the bob of helmed heads and the glimmer of ornamental swords. Beyond, the night was like ink. What was this talk of dragons?

A gout of flame suddenly lit the distant darkness. Fire poured from a gigantic maw. It showed up a huge, preter-natural serpent. The dragon was as large as a house. Red jowls and wicked whiskers glowed in the blaze. The roar of the beast shook the earth. Flames rolled out. . . .

They struck something—a great curving shield of magic cast on the wind. Behind that magic shield stood Merlin, outlined in crimson. Beside him was Arthur.

"The king and royal mage are beset!" Ector shouted.

Armsmen swore bravely and rushed to defend Arthur and Merlin.

Kay did not follow, still cradling Ulfius's corpse. This was only one dragon, and Merlin was more than a match for a single dragon. But there had been talk of more. Striding to his father, Kay said, "Where are the others?"

"The other what?" the lumbering man asked.

"The other dragons—" Even as the words formed, another wall of flame erupted in the dark distance.

A second dragon. It spat blue fire, hotter and more pow-erful than red. Killing breath jetted from a mouth twice the size of the first dragon's. The scaly bulk of this serpent was as large as an inn. Azure eyes stared balefully above the dragon's hoary snout. Its roar rattled the breastbone in every knight's chest. A second gout of blue flame roared down.

It outlined a maiden—Guinevere! Her silhouette stood clear against the blaze for a moment before it swept around her and she was gone.

"No!" Kay gasped out in terror.

"The q-queen!" Ector stammered.

Blue flames receded. Guinevere emerged from their midst. She stood unharmed, guarded by a scintillating aura of Tuatha magic.

"Thanks be to God!" Ector said.

"Thanks be to Avalon!" Kay corrected.

Many more armsmen ran to help her fight this larger beast. Kay stooped to lay down Ulfius, intent on joining them.

A third firestorm erupted in the distance. White-hot, it cascaded down from the largest maw of all. This serpent's head towered at the height of a steeple. Flame sluiced past teeth as long as lances and as wide around as men. Leather wings blotted out the stars. Its roar sent knights to their knees. White flames cascaded down to engulf a tinker's cart. Wood flashed away to soot. Pans fell in puddles of iron. An old man cringed behind, trapped between fire and stone. He hopelessly clawed at the wall that enclosed him.

"That poor, helpless man!" Ector exclaimed

"Let's go help him," Kay said.

Ector, Gawain, Agravain, Gareth, and a number of others headed toward this last and largest monster.

Kay crouched, tenderly laying Ulfius's corpse on a quiet embankment. He drew his sword and glanced toward the white dragon. "That is the fight you would have fought, Ulfius, my friend. I go to avenge you."

Kay rose and charged into battle. It was hopeless, he knew. Dragons? He had thought the beasts mere legend, but who knew what horrors Merlin had awakened from the deeps? Sword raised high, Kay ran.

The air rippled and roared before him. His father and the sons of Lot and two score others disappeared in another storm of white fire. Only their swords remained, jutting defiantly from the creature's gut.

For all the heat, for all the tears, Kay could barely see. He would join them—Ulfius and Father and all the others—and bury his blade in wyrm flesh before he was burned to nothing. He would die defending Britannia.

Kay's feet pounded down the slope. He brandished his blade. He was only three strides from that white wall of scales when the fire burst over him—

It was so hot, he could not feel it, so loud, he could not hear it.

And then, just as suddenly, he was in heaven among them—Father and Lot's sons and a score of others. They seemed in a merry mood, lifting tankards of ale and laughing between draughts. Perhaps this was not heaven but Asgard, with its warriors' revels. But no, it was not even Asgard. It was a tent—another royal pavilion, decked out identically to the last—the *selfsame* tent Kay had just left!

Ulfius greeted Kay happily, offering him a foamy tankard of ale.

"Ulfius?" Kay asked, numbly receiving the ale. "I thought you were dead! I thought I was dead! What is all this? What has happened?"

The chamberlain shrugged sheepishly. "A test. Arthur devised it and Merlin realized it. I helped, as did Guinevere and your own father."

"A test?" Kay echoed.

"An illusion. All of it. Arthur wanted to see what choices his knights would make."

"Choices?"

"To go fight the red dragon—this showed that a man lacked judgment and perhaps excelled in sycophancy. The king needed no greater defender than Merlin against that smallest dragon. Those who ran to his aid found themselves only in the empty darkness of the Cadbury Hills."

"What of Guinevere and the blue dragon?"

"That was a better choice, though it was clear the land guarded Guinevere. Those who ran to her aid have won Arthur's gratitude, and will be offered positions of honor among his armies. But they did not choose the best fight—"

"The white dragon and the tinker," Kay said, smiling beneath a mustache of foam.

"Yes, the greatest threat and the most sorely pressed victim. Arthur seeks knights who will defend the lowliest Briton as they would the very king," Ulfius concluded, taking a sip from his own tankard.

Kay laughed, shaking his head. "Arthur seeks complete fools—"

"Ha!" Ector congratulated his son, pounding the young man's shoulder, "you passed the test! You'll be a knight of King Arthur's court!"

Kay could not help smiling, a dazzling expression even with the foamy mustache. "And you, as well!"

Ector shook his head, laughing. "Oh, no. I'm pleased to have been invited, and even more pleased to have aided in the test, but I am needed in Chertsey. I'll leave all this chivalry to you young folk."

"And you, Ulfius?" Kay asked.

"No, I am busy enough as it is." The chamberlain's brow canted. "I am one of the more restless dead."

Kay nodded, noting only then that the illusory blood was gone from his tabard.

"Thank you, by the way," Ulfius said, "for your kind words and deeds when you thought me a corpse."

Smiling sardonically, Kay clapped him on the back. "Next time you die, I'll do just the same."

42

Courting Guinevere

*A*rthur watched her.

Guinevere strode among the foundation stones and pediments of the royal palace. She knew the plans well. She had pored over floor diagrams and elevations. This place was new, though. It had not been on any of the previous plans. It seemed almost an open air stage, but a wall separated it from the rest of the grounds. The wall grew brick by brick as she watched. Workers toiled at building it.

Guinevere approached one.

Arthur followed, moving secretively behind a wagon.

Guinevere reached the bricklayer. His tunic and breeches were crusted in mortar. A trowel and bucket sat to one side. A pile of cut fragments lay to the other.

"Excuse me, but what is this to be?"

He looked up at her and blinked a compliment. Dragging a shapeless cap from his head, he said, "Why, a wall, ma'am."

She smiled sweetly, and the look brought a similar smile to the bricklayer. "Yes, I know it is to be a wall. But a wall enclosing what?"

Arthur edged closer, wanting to see her response.

"A garden, ma'am. A raised garden. Rose trellises and bowers and even a balcony."

"Roses?" she wondered aloud. "What do knights want with roses?"

"Oh, they ain't for the knights. They're for looking at from the balcony. They're for the queen."

Arthur stepped up behind her and softly slipped his hands about her waist. He whispered in her ear, "You mean more to me than the power of the land. You are the beauty of the land too, and the soul of it."

She did not startle, but neither did she melt into his embrace.

Arthur went on. "Just because we would be united does not mean you would lose your power. You would be my wife. You would have power through me."

At last, Guinevere turned, eyes welling. "If we joined, neither of us would have power. I am queen only so long as I am not called queen."

"What of a chaste marriage?" Arthur pleaded desperately. "We will cleave to each other, but never have one another."

"How could we be chaste in marriage when we want each other so terribly? No. You are to be king of this land, and I to be the power of the land. We were destined so from birth—ever entwined but never touching. There is no other way." She pulled free of him.

His arms had lost their will to hold on.

Guinevere fled away among pediments and piles of stone.

Alone, she gives birth. She believes, truly believes, she is not alone, but immersed in the woodlands around her. But Morgan has never trusted herself fully to others. She is her own midwife, this proud and brilliant creature. For nine months she has arrayed about herself the herbs she would need, the knives and thread she hoped not to. And should the worst happen, she has Rhiannon, the healing scabbard.

But this child is no easy child. He is a brutal bastard. Already she clutches the healing sheath, already it has knit her together thrice. He kicks her spine. He claws outward. He tears her wide—

And if this is how Mordred treats the mother he loves, what will he do to the father he hates?

Merlin made sure to exit the ley-line highway well back from the stone henge. Over the past year, it had become chaotic and dangerous—and enormously productive. The southern edge of the thing sported a sprawling smithy, complete with twenty-three anvils, sixteen forges, and a coal bunker two stories high. The eastern edge hosted another smithy, this one clean and bright and tidy—antithesis of the blacksmith shop beside it. The western henge was dominated by a wood-wright's shop—saws and vises, benches and cases. These three workspaces, day and night, thronged with apprentices busily working, goaded on by the three-headed god.

On the northern side, raw materials arrived in a steady stream, and finished goods departed just as steadily—though not steadily this evening.

As Merlin coalesced on the grassy hillside, he spotted five ogres in the northern staging area. They argued in bellicose voices. The three-headed craft god stood atop the henge and returned their shouts with equal fury. Four of the ogres bore enormous wet bags of burlap, filled with something that oozed orangely onto the ground. The fifth carried a huge mallet over his broad clavicle. All were wet through, regular waterfalls coming from their clumped masses of black hair. Sunken eyes peered over bulbous noses, and fleshy mouths yammered out threats indecipherable. Goibhniu's responses—for he was the god on duty—were no more lucid and no less violent. This was only the latest in an hourly spectacle of Otherworld disputes.

Merlin had not come to settle the argument, but one blow of that hammer could kill the triune god and fell henge stones like kegels. Goibhniu's tact almost assured that outcome.

"You bring me wet ore," Goibhniu raged, "and want to be paid by weight? You want me to pay for *water*!"

In the brooding language of ogres, the brute with the ham-mer replied, "Of course is wet. This Atlantean ore. This from great war room of Atlantis. Of course is wet. You pay more for ore and water."

"Ore is ore," Goibhniu insisted. "Water is water. Maybe I will pay you the weight in wet coins. Maybe I will spit on them one by one. You sell dry ore, or none at all."

Shaking his head in mild amusement, Merlin remembered

a time when he allowed himself the luxury of lunacy. Conversing with tree stumps, listening to the songs of mice, eating mud soup, speaking comfort to the mourning wind—Merlin was surprised to realize he missed those horrible days. He floated into the air and drifted toward the top of the circle of stones. En route, he passed above the massive hammer that the ogre brandished.

"I give you solid iron!" the ogre growled. The hammer trembled with anger.

Merlin landed on the metal head of the thing and cast a spell that made himself heavy. The ogre struggled to bring the hammer arcing forward, but Merlin was an immovable object.

In a wry voice, he said, "Now, now, you two. Let's discuss this reasonably lest I call down lightning to test this ore . . . and those who squabble over it."

The appearance of the now-famous archmage had opened the mouths of five ogres and three gods. His threat shut them again.

"You ogres say you gathered this iron ore from sunken Atlantis, true?"

The lead ogre grimaced under the hammer's weight. "Didn't breathe three days—a long walk. Harry got ate by a serpent."

Merlin nodded sagely. "I happen to be very familiar with Atlantis. I was Zeus in a former life, you see."

The ogres swallowed in unison. Their eyes narrowed, shifting uneasily.

"You say this ore came from the war room—do you mean the royal armory, where all the swords and spears, shields and armor were kept?"

"Yes. That war room," the ogre said eagerly.

"Ah, so you had to defeat the Gorgon to gain entrance?"

"Yes. Harry got ate by him as well."

"By her," Merlin corrected mildly. The look of apprehension on the ogre's faces turned to downright fear. Goibhniu crossed arms over his chest and smilingly nodded. Merlin continued. "She certainly is a beauty, that Gorgon."

Enthusiastic nods came all around.

"I see," Merlin replied. "Well, you are liars. There is no Gorgon guarding the armory of Atlantis, and if there were, she would not be beautiful, and she would not eat Harry, but turn him, and all of you, to stone."

The ogres let go their bags of ore and crouched back from the sky, expecting a lightning blast.

Merlin went placidly on. "I presume, then, that this ore was pillaged from the various sacred pools that have been desecrated lately—remains of weapons sacrificed to the local gods. I presume that the ore in those bags will have, mixed among it, freshwater fish, not saltwater ones."

The ogres bowed their heads in guilt.

"I could kill you now. Instead, I will spare your lives, if you return this ore to the pools whence you took it."

Glad relief flooded the faces of the beasts.

"And, since King Arthur has need of enchanted iron, the only price I will exact for your treachery is this lovely hammer. There should be fifty fine swords in this—plus ten shields and perhaps a suit of armor."

A growl of rage erupted from the lead ogre. At last overcoming the tremendous weight of Merlin's spell, he swung the hammer in a mighty arc overhead. That one blow could smash wizard and henge and craft god, all.

Another blow struck first—a white-hot jag of lightning. It leaped down from clear heaven, somehow missed Merlin, flashed through the metal hammerhead, and sought ground. En route, it vaporized every fleshly thing—the wooden haft, the hand that held it, the arm that held the hand, and so forth. The craven creature's skeleton showed in lurid flashes through his meaty limbs, and then showed through in truth as muscle turned to ash and sloughed away. Bone followed thereafter. The lightning lingered a moment more, as though to assure that all that remained of the ogre was a crooked smear on the ground.

Liberated from its haft, the massive hammerhead vaulted into the midst of the henge. Goibhniu ducked. His comrades awoke and also ducked. The vast hunk of metal fell to ground in the center of the temple and rolled, smoldering, to a stop.

Merlin hovered contentedly above it all. He turned storm-bright eyes on the remaining four ogres. "Well, then, off you go!"

Without pausing for protest, the four monsters hurriedly shouldered their dripping sacks and rushed for the ley-line highway that had brought them. With several wet whooshes, the ogres one by one slipped from reality. For a moment, each was vaguely visible in the red flow of magic. Then, they faded out of being altogether.

Merlin turned his attention back toward the hammerhead in the center of the henge. "There you are, Goibhniu. Plenty of enchanted iron for the armory. I hope it suits."

The blunt blacksmith only nodded.

"And, Creidhne, how are you making out with that load of silver and gold the bluecaps brought by a week ago?"

Clearing his throat, Creidhne said, "A great deal of jewelry already, including cloisonné brooches and garnet-inset torcs and a few more pieces of royal regalia—"

Merlin nodded happily. "Very good. And Luchta, you can set aside the furnishings you and your apprentices have been crafting. I have a new assignment for you, direct from Arthur. He wants a large round table and fifty grand chairs. He wishes the table to be created from a single piece of enchanted wood, of size and form suitable to being the meeting place of his knightly council."

"A table for fifty? From a single piece of wood?" Luchta asked. Goibhniu obliged him by scratching the head's tousled brown hair. "There is not a tree large enough in all Britannia."

Merlin was already fading from view, following in the wake of the ogres to make sure they made amends. "Find one, Creidhne. Find one."

Over two and a half years, Camelot grew amazingly.

Even given the influx of workers and craftsmen mortal and

divine, the progress was astonishing. Already tents had been replaced by frame buildings of living wood. A spell of Merlin's had drawn fieldstones up through the ground until every street on the planners' map was cobbled. The twenty-foot-thick curtain wall was complete. Guard towers and bartizans surrounded the fey gates. Three separate marketplaces bustled with trade goods from distant shores. The festival grounds thronged with revelers in continuous joust. The garrison was overfilled with warriors seeking knighthood. They spent their days training in yards especially designed by Ulfius and Merlin. They spent their nights at table with Arthur, eagerly awaiting the great Round Table.

The grand palace itself was half complete. Built of white limestone and gold veined white marble, it promised to be a glorious vision. Already, its four grand and two common entrances were complete on the ground floor. The first of four aerial entrances towered at one corner.

Arthur's own apartments were only half done in the space above the great hall. He had directed the workers first to complete the chambers opposite his own. The last panels of red walnut went up that very afternoon. Glaziers finished a wall of glass that opened onto a broad balcony. Fat tapers filled candelabra and sconces. Tapestries from far Aethiopia draped the walls, and Caledonian lambskin covered the floors. All was in order, and Arthur held the key.

"Come, my dear," Arthur said. He took Guinevere's hand and led her up the white-marble stairway. "I have a surprise for you."

Her slender fingers clung warmly to the king's hand. A delighted smile filled her face. In the last few years, the young king had filled out, just as his city had. He was no longer the boy king, but a man—strong and tall and gracefully gallant. His thin beard had filled in, and his shoulders were now broad enough to make Excalibur seem at home. Of all the warriors in Camelot, Arthur was the most comely. Guinevere had difficulty these days not smiling when he took her hand.

"What is it?" she asked, slightly breathless. "More plans?

A new volume of lore? Another trunk of treasure?"

"Better," Arthur replied. Reaching the top of the stairs, he fished the keys from the pocket of his samite waistcoat. The iron shaft fit smoothly into the elaborate lock on the double arched doors. The click of tumblers came. "I hope you like it." He swung the doors quietly inward.

Warm, bright air spilled from the room. It flowed sweetly past them and down the stairs into the cool night.

Guinevere could not help gasping.

The room seemed a chamber of heaven. Lambskin made the floor as white and soft as a cloud. Windows glowed with a fading sunset. Satyrs and centaurs capered across wall tapestries. Red-walnut boughs formed the furnishings—tables and chairs composed of living wood. The bed was fashioned of four separate saplings, their branches braided together in a canopy. The whole space was lit by candles in wall sconces. As darkness deepened beyond the windows, the glow grew more inviting.

Slipping the sandals from her feet, Guinevere stepped onto the luxuriant fleece that covered the floor. She let out a great sigh and strode into the room.

Arthur pulled off his shoes and followed.

To one side of the chamber, behind a screen, was another small room. There, a tiled bath stood, water steaming. Guinevere approached it, wondering at the sight.

"Merlin has enchanted the water to remain forever warm and pure," Arthur explained. "And there is a basin with two pitchers, one containing hot water and the other cold and both enchanted to remain full. The bath has a view into the rose garden, just as the main room does. And come here—"

He pulled her toward the wall of windows. With a touch, he lightly swung back a large panel of glass, creating a door. He drew Guinevere out onto the patio. His arm swept outward, indicating the raised garden, filled with a riot of red roses. They seemed dark as blood in the dying light of day. "It is all for you, Guinevere. All for you."

43

Tables Turned

*N*ight hung over the stone henge, its workshops, and the shanty city. The saws were silent. No mauls pounded pegs. The apprentice wrights, blacksmiths, and gem-cutters were gone to inns in Salisbury and Camelot. They had a month's leave while their three masters worked on a secret and holy project.

Tonight, Goibhniu and Creidhne slept, their heads leaning on the special mantle Merlin had devised for them. It was a thin ermine stole that grew thicker as it was pressed upon. A head pillowed in that stole could sleep in comfort and silence through even a great ruckus. That single garment had done much to end the lunacy of the fallen god. It allowed each head ample sleep, and gave the master of the body privacy in which to work.

Luchta was the current master. He labored feverishly at the center of the henge. His chisels shaved fine-grained wood—an acanthus leaf here, a holly bough there, a fawn peering from the cover of a thistle brake, a knight in full armor. . . . His mind ran riot with carvings. Each new figure brought a smile of discovery and delight, exceeded only by the discovery of the next. Luchta felt he was not so much carving these forms into the wood as releasing them from captivity. His joy was grandest of all when he looked up at the vast expanse of the massive table.

It was utterly gorgeous. Measuring thirty feet in diameter and three feet in height, the table was in fact a solid cross-section from an enormous tree. Four thousand tight-packed rings converged concentrically to a jaggedly hollow core. The surface had been planed smooth and sanded until it gleamed like glass.

Luchta had cut fifty-one semicircles from the edge of the slab, each to become a seat for a knight of the table. The top three inches of each of these semicircles was cut free and hinged to become a seat back when the knight was in attendance. Otherwise it folded flush with the tabletop and blended seamlessly. Into the tabletop and the folded backs of the chairs, Luchta had carved ornate channels where Creidhne had poured gold and silver and set precious gems. All around the lower slab and at the base of each chair, elaborate motifs in iron moved. Hidden iron rollers allowed the seats to be drawn with the slightest pressure. Taken as a whole, the table and chair would be the grandest collaboration of the triune god.

Luchta sighed with a contentment he had not known for years.

"It is splendid, Luchta." A voice spoke out of the windy darkness. Merlin. He was wont to appear soundlessly and unexpectedly.

Luchta at last was accustomed to it. He nodded his head in glad agreement.

Merlin walked appraisingly around the table. His travel cloak was full of night breezes. "The craftsmanship is superb, the materials magnificent—such a beautiful and ancient slab of wood—and the execution . . . wait! What is this? Fifty-*one* chairs? I asked for fifty."

Luchta took a fortifying breath and looked directly into the eyes of the mage. "I traded the extra seat for the cross-section of wood."

The white-haired mage narrowed his gaze. "You traded the—"

"You said to make this out of a single piece of enchanted wood. I have. There's just one tree in all the world and the Otherworld that was big enough—Ygdrasill, the World Tree."

Merlin's skin paled to the color of his hair. "The World Tree? The Saxon World Tree?"

"This is from just a branch, of course, but it's got the

power of ages in it. And the fellow that got it for me said he wanted me to add one more chair—"

"You did not make a bargain with Wotan—" Merlin roared.

"Not Wotan," came a new voice, as black and sinuous as the night winds. "Not your sworn enemy, but an enemy of your enemy. And you know the saying about the enemy of my enemy?"

Eyes closing in resignation, Merlin swooned. He caught himself against the table. "Loki," he groaned. To Luchta, he said, "You made a bargain with the god of *bad* bargains?"

A laugh came from Loki. It raked across the table and the standing stones. He did not take solid form—Loki was no more than a trick of torchlight and moonlight. A set of eyes would appear momently in one alcove, the glint of grinning teeth in another. "Be calm, Jove, or do you prefer to be called mad Merlin these days?" Loki taunted. "This bargain was no bad bargain."

"For you," Merlin allowed.

Chittering laughter followed. "Of course. I never make a bad bargain for myself. But let Luchta tell you the terms of our arrangement, and you judge for yourself."

Merlin turned to the crafter god.

"It's simple enough, really," Luchta said. "Loki gave me this cross-section from the World Tree—and he swore there were no evil enchantments on it—in exchange for the extra seat. That seat would be enspelled so only a perfectly pure person could sit in it. Anybody else would get thrown out. That's it."

Brow furrowing, Merlin studied the eyes in the darkness.

"Since when have you been so distrustful of purity, Merlin?" Loki asked.

"Since when have you been so trustful of it?" Merlin replied.

Luchta said, "Now, what's wrong with that deal?"

"I don't know," Merlin replied begrudgingly. "But there must be something. Loki always benefits from his bargains.

It seems to me he is making a siege on our kingdom, a siege perilous in its trickery."

"Siege Perilous," Loki cried. "Ah, what a lovely name for the seat I have commissioned at Arthur's table. Let all impure creatures be warned lest they seat themselves in the Siege Perilous!"

Luchta approached Merlin. "It's no different from the other seats. You'll cast a spell on them too to receive only the warriors meant for them. This seat's just more picky than the others."

"I will allow it," Merlin growled, "on one condition."

"Name it," Luchta and Loki said in one voice.

"That you, Loki, quit this temple and Camelot and never appear in either again unless invited."

"Unless invited," the god echoed mockingly. As he vanished into the yawning dark, he said, "Done!"

It was a cool evening.

Arthur stood on the balcony of his completed apartments. They were the largest, grandest quarters in the palace, fit not only for personal occasions but occasions of state. Ulfius had even laughingly suggested that Arthur could hear petitions from his bed, as grand as any throne. It was a large bed, its posts carved of white marble instead of wood. Red velvet and gold silk canopied it, effective for keeping out cold during the winter and gnats during the summer. The other furnishings were marble, as well—wardrobes, cabinets, wash stands, dressing screens . . . all of it lovely, if cold. Every night, he fell asleep to the echo of his own breath.

Now, upon the balcony, he could see his breath. This would be the fifth autumn since he had founded his capital city. Everything had progressed well. The palace was nearly complete, a splendor visible from twenty leagues away. Its white ramparts gleamed in the light of the sun and glowed in the night like a hunk of moon. Two great halls, three throne rooms, the newly finished hall of the Round Table, a garrison and apartments for fifty knights, twelve larders, four kitchens, thirty-eight garderobes, four baths, an infirmary, and a dungeon—the palace of King Arthur was the grandest royal house since the courts of Old Pharaoh. As extensive as the place was, it was forever crowded with visiting kings and emissaries, knights and knights-in-training, squires and pages, dames and damsels.

"Still, it feels empty," Arthur muttered to himself.

He gazed blearily out over the city. It too was bustling and broad, growing day by day. A city of freemen, it was called. All had their homes, and more folk arrived every day, seeking a new start. For the most part, they found it.

"And why can't I find a new start, along with them?" Arthur wondered. He thought of Moses, who led his nation through travail and turmoil to the Promised Land, only to be denied entry himself. Everyone was starting over. Everyone was engaged but him. Even Merlin seemed young. "I am the old young king."

He turned. There, in the bank of windows that gave onto the balcony, he saw his own dark reflection. Camelot gleamed in a thousand lamps and torches around him, a wide galaxy. He, on the other hand, was only a dark and small figure, obscuring the bright center of it. Heaving a tired sigh, Arthur moved to the bank of windows, pivoted the glass panel aside, and entered his apartments.

A fire smoldered on the hearth, the only light in the room. Even its orange glow could not warm the white-marble columns that surrounded the bed. Weary beyond thought, Arthur unstrapped Excalibur and leaned it in its halter beside the bed. He shucked his tabard and waistcoat, folded each neatly, and placed them within the wardrobe. Camisia was next, tossed into a basket for the purpose in one corner. He kicked off his boots and pulled off trousers and leggings as well. The floor was cold beneath the soles of his feet. Lifting a sponge from his wet sink, he dipped it in a warm pitcher of water on the hearth, and did his evening ablutions. At last, clean and cold, he drew back the curtains of his bed, turned the covers, and sat.

"What's the point of being king when you're alone?"

He lay down wearily, let the curtain close, and pulled up the covers. Only then did he realize the sheets were warm, and someone lay in the bed beside him. He gave a small gasp. A sweet, familiar perfume entered his nose.

Guinevere.

"I've begun to agree." Her hand warmly found his. She was trembling. "What's the point of bearing the power of the land, if I must be alone?"

"Oh, Guinevere," Arthur said. He rolled toward her, his hand settling on her warm, silken side. "I love you."

"I love you too," she replied. Her voice was tremulous. "Oh, Arthur, what will we do when the land turns its back on us?"

He smiled in the curtained darkness. "I don't know. We will be together. That is all I know."

"Britannia will be a hostile place again, Arthur," she said, caressing his cheek, "brigands and bandits and pretender kings."

"We will be together," Arthur said, kissing her. "That is all I know."

She began to whisper something, but he set his finger to her lips.

"Someone has just entered the room."

Her eyes grew wide.

Footsteps moved from the doorway toward the curtained bed.

Arthur drew Guinevere away from the sound and reached out for Excalibur. His hand settled on the marble bedpost. The sword was gone.

There came a sound of steel hissing from a sheath. Air moaned as the blade sliced it. Samite curtains cut cleanly. Excalibur flashed down through the dark space and clove sheets and tick, cutting even into the marble frame.

Arthur grabbed the rent curtain, flung it back, and leaped out. He landed atop a burly armsman, knocking the man down.

The warrior crashed to ground, hauberk and plate clattering. A gloved hand still clutched the sword hilt, and it raked from the cracked marble.

Naked and unarmed, Arthur landed a vicious punch in the man's eyes. "Release my sword and live."

Roaring, the armsman chopped at Arthur's back.

The sword bit shallowly. Hot lines of blood trickled down Arthur's sides. He punched twice more, smashing the man's head against the marble floor.

Getting a knee between himself and his assailant, the armsman shoved Arthur off. The man lumbered to his feet. Excalibur carved the air ahead of him.

Arthur backed up. There was no escape. The warrior stood between him and the door. The balcony was four stories up. And, of course, he would not abandon Guinevere. He would have to use whatever came to hand—pitchers and fireplace pokers and statuary—and hope she could escape in the confusion.

Stalling, Arthur said, "At least tell me who you are, who has sent you."

A harsh laugh came from the panting man. He barked something back.

Though Arthur could not discern what he said, the words were certainly Saxon, and the last was unmistakable—Wotan.

The Saxon stalked past the bed.

A moment more, and Guinevere could flee for the door. Arthur wanted to make certain she would have a chance. Grabbing a fireplace poker and shovel, Arthur shrieked, "For Guinevere!" and lunged toward his death.

Glowing in the darkness, Excalibur descended. It cut through shovel and poker as though they had been only smoke. It bore straight for Arthur's chest.

And then, there was another light in the room, a blinding glare. It was hand-shaped, a woman's hand splayed in a star. Energy cracked on the chest of the Saxon, and it flung him back. He roared. Flashing fire from Guinevere's hand melted hauberk and plate both. Flesh and bone sloughed away. The man collapsed at the foot of the bed, a star-shaped hole smoldering in his breast. Excalibur clattered to the stony floor.

Arthur reeled and fell to his knees.

Guinevere's whole figure glowed. She stood naked beside the bed. Her eyes were like twin swords, and her words cut like steel. "We cannot forsake the land, Arthur. Not when such as these prowl it. We cannot sacrifice Britannia's happiness for our own."

"No," he said, gasping and crumpling to the floor. "No. We cannot. But if I must be king and suffer for love of you, be my chaste queen, and suffer for love of me."

Her figure was only then beginning to fade. Footsteps sounded in the hall outside. Drawing a deep breath of death-smelling air, Guinevere said, "Yes, Arthur. I will."

The whole Table Round was assembled for the wedding. In white raiment, Arthur and Guinevere were magically suspended in air above the hollow heart of the table. The high bishop of Canterbury pronounced the union. Sirs Kay, Gryf-flet, Lucas, Gareth, Gawain, Agravain, and Gaheris attended with Chamberlain Ulfius, Duke Ector, and the rest of Arthur's knights. Igraine watched proudly, and on the other side of the chamber stood Guinevere's father, King Lodegrance of Cameliard. Even Dagonet was there, snickering as he composed ditties for the dance afterward.

Arthur and Guinevere were the first to dance, of course, weaving their stately and solemn way in a circle atop the great table. Merlin supplied the music, with invisible players floating about the room.

In the midst of the merriment, though, he could not help feeling that the king and queen were both desperately sad.

44

The Council of War

"King Arthur may be a father figure to the rest of you," Kay said nonchalantly over his latest tankard, "and he's an idol for most of the Knights of the Round, but to me, he'll always be my kid brother." It was a scandalous statement, but with such, Kay had gathered quite a throng of admirers.

One was a young man recently enlisted as squire to Gryfflet. Another was an equally young priestess sworn into the secrets of Guinevere's mysteries. There were Tuatha Dé Danann there as well—fey folk who had the same lithe comeliness as the queen. Scholars and bricklayers, merchants and monks—the diverse people of Camelot retired from their daylight labors for nighttime revels in Camelot's pubs. Whatever their background, folk were hungry to hear the tales told by Arthur's foster brother.

Kay finished another tankard, wiped the foam from his mustache, and said, "I fought for Uther at the Humber before your glorious king even knew he was Uther's son."

This last claim was too much. Gryfflet's squire protested. "How can you malign our king? Look at the city he built in ten years' time! There has never been a city like Camelot in all the world! There never will be again!" In the way of the young, this squire's every utterance was an exclamation.

"I'm not maligning Arthur's city," Kay said. "I recognize what a wonder it is. A city of freemen. A city that has the power of sanctuary. A city where mortal and immortal mingle. Arthur must be a great man to build such a city, but I cannot see it. Did you know, just yesterday, he said something so stupid I had to rub my knuckles in his hair?"

The priestess broke in. "He is made great by Queen Guin-

evere. She empowers him. She empowers me, and we priestesses empower you knights." She held slender hands out
toward the Tuatha that lingered there in obscuring cloaks.
"Guinevere has even opened the path for these immortals to
reenter the land."

Her words were difficult to deny. The smoky reaches of
the cellar pub entertained fey folk more exotic than even
Tuatha—thrummy caps, bodachans, dwarves, pixies. . . .
Though such creatures were furtive in sunlight, they thronged
the dark streets. It was said that by day Camelot was a dream
made real, and by night a reality made dream.

"Yes, yes," Kay allowed, his blond mop nodding as he
received another tankard. "King Arthur is the father to you
all, and Queen Guinevere your mother—forget the fact they
are celibate. But to me, they're just a couple of starry-eyed
kids."

"He's right," came a new voice. The drinkers turned to
see a narrow, leering face. In black robes, the mysterious
stranger seemed somehow familiar to those gathered around
Kay. "He is right. Arthur and Guinevere are good, yes, but
not great."

Kay wasn't certain what to make of that. It was hard to
resent a man who agreed with him, but in the same breath
this stranger had maligned his brother and his brother's wife.
"You'd best defend that statement, friend."

A smile like glinting razors answered. "Arthur and Guinevere have cut a fine jewel here in Camelot, but fine jewels
attract thieves. The city will be taken from them soon
enough."

"What!" Kay demanded, beginning to rise.

"Sit, please, good knight," the stranger said. "I speak only
of Aelle of Sussex, a great Saxon thief who has already stolen Arthur's scabbard, and who lusts after his city."

Kay laughed. He waved an off-putting hand. "Aelle of
Sussex—a barbarian. He cannot stand against the Knights of
the Round, against Excalibur and Merlin—"

"Nor against Guinevere and the powers of the land," added
the priestess.

It was the stranger's turn to laugh. "Have any of you seen a true god? I don't mean naiads and dryads, immortal heroes and Seelie hounds. I don't even mean the Christian God, who prefers sermons to swords. Have any of you seen a god who boils the sky and brings down brimstone rain? Have any of you seen a blood-red titan who can turn into a thousand gigantic war beetles? Have any of you seen deities who fight with lightning bolts? Have you?"

A sullen silence answered from those around, including Kay.

"That is what you will see. Wotan is coming. Aelle and his folk bring the Saxon pantheon with them. These are true gods, not little tree spirits. When you see them on high, you will know that Arthur and Guinevere are good but not great. When you see Wotan and Thor and Tyr, you will know Britannia must fall."

Roaring wordlessly, Kay stood and raked his sword free. "Enough! Shut your mouth or draw your sword!" Kay towered above a suddenly empty chair.

The stranger was gone.

Loki, you are here. You are here in Camelot. How? Our bargain banished you from this city unless you were specifically invited. . . .

How have you fooled me, Loki?

Worse—you have fooled Arthur's own people. Your tavern tales make them believe in Wotan, make them fear the war to come. . . .

Yes. War is coming. Wotan is coming. I have foreseen it. War and Wotan are coming, and I will be slain.

I have foreseen it.

Arthur convened his Round Table for a council of war. It was a great company. Arthur and Merlin sat within the hollow core at the center of the table. On the outward edge were arrayed the knighthood—Brastias, Kay, Lucas, Gryfflet, Gawain, Gareth, Agravain, Gaheris, Bawdewyn of Bretagne, Kaynes, and five times as many more. Every last seat was filled except, of course, for the Siege Perilous. Arthur's pure knight was yet to arrive. As to the fifty others, they were perhaps impure, but noble and courageous men all the same—and hungry.

Servants moved among them, filling tankards and clearing away trays of eel and dolphin. The scrape of forks was accompanied by a sound even less pleasant.

Dagonet plucked a mouth harp and sang bawdily.

> "Our glorious king gets no sex in his bed,
> And so hopes to get some old Sax-on instead.
> Now gather unto him, ye frustrated lads,
> For war is the best sex that you've ever had!"

Chamberlain Ulfius, seated beyond the knightly table, released a groan into his tankard of ale. He waved, signaling Dagonet to cease. The gesture occasioned only another verse:

> "Sir Ulfius, always the worst of the lot
> Will gesture away all the sex he's not got.
> His hand should be put to more personal use
> Allowing him pleasure in private abuse!"

Ulfius glared. It was impossible to concentrate on the meeting with that imp capering about. Dagonet returned the look with a broad grin and a bow. Ulfius opened his mouth as though to frame a reply, thought better of it, and turned back toward his king.

"It has been my intention, since the battle of Bedgrayne ten years ago," Arthur was saying, "to regain Rhiannon. Excalibur is incomplete without the scabbard, and so am I, and so is Britannia. We have offered dearly to ransom the scabbard, but Aelle of Sussex has refused. Our emissaries to him have been slain. Our spies have been found killed. Even Merlin has been unable to retrieve Rhiannon. Morgan Le Fey aids Aelle, you see. I contented myself with these measures while Camelot grew so gloriously. Now, though, Camelot is complete, with fifty knights and fifty priestesses—and only just in time. My foster father brings dire new of Aelle from the east."

Ector spoke up. He had ridden hard from Chertsey, responding to the king's summons. "Yes. It is as you say. Even as word reached me of this council you called, my son, I heard reports that Aelle had marched fifty thousand upon London. It surely will fall to him. Chertsey will be next. It cannot stand against such numbers as those. Aelle will march up the Thames Valley until he can strike at Camelot itself."

Arthur's face was grim. "Could we make a stand at Chertsey?"

Ector shook his head sadly. "A token one, yes, but no more. You know the garrison there, Arthur. It could hold no more than three hundred men, could withstand no more than a day's battering by such a great force."

"Then perhaps we should bring all the men and arms and supplies out of it, so that they might aid us where we will make our stand," Arthur said.

"Even now, Diana is overseeing the evacuation," Ector said. "The wagon train will bring with it the portcullises, that Aelle's forces will not easily make the site defensible against us."

Arthur's eyes narrowed. "I should have realized you would not leave Chertsey unless those preparations were already in order—and in the hands of a capable administrator."

Ector smiled his thanks. "You know my Diana. She'll have our three hundred working like Aelle's fifty thousand."

"We must remember," Merlin interjected, "that those fifty thousand troops bring with them a powerful foreign pantheon. Wotan has massed this army, as much as Aelle. It is upon their belief that he invades. It is he who drives them. We must realize that the army that marches against us includes gods."

Arthur nodded soberly. His face darkened. "If Chertsey is lost, or soon will be, we must then select another place where we might meet this tide of Saxons and turn them back. It must be a place where we have a substantial fortification, a large garrison, and—it would seem—one or more potent holy sites to provide us defense in the divine battle."

Sir Lucas, duke of Gloucester, drew a long strand of hair back from his face. "The folk of my lands are deeply devout. They would never fall to the attacks of this Wotan."

"Thank you for your faith, Lucas, but Gloucester is too far west. We need a place halfway between Gloucester and London, where we might meet their fifty thousand with an equal force, and at a center of belief in our allied gods."

Bedivere spoke for the first time in that meeting. The one-handed knight was the equal of any two-handed man at that table. Bedivere was a noble warrior from a long and distinguished line and had proved himself a staunch and wise friend of Arthur's. "There is a great hill fortification near my homeland upon a height known as Mount Badon. It guards the intersections of five Roman roads, from Bath, Cirencester, Silchester, Winchester, and Old Sarum. The master of the castle is Duke Liddington, who had sworn fealty to you at Caerleon and to your father before you. There is also an abbey there, of Saint Patrick—loyal to you. As to other spirits, natural and otherwise, the place has a reputation for being haunted—"

"I know of this great earthwork," Merlin said. "During my years of madness, I had been summoned there by Vortigern, who struggled in vain to build a fortification atop it. He lured me, asking my aid, but tried to kill me, a sacrifice to the forces dooming the project." A grave look crossed Merlin's face. "I do not remember how I survived, but in the end Vortigern built his fortification. It is a place of metaphysical power."

Arthur asked, "Shall we make our stand there, Merlin?"

Blinking awhile in thought, Merlin stroked his beard. "Perhaps. The mound itself is a conjunction point along the ley-line highway. It is an ancient sídh. I imagine many outcast gods and powers dwell within. It has several large palisaded rings in a stepped pyramid. At Glastonbury Tor, such a form indicates layer upon layer of Otherworld, each group of deities fallen victim to those above. Perhaps it is the same at Mount Badon. Perhaps we might rally these former gods—offer them a share in our world now, and get them to fight for Britannia, to fight against Aelle and Wotan."

Arthur took a deep, fortifying breath and looked about at the collection of knights. "It sounds the perfect spot for our defense of Britannia." He lifted his tankard, enchanted by Merlin to remain ever full. "What say the rest of you?"

Twenty-five knights raised their tankards in kind and cried, "To Mount Badon!"

Even Dagonet seemed impressed. He sang out:

> "To Badon Hill we hie. We hie
> To Saxons kill. They die. They die
> Till Arthur rules the earth and sky
> And Merlin in a pig's eye, pig's eye,
> And Merlin in a pig's eye!"

45

Subterranean Journeys

The stone henge was as busy as it had been in the heyday of Camelot's construction. Day and night, the triune god drove his apprentices, turning out new and wondrous creations—ironwork cauldrons, gold gilded platters and goblets, sumptuous bedposts of living wood, railings in elaborate design, silver candelabra and chandeliers, wardrobes of imported teak, tables and settees of iron. . . .

To these natural products of Goibhniu, Luchta, and Creidhne were added other fineries they could not have made—samite robes in styles from Canaan, marble tabletops in black and gold, tiles of kobold blue and saffron yellow, velvets and cashmeres and woolen tapestries. . . . Intermittent shipments from places as far off as the Celestial Empire made their way up Roman roads to converge on the stone henge. Merchants made camp and brought their wares to sell and, oddly enough, found a very ardent buyer.

Merlin had just completed one such transaction, buying a mechanical horse fashioned of ivory, when Nyneve appeared at his side.

"And what use could you possibly have for such a mechanism?" she asked.

Merlin whirled, cheeks coloring behind his white beard. "An amusement only. Just an amusement." He nodded his thanks to the dark-skinned trader. With a deep bow, he dismissed the man.

The trader returned the bow. The three strong men who had carried the horse hence now hoisted an equally heavy chest of gold, which Merlin had made in payment.

Nyneve coiled about the old mage. "I know it is nothing for a mage of your talents to enchant a chest of lead pellets, turning them into gold. But I still must ask why? With Camelot complete and war looming on the horizon, why do you run this workshop day and night? Why do you act as though you are provisioning your own palace?"

He turned to her and took her hands. Her very touch slowly transformed him. Youth and vitality moved in waves up his arms. The tattered sleeves of his travel cloak solidified. Beneath those sleeves, his arms grew once again sinewy. The white beard fled his chin. Brows thinned and darkened. Worry lines smoothed away.

Merlin was young again. "The bygone gods of this land have homes within sídh, Otherworld havens where they live out their lives in whatever fashion best suits them. But I never had such a place. I have always, from the time I was slain, lived out my madness in the world of men. I am sick to death of it. I have helped Arthur build his paradise, and thought perhaps I should build my own—*our* own."

Nyneve searched his eyes for some sign of jest, but there was none.

Merlin led her to the center of the henge, where lay a specific flagstone. He tapped it with his toe. "I thought the sídh a bit conspicuous, though, and decided to hide our Otherworld home in plain sight." ·

He lifted his robes around Nyneve, enveloping her. With a quicksilver flash, the fabric and the folk within it dissolved into energy. Merlin spoke an arcane word known only to him. The flagstone at his feet transformed into an empty space. In bodies of light, Merlin and Nyneve plunged into the deep pit.

"Quite a front gate," she noted, "the stone henge."

"Yes. It is easy to find even in the dark, and accessible from highways both magical and mundane."

They plunged for some time, past layers of fossilized shells and three separate water tables. At last they arrived. Bodies of light took on flesh once again. Together, they stood on a cliff overlooking a primeval and illimitable view.

"Here it is, my dear," Merlin said. "The Cave of Delights."

Nyneve could not help gasping at the beauty around her. The sky above was a cerulean blue. A sun beamed gently in the firmament. Beside it, a single bright planet shone, its four moons dancing.

"Jupiter, I take it?" she asked, laughing lightly.

Merlin smiled. "It reminds me what I once was. The sun rises and sets; clouds gather and disperse, but always Jupiter remains, his four daughters attending him." He gestured toward the enormous cavern below. "And where the sky ends, the world begins."

To either side of the vast cave, magnificent cliff faces of granite rose. Between them stretched a wide and green valley. A blue river meandered across the base of it, cutting through golden meadows and chartreuse glades. The river wandered down to a deep blue lake, its surface reflecting the towering megaliths on either side.

"It is beautiful," Nyneve said. "The dappled streams, the lake and its darting finches—"

"They aren't finches, but herons," Merlin said.

Nyneve breathed deeply. "It is a glorious world you have

made, Merlin. But what of the ironworks and goldsmithing? Where have you put all the samite and satin?"

"There," Merlin said. His outflung hand pointed out a beautiful palace, perched on a shelf halfway up the side of one granite cliff. The building was a bejeweled crown, its porches hanging out over thousand-foot drops, its walls strewn with flowering vines, its archways leading into glorious gardens.

"Oh, Merlin," Nyneve said. "Let us forget Britannia and its wars. Let us forget about Wotan and Aelle of Sussex. Let us slip the bonds to the world of men and withdraw here forever."

A cloud of sadness moved over his face. "Yes, Nyneve. Once Arthur is safe, we will. Once the wars are done and Arthur is safe, we will."

The darkness of his features spread to hers. "Merlin, you know the wars will never be done. You know Arthur will never be safe. You know that Wotan will kill you before letting you withdraw into this Cave of Delights."

"I know."

Arthur knocked lightly on the door to the queen's quarters. "The council is over. I know it's late, and if you're already in bed—"

"No, I'm only in the bath," came Guinevere's muffled reply from within.

Arthur started into the room. The warm fragrance of perfumed soaps floated out to him over the screen. "I should come back."

"Is it so horrible a thing for a man to see his wife of five years in the bath?" Guinevere asked. Her words were a simple statement of fact, but also a reminder of the distance between them.

"No," Arthur replied. "Of course not."

He pushed back the door and entered the room. It smelled sweetly of her, a heady scent that always brought a flush to his cheeks and set his heart thrumming. The lambskin carpet across the floor was deep and soft beneath his iron-edge boots. Arthur bent and pulled the boots from his feet. He left them by the door, along with his stockings. The ivory-colored wool was sensuous between his toes.

"There is war coming," he said, in part to distract himself from the glimpse of pink skin beyond the walnut screen. "War with the Saxons. War with Wotan."

There came the sound of water running from a sponge over Guinevere's shoulder. "I knew this war must come. You knock down Lot and Aelle rises. You knock down Aelle, and who will rise next?"

Crossing arms over his chest, Arthur leaned back against the bed frame. "I'll fight that war when I come to it. First, I must fight this one. Aelle is overrunning London. Chertsey will follow soon. We've decided to stop them at Mount Badon. It is the best mustering place."

"And you were wondering how soon I could mobilize my priestesses to heal the men wounded in this war—"

"We fight to protect all we have built," Arthur said. "We fight because the peace of Camelot is worth sacrifice. And I fight to regain Rhiannon. Excalibur is incomplete without her, just as I am incomplete without you."

There came another long silence, broken only by watery noises. "Well, once you have slain Aelle and Merlin has slain Wotan and Rhiannon is recovered and joined with Excalibur, perhaps our world will be safe enough that you and I—"

"I know, Guin. I am tormented by it as well. There is nothing I wish more than to venture beyond that walnut screen. It is for others that we do not."

"Yes," she said quietly, "I know."

"When I was in Dumnonia, my mother, Igraine, told me a folktale of old Gaul. It recalled a king, Raimondin de Lusignan was his name, who married the faerie Mélusine. As her dowry, she granted him boundless prosperity and security within his kingship—on the condition that he never view her naked." Arthur sighed, staring out the windows at Camelot. "For a long while, they lived together in love, the king and the tribal goddess, and their land was bounteous. The people held a grand celebration in the king's honor, thanking him for their great happiness. But the king was not happy. He said to himself, 'What use is prosperity and security when I must have them forever alone?' " Arthur withdrew from the windows and seated himself on the canopied bed. "So saying, Raimondin descended to where his wife bathed, the beautiful faerie goddess Mélusine, and threw back the door. As soon as he saw her, she began to transform into a great dragon. Astonished, Raimondin rushed to cling to her, but her flesh turned to slippery scales in his hands and she flew away through the window. She took his prosperity and security with her, and was never seen again."

From the .bath came the wry words, "Do you fear that beneath my skin lurks a dragon?"

"I fear that when Wotan and the Saxons are slain and Rhiannon is regained, when I have given up crown and country to be with you, my dear—I fear that I will no longer be worthy of you."

"Arthur—"

With the furtive click of the door latch, he was gone.

Merlin and Nyneve stepped from the coruscating red light of a ley-line highway onto the grassy ground at the base of Mount Badon.

It was a grim and ancient site. The tall hill was surrounded by five rising rings—earthen embankments topped by palisades. At the crest of the hill, a large stone fortress stood. Its severe gray walls rose in angular defiance of the round hilltop. That castle was a recent and arrogant addition, an enormous cork shoved into the hill to prevent whatever lay beneath from boiling forth.

"It is an unhappy location," Merlin noted quietly.

Nyneve knelt upon the grass. She wore a gray cloak that blended with the evening. Her lithe figure moved without a sound. Dew had settled on the clover, and her slim fingers touched it. The water droplets pooled and formed a conduit, linking her to the heart of the sídh. The spirits there spoke to Nyneve, and she spoke to Merlin.

"Of old, this has been a sacred site to the powers of the land. It has long been a fortified dwelling of the sith, chased from the world. Do you see the spheres of ley energy?" She gestured toward the earthen rings that surrounded the faerie mound.

Even as Merlin looked, he could make out great, nested globes of scintillating power. Each earthen ring was formed where a defensive sphere met ground. The five rings had five spheres that arced over the mount and castle and delved through the earth beneath it.

"It was Vortigern who determined that the rings should be palisaded to guard the nearby roads. The divine spirits of the place did not much appreciate the intrusion, and plagued whatever army was garrisoned here. Vortigern did not allow ghosts to dissuade him. He built the castle atop the mound. It took him a very long while, for the towers of the castle kept collapsing."

A glimmer of painful memory came to Merlin. "It was during my days of deep madness. I remember. He laid me upon a dolmen and drove a knife through my heart. I was almost unmade by that knife—a blessed blade. I do not remember how I escaped—"

"In the end, Vortigern succeeded," Nyneve said. "This severe fortress, defiant even of the land that bears it up, is his success. The land hates it. Vortigern even established an abbey here to guard the castle against the powers below."

Nyneve withdrew her hand from the clover. She sighed, as though wearied. "Yes, it is, as you say, an unhappy location."

Merlin cocked an eyebrow. "Is there any way within?"

"Not without invitation," Nyneve said. "You must remember, Merlin, this place is no Avalon. This is a place of the dead, of rage and insanity."

"Perhaps we shall not want to invite the creatures here into the realm of the living," Merlin speculated. "Perhaps Badon will not prove the best place to fight this war."

Nyneve sniffed the air. "We shall see what we see. There is a spring nearby that bubbles out of the mountainside from the heart of the sídh. We will enter there. Where there is water, I have an invitation."

It was a short walk to the spring. The brow of twilight frowned into night. Here and there along the barbarous palisades, torches awakened. In the castle, tepid yellow light shone from arrow loops. It would be the job of Arthur to ally with the folk in the castle, and the job of Merlin to ally with those beneath.

A spring emerged from an eroded fissure of gray limestone in the mountainside. It showered gently downward to form a rocky brook that chattered away into the nearby woods. The waters were cold but clean, with a wintry purity.

Merlin took Nyneve's hand, squeezed it, and said, "Let us make our visit, then."

Together, they stepped beneath the icy flood. Water coursed over flesh, creating a conduit between hot human blood and the chill tides of earth. Liquid called to liquid. Skin took on the pellucid hue of running water. Muscle coursed away in torrid channels. Bone became only white stone in the bed of the creek. And then, hand in hand, Nyneve and Merlin flowed up the stream, into the cold, black heart of the mound.

The way was slim and tortuous. Water does not fear tight spaces or great pressures. Merlin and Nyneve were water now. They moved with quiet confidence past huge shelves of antediluvian stone, through vast and ancient pockets of buried peat, along slanting systems of shale scree, and into the lands of the fey.

At first, the creatures they passed—stone giants imprisoned alive and madly dreaming beneath vast mountains of rock—seemed more mineral than animal. Only the tepid warmth of their lithic bulk gave any indication they lived. Water squeezed past bent shoulders, crushed fingers, and stooped backs.

Beyond the slumbering giants were the burrows of much smaller folk—bluecaps, ettercaps, redcaps, and dwarfs.

Though minute in size, these creatures shared the stony demeanor and dim obsessions of their titanic kin. They lurked in strange immobility in their rocky mines. Their fingers splayed across the smooth stone walls as though sensing intrusion. Nyneve and Merlin passed in rivulets by their feet. The creatures muttered in tongues as lightless and incomprehensible as the world they occupied.

Higher up and farther in, the dank recesses gave way to wider spaces—true caves. Here dwelled the more recent exiles of the land, the spirits of dead Picts. Savage and inscrutable, the ghosts haunted fissures in the sloping sides of great canyons. Denied the bodies they once tattooed, they etched figures in stone walls. Not a square foot had escaped their frenetic scratches. Eyes glowed mournfully from hanging caves.

Nyneve and Merlin coursed up the waterway toward a great cavern. It opened at the center of the mound, an enormous space too large to fit in the sídh. A world of its own, the space was black in eternal night. Its stony vault was so high it did not even give back echoes. An inky sea filled the base of the cavern. Nyneve and Merlin emerged in its waters.

"I remember now where I went when I was sacrificed upon Mount Badon all those years ago," Merlin said to Nyneve. "I remember how my blood had been channeled down from the dolmen into a deep fissure of hissing steam, a sacrifice to the ancient creatures that dwelled below. I remember what they were. . . ."

Before Nyneve could respond, another voice spoke out of the darkness. It was vast and ancient, inhuman. "We remember you too, Merlin. We helped you escape. We helped you live. And you promised one day to return, to help us live again."

"Yes," Merlin said solemnly. "That day is near at hand. King Arthur will fight with the most ancient powers of the land. He will fight from Mount Badon with the aid of dragons."

• • •

He towers there into the skies. He straddles the puny battle-ments. His robes are stitched of the grave cerements of nations. His eyes blaze lightning. His arm calls from the clouds the soul-gathering Valkyrie.

They come for me.

I stand, old and ineffectual beneath the descending boot of a god. I am crushed and ground into the earth. I am slain a second time upon Badon. But this time, my blood does not course down to awaken dragons. I will rise again only in the crimson stalks of wildflowers.

46

Their Swords Will Blaze

L ondon had fallen, and Chertsey too.

Badon would not fall, though. Ulfius was sure of it. He sat a horse on the castle drawbridge and gazed down on the massed armies of Arthur. They stretched across the grass-lands below, from the final palisade to the woods beyond. Fifteen great armies.

The army of Camelot—Arthur's own force—was the larg-est company, fifteen thousand strong. There were five thou-sand from Dumnonia, and another five from Dyfed, Gwynedd, and Powys. The refugee warriors from Canter-bury, London, and the east country made another three thou-sand. Lot had sent two thousand, Ban and Bors another two thousand, and the petty kings and dukes of the midlands had fielded whatever forces they could spare. All told, Arthur's army numbered thirty-five thousand, to the rumored fifty thousand of the Saxons. Still, Arthur had a fortification, and the alliance of local gods and dragons, and the very belief of the people to empower him. He had Guinevere, the power of the land, and Merlin, the power of the heavens, and Excalibur, the power of God. Badon would not fall. Or if it did, all of Britannia would fall.

"A spectacular sight," said Duke Liddington, sitting a horse to Ulfius's side, "the arrayed and panoplied might of a nation."

It *was* a sight, the morning sun glinting from thousands of polished helms and shoulder pieces. Banners of fifteen separate ruling houses snapped in the breeze. Livery of every great family among the Britons shone on tents and standards.

"Yes, my friend," Ulfius said turning toward the white-haired man. "A great sight."

Duke Liddington had ruled this place during Uther's reign and the lawlessness after Uther and the fifteen years of Arthur. The old warrior had persevered despite constant hauntings. Ominous noises came from beneath the sídh. Horrible visions shone in the skies above. Any lesser man would have surrendered the spot to the spirits that owned it. Duke Liddington was constitutionally incapable of such resignation. His lean and weathered face had the solemnity of granite. His hair was as resilient as fullered wool. His hands had the steady strength of oak roots.

"They will be even greater to see on the battlefield," Liddington said staunchly. "Their swords will blaze like stars in earthly constellations."

Ulfius tilted his head in consideration. "I find warriors at battle to be a tragic sight, not a glorious one. Then every other means has failed."

Liddington turned a steely gaze on Ulfius. He spoke with a voice like twisted wire. "Yes. But when every other means has failed and men yet fight, yet throw themselves into the breech, I know the true glory of our kind. We love life, and will die to defend it."

Drawing a deep breath, Ulfius sighed and gazed out at the encampments. Fires sent black smoke coiling into the sky. "They will be grandest of all when marshaled to fight beside Tuatha and dryads and dragons and the very ghosts that have been plaguing you for decades."

Liddington gave a snort. "Yes. That sight, if ever I see it, will be at least strange, if not grand." He set heels to his mount's flanks. "Until then, there is the tournament. We're already late to start the day's festivities."

A rueful smile darkened Ulfius's face. He sent his mount after the duke's. "Yes. Let us go down and start the sanctioned mayhem before unsanctioned mayhem erupts." The two horses made their clomping way down the road, little puffs of dust rising from their hooves.

In the last year, Merlin had become a creature of dark spaces. He dwelled as much within the sídh as in the castle above. He was less the guest of men than of dragons. One such serpent filled the cavern before him.

There were but five of them in all, five remnants of a species more ancient than any other on the isles. Once, the enormous reptiles had ruled the dreams of the folk. Now, like any other slain god, they lived only in the subterranean spaces, in the cold unconscious of a forgetful people.

Most ancient of the five and grandfather to the others was Calbhiorus. He crouched on a pinnacle beside Merlin. There was hardly room for the two of them and a lit torch. A serpent the color of slate, Calbhiorus was the size of one of Castle Badon's towers. Inch-thick cataracts covered his eyes, through which he saw only ghost shadows. His claws were long since incapable of battle. His joints were gnarled with millennia. His mind was not clouded, though. Old and wise, Calbhiorus remembered when humans prayed to the great serpents, sang of them, worshiped them, feared them. He knew it was humans who had once made them live, and might make them live again.

"That is why," Merlin was saying to the ancient wyrm at the heart of the sídh, "you must show yourself to them before the war. They must see you, believe you are real and will fight for us. It is their very belief that will empower your return."

A long hiss—part laugh and part sigh—echoed through the cavern. Calbhiorus leaned toward the flickering torch. His silver mantle and hoary eyes entered the glow. Black jowls drew back from yellow teeth. Blind eyes narrowed in secrecy. He spoke words like runes carved in air. "Understand, then, old enchanter—they that sprung from me fear thee and thy kind. Thou art unto them the slayer folk, they that drove us hence. Understand—"

"I do understand," Merlin soothed. "But you must understand as well, great Calbhiorus, I am not mortal. I am more kin to you than to man. I was believed into being by them, and believed out of being by them. If ever you will see the light of the sun again, it will be with the aid—and sufferance—of mortals."

Calbhiorus blinked in acknowledgment. "I shall. Thou art wise in the ways of mortals, of surviving them and rising through them. I shall do as thou asks." His brittle words quieted to a whisper. "Tell not my children's children. They would bar the way."

"I would not tell them, of course," Merlin agreed, nodding his head in a gentle bow. "But once you have appeared above Castle Badon, your children's children will not need to be told. The belief of mortals will flood into them like sunlight through an unshuttered window. They will know."

A clever gleam entered the age-whitened eye of the beast. "It is hoped, then, that they shall not fear, but shall believe in the mortals who believe in them."

With that, the dragon shifted on his narrow perch. Fragments of stone ground loose beneath his talons. Wings spread in the darkness. Torchlight limned the edges of those wings and showed red through the blood that coursed along their membranes. Ancient muscles gathered. Ancient bones realigned. The dragon vaulted into the air. In a whirl of wing, he soared away from the pinnacle.

Merlin watched him go. The torchlight reached its wan red rays out far enough to show one more surge of those magnificent wings. Then Calbhiorus was lost to the rushing darkness. He would fly for some minutes before reaching the nests of the other dragons, miles away. There, his grandchildren would pick him over, sensing the smell of man on him and upbraiding the doddering old wyrm. If Merlin waited long enough on this pinnacle, he would hear their protests rise—

"Luckily for me, I do not have the time," he said to himself. Eoghruf, king of stone giants, was waiting below.

Extinguishing his torch, Merlin took a breath and stepped from the pinnacle. Air tore at him as he plummeted. Straight down a thousand feet lay a deep and icy lake. Nyneve lingered there. Together, they would visit the king of giants.

Kay strode excitedly from the Camelot pavilion and out onto the tournament grounds. The noontime sun shone down on a grand festival. To one end of the broad field, full-mailed knights and full-barded steeds thundered down tilting lanes. Leveled lances and darting banners glinted brilliantly. Even the splintered ends of shattered lances, even the blossoms of blood on staved armor, even the thrash of impaled men among the green grasses—all was bright and gleaming that noon. At the other end of the field, warriors engaged in sword duels. Tabards flapped and tangled in shocks of steel. Sweat sprayed from battered faces. And in the center of the field was more glorious blood. Men vied in hoisting and throwing stones, hauling weights on chains, climbing greased poles, pounding iron, wrestling, fisticuffs, and quaffing.

"Ah, it's a manly revel," Kay said approvingly.

Helmet in hand, he marched among the lines of his comrades. Yesterday's white rose, entwined through the visor of his helmet, was withered and yellowed now. The virtuous woman who had granted it was no longer entirely virtuous. Kay teased the spent flower from his helm, letting it fall in pieces on the ground. Once the visor was again clean, Kay drew a perfumed scarf from his sleeve, sniffed it in sweet speculation, and wove it into the metal grille. He would fight for a new virtuous woman today, and perhaps win her virtue from her this evening.

"A manly revel . . ." Kay hoisted the helmet over his golden locks and settled it in place as though it were a crown.

Striding toward the sword combats, he drew a polished blade.

His elbow cop struck something. Kay turned, peering through the veiled visor.

A huge warrior loomed up before him. The man was resplendent in black armor, a two-headed wolf done in silver across the breastplate. A tall comb of peacock feathers sprouted proudly across the crest of his dark helm. His gauntlets were as large as other men's boots, and his boots as large as other men's cuirasses. From his helm came a baleful scowl and what almost seemed steam.

Kay performed a graceful half bow. "Excuse me, sir. I have limited vision, what with my darling's scarf—"

"You have limited vision, indeed, stripling!"

"Stripling?" Kay said, standing up straight. "I am a Knight of the Round Table. I am the stepbrother of the king himself. Take back your words, or repair with me to the dueling grounds."

The warrior dragged a gigantic ebony blade from the scabbard at his waist. Steel grated forth with a sharp and angry sound. "I will not take back my words or go to the dueling grounds, but repair the likes of you here." Like a bolt of black lightning, the stranger's sword descended.

Kay took a step back, clasped his own blade at hilt and tip, and lifted the sword high. With the force of a war hammer, the black weapon struck. Kay reeled under the blow. Burrs of metal rose from his sword. He stepped back again, trying to get out from under the blade. There was no escape. Kay staggered and rolled aside. Lightless metal rammed deeply into the grassy earth.

The black knight roared and hauled on his stuck weapon.

Kay took the opportunity. Climbing to his feet, he jabbed at the monstrous man's side. His sword tip struck a smooth black cuisse. He drove on. Metal skirled on metal. The tip slid into a gap. Kay lunged hard. His sword punched through ring mail and deep into the hip of the warrior. It sank as though into emptiness, though it must have cut meat and sinew to go so deep.

Or not. The huge man gave no cry. No blood gushed forth.

He did not slump in agony. Instead, he hauled his own weapon free of the ground. Dark earth rained from the black thing and pattered ominously across Kay's bent back.

Kay yanked desperately, but his sword wouldn't budge.

The black blade descended again. It eclipsed the noontime sun.

Kay released his sword. Arms lifted above his head, he turned to vault away.

Something entered his calf, something sharper than winter and colder than ice. It delved through skin and sinew and tendon, and stopped halfway through bone. Hung up on cleft marrow, the blade leaked its cold magic into blood and nerve. As he crumpled to the ground, Kay felt enervating tendrils of night spread through him.

"A Knight of the Round Table?" the man mocked. He stared down in satisfaction as Kay writhed slowly from the blade that pinioned his leg. "A noble defender of Camelot? You seem more a bleeding worm, to me. Crawl, then. Crawl back to the other worms and tell them the fate that awaits them all. Tell them to follow your trail of blood back to me and be served in kind for their arrogance."

Shuddering as he pulled from the ebony sword, Kay belly-crawled away from the black-armored man. The whole bright world was turning gray around him. Not even his own blood was vivid in the fading, dying day.

47

Deadly Games

As competitors fought and bled and died, Loki made his merry way among them. It was gratifying. He was a lone honeybee in a vast field of flowers. These shiny buffoons were filled to the stamens with pride, and pride transformed into nectar with the addition of a little spit. Loki supplied the spit.

"Now, now, lads, why fight?" Loki shouted. In black tights and minstrel sleeves, he lingered just beyond sword-reach of a duel. He circled the pair, studying their sweat-speckled faces. "Were there regretful words? Did this fellow here make some comment about your nose? Something about its seeming a worm-eaten beet?"

The bulbous-nosed fighter took a moment to glance at the minstrel. That moment cost him the warty tip of his nose. The flesh skipped away on his opponent's sword.

"Because he should not talk, considering his buttocks. Shabby as a pair of gigantic cabbages. Stink cabbages—"

The other fellow gave a growl. His adversary jabbed one of those cabbage buttocks.

"In fact, he's so stinky and scrofulous, it's a wonder he's bedded your mother so often, even given how desperate *she* is—"

The fighters traded distracted blows, neither hitting particularly hard nor making any attempt to block.

"And it seems particularly mean-spirited to be ridiculed by a man who might even have fathered you—"

"Shut up!" the men shouted in an unexpected unison. They turned their attention back to the fight, suspicion blossoming between them.

The one with the beet nose growled, "Why do you care what he says? And what's this about my mother?"

Irritated, the other replied, *"What* about your mother?"

"I knew it!" Beetnose shouted. He swung his sword in a series of furious overhead attacks. "I knew it!"

"Knew what?" his foe asked, parrying. "Knew you were a bastard? A beet-nosed bastard?"

"I can't believe you said it again!" shrieked Beetnose between stabs. "You, with your cabbage arse . . . insulting my nose . . ."

Taking another nip out of it, the man replied, "It even bleeds like a pickled beet."

"Pickled? I'm a drunkard now, am I? Get close enough, and I'll pickle your arse into slaw."

Words and swords flew in sloppy, fitful, pointless attacks. Already, Loki had continued on. There were so many more lovely warriors to work into a self-destructive frenzy, so many more lies to juggle, so many more tender fingers to fall to the mumblety-peg.

Loki was celebrating his victory. With tavern talk and jokes, he had made the people of Britannia fear a pantheon they had never known. Wotan stalked British minds. Loki whispered in their ears. A good rumor was more deadly than a good sword. It had taken a full year, but today Loki's work would come to fruition. He was celebrating.

"Ah, another victim."

Nearby, a man sold roast pigeon.

With a snap of his fingers, Loki donned the Pendragon garb of a royal agent. He strolled officiously forward. "You there, meat merchant, where is your store of horse meat? Yes, horse meat! The king has made an edict. His knights are to eat only horse meat. It makes them strong. Yes. He has already imprisoned one and executed two for selling banned meats to his knights. Yes. Oh, I suggest you watch for a horse to fall in the jousts, grab it, and carve it up. Yes, that knife will serve well enough—"

What a marvelous festival! The pasties and pickles and prawns . . . a great open pantry, all this. The wine too, as potent as rye spirits. I reel under it. . . . reel . . .

I have . . . what is? Something is not right . . . I feel strange. Disjointed and . . . I cannot think. I remember feeling this way all the time before . . . on the heath . . .

What is happening to me? Or—not to me. What is happening to the land?

Arthur found Guinevere at the back of the healing tent. Priestesses moved with calm decorum among the injured men, applying poultices and wrapping wounds. There was a gentle murmur of bedside talk and laughter, a harmless flirtation among wounded men and healing maids. Near Guinevere, though, the tent was still, the air prickly. She sat beside a chest of implements and folded and refolded bandages.

"You sent for me?" Arthur asked, his voice hushed.

She lifted her eyes. Worry rimmed them in white. "Something has changed, Arthur. Something in the land has changed."

"Something in the land?"

"It is as though the soul of it is confused," Guinevere said, her hands fidgeting only the more nervously on the bandages. "It is as though the land is forgetting who it is."

"How can the land forget—"

"There's a spirit of confusion among the folk. There are strange shadows, strange visions in the people's mind, strange songs in the air," Guinevere insisted.

Arthur wrapped his arms about her. Her rigid shoulders seemed to melt into his embrace. "You've not been sleeping enough. You've been too busy among the healers—"

"It's not me," Guinevere insisted. "It's the land. It is sick. It is infected. The invaders are weakening it, softening it, before they arrive."

Chuckling to reassure her, Arthur said, "How could they weaken—?"

"Loki," Guinevere realized suddenly. "It must be Loki. He is sowing chaos and confusion before the advancing army. He is singing in the taverns and whispering at the crossroads and appearing before dogs and children. He is unhinging the mind of the people, weakening the power of the land, the power of our allies."

Arthur's complexion paled. Though he still held Guinevere in his embrace, he stared into faraway spaces. "Loki is moving among us?"

"Yes," Guinevere said. "He is. He can take the form of anyone, can speak lies from the tongues of trusted friends, can deliver false orders to your commanders. Unless we find him and drive him out, soon none of us will trust even our own senses."

Arthur's gaze returned to Guinevere. "I will tell Merlin," he resolved. "Merlin will know how to flush out that rat, wherever he might appear." He tightened his embrace. "Thank you for telling me. We'll tell Merlin, and he'll fix everything."

A cry went up from the head of the tent. A burly man in shimmering armor dragged a wounded warrior through the flaps.

"Ector!" Arthur called, recognizing the burly man. "Father!" Side by side, the king and queen hurried toward the front of the pavilion. "What befalls?"

"Kay is gravely wounded," Ector panted, bearing his son toward an empty cot. "A black-armored warrior did this. He cleaves through the ranks of the Table Round like the Reaper himself."

Sir Ulfius rode up into the joust channel, his fingers tingling. He gazed out on the hoof-torn tilt-grounds—narrow lanes, fragments of shattered lance, telltale spots of blood near the point of impact.

"A game, merely a game," he told himself. Merely a *deadly* game.

Ulfius sighed. Of late, he had felt too old for active warfare. He had fought in three extended campaigns before the king was even conceived. Now, Arthur himself was a solid man, and Ulfius was well over half a century old. He had a right to avoid needless combat. He was more important to Arthur as an organizer and leader, not a swaggering sword-stallion. During the building of Camelot and the creation of the knighthood, Ulfius had become more an administrator than a fighter. The mammoth task of uniting and forming up Arthur's forces at Badon had been Ulfius's private battle.

"And yet," Ulfius reminded himself, "I am the one who arranged the tournaments." He pulled on the reins of his steed, guiding the beast into the lane.

At the other end of the field, an enormous warrior in black armor rode to the start. Even his horse was a monster—a beast the size of a Caledonian plow horse. The black-armored warrior lifted his lance from its couch. He signaled he was ready.

Ulfius gulped, wondering if he would ever be ready. "Why do I get all the rotten jobs?" Giving the signal, he urged his horse into a canter.

The huge stallion leaped eagerly into the charge. Its rider leaned massively above the lashing mane. The black lance tilted toward Ulfius. It seemed only a wide circle growing wider. Lance, rider, and steed came on with an undeniable hunger.

With no other choice, Ulfius drove his own beast to a gallop. He lowered his lance. Between gritted teeth, he muttered, "I am definitely too old for this."

The black horseman came on. The ground trembled with his advance. Along the joust line, the crowd visibly swooned back.

As for Ulfius, he did not see horse or rider, but only that vaulting black lance.

It struck. With all the weight of the world, it struck.

The lance cracked against his shield, splitting it in two, and continued on into his breastplate. It burst open. The hauberk beneath cracked as well. The lance drove into his shoulder and out the other side. Ulfius's horse ran out from under him. He tumbled through clear air. Everything was roaring. The lance torqued between the black gauntlet and the falling rider. Ulfius struck ground. He rolled. The shattered end of the lance tossed grass into the air. He rolled twice more.

Then he stopped, impaled and broken, on the ground.

They would be coming for him, he knew. They would come bear him to the healer's tent. They would help him live, if he would live, and help him die if he would die.

At last the roaring ceased. All sound died. Every horse was still, every voice silenced, every sword loose in warriors' hands. Not even the wind spoke in that awful hush. Something huge and horrible gripped the festival.

Ulfius struggled to lift his head, but he could not. He could little breathe.

He didn't need to see. The voice that boomed out of that silence could belong to only one creature—the black-armored warrior who had slain him. The warrior stood in the saddle of his monster steed. Brimstone rolled in a cloud of smoke and blazing fire around him.

"Behold, Britannia. Your Knights of the Round are laid low to a man. Your chamberlain too. I have destroyed them, each last one. Such was their fate. Such will be your fate."

Who could this be? Ulfius wondered. Who could destroy the Table Round?

"Know that a servant of Wotan has walked among you this day. And Wotan himself shall bring his armies by dawn!"

That name, Wotan, it had come to mean all things terrifying.

Another voice spoke, the unmistakable tones of a certain mad mage. "Tell your master how much it hurt to die."

Even where he lay, Ulfius could see the great red flash that surged from Merlin's outflung hands.

The black warrior was caught up on that blast and flung overhead. He writhed within his armor, which streamed black soot from every pore. The knight crashed to earth. His armor, brittle as eggshells, shattered. It had been empty within.

Ulfius closed his eyes, silently thanking Merlin. Then as footsteps converged, he allowed himself to drift into oblivion.

The night was black, with neither moon nor stars beyond the red domes of ley magic. Even Jupiter was hid from sight.

Merlin paced the battlements of Badon Castle. In the baileys below, the warriors of Arthur gathered, shoulder to shoulder. Torchlight shone in their haunted eyes.

It had been a grim evening since the appearance of Wotan's warrior. Half of Arthur's troops had been deployed out along ley highways to hide in the woods to the north, east, and south. They would wait in reserve to strike at the flank of the Saxons. The other half had packed tents and provisions and marched up the long hill. Many of the troops volunteered to garrison each of the five palisades. The rest withdrew into the great fortification.

Among them were Arthur's own Knights of the Round Table. They were sore wounded after their encounters with the black-armored warrior. All would have been slain but for Guinevere and her healers. Still, the knights had been beaten and shamed.

Beneath a pitiless sky, Britannia languished. Doom marched upon them. Fifty thousand boots and one hundred thousand hooves rattled the horizons. As the Saxons slowly took the land, their gods took the sky.

Merlin had promised a miracle that night. He had promised the men gathered below, and the king sitting in a crenel nearby. Tonight's entertainment would have to be much more than invisible magicians. Tonight's entertainment must inspire these warriors to win the coming war.

"Enough!" Merlin shouted down to the troops. "Enough of darkness and despair. Enough of terrors. Tonight, I promised you a vision of our victory, and I will provide it.

"But first, let me remind you that you have had visions aplenty before now. There is Arthur, himself a miracle, the lost and reclaimed son of Uther Pendragon. There is Guinevere, queen of fey and power of the land. There is Excalibur, the king-maker and god-killer. There is Rhiannon, the healer. There is Merlin, onetime god of all the known world. Any of these signs should be enough to assure you we will win this battle. But mortal hearts are fractious things. It is the reason I have fallen. So now I reforge your clay hearts in steel—"

Merlin's arms swept outward. From a cistern shaft beside the wall, watery sounds came. Something boiled there. Something massive. Scales shifted among churning waves. An Otherworld shriek rose from the cistern.

The folk in the bailey cringed back. Their faces were as pale as moonlight.

The beast emerged. A giant black dragon hurled itself up into the wheeling night sky. Great wings of skin unfurled beneath the moonless heavens. They caught air and flung out along the black breezes a creature that had not breathed the world's air in a millennium. It sent a deafening cry through the air.

"Behold, folk of Camelot! Behold the risen Pendragon!"

With eyes, the folk of Arthur saw. With hearts, they believed.

48

Lightning Showers

The vision of the night before was nothing next to the vision of the next morn. Dawn brought ten red giants to the cloud-choked east. They were as tall as elms, as broad as oaks. They were armored in crimson carapace.

No one on Badon Hill had seen the like.

The giants advanced. Behind them came Saxons. In ten divisions, the armies of Aelle swept forward. They came like a black tide. Helms bobbed atop the flood. Pikes jutted in air. Boots and hooves pounded the ground in roaring waves. Fields disappeared under the inky gush. Thickets and glades fell to hacking axes. Streams turned to mud-churned channels. Farmsteads went up in flames. Sheep went down in pieces. Farmers died beneath arrows, their wives beneath warriors. Wherever Saxons went, the land and its people drowned.

The giants led their armies through vales and forests, converging on Badon. Whenever one river of Saxons joined another, their preternatural commanders melded as well. Red plate mail shifted. Muscles and bones fused. Four arms became two, twice as large. Four legs became two, stronger still. And so it was that these giants combined and grew and recombined until the few that remained were sixty, eighty feet tall.

The armies of Saxony swept at last onto the field below Badon Hill. The ten giants had become three titans. And when there was no longer a division among mortal soldiers, the three titans formed a single god. Red plates and meat and blood fused. A hundred-foot-tall warrior stood on the plains. The armies of Aelle were a swarm of black rats at his feet.

The god spoke. The language was not Briton or Saxon, but the primordial tongue of gods. Any mortal who heard that speech understood it—and was terrified and a little maddened.

"I am Tyr. I am the war god of a warring race. I have come to destroy you." The voice filled the world. It echoed out around Mount Badon and returned upon itself, a great cyclone of sound. "I am the one who destroys you." The god breathed in the fear that rose from Briton and Saxon both, and was empowered by it. "Know me. I am Tyr."

Suddenly, the figure riled. Each plate of armor transformed into a separate warrior—a creature of red carapace and scuttling legs, pincers and bulbous eyes. For a moment more, Tyr retained his massive form. Then he began to dissolve away.

One by one, the giant fighting beetles shifted from alignment. Tyr's helmeted head slumped into a crawling mound of shells and legs. Beetles spread out across disintegrating shoulders. The whole torso of the god sagged. Legs compressed into stout columns and widened along the ground. Even the moiling Saxons recoiled from the tide of warrior beetles. Like a wax man, Tyr melted into a spreading, bubbling pool.

The huge insects swept out over the plain. They swarmed toward the first ring of palisades. Saxons followed them.

A storm of bow fire went up from the defenders. White shafts arced and fell among red shells. Bolts bounced harmlessly away.

In moments, beetles reached the first palisade. Their pinchers lay hold of stout logs and ripped them from the ground. Just as easily, they tore apart the protective orb that rose from the mound.

Shafts shot straight into them, careening off their armor. A few beetles fell to those point-blank shafts. The rest tore down the barriers. Beetles flung aside logs to rip apart men.

"Archers, fire!" Arthur shouted from the battlements.

His own shaft ripped loose of the thrumming bowstring. It vaulted with legions of others into the heavens. They soared up into the gray noon. The bolts flared red as they punched through the lowest shell of protection, and again four more times. Then the shafts descended in a ring of death. Iron heads struck red carapace. Most careered off, throwing sparks as they went. Others imbedded in the crevices between joints. A rare few cracked the shells like pottery and sank into the black blood beneath.

It was not enough. The creatures tore down the first palisade. They eclipsed the slumbering power of the sídh and unraveled its orb of protection.

Arthur looked up to see the outer shell flicker and fade to nothing. "Fire!"

Another storm of arrows ascended and descended. Another ten beetles were slain. A thousand more tore into the defenders beyond the ring.

"Hold fire!" Arthur leaned on the battlements. His hands gripped stone.

Swords darted below, answered by claws. One soldier stabbed into the open mandible of the creature only to have his arm follow and his head and torso too. Another man— really only a boy—was grabbed by separate pincers and pulled apart. Stingers rammed into warriors' eyes, barbed claws raked their necks open, severed legs poured burning blood upon others. Twenty men fell to every one slain beetle. The defenders of Britannia stood for only half a minute in the verge between the palisades. Then, not a man was left alive among them.

The Tyr-beetles surged toward the next palisade.

"Fire at will until the palisade falls," Arthur ordered. His eyes blazed as he handed his bow and quiver to the archer captain. "Where is Merlin?"

The captain pointed to the roof of the great hall. "Up there!"

In the distance, Merlin scrambled over the slate roof, loaves of bread under his arms. He ripped chunks of the stuff loose and showered the rooftop. A flock of pigeons and a few murders of crows had converged to form a shabby army around him.

Arthur stared openmouthed. "No, Grandfather. Not now."

He rushed along the wall toward the great hall. A buttress provided a handy ascent. Arthur vaulted to the rooftop.

Merlin's flock had grown to hundreds of birds. He capered among them, tossing hunks of bread at every new arrival.

"Grandfather! Grandfather! What are you doing?" shouted Arthur as he fought past pigeons.

Merlin whirled, startled. He laughed. His eyes were bright, and his fingers fitfully clawed hunks of bread from the loaves. "Just let me finish. I've only a couple heels left."

Arthur grabbed his shoulders and shook him. "Has Loki gotten to you?"

Struggling from the king's grip, Merlin flung the last shredded bits of bread out to the birds. "There! They should each have had enough."

Eyes blazing incredulously, Arthur said, "If I've lost you, I've lost the war."

"Lost me?" Merlin wondered, suddenly serious.

"There's an army of war beetles—Tyr incarnate—attacking us."

"Yes," Merlin said with a gentle smile. "And pigeons and crows like to eat beetles. So I thought if I were to feed them—"

"If you were to feed them—?"

"If I were to feed them enchanted bread, and they were to—"

"They're growing!" Arthur exclaimed as a hip-high crow pecked at Excalibur.

"Yes," Merlin said. "The enchanted bread made them grow. Here, let's shoo them from the roof before it collapses."

Seeming madder still, Merlin lifted the edges of his cloak and flapped them like a pair of tattered wings. He crowed and scampered about the rooftop. The swelling pigeons and crows only looked in amazed confusion at the old man. Merlin redoubled his efforts, stomping and shrieking, but the birds would not fly.

Arthur growled. Every eye in the bailey was on them. He hauled out Excalibur and shouted, "Away! And fight for Britannia!"

In a startled flock, crows and pigeons that were the size of giant eagles—and now twice that size—hurled themselves into the air. Their wingtips rapped dryly against each other as they went.

The army below cringed away from the enormous birds.

"What if they eat our soldiers?" Arthur asked.

Merlin shook his head. "No. They prefer bugs."

The circling flock glimpsed the beetles below. In a peeling spiral, they dove downward. Pigeons and crows swooped to land among red-shelled Tyr beetles. Heads jabbed, beaks cracked shells, gobbets of bug flesh went down bird gullets. The air rattled with pecking beaks and grinding gizzards.

Poison mandibles could not pierce the birds' talons, could not fight past flapping plumage. The horrors of Tyr were reduced to tasty bugs.

"He was arrogant," Merlin said gravely as he watched the carnage. He cast a sidelong glance at Arthur, on the rooftop beside him. "Tyr thought he could win this war single-handed. He thought his army of beetles could overrun us. He was, of course, wrong."

"Will he die?" Arthur asked.

Merlin shook his head. "No. Gods don't die that way.

They die only if the people cease to believe. But, look, Tyr will not soon return to this battle—"

Most of the beetles lay now in empty shells or twitching broken bits. The final few that lived were going even then into gobbling beaks.

"But my own defenders will be gone soon, as well—"

From the press of Saxons behind, arrows rose in gleaming swarms. They fell viciously on pigeon and crow. Black shafts thudded into white wings. Birds flailed beneath the killing hail. Red wounds spread across dove-gray feathers. In spasms, they died.

"Can't you do something?" Arthur asked. "Some spell—?"

"I'll need all my spells now, lad," Merlin said grimly. "Thor is coming." He gestured to the east.

The sky there had gone black. Storm clouds obliterated the horizon. Thunderheads piled up with preternatural speed, forming mountains in air. It was as though a tidal wave came, a wave ten miles high. Its face tumbled and churned. Death's heads appeared and dissolved. The clouds ate up Britannia. Forest and down, meadow and stream—the land disappeared. In moments, the vast wave swept from distant Bedgrayne to the heights of Mount Badon, and on, toward Bath and Camelot and Caerleon.

It surged by overhead. Keening winds blasted Merlin and Arthur. They crouched, clinging to the rooftop.

"This is no natural storm," Arthur roared. "The arm of Wotan drags it forward."

"The arm of Wotan, and the hammer of Thor," Merlin shouted back. He pointed to the heavens.

Amid serpentine coils of cloud, something else moved. It was massive and quicksilver. Here, the sinews of a flexed shoulder proceeded from the clouds. There, knuckles tightened upon a gray haft. Within one black crevice gleamed something like a great eye, intent and pernicious.

Then there was a brilliant light. Sparks traced the outline of a giant hammer. Blue jags of light raced together and cascaded down cliffs of cloud. They split the sky in an avalanche of power. Lightning rolled toward the castle.

Badon's crimson spheres of protection did little to dissipate the tumbling torrent. It smashed through one, two, three, four shields, and arced toward Arthur.

The king was suddenly enveloped in rushing blackness. He tried to fling his arms out, but something bound him—tattered fabric.

Together, Arthur and Merlin struck the cobbles. They landed and rolled apart. Arthur turned over just in time to see lightning strike the rooftop.

Blue-white force hit the roof like a giant fist. Shattered slate exploded outward. Crackling energy danced across bronze filigree. Lightning gleamed in leering gargoyles and spilled into the courtyard. It boiled rain barrels and blazed through ironwork and slid down well ropes. Arcs impaled warriors and turned their innards to vapor.

Blinding, deafening death filled the yard.

Then, the blue energy was gone. Orange fire replaced it. Everywhere, flames leaped up—in the shattered roof of the great hall, in the cellar doors, on the piles of armor that once had been men.

"Bucket brigade!" Merlin shouted as he clambered sorely to his feet. He rushed to the nearest well to find that its rope and bucket had been burned away. Roaring, he flung his arm out. A great geyser burst from the well, blanketing the courtyard, hall, and all in a drenching rain.

Arthur staggered up beside his grandfather. "You couldn't use a spell to ease us down from the rooftop?"

A call came from the wall. "They're storming the palisades! The Saxons are storming the palisades!"

"Not a spell to spare!" Merlin replied.

"Look out! Here's another." This time, it was Arthur who clutched Merlin and hurled the man behind a rubble pile.

Blue-white fury blasted down from the heavens. Lightning and thunder arrived in the same moment. Stones exploded from the sides of the great hall.

Merlin clutched the rocky debris before him. "Wotan is of air, and Thor of fire. Our allies are of earth and water."

"Send up the dragons," Arthur suggested.

"No," Merlin replied. "They would be slaughtered wholly. They must fight men not gods. But how can gods of earth and water fight air and fire?" He pulled his hands away from the rubble, seeing his fingers red with rust. He grabbed the hunk of stone. Veins of iron ore cut through the white quartz. "Iron ore—"

"I must return to lead the men on the wall," Arthur interrupted, getting to his feet.

"Yes," Merlin said. "Yes! Let's go!"

Side by side, the two men ran for the wall. They crossed a courtyard occupied only by rubble and smoldering dead.

"Perhaps the redcaps can open shafts beneath the Saxons. Perhaps the stone giants can flex their backs and split the earth. Perhaps the Tuatha can sally forth on ghost steeds to terrify them—" Arthur suggested in a rush.

"All excellent ideas," Merlin enthused. "I'll tell them when I see them." With that, he lifted the tattered edges of his travel cloak and hurled himself headlong into one of the steaming wells.

Arthur skidded to a halt and stared down into the whistling shaft. There came a great splash, watery sounds of struggle, and what almost seemed to be playful voices in welcome.

An unplayful voice came behind Arthur—the vast crackling of thunder. Lightning danced all around a tower. Its blue fingers jabbed into the mortar, flinging it out in a gritty spray. The tower slumped, and then came down in a great roar of stone and gravel.

"There is no hope unless we can stop the lightning," Arthur growled to himself. Gathering his will, he bolted up to the curtain wall.

The men there were beleaguered. Sleet and hail lashed down in sporadic showers from the sky, chasing men into the guard towers and covered bartizans. Lightning followed, blasting apart the protected sections and killing the men within. Some were dying in sizzling suddenness, and others in slashing slowness, but all were dying.

"Arrows!" Arthur commanded, snatching up the bow of a fallen man. He nocked a shaft and let fly. "Fire!"

Only as others scrambled to loose a barrage did Arthur see the conditions below. The black tide of Saxons—terrestrial embodiment of the celestial storm—had nearly broken through the second palisade. A breach appeared, and a second, and a third. Saxons sluiced through the gaps.

"There, and there! Arrows!" Arthur shouted, pointing. "Patch the palisade with Saxon bodies!"

Flights of shafts arced out and descended toward their quarry. Before they arrived, the log-work defenses failed in two more spots. There was no stopping the advance.

"They've broken through!" came the alarm down the line. "Broken through!"

Arthur lifted his arms defiantly in the teeth of the storm and shouted, "Come along, Saxon bastards! King Arthur waits!"

Damnation piled atop damnation. Another lightning strike gathered itself above.

Arthur felt the hairs along his arm stand on end. The prickle of tiny sparks danced down his spine. He looked up and saw—

Blinding power coursed down out of the stormy sky. The uncoiling energy shattered the final remnants of the second shield globe. It jagged through the third, fourth, and fifth, and lashed toward the head of the king.

Arthur did not cringe from death. He stood, shouting at the heavens. The bolt filled the world with white. It roared and stank of a thousand distilled rains.

And then, it was gone.

Blinking away the spots, Arthur stared after the retreating lightning. It had seemed to turn in midair. An orange geyser had sprung from the hillside high into the sky. The gush of water rose to tickle the belly of the clouds. Like a tall tree, it drew lightning into it. The bolt intended for Arthur plunged instead into the arcing spray of iron water.

"Merlin and his redcaps, and iron-ore water." Arthur laughed to himself.

The geyser's spray arced down the mountain into the midst of the Saxon host. It bore lightning with it. Energy flashed and spun, entering one Saxon only to vault to another. Before the bolt had played itself out, it had sizzled hundreds of foes.

"Thanks, Grandfather," Arthur whispered.

More orange geysers jetted up all around Mount Badon. They drew lighting out of the sky as easily as a boy plucks apples.

"Now, we fight! Archers, to the wall! Nock and loose!" Arthur shouted, waving his compatriots in.

With a roar that was not unlike lightning, itself, the Britons clambered to their posts, lifted their bows, and let fly.

49

Birds of a Feather

Duke Liddington himself commanded the warriors at the third palisade gate. Beneath his dripping helm, the man's face was as impassive as granite. Rainwater filled his flocculent brows. With each lightning flash, his eyes gleamed like steel. He had not yet drawn his sword, but clutched its hilt in hands as steady as oak roots. He gazed past mud-mired palisades toward the surrounding armies.

It had been a strange and unholy battle so far—red titans, war beetles, giant birds, brimstone hail. . . . Such witchery meant little to Liddington. He could not fight specters. These Saxon gods were no different from the ghosts of the mount itself—to be ignored or endured, but not fought. That was the purview of Merlin. Duke Liddington was trained to fight men.

Conveniently, an army of them just now hacked at the palisades before him. Some poles burned raggedly, doused in oil under the spitting skies. Others were cracked by rams or chopped through by axes. Already, the fences were falling.

"Bowmen, fall back," Liddington ordered with stern demeanor. "Infantry to the fore." As his commands were shouted down the lines, Liddington turned calmly to see them carried out.

Pounded by rain and lashed by hail, archers retreated from the palisades. The men shook out their aching arms. Each had emptied his quiver into the advancing tide of Saxons, but the invaders were breaking through anyway. With quiet resignation, archers laid bows and quivers in the wet grass and drew their swords. Arrows could no longer save them. If steel failed as well, there would be no more need of bows.

Infantry meanwhile climbed the mound. Mud painted their puttees and rain streamed from their helms. Swords in hand, the footmen formed a wall of flesh and bone. When the palisades fell, there would be only those men to hold back the flood. Good-hearted foot soldiers.

Liddington was among them. There was no need for horses here, and without a horse, he was just another infantryman. It felt good to face a fight with his feet rooted to the earth. "Stand fast!" Liddington shouted to his troops.

The call echoed out among them. These were good boys—grim-faced and determined. They knew they were going to die today, and the realization made them only stronger. Liddington also would die. He who had survived British ghosts would not survive Saxon ones. He and his brave lads would die today.

"Stand fast!"

The roar of hail was suddenly overtopped by the shout of thousands of throats. Liddington heard the Saxon triumph before he saw it. Raking his sword out, he watched the palisade gate cave and fall before him.

Over splintered wood clambered dark figures. They had crimson eyes, these Pagan butchers, and shouting scarlet teeth. They swarmed in fury over the fallen gate.

Liddington's own fury was greater. His sword fell axlike. It cracked through the first man's steel helm as if it were porcelain, through the second man's skull as if it were an eggshell. These invaders dared to attack his castle, and they would die—as many as he could kill before they killed him. A third Saxon spilled messily at his feet. Stroke by stroke,

Liddington repaired the gap, filling it with dead foes.

He rammed his sword beneath one man's jaw. The point spitted the Saxon's tongue and cracked through the roof of his mouth. Even as he fell, Liddington yanked his sword free and slashed it across another man's throat. Blood mixed with slicing rain. Liddington kicked the corpse back and climbed up its back.

Steel clanged. A Saxon ax notched Liddington's blade. He twisted his sword, won free, and buried the tip in the axman's eye. Gore sprayed. The Saxon collapsed.

The dead man struck back from the grave. From a nerveless hand, his ax fell. It clove Liddington's cheek.

The duke reeled. Cold rain stung his lacerated face. Hot blood poured down his collar. He staggered numbly back. Gritting his jaw, Liddington had the unnerving realization that his lips no longer closed over his teeth.

A glance down the line showed that the rest of the footmen were similarly pressed. They had killed five men each before receiving their own mortal blows. Heroes, the lot of them— and soon dead men.

Liddington went to his knees. Saxons streamed past him. There was no stopping them now. The duke hissed an indecipherable curse through his ruined face. His fingers clutched the mud.

In the midst of the Saxon tide rode a red-bearded giant of a man. He advanced with a sneering confidence, a rider among shouldering pigs—Aelle of Sussex.

The duke saw no more. He sank to the earth. A moment later, his head bounded from his shoulders. Blood mixed with rain and fed the muddy grass. Saxons climbed across his back.

Duke Liddington joined the ghosts of Mount Badon.

While heroism ruled the palisades and the curtain wall, cowardice clutched the garrison. Armsmen had fled to the low-slung building to escape the storm. With stout walls and a roof of green thatch, the garrison was safe from storm and stress.

But not from treachery.

"These Saxons are fighting men, men after our own hearts," the rabble-rouser shouted from one low tabletop. He was a narrow man with severe little eyes and a perpetual snarl. He wore the livery of Dalriada, and though no one recognized him, his harangue had ensorcelled them. "They don't fight like Arthur. Not like the peace-loving, Camelot-building, can't-lay-the-queen Arthur! Saxons are men like us. They like murder and plunder and rape. And that's what they'll do to us if they find us here—murder and plunder and rape us. Is that what we want?"

"No!" the men shouted in unison. There were nearly two hundred of them crammed in the small space. A few more stood at the doorway and listened.

"Arthur gathered all of us warriors and then locked us away here as if we were vestal virgins. He thinks he can simply cloister away his army? Well, Arthur may not let us fight, but Aelle will. We can rebel, take the castle for Aelle. Are you with me?"

"Yes!" the men replied, hurling clenched fists into the air.

"Yes!" answered another voice. Dagonet vaulted up beside the rabble-rouser. Beneath his breath, he said, "Hello, Loki. I'm a great admirer—let me help!" He winked, and then turned toward the crowd. "Arthur's not worth a fingernail paring. Let's fight for Aelle! He's worth two parings and a blister!"

Loki glowered at Dagonet. "Let's be heroes instead of dead men! Let's fight for Aelle!"

The armsmen shouted their support.

"I'll fight for Aelle!" Dagonet cried enthusiastically. "A tall tankard of Aelle! A foamy Aelle for everybody!"

Nervous chuckles came.

Loki set a foot on Dagonet's shoulder and kicked him backward to sprawl atop the table. "I say we fight!"

"Oh, you want to fight, do you?" Dagonet asked. He popped back up as though on a spring. Agile as a cat, the dwarf rushed Loki, ran up the man's legs and torso, turned a back flip, and landed before him, fists raised. "I'll fight you with both legs tied behind your back!"

The crowd broke into laughter and applause. Some began chanting, "Fight! Fight! Fight!"

Loki held his hand out before him. "I will not fight a fool—"

"Better not fight Aelle then!" Dagonet shouted.

He seized Loki's arm and struggled to flip him over his shoulder. The maneuver resulted in an absurd humping motion.

Laughter filled the garrison.

"Why, you little trickster—"

"Why, you big trickster—"

"Fight! Fight! Fight!"

"Arthur's leading a sally!" came a shout from the garrison door. "Who among you would fight!"

"Fight! Fight! Fight!" The mob flooded out toward the door, each man drawing his sword. "Fight! Fight! Fight!"

Loki incredulously watched the rabble flood from the garrison. He hissed. "You're a canny one, for a fool. But you have saved Arthur at cost of your own life." He lifted his hands, and small sparks formed in the creases of his fingers.

Dagonet gave him a guileless look. "Was it truly so good? I felt such fear. After all, what ruse of mine could be worthy of you?"

A suspicious look crossed Loki's features. He lowered his hands. "How do you know of Loki?"

Waving off the comment, Dagonet said, "Everyone knows Loki. You're more famous than Christ. No other god compares. There's only one Loki. I've studied your genius, your triumphs—"

"Really?" Loki replied archly. "Then tell me one."

"What about the time you outsmarted Thor?" Dagonet asked.

"Yes," Loki said, nodding in fond remembrance.

"And the time you outsmarted Wotan. And the time you outsmarted Tyr—"

"The time I outsmarted Tyr?"

"Didn't you outsmart Tyr?"

"Well," Loki considered, "of course—"

"But what I'd like to know is how you outsmarted Arthur. How you got access to his castle, to his whole domain," Dagonet fawned. "That was your greatest coup!"

"Ah, yes. That was clever," Loki replied. He rubbed his hands, delighted to boast. "It is the Siege Perilous—the Round Table chair where only a pure man can sit. That is my chair, for I am pure—"

"Loki pure?"

The god whispered, "Yes! Pure evil. Pure caprice. Pure malice."

Dagonet giggled in delight. "Wonderful! So, as long as there is a Round Table, you have a place at it. You are welcome into the very heart of Camelot. You are a knight like any other!"

"Yes," Loki sniggered. "Brilliant!"

Letting out a glad sigh, Dagonet said, "What else have you been up to? I'd so like to learn from the master!"

Loki stared seriously at the dwarf. "Why not? What harm can a fool be? You're mad as a March hare. Come along. I'll show you where I've placed an enchantment to make the swords of Briton go flaccid an hour into the battle."

"Oh, I'd love to see that!"

"There is more. Much more . . . You know, you remind me of a certain mage—once mad. We'd been friends, he and I. . . ."

Militarily, it made no sense. What king, outnumbered and surrounded, would sally from his fort? What player of draughts leads with his king?

A player who foresees his foe's checkmate.

"Aelle is in the forefront, at the fourth palisade gate," Arthur shouted back among the mounted warriors. Rain pinged from helms and plastered tabards to hauberks. "He bears my scabbard. While he wears it, he cannot be wounded. It has made him arrogant." Arthur's steed stomped in an eager circle and reared once. The king hauled hard on the reins, bringing the mount back beneath him. "We sweep out as the fourth gate falls, surround Aelle as he charges through, and drag him back to the castle."

A warning sounded above, "The palisade gate is falling!"

"Raise the portcullises!" Arthur cried.

The rattle of chains and cranks came. Two massive gates lurched up their slots.

Arthur spun his horse and set heels to the beast's flanks. "Charge!"

Four hundred hooves thudded across flagstones. Their heavy reports became quicker, more clipped. The mass of horseflesh shouldered beneath the dripping gates.

At the head of the column, Arthur crouched low beside his horse's neck. Ulfius rode to one side of him, Kay to the other. Brastias, Ector, Lucas, Gryfflet, Gawain, Agravain, and the rest of the knights followed in tight formation behind. Within the portcullis tunnel, the roar of hooves was omnipresent. Just beyond, the sound of Arthur's force was lost to wind and rain and the fury of battle.

Below, Saxons formed an illimitable and black ocean. Waves of warriors rolled up the hillside to break against collapsing palisades. Their eyes shone with torchlight. Their hands ran with blood. They furiously tore down the gate. Amid smoldering skeletons and brimstone geysers and ravening lightning, they were no less than demons.

Mustering his courage, Arthur lifted Excalibur and shouted, "Onward!"

The drawbridge was still lowering as his steed charged across it. Horseshoes chipped wood. Ulfius and Kay, Brastias and Ector followed. The drawbridge shuddered under them. The planks were still six feet above the embrasure when Arthur's steed leaped. Three more mounts bounded into clear air before Arthur's horse set hoof to ground. The drawbridge moored itself, and out flooded the mounted warriors of Britannia.

"Throw wide the palisade gates," Arthur shouted imperiously at full gallop.

Before him, the defenders of the palisade turned to see Pendragon livery at the head of a full charge. Without question or pause, they rushed to the gate and heaved blocks up from their braces. Rough-hewn doors swung outward, giving a view beyond.

The Saxons were welling up the hillside, whelming the fourth palisade and slaughtering the defenders posted beyond.

Aelle was at their head—a huge tow-headed man on a magnificent bay horse. Rhiannon gleamed gloriously on his back. Though Aelle's steed bled through barding, the king himself was untouched in the thick of battle. Arrows bounced off him. Swords drew no blood. A British footman hacked into the king's neck, but Aelle merely batted the blade back. He cleft the man's head from his shoulders.

Leveling Excalibur, Arthur cried out, "For Rhiannon!"

He charged his steed into the Saxon midst. Excalibur leaped like lightning. It hewed a path through metal and muscle and brain.

One Saxon was cloven from left ear to skirt of tasses. Even as he tumbled, Excalibur impaled another. By sheer force of arm, Arthur lifted the man from his saddle and brought him hammering down on a third rider. His steed bulled past and tossed its head as though it had goring horns.

A sword caught Arthur in the side, ripping open his hip. Blood gushed.

Arthur wheeled on the attacker—a brown-haired Hun with bloody teeth. He thrust Excalibur between those teeth, making them bloodier still. The foe fell in the mud. Arthur uttered a Saxon expletive, ripped a hunk of fabric from his tabard, and stanched the flow.

His hands were still fumbling with gory cloth when the next foe screamed down on him, battle-ax descending.

Arthur turned, but too late. He hadn't even time to shy back from the dripping blade.

Steel flashed. The ax tumbled. Its flat struck Arthur's helm with a clang. It bounded off, its haft severed in two.

Ulfius drew back his sword and swung it violently to one side, decapitating the ax-man. "Onward, Arthur. On to Aelle!"

Arthur only nodded, gritting his teeth. Excalibur raked out to the other side, catching for a moment in the eye socket of a foe.

It was bloody work, chewing through Aelle's retinue. These Saxons were fierce fighters, though they had none of the discipline and close-order tactics of Arthur's knights. Horses fought for footing among the muddy fallen. Excalibur slew three more men before Arthur reached Aelle.

The two kings came together like a pair of rams. Lesser men fell away. Hooves churned the sanguine mud. Horses ran shoulder to shoulder. Excalibur flashed out.

Aelle's sword caught it and flung it back. The Saxon followed with a great sidearm swing.

Arthur whirled aside. The blade struck an elbow coppice and creased it. He spun his steed. The horse barged its rump against the bay. Excalibur rode on the weight of the turning mount. It slashed laterally past the Saxon's guard. The edge hewed through plate and chain, cutting deep into the king's flank.

Aelle only laughed. He dropped a dripping gauntlet onto Excalibur and clamped down. He hissed with the barbarous accent of his people, "While I have Rhiannon, you cannot kill me. And now, I have Excalibur too."

Arthur hauled hard on his captured sword, but couldn't pull it free.

With glad deliberation, Aelle lifted his blade. He brought the thing whistling down on Arthur's shoulder. The sword struck like a hammer blow. It cut through shoulder plates and hauberk, tissue and bone, carving a deep rent.

Arthur reeled back. He could not hold himself upright. The hilt of Excalibur dragged from his grip. Arthur tumbled from his horse. Rain pelted his face as he fell. Blackness closed in.

Aelle lifted Excalibur triumphantly in his bloody grip. Rhiannon glinted beyond. With a flip of rein, Aelle drove his beast on Arthur's and brought Excalibur shrieking down.

50

The Depths

*T*he Otherworld was ravaged.

Merlin swam beside Nyneve through the cold veins of the sídh. Everywhere they went, fey had fallen under a malaise. Tuatha ghosts did not rise. Redcaps and ettercaps leaned like statues on their picks. Dead gods had become little more that shadows and whispers. Even the dragons slept—insensible to pain, to threat, to doom. All of Merlin's exhortations had fallen on deaf ears.

"Loki's depredations have been devastating." Merlin said.

Nyneve's response was thoughtful. "He has only spread doubt. The British gods, you must realize, were only half-remembered legends before this war began. All Loki has done is dispel those half memories. Wotan has done the rest. Who could believe in grandfather gods when Thor lashes down from the heavens?"

"The divine army I promised Arthur is turning to stone," Merlin said as they entered another well in the cave. "If it weren't for your powers, we wouldn't even have mustered the iron geysers."

They had arrived in the halls of the Tuatha ghosts. Dim eyes glowed from holes in the cavern cliffs. Nyneve took slender shape from the slapping waves and rose onto the shoreline. Water sloughed gently from her shoulders.

"What hope have you here, Merlin?"

The old man assembled himself, sitting miserably in the

water. "Little hope, but perhaps our only hope." He stood. Water ran out of his tattered cloak. "Of all the creatures in this mound, the Tuatha ghosts are the most tied to the outer world. Each one is anchored to the place of his or her death, each prone to haunt that spot. If I can flush these ghosts from oblivion, I can perhaps send them through the land, to haunt the people and remind them—and the invaders—of the true powers here."

She leaned close to him. "Very good. You're always thinking. Meanwhile, what you said about an army turned to stone has sparked an idea in me." She kissed him. "I'm off to speak to the stone giants."

As lithe as any river otter, Nyneve dove back into the chill waters. Her dress and veils shimmered like fish scales and then flashed away.

Merlin blinked. A strange sadness came over him, an undeniable sense of loss, as though he would not see her again. "Good-bye, Nyneve."

The old man turned toward the caves. Lifting his arms, he abjured, "Awaken, O Tuatha spirits. I summon you. Awaken—"

"Who calls us?" a voice asked. It was deep and infinitely weary. It rose from ancient spaces on air that had not moved since before Caesar. "Who awakens us?"

Merlin smiled and heaved a sigh. "A friend, only. A friend with a warning."

"No harm can reach us here. . . ."

"You are wrong. A foreign king is sweeping over the land. He is bringing with him a tide of forgetfulness. The people are forgetting you. Even the places where you died, the places that killed you—even the land forgets." Merlin warned. "If this new king wins—*when* he wins—you will be gone forever."

Something new entered that weary voice. Anger. The implacable outrage of the murdered. And there were other voices, speaking in accord with the first. A crowd of ghosts seethed quietly. "We will not be gone forever. We will not be forgotten."

"You will. You nearly are."

"How do you know all this?" Rage began to pierce the spell of Loki.

"I know because I am just as you are. Because I want nothing more than to withdraw into my private cave, far from the horrible world above. But I have not—I have fought onward beside my grandson. I have lived. And I am remembered." He sighed. "You, on the other hand—who remembers you? Who remembers the murdered Tuatha? Who remembers the banished fey? Who remembers the giants of old? No one."

Every cave in the wall came to life. Agonized spirits circled within them. They seemed twisted creatures trapped in tidal pools, writhing under the hot sun.

"We would go remind them. We would go torment the places that destroyed us. We would keen their crimes, make them remember the old gods, but . . ."

It was a dangerous moment. One final dram of rage would flush them out, but at what cost? And what cost if they remained below?

Merlin watched the boiling caves. "I am too late. You are already destroyed. You were murdered once long ago, and murdered again this very hour."

With a chorus of shrieks, the ghosts flooded from their caves. Spectral and horrible, they roared past Merlin. Fingers tugged at his sodden robes. Fists yanked his dripping hair. Claws dug deeper still and plucked away bits of his soul. He reeled. The gale of ghosts scourged him, flaying his will, draining his strength. They were myriad.

At what cost?

Murdered Tuatha tore past him and one by one sieved up through fissures in the mountain. Tormented ghosts riled toward the world. Each wormed toward his or her own place of death, to the houses and palaces and roads that once were.

Merlin lay panting in their wake. He had been knocked to ground. The cold flood lapped his legs. The ghosts had nearly slain him. He had not felt so weak since he wrestled the Red Woman. It was a struggle even to breathe.

"How shall I ever defeat Wotan now?"

He closed his eyes for but a moment. . . .

I see myself in sections, cleft like meat beneath a cleaver.

Wotan will kill me when I go above.

It is a certainty now.

I have seen three deaths at his hand.

I will suffer them all, and be dead and gone.

Murdered, like the ghosts of the Tuatha Dé.

The moment Arthur was struck, Ulfius dropped from his horse. He was on the ground when the king toppled. Fountaining blood, Arthur tumbled into Ulfius's arms. He was sliced open from shoulder to chest, as wide as a butchered pig.

"He's dead," Ulfius muttered feverishly to himself. Rain mixed with blood and poured down his face. "The king is dead." He had no time for disbelief or sorrow.

Excalibur roared down from heaven.

Ulfius staggered back. He couldn't escape that blade. He pivoted, guarding the king. Even if Arthur was dead—*Arthur is dead!*—he would not be struck by his own sword, by Excalibur. Ulfius turned his back and hunkered down, ready to die.

Behind him came a huge rushing bulk and a terrible scream. From the crook of his huddled arm, Ulfius saw Arthur's own horse rear into the path of Excalibur. The noble steed took the sword blow straight on. Blood gushed in a wide cascade. Eyes rimmed in death, the creature spun its forehooves once last, dashing out the brain of King Aelle's mount. The beasts collapsed together.

Aelle was thrown back, stunned, among his own forces. The wall of Saxons closed before Aelle, barring the way to the unhorsed king.

Arthur's knights surged up around Ulfius. Swords sang bloodily in the stormy sky.

"Excalibur," came a gasp from the king.

"You are alive!" Ulfius laughed as he hauled Arthur away from battle. "You live, Arthur! You live!"

"Excalibur," Arthur repeated. Blood bubbled about his lips.

"The sword is lost," Ulfius said, struggling over the strewn bodies of fallen knights. "But you live!"

"Then . . . Aelle is king," gasped Arthur. He sagged in Ulfius's grip. "He has Excalibur . . . Rhiannon . . . he is king. . . ."

"No," Ulfius replied sternly. "You are king, Arthur. You are king." He reached the final palisade and, panting bitterly, looked back at the battlefield. It was hopeless. Seventy-some knights and warriors struggled to hold back thousands of Saxons. They fought a suicide rearguard while their wounded king was pulled from battle. Kay and Ector and all the Table Round would die in the next moments, and Arthur in the next hour.

"How do we fare?" asked the king.

"We are winning."

And then, the words were not a lie. The very earth began to rumble. Grassy ground stretched and broke apart. Brows and shoulders of stone emerged. Soil tumbled from giant boulders. They jutted upward in a great circle around the castle, rising where the palisades were falling. It was as though the earth grew teeth, a huge and ancient ring of teeth.

"Avebury," Ulfius said in wonder. "A fortress of stone."

Already, the beleaguered knights fell back behind the great circle of monoliths.

Except they weren't monoliths. They were figures, stooped figures pushing up through the earth.

"Stone giants!" Ulfius whispered.

The knights beheld them, too, and the Saxons. Bent necks and heads glowered down. Shoulders sloughed mud. Stony torsos loomed in flashes of lightning.

The battle paused. A palpable frisson moved among the armies.

As though energized by that corporate terror, the giants began to move.

Mud-crusted arms lifted up from the sides of the crouching figures. Heads blinked sand from ancient eyes. Hands raked out like massive scythes, mowing down Saxons. Flesh was wheat before them.

Saxons fell back in terror. The will of the invaders dissolved away. They slew each other to flee.

A cheer, ghastly and ragged, went up from the castle walls.

Wearily, Arthur asked, "We are . . . winning?"

"Yes," Ulfius said, turning his face away. He climbed toward the palisade gate. "Yes. We are winning."

From the well in the center of the castle yard rose a bedraggled figure. Merlin seemed a drowned cat. His robes streamed water as he floated upward.

A joyous mood filled the courtyard around. Men cheered upon the wall.

Merlin was heartened. As he rose higher, he saw beyond, where stone giants marched after Aelle's recoiling, retreating forces. The Knights of the Round Table were returning, victorious, through the open castle gates.

No—not victorious. A slumped and bloodied figure lay in Ulfius's arms.

"Arthur," Merlin gasped.

He swooped down toward the stricken king.

The throng ceased its cheers when they saw Arthur, swordless and nearly slain. A strangled silence gripped the castle.

Everyone could hear Ulfius's pleading. "Merlin. You must heal him. He's almost gone."

The wizard set to ground beside the wounded king. Merlin placed his hand in the wide wound. His face was ashen. "Aelle did this—"

"You must heal him—"

"I cannot," Merlin said, cursing. "I am too weak. Guinevere will save him, or no one."

The old mage held out the edge of his sodden cloak, enfolding Ulfius and Arthur. Together, the three rose into the air. Merlin bore them across the yard and to the window of the royal chamber. Glass and lead turned soft as soap bubbles, allowing the mage and his comrades to glide through. Cloaks brushed the sill, and glazing reformed itself as the three landed on the rush-strewn floor within.

Merlin released the others from his dripping cloak and fell to his knees, panting.

Ulfius bore Arthur to the bed and laid him on white linens. Blood spilled across them. "Someone, fetch Guinevere!"

There was no need. White-faced in dread, Guinevere swept into the chamber. Behind her came seven priestesses, each carrying the implements of healing—steaming silver cases, bottles of spirits, bandages, linens, wine, salt, and sulfur. The most powerful healing tool of all was Guinevere, herself.

She reached her husband's side and knelt beside him. Her hands were quick and expert, if tremulous. She dragged armor back from the wound. Daubing cloths and stinging spirits came next, until the cut was clean and bare. Then, unflinching, she moved her hands in the cleft, as though she could knit his flesh back together, tissue by tissue. Her porcelain fingers were tipped in red. She murmured devotions to the land.

Merlin arrived at the head of Arthur's bed and gently stroked the king's hair.

Arthur's face was clenched in pain, eyes and lips in tight lines. He gave little other sign of being alive.

Merlin spoke to him anyway. "You are back among friends, Arthur. Your grandfather is here. Your wife. She will save you."

Arthur bucked in the bed. Guinevere's hands came away from the gory wound. Priestesses pressed him gently back into the bed. He quieted. The queen resumed her labors.

"Guinevere will save you as Nyneve saved us all," Merlin continued soothingly. "She awoke the stone giants, not I. She forced them up into the light of day and into the sight of the people, made Briton and Saxon alike see and believe. She awoke the stone giants in our minds, and then in truth. She will come here soon too."

The king's teeth ground upon each other, making a cracking sound. His clenched fingers tore through linen and mattress tick to down. His eyes moved whitely beneath fluttering lids. "Excalibur . . ."

A grim look came over Merlin's face. "We will retrieve it. Once you are well, we will retrieve it."

Life seemed to flee the king. He swooned. A long exhalation raked from his lungs.

"Arthur, Grandson," Merlin said, suddenly urgent, "you must live. If you die, Britannia dies."

Eyes opening, Arthur stared bleakly at his grandfather. A small smile spread across his face. "Sometimes the king must die . . . for the kingdom . . . to live."

Stunned, Merlin backed away. He had no sooner vacated the spot beside Arthur's head than a pair of priestesses swooped in with wine-soaked sponges.

"He is in his wife's hands now," Ulfius said gently.

"We all are," Merlin whispered back.

51

The Death of Merlin

The door to Arthur's sickroom flew open, and in capered Dagonet. The dwarven fool turned a pair of somersaults, crashed into a side table, and sent metal implements cascading to the floor. He bounded to his feet and flung out his arms:

"The king of Britons soon will die,
    The mage of Britons soon will cry,
    The realm of Britons soon will fly,
    For Wotan is coming to call!"

"Out!" shouted Ulfius imperiously. "This is no time for foolery."

With a leering grin, Dagonet said, "It is always time for foolery."

Ulfius took a swipe at him, but came up empty-handed.

The fool cartwheeled up beside Merlin. "Aye, Mage Royale? You once knew that better than anyone." He cavorted away, leaping from bed to chair to table.

Merlin scowled as he watched Ulfius hopelessly pursue the little acrobat. "Think of Arthur. Think of Guinevere. Think of the nation—someone but yourself, Dagonet."

Stopping stock-still atop a leaning bookshelf, Dagonet set hands on his hips, as if outraged. "Think of Arthur? Think of the nation? Who else do you think I've been thinking of? I single-handedly prevented a castle riot, and then followed the instigator—Loki—throughout the countryside to learn what he has done. Tavern stories and bawdy songs—that's how he's winning the war. With foolery! He's started rumors about Wotan, told the people of his greatness. Now Wotan arrives and lives up to their greatest fears. Foolery. Wotan is winning by foolery!"

This report narrowed Merlin's eyes. "And what else has he done?"

"Well, he's mixed drops of the Lethe in the wells, and the folk are forgetting the old gods. It is why you cannot rouse the sídh to fight—childish pranks to win a war! Your allies are all turning to stone."

Merlin considered grimly. "Yes. Nyneve had to force the stone giants back into the people's minds. . . ."

"Oh, and Nyneve. You won't hear from her anymore. Loki has diverted the ley-line highways. In some places, he has established hermit monks—lunatics sitting and chanting all day, disrupting the flow of ley force. Lunatics! In other places, he has slain powerful Otherworld creatures to divert the channels. I would not be surprised if, even as we speak, the last ley line was diverting away from us. No fey creatures from outside the sídh will be able to remain, and none from within it to leave."

Fists clutched within his travel robe, Merlin strode to the window and glowered out.

Dagonet vaulted up beside him, nose shattering a pane of glass. He babbled on, oblivious. "That's how you should be fighting, Merlin. You can't match Wotan's lightning or his beetle armies. You're not Jove anymore. You're not as powerful as he, so you must be cleverer. Once upon a time, you were very clever—"

"I was also mad," Merlin answered levelly.

"You once were a fool, and lived through every war you fought. Now you've no sense of humor, and you're going to die.

"The king of Britons soon will die,
    The mage of Britons soon will cry—"

"All right, that's it!" Ulfius declared.

He had quietly sneaked up to the dwarf and laid hold of the little man's collar. With a swift motion, Ulfius hauled the man to the door, flung him through, and slammed and locked it.

Merlin only stood there, stunned. Nyneve was now beyond reach—Nyneve and the Cave of Delights he had made for her.

Brushing off his hands, Ulfius strode across the floor toward Merlin. "At least Aelle is routed."

Merlin shook his head, staring out the window. "Only a momentary victory. Aelle can be routed, but not Wotan. See, there? Already the stone giants have reached the base of the mountain and will go no farther. They cannot venture from the sídh where they dwell. And, look, the Saxons flee no longer."

"We've won a respite, at any rate," Ulfius said.

"No respite. The Saxons are still forty thousand strong, and they merely bide. They can kill us as easily by siege as by storm." Merlin took a trembling breath. "Wotan has poisoned the powers of the sídh. Soon, he will cut us off from

the rest of Britannia. Not even Nyneve can help us. Time is
on their side. They can wait, and we will die."

After an endless day came an infinite night. The stone giants
kept mortal foes at bay, but Thor continued his barrage of
lightning and hail. Night winds tore brutally at the castle.
Doubts tore brutally at its defenders. Chief among their fears
was that Arthur might die. Could Guinevere heal him without
the power of the land? And, without sword and scabbard and
land, was Arthur even king?

It was an infinite night. Guinevere spent it healing the
king, though her powers fled with the passing hours. Ulfius
and Merlin remained there too. It was a vigil for Arthur, and
for Britannia. At last, day dawned gray. With it, came a new
threat.

"What's that?" Ulfius asked, pointing out the window.

Something descended from the clouds. This was no lightning bolt, no shredding hail. It was instead a glorious rainbow path. It rolled down from the heights like a red carpet
before a king. The glimmering highway struck ground halfway up the sídh, and the path solidified.

From the very heart of the storm emerged a regal figure.
He was garbed in robes as white as lightning and was
crowned with a diadem of stars. The Saxon high god descended the rainbow path. His eyes shone silver beneath
frosty brows. White beard and hair riffled in the welkin
winds. He did not so much walk as glide. His wolves, Geri
and Freki, loped beside his feet. His storm crows Hugin and
Munin circled about his head, raucously calling to each other.
In one hand, he held his staff, and from the tip of it depended
the banner of parley.

"He wants to speak," Ulfius said, astonished. "Arthur cannot meet him."

Merlin shook his head. "Wotan was never after Arthur. He
wants to speak with me." The old man peered levelly into
Ulfius's eyes. "Stay here. Guard Arthur. Help Guinevere
however you can. The king must live."

Merlin stepped up onto the windowsill. He slid through glass and lead and drifted out on dark winds.

Every eye was watching Wotan's grand descent. They would watch Merlin's too. He must inspire them, bring fear to the Saxons and courage to the Britons. Their belief would empower his weary soul.

"Dagonet was right. I must be the man people know," Merlin told himself as he drifted along. "Not Jove—not another foreign god. I must be tattered and volatile and somewhat mad. It is time for folly. I must be Merlin."

He did not deck himself in raiment of light. He did not sprout angel's wings, or soar inward upon singing beams of sunlight. Instead, he floated up over the castle walls, dangled a moment in apparent indecision, and then plopped comically to earth. His gray travel cloak whirled up all around him, sending clouds of dust into the air.

Tentative laughter came from the castle walls and the Saxon army waiting below.

Merlin coughed violently within the dust cloud. He emerged as though flustered and patted great puffs of dirt from his cloak. An abject sneeze rolled out from him.

The battlefield roared with laughter.

Merlin smiled. He had come full circle. Once he had been a mad fool, feared throughout Britannia for his capricious fits. Then he had become the fallen Jove, king-maker and architect of a nation. He had had no time for folly or dreams. And now, at the end of it all, it was only folly and dream that could save him.

Like the shabby beggar he once was, Merlin shambled down the mountainside toward the rainbow highway. At one point—and this was done without any guile—his foot slipped into a rabbit hole. Merlin flopped on his face. The *ooof!* that came from him was no act, either, though he enchanted the sound so that it would echo away across the battlefield. It reverberated merrily among the folk there.

"This rabbit hole is helpful," Merlin said to himself, realizing only then how mad that sounded. He picked himself up, pounded more dust from his robes, sneezed twice, and then peered down into the hole. "Come on out. I won't hurt you," he coaxed, crooking a finger that sent an enchantment into the darkness below.

In moments, a pair of pink noses twitched experimentally in the opening. Two sets of gleaming eyes shone behind them.

"Ah, beautiful coneys," Merlin said, "I'd like you to save Britannia. Would you like that?"

The hares twitched noses in reply.

"Good. And you can get revenge on some old foes in the offing." With a simple gesture of his hand and a word spoken beneath his breath, Merlin completed the spell. "Off you go, now. Up the rainbow."

The two coneys sniffed once more, blinking. They hopped up from their burrow and dashed toward the rainbow bridge.

Merlin straightened. Only then did he realize he had forgotten to remove the spell that amplified his words. All the world had heard his conversation with the hares, and all were finding it uproarious. The laughter buoyed his tired soul.

"Better and better," Merlin told himself as he strolled toward the base of the bridge. "Better and better."

The darting rabbits reached the rainbow highway and bounded upward. Their white-and-brown haunches pumped furiously as they pelted toward the descending Wotan.

The god did not pause in his descent, but only stared at the strange sight.

Geri and Freki's lupine eyes lit with delight. Their loping speed increased. Soon the two wolves dashed full out toward their prey.

The coneys ascended all the faster. They ran into the face of the wolves.

Slavering jaws opened to clamp down on them. Jowls closed on nothing.

Rabbit backs rubbed wolf bellies. The coneys pelted on, straight for Wotan. They reached the regal god and clambered up his raiment as though he were a sack of carrots.

Whirling about, Geri and Freki arrived shortly thereafter. They bounded onto their master, jaws snapping hungrily.

Teeth closed on flesh, but not rabbit flesh. Wotan swatted the wolves down, only to have a hare wriggle through his chest. Geri and Freki leaped to the attack again. Wotan grabbed at the hares with hands that blazed fire. The flames only seared his robes and the noses of his wolves. The storm crows joined in, pecking at the hares. Moments later they flew off squawking, their feathers limned in flame.

No longer did Merlin's bunnies seem so laughable. It was Wotan who did. From the castle atop Mount Badon, soldiers jeered and shouted slogans about getting up Wotan's robes, and how he'd not gotten fluffy tail in centuries. From the battlefields below, men chuckled at the display. The sound was glorious, like the laughter that had founded Camelot, like the mad frolics that had begun this whole escapade.

The laughter only strengthened Merlin and weakened Wotan.

The high god of the Saxons roared in fury. With a snap of his fingers, the whole of his being flared incandescent. Hares tumbled out and fled in terror down the road. Hugin and Munin blindly circled into the nearby sky. Geri and Freki rolled to their backs, displaying their bellies in submission.

Merlin watched from the base of the rainbow road. A mild smile filled his features. He had toyed with Wotan enough before their parley, and dared humiliate him no further. . . . At least not yet . . .

As though nothing had happened, Wotan drifted down from the multicolored highway and stepped onto the sidh. He stood easily twenty feet high, at once ancient and young. There was no doubting this was a god.

Merlin bowed his head gently. "You called for a parley?" His voice yet bore the echoing enchantment.

The god's eyes narrowed. Red light streamed from them. "You attacked me while I carried a flag of parley."

Aged fingers spread in mock dismay across Merlin's chest. "I? Attacked? You? With bunnies? You are mistaken. I merely sent a pair of emissaries to receive you. *Your* wolves attacked *them*."

Snickers moved among the waiting armies.

"This has always been our battle, Merlin. From Saxony to Britannia, for over a century, it has been our battle. Your king is dying. We have his sword. Your folk are outnumbered three to one. You are cut off from all the gods of Britannia. It seems to me you have lost this war. Arthur and his people are crushed."

"You are a humorless god, Wotan," Merlin said disparagingly. "When I was Jove, I brought joviality to my people. And now, as Merlin, I bring laughter. And when there is still laughter, Wotan, no man is crushed. We will not surrender."

Wotan pursed his lips. "Then, only one matter remains to be decided."

"And what matter is that?" Merlin asked lightly.

"How you will die," Wotan said. In a single stride, he loomed before Merlin.

The mage waggled a finger at him. "I met you under a flag of parley."

The flag flashed away to ash that fell on Merlin.

In the next moment, Wotan's foot descended. It struck earth, shaking the mountainside. Dust motes rolled up around Wotan.

He shook his head and laughed. "So easily destroyed."

Except it wasn't dust. The motes were too energetic, too brightly colored. They swarmed Wotan, flying up his sleeves and down his robes. Glowing chiggers sank their claws and teeth home.

Next moment, Wotan scratched fiercely. He released a growl of nettled anger. His feet danced away from the spot where Merlin's crushed body would have been. Only an overlarge footprint remained.

The battlefield and castle, silent for a moment after the ominous boom of Wotan's foot, broke into laughter.

Merlin's voice came to them in myriad gnat song. "You may be of greater power than I, Wotan, but I am of greater wit."

Wotan stopped scratching. He clenched fists beside him, closed his eyes, and sent power gushing from every pore. In moments, his skin was skillet-hot, and then red-hot and white-hot.

Merlin had anticipated as much. Chiggers swarmed away and joined with each other. Their stumpy bodies transformed into attenuate abdomens. They spread their minute wings into long iridescence. Chiggers became dragonflies, which flocked about the glowing god.

Wotan swiped impotently at them. He hissed, his breath rolling out in a poison cloud.

The buzzing bugs retreated again, merging into new forms. Their glassy wings grew leathery. Their black carapace grew scaly. Dragonflies became amphidragons. From a score of mouths, the small serpents breathed fire that dispersed Wotan's poison breath. They rapidly circled him in a mad storm.

Wotan seemed a man bedeviled by bats. His burning hands gripped a pair of the amphidragons, and he squeezed. Blood and flesh jetted out from his fingers. Wotan roared in triumph—too soon.

The ooze of the slain amphidragons combined with the bodies of the living ones. A new beast formed. Vast and muscular, the winged lizard cast a shadow across the hillside. It towered over Wotan. Eyes as large as portcullises, teeth as vast as palisade poles, claws as huge as horses, wings that filled the heavens—

"Behold, Badon Hill, the purple Pendragon!" he roared.

Saxons below and Britons above shrank back from the terrifying beast.

Merlin opened his horned jowls. Blue fire poured forth. Flame mantled the figure of Wotan.

The Saxon high god stood in the midst of the assault, as Stoic as a statue.

When at last Merlin's fire was spent, he quipped, "I am of greater wit, and have better breath."

Wotan only stood there, literally smoldering.

Merlin cocked his dragon head. "So, it would seem we are well matched. Perhaps we should parley after all." Leathery wings withered into tattered travel robes, scales melted into skin, and the whole figure shrank inward. With a simple thought, the old man had regained his true form. He extended a conciliatory hand toward Wotan. "So, shall we talk reasonably?"

Without moving, Wotan was suddenly beside him, and the god's massive foot crashed down.

This time there was no chance to escape. The boot was preternaturally heavy, with the weight of mountains and glaciers and centuries behind it. Merlin's skull shattered. His brain was dashed to gruel. His spine cracked. Ribs burst. Macerated lungs gushed forth. Liver and pelvis and muscle were smashed to meal.

Wotan ground his heel into the earth. Then he stepped back. Merlin was only a bloody pile of meat and bone on the hillside.

The Saxon god turned toward the castle above and called out in a booming voice: "Those of you who hoped in Merlin, your hope is gone. He cannot save you now. He never could save you. Merlin was but a mortal mage. I am a god. It is given into the hands of the gods that they grant and revoke mortal life. Behold!"

Wotan flung his hand outward. Red energy surged from his fingers and coursed over the sanguine remains of Merlin. With a power beyond even the patient work of Guinevere, Wotan rebuilt his foe. Every tissue, every corpuscle, every fiber of nerve and thought regained its former place. Last of all, bone and muscle were wrapped in skin, from which sprouted white hair.

Merlin stood there again, blinking. A mild confusion showed on his face, uncertain what had just happened.

"Perhaps I should make my point again," Wotan said.

Sheets of magical fire shot from the god's fingers and sliced across Merlin. Blood gushed in the wake of each cut. Light fled his eyes. Then, with a grotesque wet sound, the severed sections slid across each other and tumbled to the ground.

A deathly silence came from the castle above. The Saxons below snickered at this inelegant demise.

Wotan smiled, hearing the sound. "Oh, I know, Britons. I

know how much you hoped in this fool. I know that some of you loved him. It grieves me that you should see him lying in chunks on the ground." He snapped his fingers.

The gory hunks of meat leaped up from their ignominious pile and reassembled themselves. Blood crawled back into the severing wounds, and skin sealed itself closed.

Merlin had returned once more, blinking and uncertain. He tried to smile, though his brow dipped in confusion.

"Much better that there be nothing left to grieve you," Wotan concluded.

There was a final flash of lightning. Merlin was transfixed on it. Every drop of liquid in his being sizzled away. His flesh burst into flame. He was there for a moment more, a burning column within the lightning. And then, not even bones were left. The lightning ceased.

The ash that had been Merlin settled down upon the ravaged earth.

Merlin was dead.

52

Madness Manifest

*W*otan's eyes blazed as he scanned the battlefield. Aelle's Saxons waited there, looking up at him in terror. Their fear suffused him, like blood in mortal muscle. In that moment, he was omnipotent, riding on their cresting dread.

What Wotan did in the next moment only insured his power for all time. Reaching toward the battlefield, he evoked spirit servants. They poured whitely from beneath his nails and coiled about his fingers. The ghosts gathered might. With a flick of his hand, Wotan sent them coursing down the mountainside. Over the heads of the Saxon warriors, the spirits stretched like spider webs.

They came to King Aelle, blond and giant in the army's midst. Sinking between his fingers, the gossamer strands wrapped tightly about the hilt of Excalibur. They ripped the sword from Aelle's hand. The blade whirled in air and stabbed down at the king. It sheathed itself in Rhiannon, strapped to his back. Then sword and scabbard both came away from the king.

Borne on slender spirits, Excalibur and Rhiannon soared back to their god.

Wotan caught the scabbarded sword in one massive hand. It was but a small dagger to that giant figure. Even so, it seemed to weigh heavily on him. Wotan gazed down at the god-killing sword and its mortal-saving sheath. They blazed with light. Desire and revulsion warred across his features.

"Excalibur and Rhiannon. The sword and scabbard of kings. You are mine. Your god has failed. Your king has failed. I am victorious."

Excalibur and Rhiannon emitted a heat no less ravening than Wotan's own. They jittered across his palm as if seeking escape.

Wotan would not allow it. He clasped the sword and scabbard in a tight fist. Grimacing against the heat, he lifted them high overhead. "I am Wotan, god of Saxony, the frozen north, and Britannia. Slayer of Jove. Wielder of Tetragrammaton's sword. Heir to the world. Bow before me."

With a sudden and unanimous motion, every Saxon on the battlefield knelt. Eighty thousand knee cops struck earth with a clatter like thunder. Even Aelle, deprived of his prizes, bowed before the incarnate god.

Victorious, Wotan gazed out over his nation. Excalibur and Rhiannon blazed and sparked in his hand, struggling for release. He bore it all, empowered by the terrified devotion of his army.

At his back, though, a chill lingered.

Wotan turned toward the gray-walled castle perched atop the hill. Warriors lined the walls, thicker than merlons. Not one of them bowed.

Eyes narrowing, Wotan shouted, "Bow to me, Britons.

Your wizard is dead. Your holy sword is lost. Your king is dying. You cannot last the hour against this army. Bow to me, Britons, or die!"

There was a man upon that wall, a friend of the dead wizard and the dying king. If any man should have known the peril of opposing Wotan, it was this man. His name was Ulfius, chamberlain of Britannia.

He cupped hands about his mouth and shouted, "We will bow to you, Wotan, yes! We will bow to you—but backward!"

So saying, he turned, dropped his breeches, and waggled his bent backside. With a glad shout, the others on the wall turned and did likewise.

Wotan lashed out—no slender spirit webs this time. Power roared in flaming sheets from his hand. It swept broadly up the mountain and burned away the final palisades as though they were mere jackstraws. The red orbs of protection flashed and disappeared overhead.

The blast of power continued on and crashed on the great gray curtain wall where the men stood. Rock pulverized to sand. The wall slumped and crumpled away. Men fell, their breeches still about their thighs. Britannia's warriors tumbled amid the collapsing defenses of Castle Badon. Many men were buried in rubble. The rest were lost from sight behind a rising cloud of dust.

The Saxon high god was not finished. He spun about and flung more destroying fire down the mountain.

A red avalanche of energy roared across earthwork rings and into the backs of the stone giants. The guardians broke to pieces just as the wall above had. Gravel and grit shot outward from their disintegrating forms and slew hundreds of bowing Saxons. Rocky debris cascaded to earth, paving a broad avenue of advance up the hill.

Wotan beckoned his army forward. "Stand now, faithful of Wotan. Stand and charge up this mountain and take it. Leave no man or woman or child or beast alive upon it." He lifted his fist high. It blazed like a giant torch. "Charge!"

Every throat on the battlefield shrieked in berserker fury.

The Saxons rose. Aelle's army charged across pulverized giants and up toward the breached castle.

Wotan turned. His prize sparked in his hand. Pleased, the Saxon high god ascended his ethereal road. It disintegrated behind him, breaking contact with earth even as murderous warriors flooded up the mound.

A thousand feet stomped heedlessly over ashes that once had been Merlin the mage.

I flouted my arse at a god. It was all Ulfius could think as he tumbled through the air among rocks and dust, his breeches at midthigh. And now I'm paying for it.

It was the sort of thing Merlin would have done, he realized. Just the sort of mad, impetuous, ludicrous thing that Merlin would have done. Perhaps that was why Ulfius had done it. A god who would slay Merlin, who would steal Excalibur and Rhiannon, who would send an army to kill Arthur and destroy Britannia—this was a god in dire need of flouting. No wonder Merlin had hated him so.

Ulfius crashed to ground amid pelting rocks and garbage. He landed on his bare backside. It hurt, and more than pride. Ulfius groaned and rolled to his side in the hail of stones. He clawed his breeches up about his waist and cinched the cord tight.

The chamberlain stood. Debris pinged against helm, epaulets, and breastplate. He raised an arm to shield his face. Through the storm of grit, he glimpsed other figures struggling out of the rubble. There was no telling how many lay dead beneath these cairns, but some lived.

Ulfius lived. He drew his sword. "To me, faithful of Arthur!"

There—that bruin of a man would have to be Ector. . . .

And the young knight he hauled from a tangle of wood and stone, that was Kay.

Something struck Ulfius's back. He turned to see Brastias grinning at him. The huge man's eyebrows were chalky. Dirt clung in pasty clumps to his teeth, but still he grinned.

He finished tying his breeches and said, "What now, Commander?"

"We fight!" Ulfius said.

"We dropped our trousers for you, Ulfius," Brastias said. "We'll gladly fight for you!"

The need was suddenly obvious. The roar of tumbling stone had died away, but another roar rose to take its place. It was the vast and demonic howl of Saxons charging up the hill.

"To me!" Ulfius bellowed, hoisting his sword high. "The rest of you, to me!"

Brastias joined his voice in the shout. Soon Kay and Ector were beside them, and Lucas and Gryfflet. Fifteen more knights came, including the sons of Lot. Hundreds of warriors followed. They were battered and bruised, but fires of fury blazed in their eyes.

Sword lofted overhead, Ulfius strode over the rubble field.

Knights and warriors marched after, hauling comrades from the rubble as they went. The group swelled. One by one, they began a hoarse-throated roar. Dust rolled from their mouths like the fire of dragons. They reached the crest of the rock pile and poured over it.

Through the haze, Saxons appeared.

Ulfius leveled his blade at them and shouted, "Charge!"

The cry was taken up in hundreds of throats. The knights of the Table Round descended, carving into the advancing line of Saxons.

Ulfius took off a man's head with one stroke. He batted the head aside. It struck another Saxon like a brainball, knocking him to ground. Ulfius ran over this fallen man and swung his sword axlike. It bashed back a rising blade and unmade the man that lifted it. Ulfius barged past the shrieking red beard and drove his elbow cop into the eye of another.

He had never fought with such fury, such bloodlust. The death of Merlin had broken something in him. There was no longer decorum. There was no longer honor. There was only hatred of Wotan and killing of his people. There was only the rage of a dreamer caught in a nightmare.

In the next moments, Ulfius brought bitter and eternal sleep to scores of his foes. All the knights and warriors fought that way. And Arthur's hundreds killed Aelle's thousands.

The blast from Wotan's fingers had leveled one whole side of the curtain wall, taking with it guard towers and bartizans and the men stationed in them. On the edge of that blast area, one tower yet stood. Its belly was ripped out and its conic roof leaned precariously over the slope. The structure was as safe as an impending avalanche—but it gave a splendid view of the killing.

It was the perfect perch for Loki.

The Saxon god of chaos sat on the canted slates, clicking his claws across them and gazing avidly at the mayhem. With each breath he took, a hundred men died. The air was sweet with their fleeing souls, sweet like the scent of burning flesh. It was well that these Britons were so skilled and so ferocious. They were grotesquely outnumbered. Were Saxons killing Britons as swiftly as Britons killed Saxons, the battle would have been over in minutes. At this rate, it would take hours, and tens of thousands of dead.

Loki clapped excitedly.

Rumbles came from the clouds. As inevitable as carrion birds, the war goddesses gathered. First, they were only golden flashes among thunderheads. Then, a glowing hoof broke momently through, and a gilded wheel behind it. At last, horses and chariots burst from the toiling mists—the Valkyrie.

"Vultures."

Horn-helmed and singing, the war virgins arrived to harvest the souls of the brave fallen. Soon seven huge chariots coursed through the air behind fiery, ethereal horses. They circled high through the sky, as sinuous as golden dragons. The wind across their wheels made an eerie song that drew

Saxon eyes skyward—and exposed throats to Briton steel.

"What delights!" Loki said, clapping. "The soul reapers ripen men for harvest!"

It mattered little to Wotan to lose these men. He only gained them among his divine armies. Even now, the warriors of Valhalla massed for battle, should this war turn. Their divine ranks swelled as mortal heads lifted and vaulted from their necks.

Loki snickered excitedly, his nails clicking on the slates.

"What's next, my king?" came a familiar voice behind Loki.

The lean, black-garbed god turned to see Dagonet arrive. The dwarf cartwheeled across the slippery tiles, running headlong into Loki.

The god of chaos released a groan. As gifted and entertaining as this fool was, he was also a clumsy clod. There is a time for chaos, and the time is not when you are rolling toward a god's back. "Beware, Fool!"

"Things are going splendidly," Dagonet enthused as he disentangled himself from the god's robes. "What's next?"

"Next?"

"Of course! Yes!" Dagonet elaborated guilelessly. "You've worked so hard setting up this war, sowing the seeds of chaos, singing in taverns—you've single-handedly won it for Wotan. And I thought you must have a reason. Wotan got Excalibur. Aelle got Britannia. The Valkyrie got fields of dead. What are you going to get?"

"What am I going to get?" echoed Loki.

Dagonet nodded enthusiastically. "Yes. What are you going to get? Surely you didn't win this whole war just for Wotan. Just for Aelle. What do you get?"

Loki blinked soberly, staring down at the men dying below. "Well, there is this mayhem. . . ."

An incredulous look answered. "You mean, you get nothing? Wotan gets everything and you get nothing?"

A white line of anger creased the god's forehead. "After all, I did this all single-handedly—"

"And you should be compensated for loss of the Siege

Perilous," the dwarf put in casually as he balanced along the spire of the roof. "After all, now that Arthur and Merlin are gone and the knights are getting killed, what use is the Round Table or your special seat? You've made quite a sacrifice, and what have you to show for it?"

Loki's scowl deepened. "Aside from a day's entertainment and a hundred thousand deaths—*nothing*!"

The dwarf shook his head and clucked. "It's just like Wotan. I heard he blasted you to ash in Avalon, right in front of everyone. He killed you in the same way he killed Merlin, and he *hated* Merlin. It tells you something. . . ."

"Yes," Loki hissed. "Yes, it does."

"And him, sitting up there in his heavenly hall, playing with his holy sword, drinking his mead and eating his boar and cavorting with his Rhine maidens, as if *he* had won the battle—" Dagonet spat vitriolically. "It's enough to make you puke."

"Yes!" shouted Loki. "Puke!" He leapt to his feet and, for good measure, blasted out a column of green vomit that reached solidly from his mouth to the ground three stories down. The bile splashed on shattered stone and burned a pit deep into the earth. Loki spat out the last flecks of the stuff, wiped his mouth on his sleeve, shook his fist in the air, and shouted, "You bastard! You're always using me!"

Dagonet came down from the canted peak and patted Loki comfortingly on the back. "There, there. I shouldn't have brought it up. Nothing to be done about it now."

Loki whirled, snatching the dwarf by the wrist and hoisting him into the air. Green bile still hung in gelatinous fangs from the god's lower lip. He stared into Dagonet's eyes and said, "Something can be done. Something *will* be done. Come!"

Loki stepped from the rooftop into midair. At that exact moment, bile ate away the tower's foundation and sent it crashing to the ground.

Heedless, the god of chaos and the fool of Camelot floated up out of the dust cloud. They passed above strafing and reaping Valkyrie.

"Where are we going?" Dagonet asked, dangling by one arm.

"We're catching a ride with one of the war virgins. We're going to set things right. We're riding to Valhalla."

53

The Battle for Merlin's Grave

The blood-thirst had not been quenched in Ulfius or the knights. They were bathed in the stuff from shoulders to toes. Their swords fell with the weight and unholy crunch of cleavers. It was justifiable to fight so—they would each and all die in moments if they did not. But self-preservation did not drive them deep into the ceaseless tide of Saxons. It was no grim necessity that launched sword tips into enemy mouths, or turned Saxon heads into kick-balls, or made knights howl like wolves with each kill they made. It was sheer fury.

"To Merlin's grave!" Ulfius shouted.

The Knights of the Round Table took up the cry. They surged beside him. Backed by sanguine warriors, they formed a wedge and drove downward, into the heart of the Saxons. Pressing on was fiercer work than holding ground, and yet easier. Each new kill paved the road ahead. Each hewn head or slashed shoulder or gutted belly was a step nearer to that ash heap where the unthinkable had occurred. The memory of Merlin drew them downward.

The tide of Saxons shifted to stop them. Even as the knights chanted the name of Merlin, their foes knew and feared that name. The Britons should never reach the archmage's grave. Saxon swords dammed the flood of Ulfius and the knights. Steel clanged on steel. Flesh hid beyond. Bloodied blades rang on mirror-bright ones. The taxed knights ran upon fresh warriors from the press below.

Ulfius screamed. He had slain ten men to gain the inch of ground he now fought viciously to retain. Three swords tangled with his, and five more men waited ahead. Ulfius growled, "Is it Saxons then, all the way to the sea?"

Then he saw something that emboldened his heart. Another army had joined the fray, an army that even then ate away at the rear of Aelle's forces. With delight and renewed vigor, Ulfius made out who they were—an army of fey.

Wotan could not poison the land, not really. Mortal minds were only temporarily dazzled by fearsome lies. For moments or hours or days, folk would forget the truth. In time, the old beliefs—those that survived plagues and famines and wars—resurfaced. From antediluvian spaces they arose. With rising belief came ghosts and spirits, faerie folk, eternal champions, gods.

Nyneve swarmed up the rivers of the Badon plains. She took her form from the cold waters. Only head and shoulders lifted above the flood. Hair, mantel, and gown flowed out behind her and merged with the churning tide.

In those coursing waters, more figures moved. Small in bubbles and spray came water sprites and pixies. Beneath them mounded the shoulders of selkies. Among river otters and seals coiled the scales of gigantic serpents. And darker things rose. Kelpies swam in their midst—water horses that lured riders onto their backs only to bear them beneath the waves and drown them. Water ghosts frothed among the tides. Leviathans stirred deep pools in the river's elbows.

Nyneve tasted blood in the water—coppery and mixed with sepsis. It was a taste like the poison of Loki's lies, unmistakable. Men died just ahead. Men and gods both. *"Rise, children of the waters, rise!"*

She led them. In the midst of the deep black flood, Nyneve emerged. Water streamed from her surging figure. It boiled from her brow. It geysered from her angry eyes.

She flung one hand out. A waterspout spawned. It grew as it traveled upstream—the height of a man, then of a tree, then of a column of lightning. It leapt the riverbank and plunged in among Saxon hordes. Mud and steel, bodies and blood churned up through the coiling column. Deprived of the water that had formed and fed it, the spout dissolved and flung warriors away. They fell to their deaths, some crushing comrades beneath them.

Other Saxons boiled alive in their armor, caught in the geysers from Nyneve's eyes. More were yanked from their feet by tentacles and tongues that lashed out of the tides. Giant snakes wrapped Saxons in crushing coils. River ghosts swarmed and smothered them.

Even as water creatures crawled onto land to slay Saxons, welkin spirits descended from the skies. Air elementals plucked up men in wispy claws and flung them like daisies. Will-o'-the-wisps glowed hypnotically, making men drop swords and shields and stumble in blind ecstasy. Air spirits spit razor sleet down on Saxon shoulders. Boreal winds froze men where they stood.

The fantastical creatures of Britannia swept into Aelle's flanks alongside an army far more mundane. Peasant Britons, gathered and rallied in the hundred villages about, charged the invaders. This was no regimented march, but the roaring rush of rabble. They swung pitchforks and shovels and scythes—whatever implements had come to hand. They wore no armor except odd scraps.

Still, they charged, bringing with them a most potent weapon: belief. It was this simple rabble that set naiads in the waterways and specters in the skies, that made brownies rise by Saxon feet and strike their ankles with thistles-turned-maces.

True washerwomen fought with broomsticks, and fey washers-at-the-ford trapped soldiers in grave clothes. Farm dogs tore at armor, and Seelie hounds sank teeth into Saxon legs. Backwood boys flung rocks, and Tuatha archers pinned men with burning shafts. Woodsmen swung axes, and dryads crucified Saxons on sudden trees. The lowest and highest of Britannia swept forward together and fought side by side. The armed and armored host fell before them.

Three more armies joined—the three reserve divisions Arthur had sent to the forests. They had waited for word from Merlin. Word had come, but not from the mad mage. He was dead, and nothing could hold back the angry charge.

Nyneve led them all. She rose from the river and slew without remorse. Her eyes focused on distant Mount Badon, on a scar of ash and soot halfway up the hillside. It might as well have been burned into her own heart. She would march over tens of thousands and not stop until she could fall in tears on Merlin's grave.

"Merlin is dead?" gasped Arthur, straining to sit up in his bed.

Guinevere eased him back among blood-crusted sheets.

"Yes, but you are not," she said gently. Her hand traced across the scarred flesh of his shoulder, knitted patiently back together. "Lie still, now. Your wound is closed, but you have lost much blood."

Arthur looked pale against the pillow. His eyes dragged slowly closed. "I've lost more than blood." He swallowed, stunned. "Grandfather is dead. . . . I can't believe it."

Guinevere leaned gently toward him. "No one can."

"I'm nothing without him," Arthur insisted. He stared at the ceiling. "Without him, without Excalibur and Rhiannon, I am not king."

"Even without those things, you are still king." Guinevere rose and circled the bed. Her lithe manner grew more decisive. "You cannot give up now. Your knights haven't given up. Your people haven't given up. The land itself fights for you. Your mentor, your foster father and brother, your knights and warriors battle forces that outnumber them by tens of thousands. They are driving toward the grave of your grandfather."

The king sat up and swung his feet to the floor. His back straightened. His head lifted. He stood from the blood-soaked bed. His face was horribly white, but he did not swoon. "Where is my armor?"

Mouth agape, Guinevere said, "Your armor is ruined."

"I need only a hauberk and helm," Arthur replied. He dragged a camisia over his head, and a quilted jerkin. "And I'll need a sword and a horse too. Any sword. Any horse. As you said, I am still king."

"You're not going out there," Guinevere said.

Pulling on breeches and puttees and boots, Arthur said, "Yes, I am. My folk have not given up, and neither shall I. And the fight to gain Merlin's grave is a fight I would not miss."

Dagonet and Loki cringed miserably on the floorboard of the chariot.

The Valkyrie were loud. They exulted in their job. Their braided hair streamed in the torrid wind. Their round cheeks bellowed with song. Their temples throbbed beneath cone-shaped helmets and curved horns. With each soul crammed into the enormous conveyance, their shrieks grew more strident. Dagonet wasn't certain whether the souls were dead already, or slain by vibrato.

"Perhaps that's the problem," he had shouted at one point.

"What?" Loki asked, miserably clutching the chariot skirt.

"You Saxons don't have muses, do you?"

"Muses? What are muses?"

Dagonet nodded. "No muses, no music. Only—this?"

It was caterwauling on a grand scale, as though someone were skinning the Sphinx.

The dead souls were repellent company too. They arrived on the vast golden floor of the chariot in whatever state their bodies had ended on the battlefield. There were plenty of beheaded folk there, bleeding their essences on the planks. Others had holes blasted through them, or viscera hanging out, or burns from head to foot. As unpleasant as they were on first arriving, these dead Saxons grew even more obnoxious as they got their bearings. To have died fighting Britons was a letdown. To find oneself then en route to Valhalla, though, was a thrill. One by one, the split-brained and dismembered folk rose to their feet. Those who still had mouths opened them. Those with contiguous throats began to sing. And the sounds they made—spurting spittle and blood and phlegm from punctured lungs—was as horrendous a noise as Dagonet had ever heard. They made the Valkyrie sound good.

"No music . . ."

Infested with the spirit of the moment, the dead Saxons began a grotesque parade around the gargantuan feet of the Valkyrie. The space was too crowded for any kind of movement, especially a parade of creatures that often lacked eyes or balance or continence. Needless to say, the ride from Mount Badon to Asgard was miserable.

At long last, the overladen craft groaned its way skyward. It shoved through a black-bellied cloud. The world became dark and wet for a time. Folk even stopped singing to mutter complaints about the accommodations. They passed through a kind of envelope from the material world to the immaterial. Clouds became dreamscapes. The chariot vaulted into the realm of the gods. Asgard gleamed before them. It was a golden city, unimaginably lofty. And at its center, the vast hall of Valhalla.

"Jump the first chance you get," Loki growled.

"You first," Dagonet replied, and gave the god a shove.

As luck—and Loki—would have it, they tumbled down directly above the great hall of Valhalla. End over end, Dagonet got a kaleidoscopic view of the place.

Wotan's hall was as large as all Camelot. The steeply pitched roof glowed golden. Mammoth beams jutted from gabled edges. Spires rose all around the central hall. They were impossibly tall, too slender to be built by mortal hands or of mortal stone. They seemed to tickle the stars. Around the hall, smaller buildings clustered. The city of gods spread to a distant curtain wall. Beyond, clouds roiled, and the bridge Bifrost descended to the realm of mortals.

That was all Dagonet had time to see. He struck the rooftop of Valhalla and slid precipitously down one side. The descent was steep enough that his pantaloons heated up, on the verge of bursting into flame. Mercifully, he caught his foot on an edge of tile and began tumbling instead of sliding. This provided a cooler, if bumpier, descent. Sometime during his head-over-heels journey, Dagonet dimly noticed that Loki drifted along placidly beside him. It occurred to Dagonet that the god could smooth his passage as well. He was about to request it when a hunk of cornice struck his head and removed the thought.

At last, he reached a grand fan gable at the roof's edge— and shot out beyond. Below him opened empty space, a drop of an easy thousand feet. The drop would be easy, the impact hard.

A slender and cold hand clamped onto the fool's ankle, stopping his descent. It was a jolting rescue, the sort a mackerel experienced at the end of a hook. Jangled and jerked, Dagonet hung upside by one ankle and stared at the yawning chasm below.

"Thank you, gracious master, for saving me," he managed to say. "You may pull me back anytime."

"First," Loki replied from the safety of the rooftop, "I have a task for you."

Dagonet's face grew red and puffy. "A task?"

"You hang now just before Wotan's private chambers. I would like you to gaze through the windows and tell me what you see."

"You can fly, Master," Dagonet reminded him reasonably. "Why not look yourself?"

"Because if Wotan notices anyone here, he will surely lash out with lightning. Lightning is unpleasant. The job is yours."

Dagonet drew a deep breath. He gazed into the private apartments of Wotan.

The place was opulent, but with a Saxon sense of opulence. Everything was hugely proportioned and ponderous. The friezes were carved deeply enough into the marble walls that men could hide in the clefts. The drapery cloths were as thick as a stout man's torso, and pooled on the floor in rumpled hills. The furnishings must have taken whole forests to produce.

"Wotan can be whatever size he wants," Dagonet observed. "Why so big?"

"It's better to be big. Everybody says so. Now, what do you see? Is Wotan in there?"

It was only then that Dagonet recognized the mountainous figure at the table. He sat so still and his features were so gray, he seemed stone. "Yes."

"What is he doing?"

"Nothing."

"Wotan *never* does *nothing.*"

"He has something in his hand. Something shiny. He is staring at it. It's the only small thing in the room."

Loki's voice was like steam hissing from a kettle. "Excalibur . . ."

"It's like a thorn in his hand," Dagonet said. "He holds it gingerly. He stares at it as if he is terrified."

"He's been obsessed with that sword since Merlin first brought it here," Loki said. "He has wanted it and feared it in equal measure. He knows it has the power to kill him."

Dagonet stroked his beard thoughtfully. "It has the power, yes. Now it only needs the inclination. . . ."

"Inclination?" asked Loki.

"A little curse would go a long way," Dagonet replied. "Something about Excalibur cutting any immortal hand that strives to hold it."

"You are a twisted little man," Loki said with approval.

An acrid wisp of magic flowed out of the god's fingers, across Dagonet's form, and through the bank of windows. In moments, it sank into the sword. Only a breath later, a crimson line appeared on Wotan's palm.

"He's moving now," Dagonet narrated. "He's shaking the sword off his hand. He's jumping back from the table. His hand is bleeding. He's staring at his palm in stunned shock, and now at Excalibur, imbedded in the tabletop."

Loki could little contained his glee.

A thought from Wotan closed the cut. He crept in, as cautious as a cat, and plucked up the sword. He yelped—actually yelped. For a moment the sword stood, shuddering, in the center of Wotan's palm. He clutched it in his other hand and pulled it out, only to have the treacherous blade slice his thumb. Excalibur dropped again to the tabletop, and Wotan backed away. Sniffing, rubbing his beard, the great god of the Saxons stalked forward, only to give a yip and shake bloodied fingers.

In his mirth, Loki almost dropped his narrator.

"How long do you think I'll have to hang here?" Dagonet asked.

"However long he keeps it up," Loki answered.

"How long do you think that will be?"

"Just about an eternity."

And Wotan danced back from the blade again, cursing.

Ulfius's heart was failing in his breast. For nigh upon an hour, he had fought in this one well of blood and death. The mound of Saxon bodies before him only grew. It was a barrier near impassable between him and the grave of Merlin. In that time, armies of fey and rabble and reserves had eaten their way through two miles of Aelle's forces, only to stall at the base of the sídh. It seemed neither side could break through.

Saxons still outnumbered Britons two to one.

"We will never . . . finish this fight," Ulfius roared as he clove a Saxon head. "We will never . . . break through to Merlin's grave!"

"We will!" came a voice at his shoulder.

A mounted warrior charged into the fray. He had only a visor and helm, a rusty hauberk, a common spatha, and a shouldering plow horse. But this man fought.

In one breath, he rode down three Saxons and slew four more. His horse, sure-footed in muddy grass, strode bravely over the fallen. Men turned into crimson fountains before him. He advanced.

There was space behind that beast. Ulfius fought into it.

Ector and Kay, bloodied and battered, followed the common hero too. Their swords felled Saxons en masse. Brastias, Lucas, and Gryfflet joined the charge. They fought as once they had of old, when Arthur and Merlin lived. In moments, they crossed ground they had stared at hopelessly for hours. The man on the plow horse fought like ten men, and the knights followed.

A knot of Saxons fortified the ground where Merlin had fallen, surrounding it with a wall of pikes.

Undaunted, the horseman stood aback his mount and drove toward the bristling line. He rode the horse right into the teeth of the pikes. Yanking the steed to a halt, the man vaulted. He landed in the ashy midst of the pikemen. His sword flashed, cutting them down from behind.

Ulfius slashed a pike in half. Ector turned another on its wielder. Kay broke through to fight beside the common warrior. The knights flooded inward. Swords sang in the failing light.

The Saxons fell back. Another contingent of Britons arrived from below. The fey army led by Nyneve at last broke through. As bloodied and torn as the Knights of the Round, they had made their gory way up the mountainside. Now, wolves and peasants, green men and woodsmen pushed the Saxons back along the line of attack.

Nyneve strode to the mound of ash they had fought so hard to reach. She fell to her knees. Tears crept down her face.

Beside her, the common man also knelt. He pulled the helm from his head. The golden hair of Arthur spilled forth, wet with tears.

54

Regrets Mortal and Immortal

The common man who had rallied them was the same man who'd rallied them from the beginning. The common man was the king.

In the midst of that doomed throng, Arthur bowed his knees in Merlin's ashes. Grandfather, mentor, court mage, friend. . . . Since Arthur had ascended the throne, they had been brothers, one becoming a king among men, the other a king among gods. They had fought side by side to build a city and a nation, had put away childish fancies and dreamed the dreams of grown-up men. They had found loves and pursued them. They had discovered not only who they wanted to be, but who they were destined to be.

"Destined to be . . ." Arthur said bitterly. He reached down a bloodied hand—he had not even donned a gauntlet when he joined the fray—and clutched sifting ash. Gray powder rode the air. "Destined to rise so far, only to be destroyed?"

Arthur lifted his eyes. Here, clustered about him in hesitant groups, were the loyal heart of Britannia. Knights of the Table Round, warriors on horse and on foot, dryads clad in vine and thistle, naiads in their watery gowns, Tuatha whose native slenderness and angled features and dazzling beauty made them almost unseeable, brownies and pixies lingering like dandelion down, dwarves whose dun and gray shoulders made them seem merely crouching stones, the eternal champions of legend with their lightning arrows and thundering hammers, the coiling serpents and loping wolves of the Otherworld . . . For every fantastical warrior at Merlin's grave, there were a hundred common Britons—villeins and serfs and slaves, peasant farmers and yeomen and tinkers. Arthur loved them all, this nation of mixed mettle and disparate soul.

Beyond bowed shoulders, others fought the demonic hordes of Sussex. This charge to Merlin's grave had been costly. Every warrior had joined the push, even Guinevere and her healers. The shattered castle above had been taken by the Saxons. Nyneve's armies had carved a path into the endless sea of warriors only to have that same sea sweep in and close off their retreat.

The folk of Britannia—commoners, warriors, knights, and fey—were surrounded on all sides. How could they fight any longer? What was there to fight for? Their only fortification now was this pile of ash, which they had sacrificed all to attain.

"We believed more in him than in any castle," Arthur said blearily. He shook his head and stared once again at the gray dust. "I can't believe he is gone."

A hand settled on Arthur's shoulder. He looked up to see Nyneve, dusty and tattered, so far from the water that empowered her. She gazed deeply into his eyes, her own as wide and brown as sacred pools of peat.

"None of us can, Arthur. None of us can."

Loki had given up trying not to giggle. Wotan was in a miserable state.

"He's fallen on the sword again," Dagonet narrated where he hung. "The sword has a real talent for landing point up. Ow! Excalibur went through Wotan's eye." The fool stopped to stare reprovingly at Loki.

The god was lolling on the rooftop, horse laugher braying from his lips. With each spasm, his hold on Dagonet's ankle weakened.

"If you drop me, you'll get no more commentary."

"What's he . . . what's he doing now?"

Dagonet sighed irritably. "The sword's fallen down his robes. He is doubling over, clutching himself—"

Loki pounded on a tile cornice. He couldn't stand it.

Wotan had gone mad. He had tried every means to guard himself from Excalibur but had ended up with the blade in each eye multiple times, across the throat twice, once down the windpipe, rammed beneath fingernails, skewering veins . . . and now this. Wotan had conjured gloves and gauntlets, enlarged himself so he might not be so vulnerable, shrunk himself so he might better grab hold of the thing, tried to shut it way in boxes or cabinets only to be consumed with desire to hold it again, tried to cast it away but found he couldn't. The torment had gone on for endless hours. All the while, Loki had hung Dagonet there, narrating.

But now, in gales of laughter, the god of chaos lost hold.

Dagonet fell. After so many hours of hanging upside down by one ankle, it was a bit of a relief. He tumbled head over heels. The blood that had pooled in lips and eyelids poured down his neck, through his stumpy frame, and to the much-denied ankle. The stirring air felt good. And it was nice to see the world right side up again . . . momentarily.

Dagonet caught hold of something—an oversized curl of window filigree. His sudden hold flipped him violently over and flung him toward the glass. Dagonet shot like a little rock through the window of Wotan. Shards whirled and tinkled all around him.

"That was close," Dagonet told himself placidly, only then seeing the flagstone floor ten stories down.

It seemed a good time to scream.

A large, sweaty, and much-scarred hand snatched Dagonet from the air. Fingers trembled feverishly as they closed on him. He was enfolded in darkness.

Was it better to spatter on the floor or be caught by a mad god?

Somewhat incautiously, Dagonet began to compose a limerick on the theme.

The fist opened. Light broke across Dagonet. Above him loomed a huge face with twitching eyes and flared nostrils. The god's ancient skin was blotchy, some spots suffused with angry blood and others white with rage. Eyebrows and beard stood in fury from his face.

Dagonet sat up on the god's open palm and gazed into that glaring visage. "And I thought *Merlin* was shaggy."

Lips like giant eels slid wetly across each other. They parted to admit brimstone breath. "Who are you?" The words pounded like meat cudgels.

Recognizing a divine summons, Dagonet stood, bowed deeply, and said, "I am King Arthur."

A scowl shuddered across that livid face. "You aren't King Arthur."

"Would you believe, Merlin the Mad?"

Wotan's fingers closed in a cage that threatened to crush him.

"In fact," Dagonet said hurriedly, "I am but the fool of Arthur and Merlin. I am, truth be told, the foolishness of the royal mage. I am his lunatic dreams, given human—well, *dwarven* form."

Wotan's fingers stopped short of killing the little man. "Why are you here?"

Dagonet pretended to stretch and yawn. He peered over his shoulder, hoping for salvation from Loki. The god of caprice glared unhelpfully through the window.

"I'm here to make sure the plan worked," Dagonet improvised.

"What plan?" Wotan asked suspiciously.

"You know," stalled Dagonet, "the *plaaaaan*—"

"I knew it!" Wotan shrieked, lifting the dwarf in a tremulous grip as though preparing to slam him to the ground. "The sword is cursed!"

"The sword? Cursed?" shrieked Dagonet as he clung on.

"Don't deny it! Merlin cursed Excalibur! He cursed it so that it would slay me!"

"Oh, *that* sword," Dagonet said, seeing a way out. "Yes, yes, Merlin cursed it. He cursed it to slay you. And, I must say, the plan is progressing well. You have less than an hour left."

"What?"

Offhandedly, Dagonet shrugged, "You'll be completely mad within the hour. Then you won't be able to heal yourself of the sword's cuts. You'll be dead by dawn. See? It's a two-prong approach." He held up two fingers in a sign that was very clearly understood among Britons. "Two. Prong."

Wotan's face went white. The hand that held his captive slumped away. He started to mutter. "I knew it. That canny bastard. He killed his own father—killed Saturn. He drove the Titans from Olympia. He's a god-killer. That's what. A god-killer!"

"*Was* a god-killer—"

"What?"

Dagonet stuck his head out between the god's fingers. "*Was* a god-killer. You blasted him? Remember?"

Remembrance moved like a cool breeze across Wotan's face. "Yes. I *did* kill him. Three times. And in front of his own folk." He smiled, his teeth a savage picket. "Yes, I killed him."

"Too bad the curse didn't die with him," Dagonet said, "not one of the provisions."

Wotan lifted the dwarf again into view. "Provisions?"

Dagonet nodded. "Of course. Every curse has provisions, limitations. It's part of the wording."

"And you know this wording?" Wotan purred. Threat twisted his features. "Tell me what it is."

"Oh, I couldn't," Dagonet said, feigning fear. "Merlin would kill me."

"Merlin is dead already."

"It's just a bunch of magical muttering—"

"Tell me!" Wotan roared.

Dagonet fell backward and did not need to feign terror. "Well, now. Let me see. I must get it just right. Ah . . . well. Let's see . . . Yes, now I remember. Merlin said, 'By the power of Olympus and Avalon and Sinai and Golgotha, allied now and forever in Britannia, I place this unbreakable and infinite curse upon Excalibur, that this sword will drive mad the high god of Saxons and slay him and do so by cleaving to him, that when it enters his grip it shall never leave it until he is slain, and can be removed only if borne back to Britannia by the Mage Merlin or . . . or his—' " Dagonet stammered to a halt and managed to blanch.

"What is it? Finish it!" Wotan said.

"Ahem," Dagonet demurred. "I got lost. I meant to say, 'borne back to Britannia by the Mage Merlin, period.' Ha ha. Kind of ironic that the one man who could have saved you is the one you killed. Ha ha. Kind of ironic."

"You said, 'or.' You said 'by the Mage Merlin or his—' or his what?"

Dagonet visibly swallowed. " 'Or his . . . or his assistant.' "

"Who would be?"

"Who would be me," Dagonet said in surrender.

"You? *You* are his assistant?" Wotan grinned rapaciously. "You could take the sword back to Britannia? You could save me?"

"Listen. I don't want to go back to Britannia," Dagonet said pleadingly. "I've been declared a traitor. There is a price on my head. Men and gods both seek to kill me. And not just kill me. They will torture me. They will keep my soul forever in torment for what I have done."

"What have you done?" Wotan asked.

"I allied with Loki," said Dagonet in pretended shame. "I helped him soften up the land, preparing it for your invasion."

"You allied with Loki?" Wotan said, harsh merriment coming to his mad eyes. "What sort of fool would—?"

"The sort of fool who could save your life," came a serene voice from above. Down drifted Loki, his brow arched sardonically. "*Could,* but need not, I remind you." Loki alighted beside Dagonet on Wotan's palm. "Now, shall we discuss terms of our agreement?"

Wotan's eyes flared. His fingers clenched. "Terms? I'll kill you both if you refuse!"

"And then Excalibur will kill you," Loki said, polishing his nails on his coat. "And after you are dead, there will be another high god of Saxons, who will be killed by the sword, and another. This one sword will destroy you and your people and Jove will be victorious at the last . . . unless you are willing to make a bargain."

Wotan shook his head, despairing. "Make a deal with Loki? I must be mad." He sighed gustily. "All right, then, what do you want?"

Loki cracked his fingers, relishing the moment. "First, we'll need a Valkyrie chariot."

"What?"

"We need a vehicle for carrying all the Rhine gold you will grant us," Loki explained, affectionately squeezing Dagonet's shoulders. "And jewels and weaponry—"

"And a promise," Dagonet interjected. "No more killing us."

"That's right," Loki agreed. "I'm tired of being killed by you, Wotan. You will swear never again to kill me or my protégé."

Lifting his head imploringly toward the mad heavens, Wotan said, "Anything! Just take the sword." He pulled his robe aside, revealing where it was imbedded. "I never want to see the damned thing again!"

55

Madness Maddened

The miracle did not begin among knights or naiads, nor even among Britons. It began among Saxon warriors as they hacked at the circle of defenders.

"What are they doing?" shouted a grizzled Saxon over the clang of swords. Only a thin line of Britons faced outward and fought. The rest had their backs turned. "What are they looking at?"

"Merlin," another answered as he stabbed a Briton.

"They're raising him from the dead," someone yelled.

"Grave magic!" the first man shouted in fear.

"Merlin is alive?"

"I knew we couldn't kill him."

"When he rises, we all will be doomed!"

"It was a trap!" the first said. "They drew us up this hill to slay us. Why else would they abandon the castle?"

"Merlin has drawn us here to kill us!"

"Merlin is alive!"

"He *is* alive!" shouted one young Briton in the tongue of his foes. He triumphantly repeated the message to his comrades "Merlin lives!" He drove forward with his sword and skewered the Saxon that fought him. "For Merlin! He lives!"

The cry went down the line. "For Merlin! He lives!" New strength came to flagging arms, new hope to failing hearts. With that shout, the Britons pushed back their fearful foes. "Merlin lives!"

Peasants strained inward to see the mage's return. They stood on tiptoe and pressed on one anothers' backs. They craned their necks and jostled forward. Every last one spoke in hopeful joy.

"He's alive. He lives!"

"I knew he couldn't be dead."

"I never believed he was gone!"

"Merlin lives! Merlin lives!" The crowd compacted. Separate men and women became a solid circle of muscle and bone. They pushed with a single thought toward the unseeable center. Their belief fused as well. It became a solid thing, palpable in the air. Countless voices chanted together, "Merlin lives! Merlin lives! Merlin lives!"

At the heart of the constricting crowd, Arthur and Nyneve had to brace each other to keep from being pushed over.

Arthur shook his head bitterly. "What madness!" A shove at his back sent his hand into the ashes. "*This* is Merlin!"

A beatific look was dawning on Nyneve's face. "No, Arthur. Not even his body was Merlin." She pushed back against the pressing throng. "It was only a convenience, a locus for his being, a vessel that held a fallen god."

"What does it matter?" Arthur growled in the crush. "He's dead. He's gone."

"No," Nyneve said. "A god dies only when he dies in the dreams of the people. But Merlin lives in their dreams. He lives as much as Jupiter ever lived. Don't you see? They are dreaming him. Briton and Saxon, naiad and saint, they are dreaming him. And it takes but dreams to make a god."

Arthur fell to his elbows. The ashes of his grandfather spread whitely over his face and arms. "Get off me!" he shouted. "Get off me!"

"Believe, Arthur," Nyneve cried out. "That's what he is waiting for. He wants you to believe. Your belief brought him out of madness. Your belief can bring him out of death."

The king lifted an ashy face. He closed his eyes.

Suddenly, he was a child again. Grandfather Merlin played hide and seek. He hid, invisible in the very air.

"Come out, Grandfather. I know you are there."

Arthur reached out his hands. He touched the knee-pieces of a warrior, the hem of a dryad gown, the homespun leggings of a villein, the tatter-edged travel cloak of an old fool. . . .

Arthur opened his eyes. The garment slipped away. Mad hope leaped through him. Merlin was not there—and yet he was. Arthur raked hands through the air. Fingers caught on invisible cloth. He grasped that frayed nothingness and held on with all his might.

"Come out, Grandfather. I know you are there!"

And he was.

There, in the midst of the crushing throng, Merlin stood. He wore his old travel cloak, tattered and gray. His eyes shone with capricious light. Every rumple had returned to his forehead, every tuft to his eyebrows and beard.

He was there, of a certainty, and Arthur clutched the edge of his cloak.

"There you are!" Arthur said. He rose, flinging back the crowd and embracing the old mage.

Yes, it was Merlin in the flesh—though more than the flesh. He had not been rebuilt from ashes. Even now, they pasted

Arthur's cheeks. Merlin had been rebuilt from the dreams and hopes of the people. He lived in the mind of Briton and Saxon, slave and king. He lived in truth. He was no longer mad Merlin. He was immortal Merlin. It shone in his eyes, which glinted with power. It shone in his flesh, radiant from motes of pure magic coursing within. It shone in his placid smile.

"You found me, Arthur. Good boy," Merlin said gently.

His embrace washed blood and dirt from the king. Arthur's common clothes transformed into the plate-mail raiment of the Pendragon.

Merlin opened his arms, not releasing Arthur, but bringing Nyneve into his embrace. She wrapped him in equally strong arms and clung, weeping happily.

She stroked his cheek. "Ash was not your best aspect, darling. This is much better."

He touched her face.

The grime and gore that had been there a moment before was gone. Nyneve's skin shone iridescent, like the shell of a nautilus. Her torn gown became robes of divine state. She seemed suddenly a queen among gods.

"No one is looking at my aspect, dear," Merlin said. "I owe you a dance in our Cave of Delights. But first, Britannia has need of us."

"Yes." She grinned and kissed him. Then, stomping a foot on the ground, she awoke a tiny spring there. "I will revive the powers of earth and water."

"And I, of sky and fire," Merlin said.

Arthur added, "And I will marshal the folk of field and forest, plain and mountain."

"We'll meet again in Camelot when all this is done," Merlin said. He embraced them once last, and gave Nyneve a parting kiss.

She set her toe to the bubbling spring and slid away within it.

Merlin rose into the skies. A staff sprouted from his hands. He grew and transfigured. Fiery light emerged from his staff and swept around his cloak. Flames transformed them from gray tatters to golden robes. Twin beams of cerulean blue lanced out from his eyes and swept a wide arc around the army of Britons. Saxons retreated in terror.

Merlin spoke. His voice rolled like a massive waterfall.

"Rise, Britons! Drive back the folk of Wotan. Their god is caged in madness. Your gods live and fight for you. Rise!"

Thousands of fists rose in the air, some clutching swords, some clutching flails, some clutching nothing but bare belief. With them rose a deafening cheer that drowned out even the voice of Merlin.

Arthur, in the midst of that throng, brandished his common sword and shouted above them all, "Follow me and fight!"

The crowd that had turned in on itself turned outward now.

"Ector, Kay, Ulfius, to me!" Arthur roared as he strode out among the shouldering folk. His knights formed up around him. "We will take back the castle!"

They roared their happy approval. In moments, the Knights of the Table Round reached the retreating Saxons. Shoulder to shoulder with common footmen, the knights laid in with gleaming swords. They cut a wedge in the enemy lines and pressed onward.

The last few brave-hearted Saxons could not stand before that onslaught of steel. Retreat turned to rout. The Saxon rearguard staggered backward up the hill. They stumbled over fallen Britons. Coney holes stole their feet. Saxons went down, and knightly blades pinned them there. They did not rise again. Behind them, comrades turned their backs and ran toward the shattered castle. It would provide little protection, but Aelle and his retinue were there. If any Saxons survived on Mount Badon, they would survive in the castle.

Arthur, his knights, and an army of common soldiers drove them upward. Grim smiles had replaced grim frowns. The surety of success even brought banter among them.

"Father," Kay shouted as he slashed a red-bearded Saxon, "I've run out of brave soldiers. Have you any extras over there?"

"Not a one," Ector bellowed back. His voice boomed so powerfully it sent three men scurrying away before him. "Perhaps they could lend us a few from below."

Arthur felled another foe and glanced over his shoulder to see how the battle went there. He laughed.

Slings whirled above the heads of farm boys. They hurled stones that cut like lightning into the fleeing invaders. Those Saxons who didn't flee were confronted by scythe-wielding villeins, who harvested unusual heads of grain. Threshing flails, shovels, pitch forks, hoes—all fell with the power of cudgels. Shepherds used crooks to round up a most beat-upon flock.

"Not a brave Saxon for leagues!" Arthur shouted, pressing the advance.

The common folk would have been enough to fight the battles below, but they had uncommon help.

Queen Guinevere led the fey army. Their glory had returned. The very grass beneath their feet drank the blood and swallowed the offal spilled there. The mound came to life. Swarms of pixies left dew trails across the ground, and wildflowers bloomed behind them. Dryads healed shattered stalks. Tuatha ghosts whirled about Queen Guinevere, their rage turned to rejoicing. Some of the spirits delved back into the mound to retrieve other fey. Every moment, more arrived. Stone men and green men, hobs and sith hounds, bogeys and bugaboos, bluecaps and black dogs, oakmen and Fir Bholgs and Tuatha. They entered the world from the Otherworld and felt again the bathing sun. While men fought and died, they danced. In twining, coiling circles, they danced.

The most fearsome dancers took shape at the base of the mound. From rock shards and sand, stone giants came again into being. Rocks bounded back together. Their lines of fissure fused. Nyneve's power propelled the fragments up from the ground to reunite. Life infused the tottering figures. Even as they solidified, the giants lifted their heads and looked about.

Saxons flooded in terror from their ring.

Stone arms swung menacingly at them as they went. Those same arms then swept into the dance. Feet of granite pounded an earth-shaking rhythm.

Merlin shook the heavens.

He flung out his hand. From his fingertips lanced red beams of light. Where each struck ground, a shaft opened deep into the sídh. No sooner had the shafts appeared than creature emerged from them. Great leathery wings, massive mantles of fiery hair, eyes huge and catlike in their horned skulls, claws the height of men, barbed and lashing tails . . . ancient Calbhiorus of Badon Hill emerged, and with him his four grandchildren.

Five dragons surged into the sky and circled around their liberator.

"Behold, Saxons!" Merlin called in their throaty tongue. "The five dragons of Arthur! Know that the Pendragon rules Britannia!"

And with that, the dragons spiraled down to harry the fleeing hordes.

Loki couldn't resist wearing the whole Valkyrie getup as he stood, gigantic, at the prow of the great chariot. He also insisted on singing in parody of the awful talents of the war virgins.

Dagonet did not join in—he knew it was impossible to parody something that was absurd already.

The mortal fool sat diminutively on the forward rail of the chariot. With one hand, he clutched a rein-bracket to keep from falling. With the other, he clutched Excalibur, intussuscepted in Rhiannon. Even though the floor of the chariot was loaded with Rhine gold, the beauty of scabbard and sword dimmed the rest. Gold and treasure and holy weapons provided the only light. All around, rolling thunderheads filled the world.

Dagonet felt utterly out of place. He had spent his life

looking at the world from three feet up. Now, the tiny, mortal Briton rode in a Saxon god's chariot, literal leagues above the ground.

Without warning, the clouds shredded away. Empty space yawned wide. Moonlight broke across the golden chariot. There, below, the night-black hills of Britannia spread to the horizons.

"Well," cackled Loki, interrupting his latest ditty, "there it is! Britannia! It is time, Dagonet, fling away the sword!"

Dagonet's eyes dropped wide. "Fling it away?"

"That was our bargain. Take it back to Britannia. If we don't, we forfeit the gold."

"Yes," Dagonet agreed, standing on the rail, "but what a waste—"

"We cannot keep it *and* the gold."

"Of course not. But I thought you were the god of bad deals."

Loki's eyes flared beneath bristling black brows. "I am!"

"Then let's make the deal bad. Let's fulfill our agreement and make Wotan pay."

"Say on, protégé!"

"Let's give the sword to Arthur."

"What?" Loki scowled. "Are you turning loyal on me?"

"Of course not," Dagonet said. "Now, think, Loki! What would terrify Wotan more than knowing the sword is in possession of the king of Britons?"

"Only if Merlin were given the blade would he be more upset."

"Exactly. Since Merlin is dead, Arthur's the next best choice. And if Arthur has his sword, the Knights of the Round Table will rule supreme."

"Why would I care—"

"Aren't you one of the Knights of the Round Table? Don't you sit a Perilous Siege?"

A wicked smile broke out across Loki's face, like a crack spreading along an eggshell. He extended a clawed hand beside Dagonet. "Hand the sword and scabbard to me."

Distrust filled Dagonet's features. "Why?"

"You're a clever fellow, Dagonet," Loki said.

"I'm not trying to fool you, Loki. A fool cannot fool a fool."

Loki snapped his fingers, and the tooth-clenched smile turned into a snarl. "Give it. You needn't worry. I see your true loyalties, Dagonet. But as long as you can serve Arthur while simultaneously winning me Rhine gold and giving me power in Britannia and allowing me to torment Wotan, I will not protest. Besides, a god of my stature ought to have a protégé."

Dagonet bowed shallowly, expecting any moment for his head to be plucked like a grape. "Thank you, Loki."

"Now, give me the sword and scabbard, and I will make certain Arthur wields them once more."

Dagonet reluctantly released the sheathed blade.

Loki nodded. He took the holy sword, no more than a butter knife in his hands, lifted it overhead, and flung it, end over end, across Britannia and into the vast distance.

Dagonet stared blankly after the retreating blade until it was lost to sight. "You will make sure Arthur wields it once more?"

Shark's teeth crowded in the god's mouth. "You'll have to trust me."

56

An End to Aelle

While the main body of the Saxon army retreated before farm boys and faerie folk, Aelle and his personal guard of one hundred warriors held fast in the shattered castle.

Arthur had led his thirty remaining knights in a charge up the hill. Some fifty British warriors backed them. Ten men had fallen to arrow fire in that climb, including two knights.

Once Arthur's forces had scrambled over the ruins of the curtain wall, though, the fight had changed.

In the deep gloom of twilight, Arthur's men rose like minions of the black earth. Their spathas sparked on Saxon helms. Their epaulets rammed through locked doors. Their gauntlets hurled invaders down long stairways. Room to room, Arthur's men progressed. They killed twenty-three Saxons in the initial fighting. Once the dungeons were secure, they captured seventy-some others, stripped them of arms and armor, and conveyed them below. Arthur's forces cleansed the castle, lighting a taper in each room as it was secured.

Only the highest tower remained, the northern tower—damaged and decrepit after Wotan's attack. The thing was a leaning deathtrap. Its roof was shattered wide open, and its top three floors tilted precariously, sixty feet above the ground. Were it not for the tangle of timbers inside, the whole thing would have come down. Ulfius and Brastias reasonably ordered that the area be closed off and a guard posted.

Arthur volunteered to be that guard. "These men have fought long and well for me, and I would honor them in this way," he said.

It was a slim lie, and would not have fooled Ulfius or Brastias except that they were drunk with victory.

Arthur alone remained sober-eyed. Victory was not yet his. He had personally checked every prisoner and corpse in the castle and noted the conspicuous absence of one man. Aelle of Sussex. The Saxon King had deprived him of Excalibur and Rhiannon, tried to deprive him of nation and life. This tower was the last place where Aelle of Sussex could be hiding.

No sooner had Ulfius and Brastias departed than Arthur drew his sword and ascended the dark tower. He climbed slowly. The wooden stairs were canted and held many blind corners. Each footfall creaked ominously. His ascent would be no secret.

In Saxon, he called up the stairs, "Surrender to me, Aelle, or I shall surely kill you."

No answer came—no answer except the telltale complaint of planks overhead.

Arthur climbed.

Halfway up the ravaged tower, a set of stairs had fallen away. It would be a precarious leap to the landing above, but Aelle had made that leap. Nothing would be as precarious as letting him live.

Arthur tossed his sword onto the landing. Gathering his strength, he vaulted across the empty space. He clutched the planks. His torso draped atop the landing but his legs hung in oblivion.

Looming up huge on the shadowy stair, Aelle lunged. Steel gleamed.

Arthur twisted aside, hauling his legs up. The stabbing sword struck wood and stuck. Arthur scrambled to his feet, snatched up his own blade, and spun.

Aelle freed his sword and swung. Metal skirled on metal. The impact was a hammer blow. Arthur growled and clutched a splintered support. He pivoted his blade around his foe's. The tip skidded obliquely across armor plate and into a seam of cloth. It sank through iron-hard muscle.

Aelle staggered aside and crashed in the corner of the landing. His impact cracked loose the wall anchors. Planks slumped beneath both men.

Arthur flung himself up the stairs.

Aelle lunged after. His massive weight hurled the landing away. Even so, he grappled the lowest of the next stairs and swung upward. With the speed and dexterity of a man half his size, Aelle clambered to his feet. He led with his sword, a bull in the charge, and drove upward. Wood creaked and shuddered, slowly slipping. Aelle worked his way forward with impatient jabs.

"When last we fought," he hissed through raking breaths, "I took Excalibur from you. . . . Now I will take your life."

Arthur countered the strokes with confident parries. He let Aelle weary himself. "In our last battle, you had my scabbard. Now, you do not. Now you can be cut. Now you can be killed." As though to demonstrate, Arthur stabbed past Aelle's guard. His sword slid between breastplate and skirt of tasses.

The Saxon roared and pulled free of the blade. "You are not a king. Not without Excalibur. You are nothing more than Merlin's puppet." He followed this comment with a new barrage of sword strokes.

Meeting each attack, Arthur retreated steadily upward. "You have lost, Aelle. I am king. Surrender to me."

Looking beyond Arthur in the dim space, Aelle grinned. "It is you who will die. You have nowhere left to climb!" The stairway above was a wrecked tangle of wood. Bulling forward, Aelle drove Arthur up beneath the wreck.

Agile as a spider, Arthur took to the beams. Even clinging there, he won past the Saxon's sword and jabbed him in shoulder and side.

Each blow further enraged the man. His blade fell heavily, missing Arthur but chunking bits of wood from the ruined stairs. Those notches became handholds for him. He hauled himself up, relentless.

Arthur climbed still higher. He was just below the top of the tower, moonlight slanting down through a hatchway. "Your army is routed, your gods have stolen your loot, your personal guard is captured. You have lost everything. Must you lose your life as well?"

In response, Aelle lunged. Suddenly, the whole mass of splintered wood broke free.

Arthur turned and leaped upward. He dropped his sword to catch hold of the hatchway and yank himself up through it.

Joists and braces ripped loose. The wrecked stairs collapsed. In a final surge of will, Aelle launched himself up the cascading timbers and caught the edge of the hatch with one hand. He dangled. Below him, with an horrific groan, the wooden mass plunged down the center of the tower.

Arthur stared into the thundering abyss, into the eyes of his foe. "Surrender to me, and I will pull you up."

Hissing his disdain, Aelle sheathed his sword and caught a second handhold on the hatchway. He heaved himself up onto the tilted top of the tower, knee cops denting the wood beneath.

Arthur backed away. He reached for his sword and remembered dropping it. Moonlight showed only rock rubble on the floor around him. The platform was ringed by shattered walls and roofed only by starry sky.

Into that starry sky rose a huge figure. Aelle seemed a minotaur. His lungs heaved as he slowly advanced. His blade hissed forth. "You've lost yet another sword," he growled. "Now, you surrender to me."

Arthur said simply, "I will never surrender to you."

"Then, you leave me no choice." Aelle lifted his sword into the starry sky.

Arthur raised his hand to ward back the blow.

Then, faster than the sword of Aelle, one of those stars streaked down. It leaped, impossibly quick, into Arthur's grasp.

The Saxon's sword struck not the king of Britannia, but the bejeweled scabbard Rhiannon.

Astonished, Arthur flung Aelle's blade away and drew Excalibur. With a shout, he lunged.

The huge man could not bring his sword to bear.

Excalibur rammed through plate and chain and meat and bone. . . . It sought the vast, hot muscle in that giant's breast and found it and split it. Excalibur skewered the heart of the invader king.

Aelle stood, stunned. His blade dangled in a trembling hand. Excalibur emerged, trailing blood. Aelle fell to his knees, and then slumped onto his face. He struggled to hiss something, but the air emerged through a dead throat.

Arthur staggered back. It had all happened so quickly. This sword, which felt so natural in his hand, this scabbard— where had they come from? They had appeared like a comet from the heavens.

Lifting his eyes toward the starry skies, Arthur saw Jupiter beaming down brightly. He smiled.

"Thank you, Grandfather. Thank you, Merlin."

•   •   •

Afternoon wore on toward evening before the barrel-laden wagon reached the Six Chimneys Inn. Horses stomped to a halt on the cobbles. The brewer leaped from the buckboard and began unlashing ropes. Most of his ilk had ample bellies and dirty tunics, but this brewer was whip-thin in his black waistcoat. His assistant was stranger, yet—a manic dwarf in yeoman's clothes. Still, they had come highly recommended.

Master Loki's ales and bitters were being drunk from London to Caerleon.

Together the two positioned a gangplank, climbed to the top of the wagon, and wrapped lines around the first barrel. With practiced efficiency, they conveyed three batches of ale to the cobbles. The dwarf held open the stout red door of the tavern as Master Loki rolled the first barrel through.

Beyond lay a lantern-lit taproom crowded with travelers and freeman farmers. Though food and drink filled the tables before them, no one ate or drank. All listened intently to the dark-haired soldier seated at the bar.

"I'm telling you, it's the most amazing thing I ever saw. Five dragons. They came out of the very mound. Right in front of me—" The speaker was a scar-faced soldier, one of many veterans of Badon who traveled town to town, recounting his exploits in exchange for drink and board. This fellow had gathered quite an audience and a number of dirty plates. "Merlin drew them up from the ground. From the faerie mound! And this just after the stone giants!"

"Why aren't there any dragons now?" Master Loki asked as he rolled the barrel across the rushes. A paunchy barkeep met him and helped guide the barrel to its spot behind the bar. "Why aren't there any stone giants?"

"Why aren't there—" the man echoed, caught up short. "How do you know there aren't?"

Master Loki shrugged as he levered the barrel onto its stand. "I delivered ale there three days ago. No dragons. No stone giants."

The eager eyes around the soldier darkened.

"He's wrong. I saw them myself!" the soldier protested. "Ask anybody who was there that day—"

"I was there," the dwarf said offhandedly, pounding a tap into the barrel-head. "No giants. No dragons. Just lots of killing."

Alarm flashed over the man's face. "He's lying! I saw giants and dragons. Faeries, in broad daylight. I'm telling you, I saw Wotan and Thor fight from the clouds! I saw a titan made up of huge beetles!"

Master Loki clucked disapprovingly to the barkeep. "You really should not serve ale to madmen—"

"I'm not mad! You two are the ones who are mad! You couldn't have been there!"

Lifting slim hands before him, Master Loki said, "Easy, friend! Easy! I spoke out of turn. In apology, let me offer you the first draw from this new cask." The brewer received a foamy tankard from the hands of his assistant. He handed it to the soldier.

The head of the ale gleamed like cream in the lantern light. Giving a sniff, the soldier took an experimental sip. He nodded and drank deeply. "What do you call this ale?"

"Lethe's Libation," Master Loki said proudly, "for those who drink to forget."

Gentle laughter moved through the crowd.

"But, I interrupted your tale. You were saying—"

The soldier gave Master Loki a blank stare. "I was saying?"

"You were telling of the Battle of Mount Badon."

The soldier set down an empty tankard and wiped foam from his lip. "Oh, that was just a lot of killing. Not very interesting."

"What of the stone giants? What of the war beetles?"

"Stone giants? War beetles?" the soldier echoed. "Never seen anything like that . . . Lethe's Libation, eh? I'll have another."

"No you won't," the barkeep said, irritably snatching up the tankard.

As a tussle began between the soldier and the barkeep,

Master Loki turned, his face lighting with recognition.

"Ah! Morgan!"

He strode across the taproom to a table where sat a raven-haired woman and her handsome young son. Loki clasped the woman's pale hand and lifted her to her feet. He embraced her happily.

"Sister, I have not seen you in ages!"

A wry smile crossed her lips. She whispered, "No, not since this morning."

"And this must be Mordred!" Master Loki declared, surveying the handsome lad. "He's your spirit and image. But there's also a bit of his father in him! And, my, has he grown!"

"Yes," Morgan replied as locals wrestled the angry soldier out the door. "And did you know he is to become a squire at Camelot? Some day, he'll be a knight."

Master Loki turned outward in amazement. "Did everyone hear? My nephew Mordred will be a Knight of the Round Table! Now that's a story you can be certain is true!"

Loki brings twilight to Badon Hill. Stone giants yawn and sink beneath the quilt of grass. Dragons slither down forgetful wells. Ghosts abandon the land to the living. He cannot drive them fully below, not forever, but he can make them weary, send them to their dreaming beds. They will rest awhile in dozing memory, and for dragons and stone giants and ghosts, a night's slumber can last ages. But when again they long for the world, and the world longs for them—they will wake.

57

The Cave of Delights

*A*t last, Arthur and Guinevere were home.

Mount Badon lay on the other side of Britannia, in the mists of memory. Death and destruction, for a time, were folded away. Gods had ceased their terrifying march across the land. Wildflowers and tender grass grew in their footprints. The very farm folk who had fought that battle remembered nothing of Wotan or Valkyrie—too awful, perhaps, or too unbelievable. There were only Saxons that day, and of course Merlin Magus—and the king.

Now, Arthur and Guinevere were home. Bright Camelot enveloped them. They remembered all that had happened, as did their knights and priestesses, but they had learned not to speak of those strange days when they rode the land. Even among themselves, stories of gods were spoken in whispers.

Perhaps even less than whispers. When Arthur and Guinevere were together, they spoke not at all of fallen gods and dead fey. They had much happier converse in mortal realms. They spoke of their beautiful city, their glad comrades, and each other. Even their chastity had become comfortable, ever entwined but never touching. Like an old couple joined not in lust but love, they made themselves a home in each other's hearts.

More than gods and monsters, mortals seek a home.

So, Arthur and Guinevere created the Festival of the Pendragon—a celebration of Camelot and Britannia. Their eyes, once trained on airy visions, turned now to beautiful realities.

"Come, my darling," Arthur said to his queen, extending a hand to her. "Let us go to the great hall to practice tonight's dance."

She smiled, love in her eyes. "They will not care how

imperfectly we dance tonight. They will look at you and see only perfection."

"Perhaps," the young king allowed with a wry smile, "but I will enjoy the practice, and looking at you. . . ."

Merlin entered Camelot. He'd avoided Roman roads and ley lines, which thronged with folk. All of Britannia, it seemed, flocked to Camelot for the Festival of the Pendragon. These days, even fey were connected to mortal matters—to feasts and fights, alliances and grievances.

Merlin was not. He came today only to bid farewell.

Merlin entered Camelot. He didn't so much enter—for he was already there—but took solid form. He assembled his consciousness from a thousand roving motes in the city. He wanted to remember every corner of it—travelers washing at the feet of the Bountiful Weirds, silks and swords and "Merlin's ashes" for sale in the marketplace, hearty knights and ladies trysting beneath the joust stands, cloistered colleges brimming with books, tavern talk and minstrel songs, pigeon flocks above chasing children, the cool smoothness of the cobbled lanes, the warm invitation of pies on windowsills, the spices of distant lands. . . .

I will miss this place, Merlin told himself as he bundled together the disparate strands of his being. He spoke not merely of Camelot, with its fieldstone walls and live-thatch roofs, but also—and more specifically—of the palace. White limestone and gold-veined marble, kobold-blue tiles and vast iron gates, balconies and trellises and gardens and spires, great halls and kitchens and pantries . . . Ah, most of all, I will miss the pantries.

He coalesced in one such cellar, just off the main kitchens. He found there an old friend.

"Hello, Ulfius," Merlin said gently. "Raiding the cellar?"

Ulfius startled and looked up. Since the battle of Mount Badon, the man had at last begun to show his age. He was nearing sixty now and could still swing a sword, but his shoulders and knees were stiff at morning, and his belly had begun to show the comforts of cinnamon toast before bed. "Oh, Merlin," he said, peering at the mage over a dusty wine bottle. "I hadn't heard you arrive. And I'm not raiding. Arthur asked me to select the wines for this evening's feast."

"You used to say you got all the rotten jobs."

A gentle laugh answered. "Yes. I used to say that." Ulfius sighed in remembrance. "And I have had all the rotten jobs. Still, it has turned out to be an extraordinary life."

"Yes, it has." Merlin nodded soberly. "Yes, it has."

Ulfius gestured toward a small table, where waited a corkscrew and a set of crystal. "I am to sample each vintage that I will recommend. Would you care to join me? I've never known Merlin Magus to turn down a drink."

Merlin waved away the suggestion. "Thank you. No. I have a long journey ahead of me, and there will be nectar at the end of it. You see, I am wearing my travel cloak." He held his hands out and turned around, the tattered garment fanning out to brush the dusty bottles. "I know it is ragged. I know it was burned away by Wotan. But it is comfortable to me, and familiar—the habiliments of a creature embarking on a great journey."

Smiling genuinely, Ulfius said, "You've always been on a great journey."

With another nod, Merlin said, "Well, I stopped by to say good-bye. I don't belong here anymore. My heart is elsewhere. Gods ought not to walk too routinely among people, lest they grow careless and step on them. No, I am not Merlin Magus any longer. Nor am I Jove, either. I am something new, and so must leave what is old behind."

Sadness and quiet concern passed over Ulfius's features. "We will see you again, won't we, Merlin?"

"In dreams, yes," the old wizard said. "That's where I truly live, anymore. In the dreams of the people. And I may stop by from time to time for a more substantial visit, especially if things go greatly awry. But beyond that, I must withdraw. It is little matter. Camelot has enough mystical citizens these days."

"Yes, but we have only one Merlin," Ulfius said, putting

down the wine bottle and wrapping him in an embrace. Even near sixty, his arms were still strong.

"And only one Ulfius," Merlin replied. "You've been friend and father to Arthur and me, both."

Ulfius drew back. "Good-bye, Merlin. Farewell, wherever you fare."

Smiling away the sadness, Merlin said, "Have you seen Ector and Kay?"

Ulfius rolled his eyes. "Oh, they have the task of selecting the ale and beer and spirits for tonight. They're upstairs, in the great hall—and I think they've attracted a couple of assistants."

Merlin glanced toward the stone steps that lead up out of the cellar. "Thank you, Ulfius. Good-bye."

Without taking a step, he was there, within the great hall. And a great hall it was. Its black hammer-beam ceiling hung with the banners of every realm in Arthur's kingdom. Its marble walls bore bosses with Pendragon regalia. Its long tables sported white linens, and fresh rushes covered its oak floor.

Thirty-some casks lined one wall. A somewhat unsteady group of four men moved along them, tankards in one hand and taps and mallets in the other. The largest of the men, a great, black-haired bear, knelt beside a fresh cask, positioned a stopcock at the base, and hammered it in. A foamy spray shot forth after the first blow. The second sank the tap securely. The man drew himself a pint.

"Ector," Merlin greeted him, approaching. "You know you need only *sample* each cask. . . ."

"Oh, aye, Merlin," the man said cheerily. "But it takes a whole tankard. You've got to sample it from head to dregs to know an ale—bouquet and body and finish, you know."

"It is the finish I am wondering about," Merlin said mildly. He gestured down the row of casks. "How can you possibly be fit to judge the quality of the thirtieth cask after having partaken of the twenty-nine previous?"

Kay, for he was there too, looked muzzily from under his

blond shock of hair. He stooped to fill his tankard. "We *have* been rating the last few higher."

"Perhaps we should move more quickly down the row," suggested Ector, who handed a full tankard to a gaunt man in black—Loki in his favorite human guise.

"Thank you," the god said a little sloppily. "And as we hurry, we ought to act disagreeable to make up for our increasing agreeability."

"Act pissed while we g-et pissed," Dagonet hiccoughed. The fool's body mass put him at a distinct disadvantage in any drinking contest.

"A health!" Ector cried, lifting high his drink.

"A health!" the others chorused.

As they tossed their heads back and quaffed, Merlin said gently, "I'll consider this a toast to my departure."

Ector looked suddenly sorrowful—as sorrowful as a stout warrior can look when ale foam mantles his mustache. "Arthur said you would be leaving soon—"

"Another draw," suggested Kay. "It's not a proper toast when the honoree has nothing to drink. Give him a tankard!"

"Awe, give him a whole cask!" Loki suggested. "He says he's Jove, but he seems more Bacchus to me. I heard he'll drink whole rivers for a nightcap!"

"Not any longer," Merlin said gently.

"No, in-deed," hiccoughed Dagonet. "He gave me his weakness for d-rink along with his madness."

Merlin smiled. "They make a necessary pair. Drink the next one to Dagonet. Tavern talk says this little fool won back the king's sword and scabbard—"

"True enough," Loki broke in.

"By single-handedly slaying Wotan—"

"Not exactly true," Loki said, his expression souring.

"And fathering the race of Nibelungen on Frigga."

Loki arched an eyebrow and glared at his comrade. "Someone has been tampering with the official story."

"I say, drink to the fighting men!" Kay said, his chest puffing out before him. A purgative belch somewhat diminished his pomp. He wrapped an arm about his father. "We're the ones who drove the Saxons up the Thames and out of London and right on back to Sussex. Why, if my little brother—"

"*Step*brother," Ector interjected.

"Sovereign," Merlin supplied.

"Arthur hadn't called us back, we would have driven them out of Saxony too and into the land of the Khans!"

"Merlin and his dragons helped a bit," Ector pointed out.

Loki extended a foaming tankard to the old mage. "And so, we are back to drinking to Merlin."

Merlin looked at the drink, steaming suspiciously in Loki's grip. "This is not Lethe's Libation, is it?"

"Of course not!" Loki said, cringing a little. "No forgetful ale in Camelot."

"Good." Merlin waved away the tankard. "Even so, I do not want it." He turned to Ector. "Well, good-bye, my friend. Neither the king nor I would have survived had it not been for you and your family."

Ector let the stopcocks and tankard fall from his hands and wrapped Merlin in a bear hug. "We won't forget you."

Pulling back, Merlin said, "The sweetest words a god can hear."

Kay interposed himself. "What about me? I'm the one who found you two. Remember?"

"Yes, Kay," said Merlin, embracing him. "I remember. Thank you."

He moved on to Loki and studied the fellow god. "You behave yourself. I'm the one who allowed you into Camelot, if you'll remember. I can toss you out if I need to."

Eyes turning sullen and glossy, Loki said, "Understood." He made little shooing motions. "Now, hurry on your way."

"Not before I have said a farewell to this fellow," Merlin said. He stooped to Dagonet's level. Wise, eternal eyes met the besotted gaze of Dagonet. "You and I were re-created in the same moment, on that terrible night at Caerleon."

Dagonet blinked blearily. "Was that when I got so short?"

With a light laugh, Merlin said, "No. But that was when

you became addle-pated. It was my madness that infused you—the torrent of my dreams."

"I've not slept well in y-years," Dagonet bemoaned.

"For a long while, I hadn't time for my dreams, and I unfairly let you carry them for me. But I have time now, again, Dagonet. With a touch, I can take them back from you. With a touch, I can restore you to what you were before," Merlin said, reaching out toward the dwarf.

A sudden sobriety came to the fool's eyes. He took a steady step backward. "No, Merlin. You can refuse the drink offered to you, and I can refuse the drink offered to me. I know what I was before and know what I am now." A hint of caprice curled his lip. "I do not suffer from madness. I enjoy it."

Merlin withdrew his hand. "I remember how that felt. In fact, when I lost my madness, I also lost some of my best friends—mostly stumps and fungi and . . . Loki."

Dagonet grinned. "And now, you say good-bye to stumps and fun guys and Loki."

"To stumps and fun guys and me!" Loki cried, lifting his tankard.

Ector and Kay lifted their drinks so eagerly they almost dashed the ale in their faces. The four men quaffed.

Loki had downed half the tankard he'd prepared for Merlin before he suddenly spewed. The ale geysered into the air overhead and burst into flame. It flashed away in oily smoke that drifted malignantly among the hammer beams.

Eyes were wide around the ring of drinkers. Everyone stared in shock at Loki.

Ector blinked. "I'd rate this one down."

Kay nodded. "The finish is a little harsh."

Dagonet said, "Let's save it for Saxon dignitaries."

In the laughter that followed, Merlin dissolved away.

He reappeared in a very different place—the grand throne room of the palace. Beneath a gold gilded ceiling and amid columns of red marble, the king and queen of Britannia danced. Though there was no music, they moved in perfect unison, as if they heard a private song. Decked in the gorgeous garments of state, Arthur and Guinevere glided smoothly across the marble floor. Huge banks of window cast sunlight down on them. They were dazzling. Words whispered between them reached Merlin's ears.

"I think we almost have it," Arthur said.

"I think we had it an hour ago," Guinevere replied wryly.

"I want this night to be perfect," Arthur replied.

Guinevere laughed lightly, "How could it not be? We are together—"

"Ahem," Merlin said, stepping from behind a column. "Forgive me for interrupting, my king, my queen. It's time I was on my way."

The king and queen ceased their dance and opened out toward the ragged mage. They extended their arms and said, "Merlin . . ."

Merlin walked slowly across the marble floor, reached the sovereigns, and dropped to one knee before them. He bowed his head. "By your leave, I go."

They caught up his hands and lifted him to stand.

Arthur said sadly, "You have my leave, Merlin. You have my leave and my blessing to do whatever you wish. I even understand why you must go. If my work were done, I would withdraw with my lady into a cave of delights. I can understand, but I cannot be glad, Grandfather."

"I am more your brother," Merlin said. "We've grown up together. You have become a king—your heritage and your destiny."

"And you have become a god—your heritage and your destiny."

"It is only right that we rule our separate kingdoms separately," Merlin said. "Thank you, Arthur. You made me what I am."

The king smiled. "And you, I."

"We can be unmade too easily, my lad," Merlin said in mild warning. "Do not let mortal pleasantries blind you to immortal perils. All might be lost in short-sightedness."

Arthur stared gladly at his queen. "We mortals have so

little time, Merlin, we must see what lies about us, or nothing at all."

"Watch your sister's son," Merlin replied. "I will not be here to protect you from him."

"But I will be," Guinevere said. "And it will be enough." She smiled sadly. "We will miss you here, Merlin."

"I may return, from time to time. And through Nyneve, I will remain connected to this land that is connected to you." Merlin gave one last brave smile, tears standing in his eyes. "Well, then, good-bye, my darlings."

King and queen converged on the mage and buried him in a tight embrace. The three clung to each other, unwilling to let go.

"I'm not leaving entirely. I'll remain, if only in your dreams."

And then he was gone. Arthur and Guinevere were left embracing only each other.

The Cave of Delights was less than a step away. No longer did Merlin need to travel the ley lines. He moved with a thought. And his next thought took him there, deep beneath the stone henge, where a perfect world waited. The sky was cerulean blue. The sun beamed bright, as when the world was young. Hills and trees and mountains were verdant beneath the touch of eternal spring. Waters coursed with life.

But more than a perfect world awaited him in that place. A perfect mate awaited, as well.

Nyneve folded Merlin into her arms—not the white-haired mage of Camelot, but a young man, just then emerging from the chrysalis of age. "I thought you'd never get here. I feel as if I've waited my whole life for this moment."

Merlin held to her tightly. "Really? I feel as if my life has only begun."

In the great hall of Camelot, surrounded by mortal friends and immortal glow, the king and queen danced. No one thought of dark pasts or bright futures. There was only the glad music, the perfect dance, and Arthur and Guinevere.

At last, they had come home.

Epilogue

*E*veryone seems to know me. Everyone knows Merlin. After fifteen hundred years, they remember me. I am, of course, delighted.

Look for . . .

Lancelot Du Lethe

by J. Robert King

from Tor Books in December 2001